RULED BY TAINTED BLOOD

BOOKS BY MICHAEL J ALLEN

Blood Phoenix:
1. Ashes of Raging Water
2. Ruled by Tainted Blood
3. Vengeful are the Drowned
4. Rise of the Exiled Lady
5. Razing the Last Bastion

Scion (Original):
1. Scion of Conquered Earth
2. Stolen Lives
3. Hijacked
4. Unchained

Bittergate:
1. Murder in Wizard's Wood
2. The Wizard's Bane
3. Forge of War
4. Scythe of Illusions

Guns of Underhill:
1. Fey West

Dumpstermancer:
1. Discarded
2. Duplicity

Delirious Scribbles:
(Short Stories)

- Wyrm's Warning
- Scraping Bottom
- Criminal Justice
- Dreams of Treasure
- Desperate
- The Bottom Line

COMING SOON:

Binarai Online:
1. Storm Refuge
2. Rogue Planet
3. Power Break

Wayman Chronicles:
1. Crossways

Guns of Underhill:
2. Mettle Kingdom

Dumpstermancer:
3. Decoy

Scion Rising (Remaster)

RULED BY TAINTED BLOOD

BLOOD PHOENIX CHRONICLES: BOOK TWO

MICHAEL J ALLEN

Delirious
Scribbles Ink

Delirious Scribbles Ink, Inc.

Copyright

This is a work of fiction. Names, characters, places and incidents are a product of the author's imagination or are used fictitiously. Locales, businesses, companies, events, institutions, and public names are sometimes used under fair use licensing for atmospheric purposes only and are not representative of their namesake. Any resemblance to actual people—living, dead or in between—is completely coincidental.

Delirious Scribbles Ink, Inc.
4519 Woodruff Road
Suite 4, #108
Columbus, Georgia 31904
www.deliriousscribblesink.com

Interior Layout ©2022 Delirious Scribbles Ink, Inc.
Cover Design ©2022 Delirious Scribbles Ink, Inc.
Cover Art ©2019 Andrea Fodor

ISBN 978-1-944357-42-9 (intl. tr. pbk.)
ISBN 978-1-944357-43-6 (hc.)
ISBN 978-1-944357-44-3 (epub)
ISBN 978-1-944357-74-0 (large print)

Printed in the United States of America
10 9 8 7 6 5 4 3 2 1
Ruled by Tainted Blood / Michael J Allen. — 1st ed.

Dedication

For Scott, a steadfast friend and source of both encouragement and good ideas.

For B, B & E, J, S & J, and L.

Delirious Scribbles Readers Group

Like free stories?

How about curated deals for Science Fiction and Fantasy books?

Get your first benefit—a FREE story sent right to you—by becoming a member of the Delirious Scribbles Readers Group.

Begin your journey, just scan this image with your phone camera!

Content Advisory

In order to provide my readers the best possible experience as well as be responsive to reader requests, I've created a reader-curated content advisory on my website. If you are sensitive to certain kinds of fictional representations, please check this book's listings before reading.

I hope you enjoy this story...

— Michael J Allen

To visit the advisory, just scan this image with your phone camera.

Chapter One

Fires of Rebellion

Quayla

Waking naked in the bloody waters of the fountain within our sanctum garden wasn't what I'd expected.

A low moan lamented dull, throbbing stabs of pain. My eyes refused to open. Elven blood and bone exploded behind my lids, current pain connecting to remembered agony. Even before I managed to flee the show, I knew I was broken.

"Ani?" the single word escaped in a croak.

"Shield Quayla!" Excited relief filled our Shield automata's voice. "You've returned to consciousness."

Except, she's not an artificial intelligence. She's something else.

"Yay?" I swallowed. Sucking on my tongue failed to milk any moisture free.

Dry mouth occurred in most mortal lives, especially after a night of revelry. The condition shouldn't happen to me—a mythological creature formed of water.

Questions escaped my lips in a drawn-out moan. "Is Vitae safe? Are we secure? Where am I?"

The escaping words fostered a vague sense of déjà vu, like Anima and I had already had this conversation.

1

"Vitae is fine. You defeated the main Sidhe assault."

Main?

Hesitance crept into Anima's words. "He put you in the garden fountain to help you recover."

"There was more than one assault? What aren't you telling me? Where's Vitae?"

"The assault you met hid another. The repercussions required Vitae to leave you in my care. He and Summus have gone to speak with the Sidhe Courts."

I pushed up into a partial sitting position. One hand slipped on the fountain's edge, splashing in a bare few inches of water. I looked down.

Blighted hells, Vitae's going to kill me for using up Mare's essence.

My body rested in the blood-stained dregs of a fountain once containing the last of Mare's essence. Skin puckered around impaling bone chunks and metal shards. "He just left me here? No one's here but you?"

"Th-that's correct."

Shrapnel tore skin as I shifted, further staining what remained of the fountain's waters.

Vitae just abandoned me here? After I saved him? He left me bleeding in the fountain...alone?

Heat crept into my voice. "What could be so bad he abandoned me to help a divine?"

Anima didn't answer.

It took several tries to focus my mind enough to transmogrify my body from human flesh into my native watery essence. I didn't fully transmog to my real form, just enough to make removing shrapnel less painful. The shift happened more rapidly thanks to recent reading.

I yanked shrapnel out of my body piece by piece, dumping the shards on the garden floor and rebalancing my essence to fill in the wounds. I reverted to human shape and grabbed a tiny wing on one of the five, diminutive stone angels looming over my spinning head. Casting my eyes between the small statues to the marble archangel for moral support, I struggled to lift myself. A sluggish thought brought my gaze back to the putto—often misnamed cherub—I gripped as an anchor.

The alcove between the putto's feet gaped empty.

Repercussions...Creator's mercy!

Cold swallowed me. My fingers slipped. I crashed down into the fountain, unable to catch my breath. A panicked crawl through the basin brought me to another empty alcove and then another.

My hand came down onto piercing pain.

I turned over once-more-bleeding fingers to find sapphire shards digging into fresh, pink skin. The world slowed. Gravity doubled and doubled again. My head turned toward my egg's alcove like an ancient cemetery gate.

Fragments of celestial silver and sapphire trailed from the alcove into the fountain's basin.

My voice pitched toward subsonic. "Ani?"

It wasn't abnormal to feel different in a new body. I'd chalked up disorientation to the new form and my injuries but evidence stared me in the face—just as wrong...broken...shattered as I felt.

"I'm sorry, Shield Quayla, but something broke your egg during the theft of all the others."

No. That's...that can't be possible.

I'd never been without an egg, never been without that last anchor to Creation that would've protected me against True Death.

"There's more, Quayla. I hesitate to burden you further, but your mass is wrong," Anima said. "Your nest didn't contain enough essence to grow a full-size body when you killed yourself."

Lingering cold became an ice age.

Shields varied in size, so being smaller than normal wasn't the end of the world. My lessons suggested ways to adjust mass, but the loss of my egg felt crippling.

Suffocating and on the edge of abject panic, I tried to emulate our earth phoenix Terrance's calm practicality. A quick count of limbs and digits confirmed a functional body, but no matter how hard I tried to push concern aside and find a rational course of action, I couldn't escape the reality sucking me in like a black hole.

My empty nest hadn't contained enough essence during my last rebirth. My egg had been destroyed.

A sudden sense of being crushed returned.

How close to True Death did I come?

Our sanctum had suffered attack and if the Sidhe came back, any death meant permanent Destruction.

Vitae just left me here dying with an empty nest and no egg.

I collapsed back into the fountain. An itch in my cheeks forewarned tears, but I couldn't afford any more loss of essence.

"Creator, what do I do?"

"Draw in the waters," Anima said.

My gaze fell on the fountain's remnants, head already sweeping back and forth. "I can't. Vitae will have my head."

"You need all of the strength you can gather."

Anima was right. Besides, Vitae could've used his essence to heal me before he left. Instead he'd dumped me in the fountain and left me to my fate. Despite being an unintended compliment, it reinforced one thing: my desire for Vitae's approval was just as misplaced as our air phoenix Caelum said.

If he doesn't care enough to help me after I saved his life, I'm done caring what he thinks.

I drew in the fountain's waters. The extra water steadied my head and added some mass, but didn't fill the ache left in my chest by waning anger.

I picked shattered sapphire shards and bent celestial silver, cradling the pieces to my naked breasts. Touch against the dead egg fragments no longer tingled my skin. I circled into a fetal ball in the bottom of the fountain, wrapped so tightly around what remained of my egg that the shards left blood trails painting my chest.

I saved him, did my duty, sacrificed myself for the Shield, and Vitae still abandoned me without a care whether I lived or died.

Ignis

A firestorm swirled Ignis back into existence. Flames reflected off the mirrored metal of his nest's alcove, redoubling the heat of his furious snarl. Ashes floated down around him, settling back into the stone basin. He stared into his reflection, eyes still glowing coals.

"How dare he?! I'll hunt that infernal elf down if it takes—"

Anima's voice rose from his nest. "Shield Ignis?"

"What?" Ignis snapped. "I've got to get back there."

The Shield's automata sounded hurt even though she wasn't designed with emotions. "The Shieldheart and Summuseraphi are en route to where you died. You're needed elsewhere."

"That son-of-a-bitch faerie ripped my heart out of my chest while I was still alive."

"I'm sorry for your pain, but the Sidhe ambushed each of our shields and they've launched multiple coordinated incursions. Two shields and a Divine One for a single site is overkill."

Ignis pushed open the alcove. Lingering handprints glowed on the metal. He descended the rear access steps of his apartment building's ancient dead boiler. He yanked a pull chain. The handle warped, but a short deluge of scalding water from the newer boiler cooled his skin.

Putti had reworked the boilers so that neither could be removed without compromising building integrity. They'd added an adjoining entrance behind both into Ignis's basement apartment.

A section of brick wall swung out of the way, admitting him into a large corner shower unit. A twist of a handle opened up shower heads above and around him, tepid water lowering his body temperature the rest of the way. He never used the hot water tap even during bitter winters.

Ignis stepped from the shower onto a fluffy slate grey rug and grabbed a matching, if fluffier, towel. He patted himself dry and took only a moment to double check his reflection. He was in a hurry to rip the Unseelie knight's head off, but haste was dangerous—particularly when combined with fire and fury.

A glance at the mirror showed Ignis in need of a body-wide shave, but otherwise his basic size, shape and nationality had returned to a close approximation of his former self.

Focus in his final moments had informed the makeup of his new body. He'd learned the technique from an earth phoenix that had been positively persnickety about appearance. It didn't always work and little changes crept in no matter how much time he had to concentrate, but he didn't need as many changes of clothes as Aquaylae or Caelum.

Nobody needs as many changes of clothes as Caelum.

Ignis dressed quickly and grabbed a spare hilt from his underwear drawer. The foot-long ironwood rod resembled nothing so much as a thick, intricately carved flute. Nonetheless his weapon's flexibility served him better than Aquaylae's karambit hilts or even Vitae's fighting canes.

Ignis touched an alderwood box gilt with tarnished silver on his dresser. He placed his other hand on the gem in his chest and closed his eyes.

"In service unto death I swear this life unto the Undying Light."

A gleam of white light leaked from the box's seams. Ignis opened the tiny chest, removing a golden pocket watch intricately carved with the image of an angel. He tucked his means of contacting Vilicangelus into a pocket and hurried out the door.

One hand tucked inside his jacket and fingers wrapped white-knuckled around his hilt, Ignis exited his apartment building tense for a fight. Heat clung to his new skin, blood burning in his veins. Knight Dolumii had ambushed him with the help of some Wyldfae. They'd killed him. Dolumii had stolen his heart.

If he thinks he's going to control me, he's got a lot to learn about fire.

Much to Ignis's disappointment, nothing so much as looked at him funny during his march to the bus stop.

Nothing's waiting for me here because I was the first ambush.

Ignis took a deep breath, smothering the coals of fury that started to outline his body in a nimbus of flame.

Calm, the flame of a scented candle or sandalwood and incense. Wildfires are destructive, and once unleashed, control becomes problematic—not something anyone wants in a metropolitan area.

Ignis hated taking public transit, but he wasn't comfortable storing money digitally and accumulating debt was out of the question. Without an easily-melted banking card of some sort, he couldn't call Uber or another of the cab company replacements. Seeking a banking branch for taxi cash required time he didn't have. He reached the bus stop as the MARTA bus rounded the far corner. The dirty, dented vehicle stank of natural gas. Its door opened and a wave of Sidhe taint rolled over him, masking all other smells.

Ignis licked his lips, smiled and stepped inside.

So, who's today's contestant? Fae Kissed or faerie?

No one jumped him.

He scanned the half-full seats. No one looked at him for more than a glance, but no one failed to take that glance.

"Were you going to pay?" the driver asked.

Ignis slipped his emergency five into the bill reader, ignoring the label warning him that the unit didn't give change. The bus gave a small jerk as it lurched back onto the road.

Ignis stepped between benches and seats, keeping a hand on the guide bars to ensure his balance. He inhaled as he passed each passenger, envying Caelum his nose.

Old lady—no.

Two toughs—no.

Middle-aged waitress—no.

Corporate clone—no.

Each filled seat failed to intensify the taint, but the prickle along his skin identified the magic's origin as Unseelie.

Ignis closed to the final row of seats. A fine-featured young man muttered slippery words meant to persuade the clothes off a teenage girl not long into her breeding years.

Ignis inhaled the increased taint.

He dropped into the seat behind them and leaned his arms on both chair backs. "Unless you want to bleed purple for the young lady, I suggest you sit up straight and don't say another word until we step off this bus."

"What're you talking about?" the boy said. "Buzz off, creep."

Ignis grabbed the back of the boy's neck. "You must be new to this Shield."

The girl paled, eyeing them both. "W-what's going on?"

"Everything will be fine, Miss. He won't bother you anymore. The young gentleman and I are just going to get off at the next stop." Ignis let a flicker of his anger heat his fingers. "We need to chat."

"He wasn't bothering me," she said.

The young man jerked from Ignis's grip and whipped around. "I don't know who you are, but hands off or I call a cop."

Ignis frowned. He grabbed the boy's shirt, jerked him forward and inhaled.

"What the hell, freak?"

"What's going on back there?" The bus driver called.

"Everything's under control." Ignis pulled an old wallet and flipped it open. At the distance, his spare fire inspector's badge did the job. He turned toward the girl. "Just questioning a suspect."

Her expression flickered. Then her whole image flickered.

"By the Undying Light," Ignis said. "I order you to hold and be known."

The girl looked from Ignis to the boy and back. "I-I'm not sure what you're talking about."

Ignis's eyes narrowed. "I think you do. After the boy's gone."

"Who're you calling boy? We're basically the same age."

Ignis smirked. "Would you care to repeat that? Are you telling an enforcer of law that you're a twenty-year-old male trying to seduce a teenage girl?"

"Um, well, I said basically the same, I-I'm seventeen, so—"

"ID, please," Ignis said.

A little ring heralded an impending stop.

"I didn't do anything. I've seen TV. You can't question anyone underage without a parent or guardian present."

"Show me your ID to establish your age, and I'll let you go."

"Screw you." The boy lurched out of the bench, grabbing a rail as the bus pulled up to a stop. He rushed out the door before Ignis could follow.

Ignis didn't bother.

He turned to the girl.

Her image vanished with a pop. A grizzled-looking pixie scowled around the cigar parting his salt and pepper beard. "What's the deal, bird? Do you have any idea how much fresh wafer semen goes for at the Goblin Market?"

"Ensorcelling a mortal's mind violates the Articles of Ararat." Sightline blocked by the bus seat, Ignis slipped his spare phone from one pocket and an elderberry thorn loop from another.

"I didn't do a damned thing to his mind. I didn't offer him any deals. Hell, he was practically begging to put his little worm in my hand." The pixie grinned. "Besides, nothing happened thanks to you. No slime, no crime."

"You're wrong—plenty of slime in that seat." Ignis tossed the loop into the seat next to the little pixie.

The faerie leapt up, flitting away from the loop. He raised his eyes back to Ignis in time for Ignis to snap the surprise photo.

"Name, Sidhe," Ignis said.

"Cember, bird."

"This is an official warning. Leave the mortals alone and return home."

"I am home," Cember said. "Next stop."

Ignis tensed. "There's an Arch at the next stop?"

Cember's brow wrinkled. "Not that I know of, just my apartment."

"You don't live in Faery?" Ignis asked.

"Cember fetch this. Cember do that. Cember lick my ass so I don't have to bathe. Thanks, but no thanks."

"How'd you pay for the apartment?" Ignis asked. "Fairy gold?"

Cember snorted. "Greenbacks, pal, and before you ask, they were as genuine as winter rain. Earned fair and even, disgusting as that is."

"How?" Ignis asked.

Glamour changed Cember into a grizzled, middle aged man.

"I'm a private dick—surveillance, lost objects, just like in the Philip Marlowe books. Getting candid pictures is easy when you can fly into the room with an invisible camera." Cember rang the stop request and stood. "I've been warned. I'm going."

"I don't like the idea of an Unseelie running around the city unsupervised," Ignis said. "What's to stop you from converting mortals?"

"I can glamour, okay, but wishes aren't my bag. Hell, who wants the administrative headache of keeping track of all those deals? Besides, if I were dealing, I'd have to answer to the Court, and that means losing my anonymity. Thanks, but no thanks." Cember headed for the exit.

Ignis didn't stop him. He retrieved the thorn loop and sat back in the seat thinking about the encounter. The bus pulled into Dunwoody station. He rode the escalator up to the train platform. Along the way, another taint played across his nose.

Lingering from Cember or something else?

Taint stench grew then faded.

Ignis followed, still itching to vent his spleen while waiting for the next train. A strange graffiti tag marked the foot of another stairway. The stylized goblin's head resembled a badly depicted house elf. Symbols rode a silver headband across the cocked head: a bag of gold coins and scales—typical of a Goblin Market; a birdcage; and a triangle composed of three smaller shards or possibly daggers. The bubble depicted around the head made less sense. Tiny marks shaded the bubble into a sphere. Violet and green goop graphically clung to its exterior.

That's pretty intricate. How'd they get this painted without getting caught?

Ignis cradled his face.

Glamour, you idiot, hence the taint.

He took a picture. The sound of an arriving train called to him. He hurried back to the platform, arriving as the doors closed. Plunging an arm between closing doors triggered a safety buzzer. The doors reopened. He claimed a seat and drew out his headphones before the train lurched forward. The new Sanderson audiobook filled his ears, taking Ignis into foreign battlegrounds as MARTA whisked him through the city toward his Camaro.

Caelum

Caelum surveyed the carnage around his motorcycle. The dwarfish figures bled pools onto the parking bay floor, revitalizing the blood-red of their vests and berets. They'd ambushed him when he stopped to replenish empty clips en route to headquarters.

He'd barely parked when the redcaps assaulted him—his second ambush that night. He piled their footman picks and Freddy Kruger gauntlets nearly to the top of his rear tire.

He headed over to the closet where he kept jugs of water, envying Quayla's more efficient methods of clean up.

"What's going on—oh my God!" the woman shrieked.

Caelum whirled around and bolted in the direction of her

scream. He threw his hand in her direction, wind sweeping around her cry in an attempt to muffle her scream.

Probably too little too late like those first gunshots.

He bent wind around her, sweeping air from her lungs' reach. She gulped like a landed fish, grabbing at her throat. Almost a full minute later, her eyes rolled back. Her body followed suit.

Caelum's essence propelled him to double speed. A feet first slide caught her head moments before she hit concrete. Her head slammed a little too close to home, but he shook off the pain and lifted her from the ground. Wind fed and starved her, keeping her momentarily out while he rushed her to the stairwell.

Damn but it'd be nice to have Glamour sometimes.

Caelum laid her down and beckoned air to her lungs. She stirred almost at once. "What happen? Oh, God, dead bodies. There were dead bodies."

Caelum smiled. "I may not look my best, but I assure you I'm not dead."

"I saw...what happened?"

"You fainted, hit your head pretty hard." He flashed her a charming grin. "It would be my pleasure to escort the lady to a doctor."

"No, we need to call the police."

"For a little bump on the head?" Caelum asked.

A man's voice boomed deeper in the parking bay. "What the —hell, yes! I'm going to be rich!"

"Shit. It'd be so much easier being a faerie sometimes." Caelum pulled a small white feather from his back pocket.

The woman shrieked again as the down glowed to life.

"Vilicangelus, Vilicangelus, Vilicangelus," Caelum watched her staggering retreat transform into a shrieking sprint. "We're going to need some rewrites."

Chapter Two

Cleaning Up

Ignis

The bus slowed toward the stop nearest his death. Ignis chaffed as another car pulling out of a parking lot held up the bus, but the bus driver wouldn't open the door until he'd parked inside the stop's painted boundaries. Ignis bolted the moment the door hissed open, bowling over an alpha Barbie too engrossed in her phone to pay attention to those around her.

Ignis didn't apologize.

He turned up the street and sprinted for all the unaugmented speed his body was worth. Vitae's Mercedes parked behind his own Camaro, but Ignis didn't hear any battle sounds.

Could Dolumii have killed Vitae and Summus too?

A scent of fire and charcoal wafted from the church ruins. Taint lingered on the wind. He inhaled deeper.

It doesn't seem as strong as before, but they hid it sufficiently the first time to ambush me.

He eyed the church.

Blood burned through his veins. The long trip had calmed his fury, but it lurked near the surface ready for his call. He wanted to charge in like a hot head.

He didn't.

Two others had been dispatched out to this site. Vitae's Mercedes confirmed their arrival.

Ignis resisted calling out to them in case his killers lay in wait. He drew out his hilt and approached the cars.

The Mercedes was empty.

He pushed essence into his hilt. He didn't manifest a weapon, but readied one like priming a flint lock. He opened the Camaro's passenger side door and whispered to the bronze angel statue.

"Anima?"

"Shield Ignis, please report your status."

"I'm at the site of the ambush but haven't entered yet. Vitae's car is here, but I don't see anyone."

"Summuseraphi just arrived, delayed by a call to assist Caelum with a quick rewrite," Anima said.

"And Vitae?"

"The Shieldheart slew himself in an attempt to defend our sanctum from incursion."

Flashfire shot through Ignis. "What? Who attacked our Shield?"

"Knight Dolumii and Knight Gherrian," Anima said.

"Our Shield is under attack and Summuseraphi attended to a re-write instead?"

Is he really that young? Divine should have more sense.

Ignis sprinted around and leapt into his car. "I'm on my way."

"We still have Veil breaches in progress. You're needed to quell the incursions and then instructed to gather your nest and bring it to headquarters," Anima said.

"Understood."

"Understood as in you need the address to the closest breach, or understood, but you will ignore your instructions...again?"

"Our Shield is under attack and Aquaylae is there too weak to defend herself. The rest of the city can burn down again for all I care." Ignis took a turn at twice the safe speed, his fire department light flashing the same color as his temper "I want a piece of Dolumii. We can deal with the breaches once our Shield is safe."

"Shield Aquaylae didn't leave many pieces of appreciable size," Anima said.

Ignis slammed the brakes and swerved around a wafer too important to let an emergency vehicle through an intersection first.

"Dolumii's dead? What about Gherrian?"

"All invaders have fled or been dispatched," Anima said.

Ignis slammed a fist into his dashboard, dented plastic melting.

Not sure if I should congratulate Aquaylae or be cross with her.

His voice came out a growl. "Where do you need me?"

Anima provided him an address. A few hard turns had him running in the right direction.

Ignis

Ignis stepped off the elevator into their sanctum. Palpable tension and doubly-thick taint slammed him back. Memory replaced missing items and traced structural damage around the foyer and up the stairs. Signs and experience described a pitched battle originating in the upper level, descending the stairs and eventually ending in Vitae's bedroom.

We've been assaulted, and I was the initial distraction.

Fair-haired and handsome Caelum stood in the bedroom entrance. Blood stained a bedraggled corporate suit and concern rumpled Caelum's normal breezy, devil-may-care expression.

Ignis joined him.

"It's like the Joker exploded, Iggy."

Ignis chuckled at a jest not far from truth. Vitae's gentlemanly décor had been shredded. Dried green and violet blood painted every surface. Faerie bone and armor fragments pockmarked walls and even some of Vitae's hardwood furniture.

"Aquaylae and Vitae?" Ignis asked.

"Vitae and Summuseraphi haven't yet returned from meeting with the Courts," Anima said.

"Quayla's in what's left of the greenhouse," Caelum faced Ignis more fully. "It's bad, Iggy. She should be True Dead."

Ignis's inner flame suddenly banked. "You're not making sense. Her egg—"

"Shattered," Caelum said. "The others were taken."

Ignis surveyed the carnage with new eyes. Vitae's nest was half full. Considering the Shieldheart's fastidiousness, the level meant Vitae died more than once.

"Where are the rest of the Knight Dolumii's remains?" Ignis asked. "He took something I need back."

"Vitae took both knights' swords with him," Anima said. "The rest is as you see it."

Ignis cursed and mounted the stairs. He hesitated at the top, assessing the carnage. Rippling plastic sheets replaced yard after yard of glass, trying to keep in the air conditioning. Terrance stepped out of Aquaylae's bedroom, the stolid Moor's dark face bent and grim.

"She's well?" Ignis asked.

"It took nearly more strength than I have to tear her away from the shards of her egg," Terrance said. "She is as shattered. It would be well if her paramour were allowed to tend her."

"Vitae will never permit that," Ignis said. "Besides, I thought you didn't approve of dating wafers."

"I don't, but she needs comfort right now, familiarity."

There is more you're not saying. What about this wafer changes your mind, old brother?

"I can supply the dashing good looks,' Caelum said.

Terrance sighed. "I fear even being her brothers all these years, we will not prove enough."

Ignis followed Terrance into the garden. Spiderweb cracks

splintered thick glass protecting the garden. More plastic covering the small holes in the resilient panes expanded and contracted like lungs.

Characteristic grime of the diminutive putti seemed to shadow the white marble archangel and his little attendants. The stone wasn't dirty, but the violation of their sanctum sullied his impression nonetheless. Blood pinked the dry basin next to Terrance. A hitch caught Ignis's throat. Nothing remained of Mare's essence.

Even centuries after her loss, even knowing all that time that she'd never return, even knowing Aquaylae had added her essence to refill what evaporation stole from the basin, losing the last bit of Mare hurt to rival the loss of Ignis's heart.

His putti drew Ignis's eye. The empty alcove knotted his twisted guts into a Gordian knot.

Gone. Taken, but by whom and for what purpose?

Caelum's expression hardened. "They violated our sanctum."

"Killed us and stole what's precious," Terrance said.

Caelum's voice fell to a whisper. "They nearly took Quayla from us too."

Cold blue fire shot through Ignis, but he stood as still as the statuesque angel on the fountain. "Why?"

"I don't know," Caelum said. "After I dealt with the grendlings, a bunch of redcaps ambushed me."

"More Wyldfae," Terrance said.

"Grendlings, redcaps, a half ogre and efreet," Ignis said. "Did they all work for Dolumii? Gherrian?"

"Or were some of them random incursions exploiting the rest of the noise?" Caelum asked.

Vitae exploded from nowhere, charging into Ignis's face. "Salamander, not efreet. You're our Pyri, a Phoenix of Flame. How can you not tell the difference?"

Emerald lit Vitae's brown eyes until they glowed like neon. Anger darkened his olive skin and Vitae's centuries-old Edwardian suit was in disarray. The furious phoenix hulked over Ignis's new body despite little difference in size, but a fragility undercut Vitae's bullying demeanor.

Ignis narrowed his eyes, trying to understand what he was seeing. "I was mistaken, Vitae, nothing more."

Vitae shoved him. "You were lazy! Incompetent! You cost me lives. You practically handed them our eggs!"

"Easy," Caelum said. "They're both shapeshifters. For all we know they imitated efreet to fool him."

"He should know the difference," Vitae snapped.

"Vitae, calm yourself," Terrance said.

"This Shield is a disgrace," Vitae paced. "We're not a laughing-stock anymore, it's gone far beyond that now. Our Aquaylae's shacked up with a wafer, paying more attention to her sex life than her nest. Our Ignis can't tell the difference between sala-mander and efreet. Neither our Ignis nor Caelum can be bothered to ensure that our sentry net remains complete, and you..." Vitae narrowed his eyes at Terrance. "How is it you weren't ambushed? Collusion?"

Terrance's lips pressed together until they all but disappeared.

Ignis stepped between them. "That's enough, Vitae."

Vitae rounded on him, gesturing toward the fountain. "Our eggs are gone."

"Which is not Terrance's fault," Ignis said.

"Oh, no. It's not his fault. It's mine. I'm the Shieldheart. I let this disgrace happen, but no longer. You're all ordered to relocate your nests back into our headquarters."

Caelum snorted. "Not hardly. You don't rank any higher than the rest of us. Besides, what's the big deal? We have a full Shield, we'll just make more eggs."

Ignis shook his head. "We're linked to them. The only egg we can remake is Quayla's."

"Not until she is stronger," Terrance said.

"Why can't we make a second? What's bad about having two of them as a failsafe?" Caelum said.

"You see, an elf couldn't have proven my point more elegantly." Vitae shoved a finger into Caelum's chest. "You're centuries old and as ignorant as a new hatchling—you and that incompetent—"

Anima's voice inherited the anger in the air. "That 'incompetent' saved your life, Vitae. Quayla sacrificed herself to protect this Shield and she, not you, slew both Sidhe knights."

"Aquaylae!" Vitae roared. "Her name is Aquaylae and it was luck that she managed to ambush them after I'd injured them nigh unto death!"

Caelum mouthed. "Nigh unto death?"

"I won't stand for this anymore. There *will* be order in this Shield!" Vitae said. "Since the rest of you lack the sense the Creator bestowed, I'll provide it. You will relocate your nests into headquarters at once."

"Screw off, Vitae," Caelum said. "You're not Divine."

Emerald light pulsed around Vitae as he lunged toward Caelum.

Ignis set a restraining hand on Vitae's shoulder.

Vitae slapped him away.

"Anima, something is wrong with Vitae," Ignis said. "Summon our Praefectus."

Vitae rounded on Ignis. "There's nothing wrong with me a little of the respect you promised wouldn't cure."

Terrance stepped up shoulder to shoulder with Ignis. "Then you will calm yourself, or I will call for Summus myself."

Vitae seethed, but his aura dampened.

Ignis sighed, turning to Caelum. "Caelum, I would appreciate it if you would show Vitae the respect he is due."

"That's a two-way street," Caelum snarled.

"As the younger, yours should be the first step," Terrance said.

"And Vitae is correct that you must attend to your studies better," Ignis said.

"How about the Cliff's notes version?" Caelum said.

Vitae threw his hands up.

"The Bible speaks against a man serving two masters,"

Terrance said. "To link two eggs would be to pull both mind and soul in opposite directions."

Caelum frowned. "Is that two directions or four?"

"You'll have plenty of time to construct understanding once you've relocated," Vitae said.

"No way," Caelum said. "I like where I live, besides it's close to work."

"There will be no more work in the mortal world. You will focus exclusively on your duties to this Shield," Vitae said.

Caelum glanced at the other two. "You're just going to stand there and put up with his megalomaniacal ranting?"

"Anima, do we have any clues regarding the missing eggs?" Ignis asked.

"Power loss disconnected me from the Sanctum's systems, but we know mounted knights of both Seelie and Unseelie Courts invaded the sanctum," Anima said.

"Why doesn't she have backup power?" Caelum asked. "You know we should get Dylan to check out the system and—"

"No," Vitae said. "That mortal is to have no further contact with us. I've requested he be rewritten."

"You what?!" Quayla's voice cut across the garden. She stormed across the intervening space with all the grace of a newborn foal. She shoved Vitae with all her momentum.

Ignis lurched forward, colliding with Terrance but both still managed to catch her.

Vitae recovered. "You saw. Anima recorded. She assaulted me over a filthy wafer."

"Dylan is twice the man you are, you...you...dickless Vulcan!"

Caelum laughed.

"She's ill," Ignis said. "Too weak to be held accountable."

"I will not let you harm, Dylan," Quayla said.

"I demand a quorum," Terrance said.

Silence filled the garden, broken only by the sound of wind-rippled plastic.

"No action may be taken against the mortal Dylan Snyder

until decided by quorum," Terrance said. "After Quayla's been deemed strong enough for duty."

Ignis eased Aquaylae onto a bench. "We must focus on what's important."

Quayla opened her mouth, but Ignis quieted her with a smile and finger to her lips.

"Ignis is correct," Terrance said. "Recovering the eggs must be our first priority."

A blinding blaze of light resolved into a phoenix, then a winged man and finally the golden-haired youth that served as their new Praefectus. "Not entirely. We must also deal with the diplomatic ramifications of two Sidhe knights dying in our sanctum and the lingering demand for Quayla's apology."

"They invaded us, how're we responsible for diplomatic ripples caused by their actions?" Caelum said.

"And they ambushed us," Quayla added.

"With few exceptions, it was Wyldfae that attacked us, and those exceptions are dead," Summus said. "Neither Court will accept blame for the actions of the Anseelie."

"I witnessed Dolumii give them orders," Ignis said.

"Your word against his," Summus said.

"He's dead, he doesn't get a say," Caelum said.

"His honor in their Court, his reputation, perhaps even his kin all against the word of one phoenix," Summus shook his head. "They took exception to Vitae's possession and refusal to surrender their so-called Champion blades. To make matters worse, when Vitae and I revealed the theft to them, they blamed each other and declared war."

"Great going Vitae," Caelum said.

"We must proceed carefully," Summus said.

"Kiss their Glamoured asses?" Caelum asked. "No way."

"I will speak with Vilicangelus for guidance," Summus said.

"What about the rest of us?" Caelum asked.

"They're likely to bring their war into the mortal world," Summus said.

"Sure, why mess up your yard when you can crap all over your neighbor's?" Caelum asked.

"Be vigilant, and in the meantime," Summus fixed Caelum with his gaze. "You and Aquaylae will attend to your studies while she recovers."

"And everyone will move their nests back here," Vitae said.

"I gave no such instruction, Shieldheart. This Shield determined together that this way best protects your charges."

Vitae scowled. "Obviously, that decision was flawed."

"Yeah, being reborn here really helped you stop the assault," Caelum said.

"Caelum," Terrance cautioned.

"Oh, right, it didn't. Quayla had to risk True Death to save your ass," Caelum seethed.

"Caelum," Ignis said.

"Starting to see a pattern here, you like sacrificing Aquas—"

"Caelum!" Ignis, Terrance and Summus snapped in unison.

Vitae stood rigid, energy nearly crackling in the air around him. White-knuckled fingers strangled the hilt of the Unseelie Champion blade. His eyes darted to Summus and his lips pressed into a thin line. "Shield Caelum."

This whole situation is already a powder keg.

Summus glanced at Ignis for support.

"Vitae, a word?" Ignis asked.

Vitae ignored him, continuing on in a lofty, self-satisfied tone. "It seems it falls to me once more to remind you that it is your turn to clean our sanctum, including my bed chamber."

"You're the one that got blood everywhere," Caelum said.

"Vitae is correct regarding the rota." Terrance eased an arm under Aquaylae. "Come, little sister, you must return to bed."

Aquaylae's physical state proved out Anima's claims, but it was her shredded emotional state that knotted Ignis's gut, squeezing heat outward until it fogged his eyes.

We must seek out our attackers with haste, punish them and then tend to healing this Shield and all who serve it.

Vitae

I stormed away from the others and into my bedroom. The door hadn't survived. I yanked the bloody coverlet from what remained of my bed, snapping it to dislodge clinging detritus. I pushed one corner of the fabric to the wall.

A moment's concentration grew a slender spike of essence from the top knuckle of my hand. I punched the stiletto through the coverlet and wall, moving on to repeat the process several more times.

Cut off from my unreasonable shield brethren, I allowed myself a moment to drop my guard. We were birds of prey. Showing weakness to another predator enticed violence, and my brethren were already after my throat.

Rallying around Aquaylae against me.

Several deep breaths centered me. Invasion and battle, shocks and surprises had bombarded me nonstop since Ignis's death. I'd been forced to sojourn surrounded by incompetence and sedition. I'd had to show the insufferable Sidhe Courts strength while resisting the desire to drive one of my new swords into their disrespectful hearts.

I'd prevented a truth that shook me to my core from vibrating me apart through it all.

Mare's still alive.

I drew both Champion blades, discarding Gherrian's to cradle the Unseelie blade stolen from Knight Dolumii. I gripped it with both hands, my right tightening around the blade until it cut into me.

"Vitae, you are cutting yourself," Anima said.

"Leave me be. Cease monitoring this chamber."

The troublesome automata didn't respond. Unlike Aquaylae, it could be trusted to obey. Our new Aqua would cease to be a problem very soon.

Mare?

Nothing.

My whispers cracked. "Mare? Can you hear me?"

Silence.

I sniffed back tears. I'd heard her voice holding the Unseelie knight's blade, the very blade that had torn her soul from her flesh. I had to free her.

Aquaylae had used up the essence transferred from Mare's nest to the fountain, but there was another way to bring her back.

I rounded the bed to the far corner, snatching the antique table and hurdling it out of my way. I knelt, laying the sword on the ground to wrench open a secret compartment with bloody fingers.

Fingers shaking with anticipation, I drew out an antique key.

I slipped only my face through the coverlet's folds, ensuring none of the others in sight or waiting for the elevator. Hasty steps brought me to Mare's bedroom door.

The key shook violently enough that inserting it into the lock took several tries. The click of the latch releasing stole my breath. I pushed the door open, hesitant despite Mare's centuries of absence. I stepped into a veritably separate world—a shrine.

No one but I had entered Mare's bedroom in the many years since her death, and even I hadn't dared to brave her chamber often. A preternatural chill hung in the air, opposite the warmth of our former Aqua.

A rough whisper escaped me. "Forgive me this intrusion, milady."

"Vitae?" Anima asked.

"I told you to leave me be!"

No one except me had been permitted inside Mare's room since her death. Even though the others refused to live within the sanctum, I'd conscripted the putti to rebuild other sections of our headquarters, carving out a small bedroom that eventually became Aquaylae's chambers.

The others witnessed the construction, but never questioned me. They never attempted entry. They never requested the key.

An ancient fan hung from the ceiling. Huge leaf-shaped blades spun languidly, propelled by a tiny whirlwind gifted Mare by Caelum's predecessor. Handwoven rugs blended the greys and browns of a storm-tossed ocean, covering stained hardwoods. Royal blues befitting Mare's character curtained the windows and the four-post bed.

I parted the gossamer, baby blue lace separating her bed from the room. Mare's egg rested in the beds center, nestled between pillows of sapphire or ice blue.

A soft glow fainter than a will-o-the-wisp lit the egg's interior. Without a heartbeat to match, the glow of Mare's essence didn't brighten and fade like other eggs.

With care not to wrinkle Mare's quilts, I lifted her egg from its nest with exaggerated care. I cradled her egg to my chest, noticing blood from my cut hand marring the gorgeous blue.

Fury rose.

How could I be so careless! Soiling her egg is totally unacceptable.

Tears edged from my eyes. I laid my cheek against Mare's egg, hoping they would cleanse away my unforgivable mistake. "I'm so sorry."

Anger drained away into the soothing cool silver and sapphire pressed to my skin.

"Mare, please hear me."

The egg had never answered no matter how many hours I begged it. Bringing the sword hilt to rest against Mare's egg, I whispered once more.

"Mare, hear me."

No response.

My essence could rejuvenate an injured phoenix. I pressed sword and egg tight to my chest and transmogrified until I could press the two of them into the red and gold plasma of my body.

I called Mare to me, called with my mind and my voice and

my heart. I pushed essence into the sword, fully aware the blade might take a liking to me and rip my soul from my body as it had Mare's.

At least we'd be together.

I tried time and again, fed the blade essence over and over, begging again and again.

The blade drank down my blood, but gave nothing in return.

I wanted to hurl the blade from my sight, to break it once and for all. Doing so could conceivably destroy any chance to liberate Mare from her prison. I wouldn't risk her nor let her go.

There's a way to free her. I will find it. I will free her no matter the cost.

Caelum

Caelum entered the Goblin Market and handed each of the billy goat guards a case and three bars of Bit-O-Honey candy.

They took turns eyeing the gateway behind him.

"She's not here," Caelum said.

The guards snorted.

Caelum dragged the foldable cart filled with milk and candy bars to one side. He unfolded his ether silk handkerchief until it stretched to a shimmering, constantly-changing rainbow of colors the size of a throw rug. Above him colorful silks wrapped an ancient tree, serving as gangways and tents, boundaries and shopping stalls. Faeries of all kinds stood stock still where they'd been perusing shops on the ground and each of the five levels rising upon silk like his carpet.

He held up his hands. "I didn't bring her along. I'm not here to cause a fuss."

Faeries returned to their shopping.

Caelum sighed and sat on his rug. A few whistled notes tamed the ether silk like one might mesmerize a cobra. He rose slowly, taking extra care to offer right of way to every faerie around him if it was their due or not.

It took far longer than normal to reach Oshyn's booth—long enough that his temper frayed by time he reached the first-tier shop.

You'd think a water phoenix would be calm and patient, not ruin my years of work building a rapport in the Market.

A half-sized elf garbed in silver and white silks eyed Caelum with wary unease. Behind Oshyn, high-pitched mutters coursed through a line of knee-high brownies. The miniature Cousin Its resembled a gaggle of decapitated old mop heads, arranged by hair color in ascending heights.

"I greet you, Oshyn, and hope I find you well and your endeavors profitable."

"Well enough Shield Caelum, though it is my burden to inform you the Market's current sovereign has decreed that you must pay thrice and thrice again in all the Market, even my humble shop."

"Understood." Caelum drew a crate of milk and several boxes of candy from the cart. "And I will pay thrice and thrice to honor your sovereign and the good work of your gentle brownie helpers."

A visible shiver ran down the hairy ranks.

"I need a one-time cleanup performed." Caelum added a half case of Bit-O-Honey. "Rush job."

Oshyn raised his nose, pointedly not looking at the barter collecting in Caelum's hand. "I see. We are very busy. Booked long into autumn, you know. Far too busy to clean up after anyone so dishonorable as Shield Aquaylae."

Little disgruntled squeaks escaped the array of tiny living mops, rippling the hairs along their curl-toed boots.

Is that so, my little friend?

"Oh, that's too bad." Caelum tossed the candy back into the box and replaced his milk. "The job didn't have anything to do with Quayla, but if you're busy I understand. I'll see you later, Oshyn."

His whistle turned the carpet around the other way.

"A moment, brave shield, we might fit you in...for a small surcharge," Oshyn said.

The Cousin It army sighed its relief.

"That's okay. There are plenty of modern cleaning companies who won't have to upset their appointment schedule."

"Wait!" Oshyn bounced from silk to branch off a goblin merchant's feathered hat and onto silks in front of Caelum's carpet. "It was a jest, just a summer frolic. We have plenty of time to help Shield Caelum."

Caelum frowned. "I don't want to be a bother."

"No, no, nothing of the sort. Perhaps I confused the good shield with my poor humor, a discount, yes, a discount, only one thrice."

The army stiffened.

"That wouldn't be fair to your brownies," Caelum rubbed his chin in dutiful manner. "Far be it from me to insult your sovereign's hard workers or her command. Perhaps only one thrice candy?"

Oshyn's eyes widened. He squeaked. "One thrice candy?"

Caelum held up a hand. "You're right. I should stick with mortals. They've got all those new chemicals and machines. Probably do a much better job."

Oshyn stomped a foot, making the silk streamer beneath him ripple. "I insist you let us handle this job, full milk and one thrice candy. Declining this offer would dishonor the whole line of my ancestors."

"The whole line?" Caelum smirked. "Nobody would be like, meh? Not even your sovereign?"

"The whole line, Shield Caelum."

"Okay," Caelum smiled. "If you insist, the job's yours."

Oshyn bobbed his head once in the affirmative. "Good, what is this rush job?"

"Shield Sanctum, standard full cleaning...oh, and a bit of blood."

Oshyn stuttered. "Sh-shield S-sanctum?"

"Which blood?" a brownie asked.

"No witches, just Sir Dolumii's, Sir Gherrian's, our Vitae's, a bit of wyvern and griffon blood mixed in... oh, Quayla might've bled here and there too."

A wave of groans rippled hair along the line of brownies.

The rest of his trades went just as smoothly, slowly dwindling the boxes of candy. He traded whispers and secrets, gems and jokes, filling the empty milk crates with all the odds and ends he needed—including a pair of replacement karambit hilts for Quayla. One whisper seemed to pertain to the shelter thefts, but the slightest inquiry saw him sent away.

Too much scrutiny on me this trip. Next time.

Caelum returned to headquarters. He called out as he stepped off the elevator. "Ani? Is Vitae back?"

"Not yet," Anima said.

"Good." Caelum blew an elderberry whistle.

"Caelum, there's an Arch forming in the foyer. We're under atta—"

"Hey, hey, easy there, my beauty. It's just the janitors."

Brownies whirled out of the Arch like a flood of tiny, chittering carwash brushes. Their hair whipped round and round in all directions, scouring dirt and blood out of existence.

Chapter Three

Unexpected Magic

Vitae

Burning sandalwood and white sage assaulted my nose the moment I reentered headquarters. A hint of taint undercut the other smells just at the edge of my awareness. The others might not have noticed under the other aromas, but the tickle of unnaturalness pricked my skin like gooseflesh.

A little voice whispered suspicions.

I strode up the stairs, eyes tracing walls far too clean. Caelum wasn't anywhere near as troublesome as Aquaylae, but the wild wind shield also wasn't what anyone would call thorough.

Only his goldbricking is this thorough.

My immaculate bedroom gave certainty to my doubts. Even my fighting canes gleamed with a fresh coat of polish.

There's only one way Caelum did all of this.

I checked Aquaylae's room, finding it empty of both mess and the untidy water phoenix. "Anima, where's Aquaylae?"

"The library," Anima said.

A flash of irritation increased my pace. She needed to be resting. The only other activity she should've been permitted was filling her nest. Instead, once more she insisted on ignoring what was best for my Shield. She insisted on pursuing her own wasteful agenda rather than accept that only judicious employment of sleep, slurry and sacrifice would fill her nest in a timely manner.

It seems I must once more remind her of her priorities.

I strode down the stairs. "Anima, where is Caelum?"

"Shield Caelum departed an hour ago."

No amount of old-fashioned elbow grease could've achieved the resultant scouring. Caelum's departure so long ago meant he'd misused his essence to speed the cleaning. With the resistance I'd encountered earlier, I needed to ensure I had evidence of Caelum's excesses to convince the new Praefectus to enforce stronger discipline. "How is it he managed to clean up with such alacrity?"

"He hired a troupe of brownies."

I froze mid stairwell, shock and fury vying for supremacy. My teeth ground against each other, inhibiting speech. "He invited faeries into our sanctum?"

"I assure you, Shieldheart, I monitored their every action."

"Did Caelum?"

"No. He entrusted the task to me since, as he pointed out, I would've monitored them even if he were supervising."

"While that sounds like Caelum's brand of reasoning, you'd do well to lend following his example less weight than your operating instructions."

"If you so say, Vitae," Anima said.

"I do." I completed my descent and braced myself to enter the library. A sudden thought plunged me almost physically into a bog of despair. "Anima, did the brownies enter Mare's room?"

"No, Vitae."

Breath and heartbeat raced. "You're sure? *Absolutely* certain."

"Yes, Vitae. They cannot have entered without me knowing."

Dealing with Aquaylae was trying at the best of times, but more so inside the library. Before I braced myself for the coming encounter, I hurried to Mare's door.

It remained locked.

I breathed a sigh of relief and turned toward the library.

Aquaylae and the other shields needed to reside within the sanctum. Only under constant supervision could they be rehabilitated and the Shield returned to acceptable standards. Until I managed to free Mare, having Aquaylae under restricted to headquarters meant tolerating her underfoot inside the temple of knowledge Mare and I had built.

She must be persuaded to select study materials and depart without dawdling.

The opening elevator halted my march. I framed a reprimand for Caelum only to find Aquaylae's mortal. He eyed the foyer with a mixed uncertainty and awe.

My anger at Caelum's transgression blossomed into fury at the insolent mortal. "What are you doing here?"

"I came to check on Quayla," Dylan entered the foyer.

I closed until we faced one another nose to nose. Nails dug into my palms, a growl adding to the force of my words. "I told you she is no longer allowed to associate with wafers."

"I heard you the first time, and I allowed you space to stabilize her, but I'm not about to walk away on your word."

"How did you gain access to this floor? Mortal piracy?"

Dylan lifted a security card. "You left Quayla's purse behind."

I snatched away her card. "I made our position clear. Be gone."

"You don't intimidate me, Vitae. I'm not leaving."

While finding fault in his tenacity remained beyond me, his blatant refusal to accept his place lit my eyes with power. He would learn proper deference. Once he cowered, eyes open to the realities, I'd see him rewritten.

"You should be afraid."

Dylan stiffened, his countenance hardening.

"You are an insignificant mortal trespassing in the halls of giants. Your casual lusts—"

"I love her."

"Fine." I pressed my lips together, holding tight on the

pulsing power rising within me. "Your *love* distracted Aquaylae from her duty, risking her permanent destruction. Her purpose is too important to allow your feelings to jeopardize her. She won't be returned to that apartment or your bed."

"Is she all right?"

"Try to grasp your own language, mortal. Aquaylae has no further use for you. Be gone."

Dylan's voice rose. "I will only leave once I hear her send me away with her own lips."

I seized him, drawing him close enough to smell his horrid breath. My skin tingled in hot pulses "You're not good enough, not welcome and not wanted. You *will* see reason."

My anger vanished, leaving me awash in sudden cold calm.

Dylan's expression went slack. He turned, glazed eyes wide. Aquaylae's reflection filled his eyes, disgust bending her features.

Tears slid down his cheeks and his face screwed up in pain. "Q-Quayla...how could you say something like that...I thought you loved me."

The space in front of him remained empty even though Aquaylae stood reflected in his eyes.

"Fine. You're not thinking, not making sense, but I'll give you space." His angry retort brought me back to the present.

Aquaylae emerged from the library. Her expression brightened. "Dylan? I thought I heard you." She hobbled across the intervening space. "I'm so glad to...Dylan, what's wrong?"

Dylan's head snapped to one side, swinging back and forth between Aquaylae and the reflection. "How are there two—" His face contorted. He smashed Aquaylae's phone against the marble tiles. "Fine, you can *both* burn in hell for all I care."

Aquaylae's voice cracked. "Dylan?"

The mortal whirled toward the closed elevator only to turn back. "Well? You wanted me gone, so let me out of this birdcage already."

I stepped forward, swiping my access card.

"Wait!" Aquaylae shambled forward.

I caught her, restraining her until the closing doors removed the troublesome mortal from our lives. "You're better off without him."

"He makes me happy."

The corners of my mouth bent downward. "If your happiness comes from external indulgence instead of duty and service, you've greater issues to conquer."

"How could you drive him off like that? What did you say to him to turn him against me?"

"Only what was necessary. Nothing of consequence."

Aquaylae shoved a finger into my chest. "I don't believe you."

"Vitae stated Dylan was not good enough, not welcome and not wanted here," Anima said.

Aquaylae slapped me across the face. "I'll *never* forgive you."

She stormed off, leaving me to rub my cheek.

"Thank you, Anima."

"You were rude, but I saw no reason for Dylan's reactions," Anima said.

No, his response was all due to what was reflected in his eyes... something no one else saw. How was such an illusion possible?

I turned my tingling fingers over and again.

"Anima, one of Caelum's brownies must still be here."

"I assure you Vitae, I kept ceaseless track of their activities. After confirming their departure, I ran an additional deep scan. There are no faeries present in our sanctum."

I nearly ordered Anima to run another scan, but a horrifying thought stopped the words in my throat. I stormed into my bedroom and knelt next to my basin. I inhaled. The sweet coppery tang of my blood covered the contamination, but it couldn't mask the Sidhe taint from prickling my skin.

I reenvisioned my deaths and rebirths.

Faerie blood must have contaminated the essence from which I was reborn.

Horror and disgust warred with curiosity and delight.

Such contamination explained the sudden influx of selfish

thoughts and quixotic temper. More importantly, it further explained what I'd considered strange attention I received when visiting the two faerie Courts.

My eyes shot to the wall separating my and Mare's bedroom. My smile blossomed.

The influx of Sidhe blood in my reborn body seemed to have granted magical side effects not least of which control over mortals. If I were able to turn such abilities to my conscious control, I might be able to control the Unseelie sword enough to free Mare's soul. She could be reborn. In the meantime, enhancing my abilities allowed me to shore up our defenses, shoulder some of Summuseraphi's growing burden and prove myself worthy of ascension.

"Vitae?"

"I apologize, Anima. I thought the mortal's behavior a reaction to magic, but as I am unable to sense any faerie hiding in our home, I must've been incorrect."

"With all respect, Shieldheart, my own senses are far superior to yours for this purpose."

"I apologize for not trusting you." I headed for the elevator. "I will return once I have satisfied a query or two."

Quayla

My bedroom door didn't slam anywhere near as hard as I intended. Tears streaked searing, angry lines down my cheeks. I threw myself onto the old four-post bed, knowing but not caring how much I needed those tears to refill my nest.

I'd barely landed on the coverlet when I rolled off and paced the confines of my antique-appointed cage.

Vitae—who'd betrayed and abandoned me—had also jailed me within the sanctum, refusing me all exit until he deemed my health and my nest sufficiently recovered.

"Shield Quayla?"

"Not now, Ani, please."

"I just, well, is there anything I can do?"

"You can let me leave."

"I am truly sorry, but I cannot," Anima sounded sorry too.

Fine, if I'm not good enough for Vitae's Shield, then I'll leave.

I forced my weak legs over to my nest, snatching up both hilts. Fury flashed my flesh to essence in moments. I planted my left leg in the basin's center, positioned my curved knives on either side of my leg and scissored them through my thigh with an agonized shriek.

"Quayla!" Ani cried.

I teetered away from my still standing limb and smashed my lower back against the bureau. I hopped back into my nest, bare foot splashing in the liquid from my leg and sliced my karambit across the other leg.

As I teetered atop my severed leg, a solid two-handed shove launched me backward. Lightheadedness assaulted my tumble.

"Quayla, you have to stop," Anima pleaded. "That's too much essence at once."

I wanted to demand how she could possibly know, wanted to scream how impossible it was for her to know what is was like to be alone, mistreated and abandoned. My shock-befuddled brain refused to form the words. A high-pitched whine sent ripples through my essence. I bore down, demanding my watery substance to rebalance and regrow the lost legs.

Unconsciousness beat me silly before I learned whether or not my essence obeyed.

Detective Foxner

Sabrina Foxner sat in her car, staking out Quayla Buckler's apartment. She'd parked kitty corner a little way down the street

—as close as she dared after her Captain had ordered her to close the unsolved case.

I've never let a case remain unsolved before and I'm not starting now—besides, he can't tell me how to spend my personal time.

The Johammer electric motorcycle remained in the otherwise empty parking space. Nothing moved behind the curtained windows. No lights snapped on to illuminate the third-floor apartment. The motorcycle never moved. There'd been no sign of Buckler or her boyfriend at all.

The lack of activity made no difference. Her Captain's orders weren't enough to change the fact that Buckler was guilty—new body or no new body.

Nothing about this case makes sense, why should this? I know I'm right. She's the one I want.

Sabrina's thoughts drifted back to the off-balance coroner's assistant—Brantley something. He'd been adamant the odd ritual weapon had been made out of troll, something from horror films and apparently the world of super-geekdom. He insisted the bone grew before their eyes. Nothing grew that fast, not even the beansprouts they'd made them all grow way back in school.

Nothing natural anyway.

Brantley had been just as certain about the weapon as she was about Buckler's guilt. She shook the thoughts from her head.

I'm grasping, desperate to prove my instinct right even if that means embracing something as ridiculous as magic.

Sabrina would wait. She'd catch Buckler. All she needed was an excuse to enter Buckler's apartment one more time.

Vitae

I sat in my car for several minutes with my eyes closed, trying to feel the power I'd used to make Aquaylae's mortal more malleable to reason. Like the others, my essence thrummed with the power of Creation. Discerning the foreign power gifted me by a tainted rebirth proved a search for a specific needle in a canyon filled with them.

My importance as a life phoenix often relegated me to over-watch from the sanctum. It wasn't a matter of being weaker than the other shields, but only I could enhance the raw elements corresponding to the other shields' essences in order to empower or heal them.

Case in point, I had the ability to help Aquaylae back onto her feet. I simply had no intention of rewarding her laziness. We needed a strong Shield in the face of Sidhe war, but even at full strength Aquaylae would only be a weakness, a drain on our resources.

We need Mare. If I can access Sidhe magic, I could bend it to my will, make it serve the greater good...make Dolumii's sword release Mare back to us.

I pondered the ramifications.

Sidhe taint corrupted life, and there wasn't anything to me but life. If taking Seelie or Unseelie essence into myself granted me addition abilities, made me a stronger shield, then it offered a mechanism for shoring up our defenses.

First, I must determine if the feat is repeatable.

Both Anima and my nest were tied into the angel network. I knew of no way to separate the automata from that network, and the runes carved into my nest's basin and enchanted couldn't be removed. Anima would sense any rebirth. The automata would record the information, querying me for the cause of death for its report to our Praefectus.

Experimenting with Sidhe blood wasn't forbidden in the strictest sense, but our new divine didn't have much sense to start with. Our creation had equipped us with a certain amount of free will, promoting inventiveness in the cause of duty. Protecting my Shield and the Praefecture of Atlanta was my duty.

If pursuing mastery over magic offers the slightest chance of rescuing Mare, I'll pursue this through hell itself even if harnessing Sidhe magic serves neither Shield nor Atlanta.

There was an element of risk involved, but the worst-case scenario seemed death and rebirth. Like Mare—and unlike Aquaylae—I was willing to discomfort myself for the greater good.

All of which remained hypothetical until I acquired a source of Sidhe blood. The obvious avenue for acquiring such dwelt in the Goblin Market. Unfortunately, Aquaylae's gauche assault in that quarter effectively closed the Market off as a source.

Probably for the best. Purchased blood wouldn't include species, age or gender statistics, hampering analysis with a large unknown variable.

Fortunately, Sidhe activity was higher than normal.

"Anima, please provide me the location of the sentry net's largest dead zone."

"There is a large unmonitored area on the North perimeter, near the King and Queen buildings."

"Of course." I started the car. "Thank you."

"Do you require backup?" Anima asked.

"No."

I exited the garage into moderate traffic. Like it or not, over the last century Atlanta had grown in leaps and bounds. The addition of the automobile created a constantly worsening situation that outstripped road capacity, exacerbated by American entitlement to operate vehicles solo rather than the more community-minded transit paradigms in Europe. Little could be done about surface streets short of demolishing whole blocks and redesigning the system. A few of the other metropolitan Shields reported attempts to create multilevel surface streets. Citizens unwilling to pay higher taxes or suffer commuting inconveniences combined with ever present governmental misappropriation stymied those projects.

Eager as I might be to experiment, there was no rush or rage. I would arrive in due time, enjoying the best of mortal composers along the journey.

Part of me hoped for another breach in the Veil. I hadn't had the opportunity to test my captured elven blades in combat, and there were no guarantees the large dead zone in our net would hide readily available Sidhe.

I reached Atlanta's northern perimeter without Anima reporting any incursions. The corporate bastion remained busy even as evening came into its own. Commercial businesses served workers, commuters and companies running round-the-clock business models. Mortals bustled hither and yon, pursuing their little hordes of wealth, power or pleasure.

And there will be a Sidhe in their midst somewhere trying to make a deal.

I cruised along streets, keeping an eye on my surroundings and listening to my essence. Sharply-dressed and beautiful people amid the masses offered prospective suspects.

A turn off of Ashford-Dunwoody onto Hammond brought me close enough to feel a Sidhe. It took longer than acceptable for me to sight the faerie. I'd been looking for glamour and flash, not a shamble.

Vilicangelus postulated that a shamble encounter had inspired Charles Schulz's Pig-Pen. The Sidhe creatures lived and breathed filth. It clung to them like an ever-present cloud, only settling when they went immobile.

I drove into the parking structure.

A practiced beggar would've waited near the pay stations, where people had their currency at the ready and slow exit processing piled up the vehicles. The shamble lurked off to one side. The carrion feeder didn't care about currency, only easy prey.

"Anima, please see if you can find any indications of missing persons in my current area."

The shamble turned its back and wandered away the moment it saw or—more accurately—sensed me.

"There have been a number of missing persons reports around Perimeter Mall."

Parking in a reserved spaced guaranteed my vehicle would be towed if I lingered. There wasn't any reason for concern. I'd finish the shamble easily. I jogged up the shamble's filthy wake, drawing my Seelie Champion blade. The Unseelie creature had derailed my search, but I could not allow the vile beast to wander Creation. Technically, a shamble was a Sidhe creature, but the idea of infusing the filthy thing's blood into my essence was unconscionable.

"In the name of the Undying Light, I command you to stop."

The shamble groaned something, but didn't slow its retreat. I picked up the pace.

"I commanded you to halt." I tightened my grip on the sword despite how it fitted itself to my hand. "Continued resistance will require me to take aggressive action."

Much to my disappointment, the shamble stopped, turned and gave me a filthy look. "Ain't doing nothing."

"You are outside Faery, and I have reason to believe you've been preying on mortals."

Up close, shadows and phantoms slipped the shamble's control, betraying the creature's disguise of a homeless human. Phantasms swirled and vanished: a shrieking woman, an elderly man and a Nubian corporate professional. Their appearance lasted less than an eye blink, but I needed no further evidence that the shamble had murdered mortals and kept their souls.

In my younger days, I might've pretended not to notice, closed peaceably for a surprise attack. The sight of stolen souls bit deep. Heat washed down Gherrian's blade into me and back over the sword in a swirling red and gold corona.

I rode the wave of fury straight for the shamble's throat.

The shamble slipped under my strike, moving far faster than its name implied. It dropped its glamour, revealing the mishmash of detritus that made up its body. I positioned for a thrust only to have the beast hurl a woman's soul into my face.

Her terror hit me like a runaway Clydesdale. My battle cry became a shriek of terror. In the moment of distraction, the shamble swung both arms. A sickening energy colored like a black eye bound two thick limbs launched from the Sidhe like a zombie bola.

They hit my shoulder and ankle hard enough they knocked me horizonal. Arm bones snapped. Leg bones shattered. Cracked ribs threatened to puncture my innards. The flesh bola snapped back like it had been connected by a bungee cord as a shamble leg curved itself up in an uppercut to catch my airborne body in the hip.

More bones broke and broke again as I hit the concrete. I rolled a painful retreat, using the time to check our surroundings. Hidden behind a minivan and invisible to the road thanks to a retaining wall, I transmogrified my flesh to essence and back to restored flesh.

The shamble stomped my back.

Most shambles I'd faced would've taken the opportunity to flee, trusting camouflage and glamour to lose me.

I rolled toward the beast and thrust Gherrian's blade into its torso. Energy sheathing the blade flared through the faerie like nuclear fire. Souls filled my head with ear-splitting shrieks most mortals couldn't hear.

The blade's corona intensified, dragging anguished souls into itself. The guard bubbled and shifted, liquid yet metal. Faces of the shamble's victims filled in blank spaces on the hilt, their features bent in torment as they receded into the metal to leave only eyes behind.

I stared, my soul colder than the night I'd spent in Antarctica.

My gaze came up, fixating on the scattered remains of the destroyed shamble. For a moment, I empathized, feeling just as scattered as the dead faerie.

Chapter Four

Seeds of a Trap

Ignis

Ignis returned to his Camaro with another two fire extinguishers. He propped them on his bumper and dug another nested, three-chamber disk from the toolbox in his trunk. He applied Gorilla glue to its base, careful not to block any of the holes exposing the encapsulated ashes to air. He attached the disk to the extinguisher's bottom, repeated the process and carried both back to the restaurant.

The restaurant manager accepted an extinguisher with a frown. "I don't understand, inspector, we just had those certified three months ago."

"New regulation." Ignis shrugged, handing another over. "Politicians love to tweak rules. This alteration doesn't affect their certification and it's free. So, just hang them back up."

Ignis finished adjusting the other extinguishers and bought a to-go order for a late lunch or early dinner. He stepped into twilight, inhaling deeply to test the new seeds. Garlic, almond chicken made his stomach rumble. He popped a piece into his mouth and settled in behind the Camaro's wheel.

"How's does that look, Ani?"

"That mends the last hole for that sector, though we're still a little thin on the eastern edge."

"I already seeded that area." He gobbled another chunk, pulling a plastic fork from inside a napkin roll and attacking the accompanying angel hair.

"The shortage is not yours, Ignis."

He swallowed a too big bite in his rush to fill the ache in his stomach, scratching his throat. "How's Quayla?"

"Her nest is full and she is recovering slowly, but headquarters has felt like a demilitarized zone since yesterday," Anima said.

Vitae should've tasked her to handle her paramour. Taking it upon himself and with such vitriol only worsens the rift among us.

Ignis shook his head.

Should've gotten myself a drink too.

"We have a Veil breech six blocks north of you," Anima said.

"We just patched that area." His attention shot to the small archangel, one arm pointing the direction. He clumsily closed the to-go container and dropped it to the passenger floorboards. "Always when I'm eating or in the bath."

He pulled out in a rush, causing a near collision with a driver that'd whipped around the corner without slowing. Ignis left the blaring horn behind a layer of rubber, slapped his emergency light on the dashboard beside the angel statuette, and turned on his siren.

"You bathe?" Anima asked.

Ignis chuckled. "You're hanging out with Caelum too much. His influence on you is becoming problematic."

"We have a second Veil breech in the alley north of the first location," Anima said.

Ignis took a hard right, whipping around a taxi dropping off its passenger. The archangel figurine pressed both hands over its face.

"Not sure how I can minimize my contact with Caelum," Anima said. "I'm stationary."

"Touché." He pulled to a halt in front of a hydrant near the mouth of an alley leading to the detected breach. Ignis threw his inspector's parking card onto his dash, grabbed his weapon rod, and leapt from the car.

"Take caution, Shield Ignis. Do you require backup?"

He called over his shoulder as he ran. "If you don't hear from me in fifteen minutes, call in the cavalry."

He charged up the alley behind a force of elves, pixies and gnolls. The screech of hasty breaks and sounds of crashing metal filled the air ahead of him. Another Sidhe force poured out of the far alley—goblins, Unseelie elves and a two-story ogre. The two factions crashed into each other. The ogre seized and hurled cars —at least one occupied—from his path in his hurry to reach his enemies.

Damn peace-preserving conventions.

Heat kindled beneath his skin. He pushed it into his weapon. Flame danced out both ends, curving back toward him. Twin sparks shot from the ends toward one another joining in the center. He pulled back the bow string, detaching a starburst mote of his essence and extending one point into a long, feathered shaft.

I hate warning shots.

He loosed the arrow above them. The starburst head exploded like a July skyrocket.

"By the Undying Light, I command you to repair this damage, Glamour your appearance and retreat back beyond the Veil."

The ogre threw a jogger and her dog at Ignis.

Ignis threw himself forward, building power as he ran. He leapt, transmogrifying mid-air to catch both in extended wings. Force threw the three of them backward. He hit the ground as a man with the woman and dog in either arm. He charged forward once more. Essence extended from one end of his rod into a flaming scimitar.

The dog—leash free of his owner's hand—chased Ignis down

the alley with excited barks. Gnolls turned toward the offensive animal, growling objections to whatever it barked.

"I warned you." Ignis's blade quartered the first gnoll. He turned it on the second. "By my authority as Shield Ignis, I sentence you to summary punishment."

An elven blade intercepted his, bright magic holding off Ignis's flaming edge. Blades clashed. The second gnoll thrust a barbed spear at his gut. He parried a low cut, sidestepped the spear and ignited the gnoll's forearm with a nimbus-shrouded hand.

A second elven knight leapt to his companion's aide. A hurled goblin slammed into the elf's back as she lunged at Ignis. The flame phoenix took advantage. Sweeping his weapon upward, he decapitated the goblin, sheered the top off an elf's skull and beat aside first elf's attempted head cut.

An Unseelie knight stabbed a serrated blade shimmering with dark magic into the first elf. Ignis cut at its arms, weapon deflecting off enchantment-shrouded bracers. The Unseelie swept its blade up in a salute, separating his sword into two lighter blades and engaging both the injured Seelie and Ignis. Pain sliced across Ignis then up his veins as the poisonous magic sank into him.

The wafer's little dog jumped around the fight, yapping and growling with an annoyance factor far outweighing its size.

Ignis batted aside a strike, leaping backward in a series of end over end flips. He transmogrified in the last flip, burned the magical venom from his system, and transmog'd back. He landed off balance, dropping to one knee as he wrenched a mote of essence from himself and fired an arrow into a charred, charging gnoll.

A massive blurred shadow entered Ignis's peripheral vision with a roar. He rolled sideways, imagining a colossal ogre fist hammering him into the street. He unleashed another arrow at a goblin already lined up in his sights before shifting the weapon back into a scimitar.

Blood exploded in bursts of green and violet as the shape split into two parts. The first flipped into the air, wings appearing then disappearing as quiet bullets spit at faerie in triplets. The motorcycle slammed into several goblins and the ogre.

"Nice to see you," Ignis charged the Unseelie knight.

Caelum dropped his machine pistols and pulled twin M1911 semi-automatics. "You didn't tell me we had a party on the calendar tonight."

"Fire is often unpredictable." Ignis jumped back out of the knight's slash, twisting to avoid goblin javelins.

Caelum blew holes in two goblins then double shot an elven skull. "Pity our opponents aren't."

"Aren't those guns outmoded?" Ignis said.

"Says the guy who uses a sword," A goblin shortsword slashed Caelum. He grimaced, shooting it in return. "Besides, some things never go out of style."

An ogre fist came a feather's breadth from reducing Caelum into bread dough.

"Any others on the way?" Ignis said.

"I was scouting a research location not too far away," Caelum shot Ignis's opponent in the back of his helmet, painting Ignis in violet. "Ani said you might need a hand."

"We're going to need a lot of rewrites," Ignis hamstrung a Seelie elf trying to flank an Unseelie.

"Wouldn't want Summus to feel unneeded." Caelum reloaded, pausing to slam hot steel into a goblin nose. "You know we'd be in trouble if they teamed up against us."

The remaining Seelie and Unseelie exchanged glances. They charged together.

"In future," Ignis took a thrust to the gut and answered by severing the limb holding the dirk. "You can keep those kinds of comments to yourself."

Caelum raced up an alley wall, firing downward as he leapt. Three javelins caught him dead center midair. He slammed to the ground with a heavy grunt.

"Back off and transmog," Ignis pressed two attackers.

"We can take them," Caelum struggled upright, shooting a charging faerie in the knees.

"It'll rebalance your essence, idiot," Ignis leapt over Caelum, scimitar cutting a blazing butterfly pattern.

"But the wafers will see."

"Cat's in the aquarium at this point," Ignis said.

A flash of light and burst of wind told Ignis Caelum had done as instructed. Caelum cursed. "My pistols!"

Amateurs, him and Aquaylae both.

Ignis cut down the last Seelie. He turned to face three wounded goblins and one very angry ogre. He took a deep breath, backing away slowly. "We can end this peaceably if you'll do as ordered."

"Only bird orders of I want come with a side dish," the ogre bellowed.

Great, I'm surrounded by stand-up comedians.

Ignis shifted his weapon once more and impaled two of the goblins with fire-burst arrows.

Caelum bellowed and charged the ogre. It cocked its head at him as he dove between the ogre's legs. The ogre shoved its knees together like an outfielder catching a ground ball. It scooped Caelum up, opening wide jaws.

Ignis sent an arrow into the ogre's mouth. It dropped Caelum and growled through a smoking grimace. Ignis charged, cutting down the last goblin with his flaming blade before dancing around the ogre. It picked up a car and slammed it down atop Ignis. He rolled out of the way, all too aware he wouldn't be in time.

Two explosions deflected the deadly Hyundai.

The ogre fell forward on shredded knees. Caelum stood behind it, cocking his shotgun for another blast.

"No pithy one liner?" Ignis rolled to his feet, cutting at the vulnerable ogre. "No boom stick jokes?"

"Too tired," Caelum blasted the ogre in the small of its back.

They made quick work of the brute after that.

Ignis surveyed the carnage, extinguishing his weapon. Sirens screamed their way from multiple directions. "Get gone, call in Summus as quick as you can."

Anima's voice escaped the statuette between Caelum's handlebars. "Caelum, we have two more Veil breeches. Make that three."

Caelum yanked his motorcycle upright and sped away.

A part of Ignis wanted to race to his car and join Caelum, but the injured mortals needed him first.

A Shield is never just one phoenix.

He rushed from wafer to wafer, doing quick triage before offering medical assistance to those most in need. A fire truck, firefighters and their firehouse paramedics arrived on the scene. A few of the younger ones stood back in shock and confusion, but old hats dove in to help the injured.

"What the hell happened, inspector?"

Ignis grimaced. "Not sure, Lowe, I was a couple of blocks south when I heard screams. You, bring me your bag. I need a better bandage."

"Good ears," Lowe said.

"Loud screams."

A young paramedic pushed his bag into Ignis's hands. "What are those things?"

"Concentrate rookie! Help the injured!"

"Stop gawking and get in the game, Billy," Lowe snapped.

A blinding flash of light filled the scene.

"Holy Mary Mother of God, what the hell is *that*?" Billy asked.

"Behold, Summuseraphi Divine Messenger of the Undying Light," Summus announced. "Seek my light and see truth anew."

Judith

Judith paced back and forth behind the counter. The scent of cloves and honey wafted up from the cup of chai sitting next to her own empty coffee. Dark clothes clung to her as her short, straight hair whipped her cheeks with each angry pivot.

The chai had been a peace offering, an apology for the horrible things she'd thought about Quayla for making Judith tend the shop alone. Quayla made a habit out of being late, but she'd never been absent without a word for days on end. It wasn't like Judith managed Ponds de Leon Flowers. No one did.

Sure, officially there was a manager, but Judith hadn't ever met him. She'd called him after Quayla's second day of absence. The number had rolled to voicemail. An internet search turned up the number was hosted by Google Voice, but no owner. She'd left message after message, but no one had called her back.

Something's wrong. I just know it.

Judith played aloof, but she really did care. She cared too much in fact. One of her lifelong failings came from a habit of becoming emotionally invested too readily. She fell in love too easily, and every time she cared about someone or something, she got hurt.

I decided to be smarter when I started Georgia Tech, but I just can't shake the feeling that Quayla is in trouble.

Judith glanced at her reflection in the flower chiller. Circles cradled her puffy eyes leaving the rest of her pale skin to look pallid against her plain, black clothes.

The bell over the door spun her around. An ugly, dark-skinned midget in a foreshortened trench coat hobbled into the shop, cleared his throat and addressed her with a thick, gravely accent. "Is she here?"

Judith braced herself against the guy's aroma and took a deep breath. "No. Perhaps you'll let me assist you this time?"

He shot Judith a nasty look and hobbled back out of the shop.

"Whatever." Judith rolled her eyes. "Like I care."

She called the manager's number again only to be told that the voicemail box was full.

Screw this.

Judith grabbed her clutch, Quayla's chai, and a unicorn-decorated motorcycle helmet. She shoved the gift Quayla gave her last Christmas onto her head and stormed out of the florist shop. She paused a moment to lock the door, pinning her lip beneath her teeth in sudden indecision.

If Quayla can get away with being absent, then he'll just have to deal with me closing up early.

She jumped on her scooter and headed across town to the address she'd dug out of Quayla's personnel record.

Judith pulled up in front of Quayla's apartment. She took off the helmet, shook out her hair and ran her fingers through it to comb out any tangles.

Not that I care about looking good for Quayla.

Judith used the whole cross-town trip to build her temper into a tempest. Anger kept the worry at bay, and if she found Quayla lounging around at home Judith had every intention of letting Quayla have it.

She stormed up the stairs.

If Quayla was fine, Judith intended to get answers.

Quayla had left her alone without a word. Her absence forced Judith to stay near the florist shop, forgoing coffee and lunch hour study time. She'd had to stay late, unsure where Quayla was or why she was forced to close up the shop alone.

I had to do the whole inventory myself. If I hadn't ordered flowers, we wouldn't have had any for orders.

Worse, Quayla'd left her to worry without any idea why she'd abandoned Judith to deal with people—horrible, terrible, normal people—all by herself.

She pounded on Quayla's door. "Open up."

No one answered.

"Quayla, you owe me some answers, damn it. Are you even all

right? Never mind. I don't care. Just answer this door and promise to come back to work."

No one answered.

She pounded again. "You just up and left, no note, no message. You left me taking care of everything. You left me to deal with the police. I'm not the manager. I'm not the owner, but you made me lock everything up. I—"

The door swung open.

A chill froze Judith's words in her mouth.

Blood ran a path from the door to the couch.

Judith felt as if her insides had shriveled up like a raisin. She stepped inside. "Quayla?"

Please don't be dead.

The blood stopped at the couch, but Judith didn't. She checked the rooms one by one, each tightening the vice around her heart. In some ways, the lack of Quayla's body compounded her fear.

I have to do something.

Judith hurried out the door only to be brought up short. One moment the stairwell was clear. The next the ugly man from the shop growled at her. "Is she here?"

Judith screamed and darted around him. The throb of blood hitting her ears drowned out her wedges hitting the old wooden stairs. She made it down three flights, onto her scooter and into traffic without remembering to breathe.

Police. I need the police.

Detective Foxner

Sabrina directed the purse snatcher deeper into the precinct. She should've been taking him to processing, but he'd offered her a series of apartment thefts. She hated making deals with criminals, but the break-ins had resulted in the hospitalization of an elderly man.

Things in homicide were better, cut and dry. Murderers went to jail. No deals. No pressure to let a criminal escape justice.

"How many times do I have to tell you, Quayla Buckler!"

Sabrina froze in her tracks, jerking her handcuffed informant to an abrupt halt.

"Hey!"

She ignored him, instead seeking out the familiar voice. It took several moments to recognize the animated woman as the thin, impersonal shop attendant Judith...something.

"Someone needs to help," Judith said.

"I already explained this to you," the desk sergeant's tone indicated the imminent death of his last nerve. "We will assign your report to one of our officers to investigate. I'm sorry, but missing persons aren't the highest priority on our plates today."

"There was blood."

"I know. It's in my report."

"Stay here," Sabrina stepped toward Judith. Second thoughts stopped her. She flagged down a uniformed officer. "Hey, take this suspect to my desk. I'll be right there."

If the younger officer objected to being ordered around by a detective, he didn't make it obvious. He inclined his head, took the purse snatcher by his bicep and left Sabrina to approach Judith.

"Excuse me—"

"You're the one that came by asking questions about Quayla," Judith said in a rapid stream with barely any gaps. "She's missing. There's blood in her apartment. I need—"

Sabrina held up a hand, resisting an urge to grin. "All right. I understand. If you can give me a couple minutes, I will come with you to check this out."

Judith gave the incredulous sergeant a nasty look.

Sabrina gestured for the sergeant to let it go and escorted Judith deeper into the precinct. The formerly dispassionate woman rattled off information on fast forward and seemingly endless repeat. Sabrina barely listened. Judith's report meant sufficient probable cause to get her back into Buckler's apartment. It wasn't burglary, but, "Did you notice anything missing from Miss Buckler's apartment?"

"Besides Quayla?"

"Yes," Sabrina asked.

"How the hell should I know? I've never been in her apartment. Besides, what does that matter?"

"Could anything be missing?"

"Yes, Quay—"

"Excellent," Sabrina cut her off. "Have a seat here. I have to finish up with that suspect, but I will be with you as soon as I am done."

"Someone needs to help now."

Sabrina gave Judith a flat look. "The desk sergeant was sending you home. I'm offering to come with you as soon as I finish one thing. Be grateful I can squeeze you in."

Judith's face dropped. "You're right. I'm sorry. I'm just really worried about Quayla."

Sabrina forced a smile. "I understand."

It took longer than Sabrina would've liked to deal with the purse-snatching stool pigeon. He seemed interested in anything that dragged out the interview while Judith paced back and forth in front of the line of chairs near the wall.

Sabrina cut him off. "You've already told me that. I'm starting to think you're stalling so by time I get to the location you gave me, the evidence will be gone."

"No, nothing of the sort."

"Good, then I'm going to put you in holding so you can't warn anyone before I get there."

"Wait, you didn't say anything about me being stuck here."

"Must've slipped my mind."

After the dirt bag was off to rot in holding, Sabrina turned her attention to the impatient florist. One surprise inspection of

Buckler's apartment would tie up the case with enough time to raid the address provided by the purse snatcher. After a short discussion, Sabrina agreed to meet Judith at Quayla's apartment. The woman's scooter meant not being restrained by Atlanta traffic, soon escaping Sabrina's sight. Sabrina breathed a sigh of relief when she pulled up to find Judith waiting.

If Buckler's landlady discovered Sabrina on the premises, she'd likely demand a warrant. Judith's presence meant not needing one. She followed Judith up the stairs.

"There was this guy who kept coming into Ponds looking for Quayla. He followed me here."

"I remember you telling me about him."

"He might still be here."

"Let me go first," Sabrina said.

They reached the third-floor landing. Buckler's apartment door hung open just enough to display a dark sliver. Sabrina pushed the door in, hand on her undrawn sidearm. Old bloodstains marred the floor, but they'd been present the last time Sabrina had searched the apartment.

No reason to tell Judith that until after I've searched.

"Miss Buckler? It's Detective Foxner and your coworker. Judith's concerned for your safety, so we're coming in..."

The door opened to reveal a crowd of small, malformed naked men. They turned as a nasal tone filled the quiet. "You incompetent jackass. You told me you dealt with her."

A blur of motion left a glittering trail of fairy dust as an impact against the foremost ugly, dark-skinned midget's head sent him toppling. The others tensed but didn't move.

A male Tinkerbelle rocketed from Buckler's couch to the door. Sabrina drew her sidearm, an order on her lips. A plume of golden dust flooded the doorway.

Sabrina spasmed. Her gun thunked to the floor as her body arched in a body-wide stretch. Her nipples tightened as phantom fingers caressed her breasts exactly the way she liked. Wetness collected between her thighs. Something triggered her clitoris and every muscle spasmed in orgasm.

Somewhere distant another woman, probably Judith, moaned in ecstasy.

The fairy grew to a full-sized man dressed in a tidy business suit. He gestured. "Put them on the bed while I figure out what to do with them."

Sabrina's orgasms intensified until her muscle spasms grew to the verge of painful.

"We can dispose of them," the ugly midget licked his lips. "At least, what's left."

"No eating them...or tasting for that matter. Just put them on the bed. The spell will keep them quiet," a grin flashed across his face, "well, not quiet, but pliant until I find out Her Highness's desires."

Chapter Five

Revelations

Vitae

Both Champion blades had formed themselves to fit my hand when I'd first claimed them after my defeat of their Sidhe owners. It seemed clear they'd responded to the Sidhe essence mixed into my new body. Dolumii's sword had refused to give up Mare—theoretically due to my exhausting the faerie magic within me. Without magic to command their function, Gherrian's sword never should've drank in the shamble or its captured souls.

My use of glamour against Aquaylae's paramour hadn't been conscious, but I had desired the mortal to see reason.

I did not wish this. It should never have happened. I will not accept this.

I held Gherrian's sword in both hands. Horror-backed will commanded the Champion blade to release the souls I'd inadvertently captured. I strained against the sword to no avail, thwarted by what almost felt like a smug stubbornness.

Impossible! Weapons don't possess wills of their own.

Slamming the blade into its sheath, I returned to relocate my car's parking place. The extensive dead zone hadn't been managed by a single shamble. North perimeter hid the Sidhe I desperately needed. If I climbed to the MARTA transit system and rode on their filthy trains, I'd discover another faerie sooner or later. Long hours on plastic seats held no appeal, so I investigated the nearby shopping mall first.

I held a heavy glass door for several young ladies deserving the courtesies due a lady despite indecent attire. Two youths in desperate need of belts barged through the opening, cutting off the ladies.

My jaw tightened enough to hold back a scathing rebuke.

Once the thankless ladies were on their way, I located a map. Running my finger down the various eateries identified two spots likely to draw in pixies—a candy shop and a bakery. I oriented on the bakery first, counting on the pixie love for honey to provide quarry.

I hadn't traversed to the half-way point when the warm aroma of cinnamon, butter and sugar caressed my nose. A small shop to my left—drolly named Cinnabon—offered baked sweetbreads and some kind of citrus drink named after a Roman emperor.

I stopped, closing my eyes to feel for any pixies or sprites drawn in by the tantalizing aroma.

A youth knocked me forward. "Watch where you're stopping, old fart."

In bygone days, it would've been compulsory to redeem my honor while teaching the youth proper manners. Unfortunately, dueling had been outlawed in recent centuries, and as such, doing so risked unwanted attention.

A tickle against my essence lifted my eyes to a hole in the ceiling just behind a support girder. Since mice seldom flew and frequent climbing to such a home would be too exposed, the only logical explanation seemed a pixie hollow.

I regarded the bakery once more, noting an employee cutting open a bag to apply icing to a freshly-baked tray of rolls. The employee's skill with icing the buns, compounded by the prepacked icing itself disqualified the youth as a baker's apprentice.

And thus, those sweetbreads are some modern convenience, a counterfeit of true craftsmanship with undoubtedly an equally slap-dash flavor. How can these mortals have forgotten the richness of handcrafted baked goods?

The answer was one of caring. Mortals didn't care the flavor was inferior because having a sweetbread without even a moment's effort is convenient. They didn't have to work for the treat. Someone else performed the work for them.

Better flavor and a sense of accomplishment no longer warrant personal effort. These mortals are entitled to their inferior sweets and to have them without any effort.

I withdrew a wallet from inside my coat. The two five-dollar bills contained in the folded leather had sojourned within for almost a century. The price of the so-called confection would exhaust one—obscene for a single roll, but ready bait would lure the pixie faster than more hunting or returning to the sanctum for honey.

"My good fellow, I would purchase one of your confections."

The employee gave me a strange look, but his fingers created beeping noises on a computer. "Visiting from out of town?"

"Nay, I've lived in this city for some time."

"If you say so. That'll be five thirty-two."

"The price board indicates four dollars and ninety-six cents."

"Sales tax."

I pursed my lips, added the second bill and offered both.

The employee gave me a shifty eye. He extended the bills "Look, I don't want to call a cop, all right. How about you just leave?"

"I require the confection."

"And I need you to pay for it."

"That is legal tender."

The employee yanked another five-dollar bill from his drawer, tapping a finger on the green seal. "If you're going to counterfeit, do a little research."

Heat burbled in my stomach. "My good sir, this is legal tender in these United States you call America."

"Fine, just a minute," the employee stepped into the back.

The delay was irksome, but at least the boy had come into line.

After an interminable wait, a lady addressed me. "Excuse me?"

I turned to find a woman dressed in a local law enforcement uniform. I inclined my head. "How may I assist you, madame?"

She sucked in breath. She tucked stray hair into place, her smile flickering to full strength. Widening pupils traced up and down my body, lingering a moment near the swords without actually locking onto the weapons.

The sweetbread vendor came out from behind the counter and pushed my two bills into her hands. "He tried to pay with these."

My temper rose. I'd been put off so that he could summon law enforcement and accuse me of criminal activity.

"Please remain where you are, sir." The officer turned the bills over in her hands, brows rising first at me and then furrowing at the boy. "What do you think is the problem?"

"They're counterfeit." He offered the same bill he'd shown me. "He didn't even bother to get the seal the right color.'

She gave him a flat look. "The bill in your hand is worth five dollars. These are over a century old and probably worth far more considering their condition."

She handed me the two bills. "I recommend you trade these to a collector rather than just trying to spend them."

"I see." I pursed my lips, frowning at the currency she handed back. "Thank you, madame."

"Is something wrong?" She asked.

Many things piqued my temper. The sweetbread vendor had accused me of being a lowly knave—something I couldn't settle via challenge. My own mistake using old currency had gathered unnecessary attention.

We carried toothless weapons to avoid legal entanglements or drawing attention. We only employed essence to arm ourselves in the face of faerie adversaries. The law keeper had noted my swords, but for whatever her reason chosen to overlook the bladed weapons.

Both mistakes and my ignorance of sales tax grew out of limited exposure to current mortal life.

There may have been some merit in Mare's arguments after all.

"Sir?"

"My deepest apologies, madame. I'd intended to purchase a confection as a treat for a...little one, but it seems it would be imprudent to purchase such with this currency."

She smirked at me and drew a wallet. She handed money over to the boy. "Get his order." She turned back to me. "I love your accent. Are you a British movie star?"

"I am not. While I appreciate the offer, madame, I cannot allow you to give me charity."

Her eyes flicked away. "A trade then? You buy me dinner."

Do all mortals think only with their hormones?

"Once more, I appreciate the gesture but that isn't possible."

"Oh." She made a dismissive gesture. "Just pay it forward then." When I didn't immediately respond, she added more. "You know, you do something nice to help someone else."

"I shall do so. You have my gratitude."

The boy pushed a box into my hand and coins into hers. He huffed at both of us and stormed back into his shopfront. The lady shield hurried way, glancing backward twice.

I seated myself at the nearest bench with my back to the shop. Opening the carton wafted cinnamon-spiced steam into my face. Despite the attractive aroma, I knew tasting the sweetbread would ultimately provide only disappointment.

A moment's focus extruded essence, allowing me to drip it upon the roll. I settled the roll's container on the lip of a trash receptacle with the cardboard lid open. A finger brushed the thick icing and I brought it to my mouth without thinking. Incredibly smooth sweetness touched my tongue, undercut by the tang of cream cheese and a hint of vanilla.

Inferior—as expected.

A silk handkerchief from my vestment cleaned the residue from my fingers. I leaned in an alcove beneath, but behind the pixie hole and went quiet, damping my presence.

Between the free sweet and my vital essence, the pixie took almost no time to poke his head out of his hole. He glanced around, tiny nose sniffing and antennae twitching back and forth. His eyes narrowed toward the abandoned confection.

A surge of magic took me off guard, causing an involuntary gasp. The spike far outstripped what I'd heretofore felt from any faerie of his size.

Glamour cloaked his dive, but the wind of his passing washed over my skin. Impact slid the carton a finger's breadth. A mammoth bite—for a pixie mouth—disappeared from the iced bread.

After allowing several moment's gorging to foster lethargy, I approached with a swift, silent gait. I snapped the box closed on him. The box buzzed and jerked, foul-mouthed oaths spilling from the container's seams.

I shook the box once. "You will be still, Sidhe."

"You bent my wing! Whoever in the blighted hells you think you are, you're not giving me a lot of reasons to grant you your heart's desire. Let me out this instant or there'll be no bargain."

I rattled the box again, striding out the nearest exit

Teeth sank into my finger where he'd chewed through the carton and into flesh. I didn't jerk my hand away, but I did address him. "Assaulting a shield will not improve your predicament, faerie."

An involuntary squeak told me I'd shut down his teeth for the nonce. It took considerable juggling to open my Mercedes's door, remove my swords and enter without allowing the Sidhe escape. Doors closed and locked, I set the container on my passenger seat.

The top popped open. The pixie hovered just over the confection, shaking like a dog. Icing shot in every direction, dotting calf-skin leather and dashboard controls, pristine carpet and my suit.

Heat built up, escaping in a growl that wrenched the pixie's eyes up to mine.

He cringed, casting around and squeaking in a piccolo voice. "No napkins?"

I removed my handkerchief and cleaned a glob of icing from my cheek. "No."

It puffed itself up. "I demand to know why you trapped me. I wasn't doing nothing?"

"Sidhe are not allowed to abide within Creation, certainly not in a public shopping area where mortals might witness them."

"Fine, fine, spare me the lecture. Release me and I will return to the Courts."

"I have queries first."

"I won't rat anyone out," he crossed his arms.

"You invoked glamour to disguise yourself when you went after the roll. How did you go about that?"

"I just did it, okay?"

"No, you had to have learned some process or mindset to allow you to create the illusion you desired."

"Maybe, I don't know, look, what's it to you?"

"I wish to understand more about faerie magic."

His gaze narrowed and he sniffed loudly. An instant later, his head shot sideways to the blades lain in the back seat. I wasn't concerned he could turn the blades against me so I made no move to prevent him from investigating my swords.

Instead, the little pixie stepped closer to me and inhaled. His eyes widened until they threatened the limits of his head. "You've got faerie blood. You're trying to use our magic!"

He bolted for the back seat, burrowing through the seats toward the trunk. I craned around, snatched him in my left hand and pulped his body with a tiny crunch.

"Tedious." I turned back to a comfortable sitting position.

I shifted my hand from flesh to essence and absorbed his fluids into my own. His mass didn't add a substantial percentage to my overall balance. A surge of magic coursed through me, though it didn't seem as strong as his glamour.

Perhaps he exhausted his strength remaining unseen.

Success in all things came down to discipline and will, so even though he hadn't provided instructions I determined to use his magic. I turned my left hand over, and concentrated. My fingers faded from view one by one.

I took a moment to shift and rebalanced my essence. Spreading the taint which accompanied his magic would hopefully limit notice by the others and possibly allow for more dramatic glamour experiments.

I started the car and pulled out of the garage. Fingers of my right hand absently slid through the icing, lifting the buttery sweetness to my mouth.

I smiled.

The limited essence of a mere pixie, absorbed rather than part of a rebirth, had granted me power I could feel. With practice and more Sidhe blood, the possibilities for making an increased difference in the war against the Sidhe offered just and delicious desserts.

Terrance

"I'm sorry, but no, severing essence never really gets easier, little sister. Death must carry a cost, even for a phoenix." Terrance cupped her icy hands as her shuddering, emaciated frame quaked with grief. "If it is of any comfort, you will eventually become inured to the pain."

"So, I just have to stop feeling." A tear trailed down Quayla's hollow cheeks. "Vitae will be pleased."

The wounds she'd suffered defending the Shield and rescuing

Vitae had healed. And yet beneath her mended skin, young, caring Quayla seemed more holes than heart.

"When Anima informed me of your actions, she did not convey how drastically you'd overdone severing essence."

She refused to look at him.

The essence in her stone basin rose to the very brim. Junk food wrappers haloed her nest, but her emaciated body bore not even a single extra ounce. Her legs shook, barely able to keep her upright.

Even a peapod pixie would represent a mortal threat to her in this condition.

"If faerie's war hadn't monopolized our time, one of us might've looked in on you sooner."

"I'm fine."

"You are not fine." Terrance eased the stone from his voice. "Why have you done this to yourself, little sister?"

The venom in her tone belied her body's weakness. "I will not listen to Vitae call me lazy or incompetent any more. I will not listen to Anima announce an incursion and then stand idle waiting for the death cry of one of my brothers." She pointed a shuddering hand. "My nest is full, make Vitae release me."

"We're not made for cages, true, but lend not your thoughts to foolish notions."

Her eyes hardened.

"I know, little bird. It's been only a few days, but young wings yearn to fly free in open sky." He pulled her close. "Vitae's treated you poorly. We're under assault. There are many reasons you might wish to flee the coop... perhaps to never circle back?"

"I don't get that choice," Quayla said.

"We have all felt as you do, been plagued by a desire to fly free without the chains of duty to hold us captive."

"Really?"

Terrance nodded. "I felt much the same in days before our Vitae's birth. Youth always seeks freedom they feel their elders are unfairly withholding."

Caelum entered her bedroom with grocery bags in both arms. His smile lacked its normal vitality. His clothes remained disheveled from tangling with another breech somewhere between work and headquarters.

"Hello, beautiful, come here often?" Caelum asked.

Quayla smiled. "Hello, Caelum."

"I was talking to Terrance," Caelum said.

A thin, weary giggle escaped her lips.

Caelum's answering smile hid his own exhaustion. Even the way he carried himself advertised the toll the opening salvos of the Seelie-Unseelie war had wrought on Atlanta and their Shield.

"I brought more contraband. Terrance and Ignis both contributed, so I bought you some really decadent treats." He flashed another grin. "I left that stuff in my apartment and brought you this instead."

Quayla gave Terrance a pointed look. "Thanks, Caelum, but since my nest is full, I'll head over to your place and grab it."

Caelum raised his brows.

We are in desperate peril, but no matter how much we need her at our side, we cannot allow her to leave until she's restored body and soul.

Pain ran wide paths from her eyes into the depths of her soul.

"Not until your egg is remade," Terrance said. "Rest up. We will come together as soon as the Sidhe allow."

Caelum tucked the bags inside her bedside cabinet.

"Vitae requires your immediate attendance in the garden," Anima announced.

Quayla stiffened.

Terrance offered a smile as a peace offering. "Vitae is weary from battle. He speaks without thinking."

"Thinking has never been his strong suit anyway," Caelum said.

Rather than laugh, she darkened. "Thinking of others might cost him something."

"Shield Quayla, that accusation is unfair and unworthy of

you," Anima said. "Especially considering the weight he has carried on your behalf."

Quayla opened her mouth to retort, but Terrance placed fingers over her lips. "Peace, little sister. Be the dappled pool, not the roaring waterfall."

She pried herself from his embrace and staggered toward the garden with her jaw set in a taut line.

Terrance sighed.

"We need to do something," Caelum said.

"I know, but it is so long since I have been only two centuries old, I fear I don't remember how she feels well enough to help."

"Vitae summons you all," Anima said.

One trouble at a time.

Terrance led the way, pausing to help Quayla up the last few steps. She threw him off the moment they reached the landing. He tried not to take offense, but her attitude left his feelings bruised.

Caelum offered a reassuring smile on his way past.

Putti had repaired the outer greenhouse, but there'd been little time to clean up after the battle and even less to heal the garden itself.

Vitae and Ignis stood on opposite sides of the fountain, both closed off behind folded arms. Ignis's new body had grown a few inches and become more muscled while remaining Asian. That his dark eyebrows and a thin stubble on his head remained spoke to the constant onslaught of faerie incursions. The older warriors hid their fatigue better. Ignis had fought twice as many battles as all but Terrance himself. He'd rescued both Vitae and Caelum, though on the last he'd arrived a moment too late to prevent Caelum from dying.

Vitae wore fatigue like a cloak. An unknown burden bent his shoulders. Several diplomatic trips to the Courts had increased the incursions rather than rein in the Sidhe. The Wyldfae envoy Thatch had reportedly failed to uncover any hint of their eggs' whereabouts.

Vitae shot Ignis one last dirty look and beckoned them toward the fountain. "Come to order and praise the Undying Light."

They rose, each bowing to the fountain's statue. Summus appeared in a blaze of light. It died away, leaving the sparkling, shining Divine Phoenix nonetheless shadowed by the efforts of his first month on the job.

Caelum helped Quayla genuflect as they all bowed and spoke. "Summuseraphi."

Vitae stepped into their center and lowered his head. "I address this Shield feathered in shame."

Terrance glanced at Ignis.

The flame phoenix wore a hard scowl.

"I have acted badly, treated members of this Shield and yay even Divine Summuseraphi with disrespect. I offer apologies without excuse, though I've discovered some cause for my erratic actions."

"What are you talking about?" Caelum asked. "You're always grouchy and besides, we've all died this week—except Summus."

"And Terrance," Quayla offered him a proud if weak smile

"Hard to beat blood out of a stone," Caelum said.

"May I please continue?" Vitae asked.

He waited until every head granted him permission before forging on, the image of humility. "When Knights Dolumii and Gherrian exploded in my room, Sidhe blood tainted my nest."

Caelum and Quayla shot each other looks.

Ignis pressed his lips together, head nodding slightly.

I knew Vitae was acting out of sorts, but this makes much more sense.

"While I imagine tainted essence would have negative affect on anyone, as my own essence is also lifeblood, it created a potent reaction. I would ask you to forgive me for not realizing sooner and taking measures to ensure I remained the best Vitae I am able."

Vitae crossed to Quayla and knelt. "I wronged you, little sister, and ask you especially to grant me pardon. Ignis has convinced me your mortal has a good soul and a visit would ease your convalescence."

A pensive scowl furrowed Ignis's brow.

Something's amiss. Could Ignis have convinced Vitae without realizing it?

Indecision warred behind her eyes. Water was easy going, taking the path of least resistance in most things. Just the same, once the river raged it could rend even the mountain.

Quayla refused to meet Vitae's eyes, but she nodded. "I choose against wisdom to forgive you—once Dylan forgives you for every wrong you did to him."

Vitae stiffened.

"And I want my phone replaced," Quayla said.

Terrance smirked.

Rage and gentleness in a single breath.

"Does this mean you're going to stop trying to reverse our right to keep our apartments? Our jobs?" Caelum asked.

"If you desire to take the risk," Vitae said.

Ouch, Quayla must've stung him deeper than I thought.

"How about letting me travel a bit for work?" Caelum asked.

Vitae's gaze shot to Summus. The archangel cleared his throat. "Things are too dire within this Prefecture to permit being shorthanded."

"The picnic next week?" Caelum asked

Vitae's lips pressed together.

That's enough pushing.

Terrance cleared his throat. "We can discuss that later, once things have calmed."

"Shield Terrance speaks wisdom," Vitae said. "To business. Ani, please recap this week's activities."

"In the past five days, we've repelled armies from both Courts, sealing forty-two of forty-nine Veil breeches...did you call me Ani?"

"I meant no offense," Vitae said.

The garden went silent.

"Anima, please continue," Summus said.

"Yes, of course Praefectus. We've died six times. Nest levels for Terrance, Vitae, Ignis, Caelum and Quayla are as follows: full; ninety percent; eight-four percent; ninety-seven percent and full."

"Excellent work, Quayla," Summus said. "Are you strong enough to reform your egg?"

Quayla opened her mouth.

Terrance spoke first. "She's worked hard this week, but exhausted her essence too far for such an ordeal."

"Soon though, I think," Vitae said. "Aquaylae has found admirable focus. If only the rest of you emulated her."

Ignis's normally lighthearted tone crackled with bite. "What do you mean by that?"

"I mean that Aquaylae is showing the drive, the fire of a true Shield of the Undying Light, while her brothers have failed to find even a whisper of our missing eggs."

Ignis marched up to Vitae. "So says one of her failing brothers."

Caelum stepped between them. "Hey, we've been a little busy."

Vitae folded his hands. "Events have distracted us. This mustn't continue."

Ignis's jaw hardened. "What exactly do you expect from us? Abandon the mortals? Quit our jobs? Terrance's work is in service to the Isaac. I'm using mine to seed the city."

"Maybe we could get help from another Shield," Caelum said.

"This war has spilled into other jurisdictions," Summus said. "The Courts seem almost happy to have the distraction. We must handle this issue on our own."

"We must interrogate wrong doers, not just drive them off or slay them," Vitae said.

"Oh, I see," Ignis paced away. "We're not imperiled enough for your satisfaction, so we need to focus on maiming the armies of Faery so we might question one or two."

"Warriors of our experience should have little trouble saving one or two," Vitae said. "I've questioned several."

"And have you learned one damned thing?" Ignis asked.

"Shield Ignis, have a care with your tongue," Summus said.

Caelum stepped onto the fountain's edge, gathering eyes to him. "Taking the little ones isn't too hard, but they don't know anything."

Terrance gestured Caelum off the fountain. To one side, anger and fright fought for Quayla's expression.

I must do something to quell this.

Terrance crossed behind Vitae toward Quayla.

Ignis's voice cracked and popped like a bonfire of green wood. "How do we know you aren't still corrupted? You could be lying or working against us."

Terrance's gut became a glade plunged into deep winter.

Vitae stood ramrod straight. Tension bunched his shoulders. Anger-knotted fingers clasped behind his back where only Terrance had the angle to see.

A flickering nimbus haloed Ignis as he paced back and forth in front of Vitae like some kind of inquisitor.

Summus stood in arm's reach of both, but indecision and inexperience froze any response.

"Bide." Terrance's basso fell heavier than intended. "This family is fatigued. It is wounded and weary and thus our words are the snaps of an injured and cornered animal. We must stop this."

"We?" Caelum asked. "You never opened your mouth."

"A trait one hopes is in your near future." Vitae closed his eyes, mouthing curses. "I am sorry, Shield Caelum. I regret hasty words."

"We must find our eggs," Terrance said. "To achieve this, perhaps it's better to adjourn, take food and rest, and return to council with eased spirits."

"Shield Terrance is wise," Vitae said.

"You two have your little tea party." Ignis scowled at Vitae.

"I'm going hunting, lest *my* dedication be openly called into question."

Ignis stormed out of the garden before Terrance could object.

Vitae strolled away, shifting folded hands to his front and turning his back to the others.

Summus tightened his jaw and vanished in a flash of light.

Quayla shoved Vitae from behind. "How could you say such things to Ignis? He's fighting harder than any of us."

Vitae's brow rose. "Us?"

She balled her hands together once more, knuckles whitening. "I understand you thinking you have some right to bully me around, but Ignis is everything you keep telling me I'm not."

Vitae chewed his words.

I have to stop this before it gets any worse.

Terrance rushed across the garden.

Vitae lowered his head in deference, fixing her with his gaze. "You are perhaps correct. Thank you. I appreciate your candor and willingness to assist."

Quayla blinked at him.

"If you'll please excuse me." Vitae exited the garden.

Terrance replaced him at Quayla's side, feeling almost as confused as her expression.

Caelum ambled over to them, caressing Quayla's cheek. "Rest quickly, sis. You're missing...not all, but at least most of the fun."

Chapter Six

Hidden Omens

Vitae

I marched into the downtown high-rise, still tingling from the two Seelie sprites I'd used to counterbalance an Unseelie pixie whose essence I'd absorbed. Wafers gossiped like a gaggle of hens in the foyer. I pushed through them without even offering what would've been insincere apologies and strode to the security desk.

An older woman with iced golden curls smiled up at me. "May I help yo—:

"You will fetch Dylan Snyder."

"Do you kno—"

"I've invested more than sufficient breath to provide what is needed for you to execute your task."

"Sir, you don't understand. We have over twenty thousand employees. I need you to—"

Impudent, waste of—If I'd brought my swords, I could've disemboweled the wafer with barely a—

I met the woman's eyes and pushed like I might when squeezing my essence. The world spun and the woman blurred. "Be about it."

She blushed, pushing at her hair as if to straighten it. "Yes, milord. It'll be my pleasure."

A much larger security guard crossed to us. "Is there a problem here, Manda?"

I met the man's eyes and summoned my essence once more.

A hand rested on my shoulder. I spun around with a cutting, pithy retort on my lips. My eyes locked on a vast emptiness framed by leathery, wrinkled sockets. A voice of fathomless depth whispered. Each word settled on my chest like an entire atmosphere of water. "This is not the path, Vitae. Walking it will destroy everything you desire to accomplish."

Time seemed to slow.

Stars and brilliant clouds of color floated in the enrapturing darkness, easing from the speaker into me. Countless brilliant flares of life sent my heart into inhumanly fast sprints.

The blackness cradling all of the color and light slipped into me like zephyrs of shadow. All of the life infusing me vanished in an instant, snuffed like a single candle. My heart stopped for a breath that endured without visible end.

"Sir?" Manda said. "Mister Snyder is on his way down."

I sucked in breath that seared its way into my lungs. I shot my head side to side then whirled to the woman behind the counter. "Where did that man go?"

"Jimmy? He went back over to his station."

"No, the man who placed a hand on me."

She frowned, glancing around. "I'm sorry, sir. I must have missed him while contacting Mister Snyder." A mischievous grin lit her face. "I'd be happy to make it up to you. Anything you want...day or night."

"I would sooner rut with a diseased animal." Anger flared in my chest, but was snuffed out when her pain surged into me.

I'd never been connected to a mortal in that way. My insides—already ravaged raw by the otherworldly experience—writhed with her tumultuous emotions.

I have to make this pain stop.

I pushed my will into her once more, heedless of the warning I hadn't shaken off. "You'll forget my last words, instead you'll recall a polite excuse that will leave you mildly disappointed."

Energy washed out of me.

She refused to meet his eyes, addressing Vitae in a flat tone. "If you would fill out the sign-in sheet, I can prepare you a temporary visitor's badge."

"What?" I registered her comment a moment later, but rather than answer stepped away.

"Oh, it's you," Dylan said. "What do you want?"

I stiffened. A red rage seared up and down my veins. My hands itched to wrap around the impudent wafer's neck and snap his head clean from his shoulders.

I moistened my lips, pushing the rage down. I lowered my head so the mortal could not read my eyes. "I've come to apologize."

"What?" Dylan asked.

"I apologize...Mister Snyder. I should not have spoken the things I did. A-Quayla wishes you in her life. The Shield requires your expertise, and I have come for your forgiveness."

Because I've been ordered to obtain both.

Dylan stared.

I produced a security card, holding it out with only a slight tremor. "Quayla has not fully recovered from her most recent death so—"

"She died again?"

I lowered my head once more. "To save me and our sanctum."

"Doesn't sound like the sanctuary you tout as safe—"

"You worthle—" I forced my voice to soften. "You are correct. It is for this reason we wish to enlist your services to improve the technology protecting Quayla."

"And the rest of you," Dylan said.

"Yes."

"Which makes your mention of Quayla a way to manipulate me."

A talon across his carotid artery would silence this wafer in instants.

I made my shoulders sag and refused to meet Dylan's eyes. "I would never intentionally do anything that would make you feel manipulated."

"Is that because you don't wish to manipulate me or you just wished you didn't suck at manipulations so badly that I can see right through you?"

I tucked away the card. "If you don't wish to help, I understand. I am sorry to have wasted your time."

And mine.

"I'll think about forgiving you—after I talk to Quayla." He extended a hand. "The card please."

I produced the security card.

"Anything else?"

"It would be a kindness to Quayla and myself if you could procure her another mobile phone on my behalf. I can provide moneys through my delegate, but my knowledge of tech—"

"Would have her lugging around an eighties car phone with no service," Dylan said.

"Does this mean you will choose one best suited to her needs?"

"Yeah, I'll bill you for the phone after I decide what to charge for evaluating your systems." Dylan turned on his heels and marched toward the elevator bank.

Sunlight entering the foyer through the windows took on an orange tinge.

What would the Sidhe Courts do with the knowledge that a shield is fond of that wafer? Especially if she refuses to apologize in the manner that they desire?

Caelum

A whirlwind blew Caelum's new body together inside his nest. Balloons swirled within the alcove on circling currents of essence. He cursed and turned to the freestanding mirror just off to one side. He frowned.

Taller, skinnier...ugh! I look like a gangly adolescent, I'm really going to have to hit the gym, right after I dye my hair. Blonde isn't a manly color—even with angelic looks, besides, it makes me look pasty.

He snatched a long pin from the nearby table and popped several balloons. The stored essence joined with the whirlwind, topping off his nest once more.

Caelum turned his back on his reflection, He stepped out of his basin and rounded a privacy screen into his modernly-appointed bedroom. Unlike headquarters, the only items older than a single year hung on a wide wall populated with firearms.

He snatched down a sawed-off shotgun, dropping it on the bed and grabbed twin MAC-10 submachine guns. He added two newer and only slightly less loved M1911A1 semiautomatics to the growing pile on the bed. He yanked a drawer in the wall open and plucked several full ammunition clips from its recesses. He slid the first into a back pocket that wasn't there.

Caelum chuckled.

Right, pants. Well, going out like this would prove clothes don't make the angel. Then again, having arrest photos go viral probably isn't good for my career at Circlestone.

Instead of his normal business casual attire, Caelum dressed out in fatigues. He snagged a belt from his dresser drawer to hold his trousers up on a narrower waist. He paused before closing the drawer to touch an alderwood box gilt with tarnished silver. He touched the gem in his chest and closed his eyes.

"In service unto death I swear this life unto the Undying Light."

An answering thrum of power delivered the small down feather from the Shield's divine.

Plucking Summuseraphi's ass now, I guess.

He turned it over in his hands, unable to discern any real difference before tucking it into a back pocket, pulling on a shirt and loading up for a night of faerie-splattering reprisal.

How do I get back with all this hardware? Can't exactly catch an Uber.

He thought, idly grabbing empty balloons from his bedside. With a moment's effort, he inflated them with essence-enchanted breath. He tossed each into his nest until out of breath. He cherry-picked a prepaid phone from several in another drawer.

"Ignis, Caelum. Can you pick me up at my place? I died."

He hung up and filled another balloon.

I'd best keep as much essence on hand as I can.

Vitae

I parked outside the small warehouse. The rental wasn't far enough from Hartsfield-Jackson Airport to escape the roar of landing aircraft. I hadn't yet bothered to figure out the conventional security system, but had set a series of seeds to give me warning of intrusions both Sidhe and Angelic.

"Anima?"

The automata's voice emerged from my bronze statue. "What can I do for you, Shieldheart?"

"Please send Nuntium to Thatch in the Sidhe Court and inform him that after giving the Courts' request as much consideration as they've given ours, we are declining the form and flavor of apology demanded."

"Yes, Vitae, but I don't think they're going to like that answer."

"They are welcome to send me another emissary to discuss the topic further if they wish. Though considering the war they're waging, I cannot vouchsafe his safety."

"Understood. Shall I also inform Shield Aquaylae?"

"Quayla doesn't need any more distractions from her convalescence. I'm sure she'll waste enough energy rutting around with the wafer when he visits."

"He accepted the security card then?" Anima said. "Shall I activate it and inform her?"

"Activate the card, but it would be best for Quayla's feelings that we keep this a surprise...just in case her wafer refuses to come."

"It may not be, my place, Shieldheart, but I commend your willingness to apologize and make peace for the benefit of your fellow shields."

I cannot believe I am being condescended to by a mortal device.

"Thank you for your kind words, Anima."

After taking a moment to verify my seeds, I drove my Mercedes into the warded warehouse.

"Anima?"

The silence after my second call evidenced the wards, functionally separating the statuette from the angelic network. I climbed out of my Mercedes, knocking a heavy briefcase against the door frame. Giving the jostled contents little thought, I stepped over a magical circle drawn on the concrete and dropped the case onto an old wire spool serving as the only table in the otherwise unfurnished space.

A control just inside the warehouse proper closed the accordion-style doors. I retrieved the briefcase en route to the workshop sectioned off on one side of the large space. Dropping it onto a worktable beside a nearly-completed stone basin evoked a yelp and an angry buzz.

The case opened to expose a small crystalline cage, a bruised and battered pixie imprisoned within, and my original volume of the *Shieldheart's Guide to Nests.*

The faerie assailed me with insults and so-called curses

I rolled my eyes, checking over the precious book. I'd written the guide centuries ago, but as I explained in the forward notes trusting memory with something as vital as nests was the same as leaping unarmed into peril. I opened the tome to the appropriate section, tuning out the angry Sidhe's grating, high-pitched droning.

I circled my new nest, comparing runes stenciled in place from memory against my notes in the book. Several runes proved missing, but not due to absentmindedness. I'd omitted runes responsible for connecting the nest into Anima's sentry net—the same connecting runes I'd left purposely absent from the seeds placed to watch my warehouse.

I stopped, staring from the book to the basin and back in shock.

I'd forgotten to prepare runes locking the nest to my sole use. A shiver went through me as I considered the potential mess resulting from lazy, weak-willed Aquaylae gaining access to the powers I'd be imbuing into anybody reborn from the basin.

Once I'd confirmed the final arrangement of runes and added a precedence sigil to mark the new nest as my primary rebirth location, I set to work with a tiny bejeweled hammer and file. Time, practice and patience carved exacting runes into the basin's stone. One feather-shaped leaf of divine silver at a time embossed the markings. Hours of tapping and layering and finishing brought the nest to completion.

Magic and a sense of connection shrouded the new nest. It might've been overkill, but I double-checked each rune an exact duplicate to those in my book one last time.

Perfection is worth any labor.

The work had been tedious and draining, but giddy anticipation filled me. Prior to the nest's completion, faerie blood experiments had been limited to direct absorption. The new nest allowed a whole new phase of tests. In theory, being reborn with Sidhe blood purposely mixed into my essence allowed me to regenerate magical strength just as the faerie did. Instead of exhausting the absorbed magic and being forced to draw in more, I'd generate my own.

I carried my new nest onto the main warehouse floor, setting it down at the precise geometric center of a circle drawn and rune-decorated with now-dark blood.

The next logical test required courage. It would prove my dedication to my Shield, my worthiness to ascend into the ranks of the divine and prove my dedication to Mare as the highest form of agape love.

I'd been polluted by Sidhe blood unawares. To protect my Shield and have any chance of freeing Mare from Dolumii's blade, I had to master Sidhe magic. I had to arrange death and rebirth from essence purposefully contaminated with Sidhe blood.

I squared my shoulders, summoning my resolve.

Tainted essence had left me vulnerable to the capricious tempers and tastes of Faery. But the Sidhe blood mixed into my nest had also granted me advantages, had made it possible for me to sense Mare. My Shield needed stronger shields in this time of conflict, but even more important, Mare needed me.

There's nothing I won't risk to free her.

It would've been better to include Ignis and Terrance in my experiments. Properly empowered, the three of us could've forced the Unseelie Champion blade to relinquish our fallen shield.

Unfortunately, lazy living and fraternization with mortals had weakened the others. Complacent and modernized, they lacked the fortitude necessary to devote themselves wholly to their duty let alone to what was needed to free Mare.

I did not share their weakness.

Mastering Faery blood will free Mare and give me the strength to dominate the Sidhe once and for all.

I fetched the caged pixie from my brief case and carried it into the back part of my warehouse. Mostly occupied cages specially designed to hold the denizens of either Sidhe Court dotted the area.

"You cannot hold us here, bird," a winter elf shouted with a hoarse voice. "You're in violation of the Articles of Ararat."

I folded my hands together, tilted my head and regarded one of the faeries I'd captured assaulting Atlanta. "I believe if you were to review that armistice, you'd find your rights forfeit by assault upon mortal noncombatants."

"We were attacking the Seelie."

"Did you or did you not slay a family of three shortly after your entrance into this plane?" I asked.

The knight chuckled, shrugging one shoulder. "They happened in the way. Totally unintended."

I bristled. "Allow me to assure you, sir. What happens to you will be absolutely intended."

It took all of my will not to choose the elf for the next test. Fortunately, logic overruled passion. I wasn't ready to test at that level. Early experimentation suggested the power within an elf equivalent to approximately three dozen pixie-sized faeries or three grendling-sized Sidhe. I needed more of each type to develop a reliable quantification system, but observation advised prudent caution. Before I utilized another elf for my experiments, I needed to satisfy two conditions.

Limited experimentation with the blood of only a single court had granted me marginal powers at the cost of enduring the influx of overriding faerie emotions and desires that threatened to thwart both my balance and my control.

Not that I'm weaker than faerie whims.

Thus first, I needed to acquire an elf of the opposite Court that the Seelie and Unseelie natures could cancel out the influences intrinsic to their specialized natures.

Second, my ability to channel their magic needed to be advanced sufficiently so that I could utilize the amount of magic contained in their beings.

I turned my attention to a set of small metal birdcages. The sight of wilted little faeries made a part of me cringe.

The winged should never be caged.

I sized up the new pixie. He looked too healthy to match up with another pixie from an opposite court. I set down the newest captor and evaluated my prisoners for a pairing of like size and condition.

I am sorry to do so gruesome a harm upon you, little faeries. If this necessity casts me with villainy's shadow, I shall bear the shame. Protecting this Shield requires that I free Mare.

I chose and carried my prisoners into the main warehouse. They'd been imprisoned long enough that curses and oaths had surrendered to natural curiosity. They bombarded me with questions, flying against the metal bars to add burning pixie flesh to the taint escaping their ceaselessly chittering mouths.

I set them down inside a large blood circle. A tome of Egyptian blood magic retrieved from my inner pocket allowed a review of the chapter on activating circles. After several minutes rereading, I brought a small pool of essence to my fingertip and touched it to the circle. Runes inside and out flared to life. A softly glowing glisten ran around and around the circle in an endless wave.

A smile crept across my face.

I turned to the cages.

This is necessary. The Courts refuse to return our eggs. They play at war, staving off boredom by slaughtering innocent mortals. They deserve this—the honor of contributing to the cleanup of their mess.

I opened the first cage.

The pixie bit me and darted out the opening singeing one wing in the process. He rocketed toward freedom only to slam into the circle's edge.

I snatched the dazed fairy from the air, snapped its head off and drained its blood into my basin. An uneasiness pushed fingers into my gut and twisted. I pushed away discomfort, stiffening my resolve.

For Mare.

The other pixie went mad.

High-pitched, rapid-fire chittering filled the circle with insensible begging and bargains that seemed to split my head. I opened the second cage. Instead of racing out, it darted side to side against the cage, trying to avoid my hand. Damage to its wings eventually rendered it flightless.

The little faerie lowered its head and walked into my hand. "Why, Shieldheart?"

My head tilted. "I must free...I must protect this Shield. Faerie blood will increase my ability to protect mortals from your war."

"We're only playing at war," he said. "It could be so much worse."

"You're playing out your war on mortal soil, killing innocents I'm charged to protect in the bargain."

It shrugged. "Wafers breed like rats. Given the choice, would you destroy your own lands when another battleground awaited as surrogate?"

I considered. "You and I are of like mind. You war on surrogate land. I take your blood as a weapon against your kind."

"I watched you choose us. Why one from each Court? Did you choose only males purposefully, or by coin's toss?"

"You're a quizzical little fellow," I said.

"I'm stalling," he said. "I don't want to die."

I nodded. "I experienced a number of negative side effects from reincarnating from blood tainted more strongly with one of two tainting Sidhe blood types. My first experiments of absorbing alternate Sidhe essences allowed for some less detrimental balancing. This time I shall reincarnate from essence augmented by balanced taint. I chose your kind for this test due to your weaker magic."

"A faerie is a faerie, be it cold or nay. Beware. A faerie nature may twist your will, bent in shapes it doesn't desire to fulfill."

"Nicely rhymed." I snapped its head off and dumped green blood in with the violet pooled at basin's bottom. A container of my essence filled the basin enough for a single rebirth, though the green and violet swirled atop the red like oil atop water.

I slid a knife's blade up and along one wrist and bled into the basin, mixing the blood with my other hand. Vertigo and nausea seized me. I repositioned so that the blood flowing from my wrist could not go astray and waited for death.

These amoral monsters must be stopped. For the good of my Shield...for Mare...

Chapter Seven

Seeking Answers

Terrance

Terrance pulled into the carport behind his Paulding country home. Vitae chaffed at Terrance's choice. He disliked the earth phoenix living so far from the polluted population center.

I've never failed at my duty. I will not be bullied by a Shield-heart decades my junior.

He dismounted his raised truck and slid shut the accordion carport doors. The former pool turned garden called to him.

Too tired for a soak anyway.

He badged the security lock and keyed the passcode, allowing access to the square house design imported from Florida. He walked over and slid open the steel-framed, double-thick, bullet-proof glass door seamlessly blended with the back wall facing the backyard. The warm wet scent of growing things washed lingering taint from his nostrils. Another square of like glass surrounded the cherished center of Terrance's home. He strode down the left hall past sliding doors of polished wood, eager to enter the house's atrium heart.

Terrance keyed another security lock.

Entering the open-air garden triggered soft lights lurking beneath plant leaves and behind stones. His nest rested in a cluster of plants flourishing in the essence rich dark soil. He pressed fingers into the earth, checking the shared earth to ensure his spare essence remained potent and nutrient rich.

Need to replace some and seed a bit more crushed quartz.

He glanced upward. An intricate and all but invisible edderkopp webbing protected the private glade, still charged with Wyldfae magic bartered from the net's creator.

He circled the atrium collecting a wooden mug of water from a freshwater spring, fresh green onion and some toadstools from a fenced patch at the very front.

Terrance rounded his nest and settled the objects on a flat stone at the foot of a waist-high henge. He seated himself on a low stone opposite the hedge, closed his eyes, and placed both hands flat on his seat. He reached for the solid rock, drawing its peaceful solidity symbolically into his soul.

Terrance whispered. "Yarque. Yarque. Yarque."

The ground rumbled beneath his feet. The center of the henge parted. A diminutive old man crawled out of the crack. A footlong eggplant serving as a hat halved again the grizzled old faerie's height. Despite its entrance through a crack in the ground and a dirty, bearded grin, not a speck dirtied his Zwiesel-style clothing. He glanced around, reflexively dusting its evergreen vest and the matching leather *bundhosen* which made up the regional *tracht*.

Yarque bowed to Terrance, doffing his hat. He strode to the flat rock, scooped the offering into the hollow eggplant chapeau and hopped up onto the henge, feet dangling.

"Terran."

"Yarque."

"Mind if I eat first?" Yarque asked.

"Have I ever?"

Yarque grunted, chewing mushroom and onion in turns.

"One of these times I'm going to sauté those for you first," Terrance said.

"So you keep saying." Yarque shoved a mushroom into his mouth, spraying chunks of it as he spoke. "You've shown better sense thus far than to ruin perfectly good grub with fire and fat." He scanned the rock platter. "You don't by chance have any grub?"

"I do not."

Yarque harrumphed. "Been wondering how come you hadn't called."

"Been busy."

"Going to be a damned sight busier before long."

"So you're aware of what's happening?" Terrance asked.

Yarque rolled his bushy-browed eyes. "I *am* a kobold."

"I'd hoped you might have some insight."

"Of course I have, but I cannot construct your understanding."

Terrance scrutinized his kobold guest. He hadn't bound him to guest conventions with bread and salt.

Yarque would refuse to eat them anyway and never return.

"I see a mind sharp as obsidian behind those eyes, and I am sorry, boy, but I *cannot* give you the answers you seek."

"You're bound, but by who? Is there perhaps a royal among the Wyld at last?"

"Can't say. Couldn't say." He shook his head. "No. As you know, only Seelie and Unseelie royals are allowed. They insist it's so."

Terrance considered. "Can't say anything? *Can't?*"

Yarque grinned. "The Exiled Lady binds me so."

"She's not Wyldfae."

"No," Yarque's grin widened. "And yes."

Not Wyldfae, but rather royalty in exile. Could the Wyldfae have taken her to lead them?

Terrance watched the little kobold's delight nearly glow. "Why are the Wyldfae attacking us?"

"Not you, not the shields within the Shield. Wyld want you where you are, serve and protect....so important." The kobold stuffed a mushroom into his mouth, chewing dutifully.

"Yarque?"

He pointed to his full mouth and grinned. The grin slid from his face as his eyes widened. Terrance whipped around, arms tingling in expectation.

Nothing threatened.

He turned back to find the stone platter clean and the kobold gone. Terrance slapped a hand across his face.

Yarque is a Power. Nothing on Earth can frighten the former putto...and you let him distract you with the first trick in the book. How old are you?

A chuckle rumbled up from Terrance's gut.

So old a trick the little bastard may have invented it.

He trudged across the atrium toward the keypad and bed.

"Terrance." Anima's voice emerged from his nest. "We have two Veil breeches near you."

Bradley

Bradley Sky cruised slowly up and down the east Atlanta neighborhoods where most of the recent influx of magical bodies had originated. A heavy, bastardized remote control rested on the dashboard, wedged in place so that the globes of contained gases faced forward and right.

Unable to see around the brick of duct taped AA batteries, Bradley eyed the reflection for the tell-tale illumination within one of the spheres. A cord ran down to his cigarette lighter port, dimming his head lights but easing the drain on the thirty-two jury-rigged batteries.

A hungry snarl escaped the back seat.

Bradley cursed.

Over three hours of searching, he'd exhausted four pounds of hamburger and a half-dozen chicken sandwich patties picked up from a burger joint half an hour before.

Maybe I should've left Whiskers back in the morgue, but I wanted to be ready for anything the rattler picked up.

One of the rattler's globes lit up blue, the light dying a moment later. Excitement mixed with trepidation. Bradley braked, snatched up the remote and swung it backward.

A horn blared several short blasts behind him.

Bradley cringed, but flashed a look back up the sidewalk. Three youths in gang clothing had stopped a grizzled mid-aged man in a trench coat.

The rattler lit up blue once more.

The driver behind him laid on the horn.

Bradley's engine stuttered.

He whipped around to face front and hit the accelerator, barely resurrecting the engine before it spluttered into silence. Engine acceleration overwhelmed the pressure he had on the brakes. He lurched forward. It only took a moment for Bradley to even out the car's forward motion. He took the first right to let the other car past and searched both sides of the street in vain for a parking place.

He whipped around the block as fast as he could manage with traffic and traffic lights. He spotted a parking spot on the next block a moment before he turned right once more. The light turned yellow.

He gunned the accelerator, running straight through from his turn lane. A yellow minivan bolted through the light too, forcing Bradley to brake mid intersection or slam into the other car going for the single lane on the next block.

The engine spluttered.

Another car horn blared from his right.

He revved the engine to follow the minivan only to have a Prius run the light and nearly sideswipe Whisker's door. He checked over his shoulder in a rush and followed the Prius out of the intersection he was blocking.

The Prius took his space.

Bradley's curse echoed the irritated growl from the back seat.

He found another spot two right turns later. Bradley grabbed the rattler and the reinforced cat carrier, hesitating at the parking meter.

Forget it, what are the chances of a meter maid working this late.

He hurried up the street, sweeping the rattler right and left. Adrenaline left his skin tingling and heart racing. The rattler had detected one of the murderous blues killing Atlanta's citizens. All his work developing a magic detector had paid off. He was about to find the culprits—whatever they were—and stop them with the help of the dead cat he'd reanimated with troll bone marrow.

This is better than the time we raided that dragon lair in high school.

He stepped onto a corner of the block where he'd detected the blue. The rattler swung left and right. None of the globes lit. He scrutinized the detector, confirming both gas and battery power remained.

Not close enough?

Bradley hurried toward where he'd seen the three toughs.

They rose off the front stoop of their apartment building, mischief in their stances. He swept the rattler toward them.

No reaction.

"That some kind of homemade taser?" The first asked.

"What's in the bag?" the second asked.

"No," Bradley turned to the second. "You don't want to know."

"I think I do," the second said.

Bradley backed away, checking battery levels to confirm the rattler had enough power to detect any magic on them.

The third jerked the cat carrier out of Bradley's hands and

tossed it to the second. He caught it with an oof, and grabbed a zipper.

"Don't," Bradley warned.

Two tore open the bag. The cat slammed itself at the cage, nasty claw raking the tough's arm. He dropped the case, cradling an arm.

Three swore.

"Jesus," the first said. "What the hell is that?"

The cat threw himself at the impact-warped cage, eyes glowing a sickly green. It went wild, hammering the cage with its scaly body. Back spines caught in the metal, some breaking and sending the animal into a greater frenzy.

They bolted into the building.

Bradley dropped next to the cage, setting the rattler on the concrete. He grabbed the cage, trying to simultaneously sooth Whiskers with his voice while bending the cage back to its original shape. Claws slashed long furrows down his arm for his trouble.

He winced and shoved a hand into one pocket. The appearance of a green water pistol changed snarls to hisses. Whiskers backed away as far as the cage allowed.

Bradley used the cat's retreat to close the bag once more. He cursed the searing pain in his arm and retreated back to his car with Whiskers and the rattler. He shoved the bag into the back, grabbed a hefty first aid kit and sat in the passenger seat with the door still open. He lowered his arm to hang over the street and cringed.

Pain shrieked like a banshee as he poured rubbing alcohol down the cuts. The alcohol sizzled and frothed like baking soda mixed with vinegar. When the bubbles subsided, Bradley poured iodine over the cuts, patted them dry, applied antibiotic gel and wrapped a bandage around the injury.

You know, if I injected myself with some of the troll marrow I would probably regenerate a whole lot faster.

Ignis

Ignis slashed, bringing the fiery blade down with exaggerated slowness. He turned, thrust, turned again. With his eyes closed, the subtle ridges beneath his bare feet seemed more pronounced.

Small water pipes ran throughout the floor. Narrow ceramic tiles laid between each run evened his footing. Noise cancelling ear buds drowned out every sound but his heart.

The new heart wanted to thunder like mustangs across the land. It wanted to force burning blood through veins and arteries until fury coursed through every cell.

I know better.

He pushed his essence downward through the bottom of his hilt and swept the blade upward in an underhanded cut. He followed up with a downward cut and a lunging step.

Like the essence blade, Ignis squeezed his anger and frustration down through the soles of his feet. He focused on slow, practiced motions. A back flip took him from the ground, separating him from the heatsinks and letting the fury pool. He pushed some of his temper out in the essence extending from both ends of his hilt. The arms of his bow stretched outward, pulled back with an arrow of blazing heat that threatened to crisp his eyebrows.

Damn Vitae! Insufferable, arrogant, tight ass.

Ignis took a deep breath, sucking essence and temper back into himself. He pushed the latter out his feet, focused on breathing and stepped into the next form.

Anger is the enemy. Fury is a thief.

He'd had problems with his temper since hatching. Quayla and Caelum had nothing on that younger Ignis when it came to wild, impetuousness. He'd worked against the impulse since his creation thanks to a wise water phoenix.

Old Quayl had been worlds worse than Quayla—and better in some ways for his wisdom. The water phoenix had felt even more deeply than Quayla. He'd seemed a calm, wise mentor and the next instant he'd been a tsunami with more roar than a volcano.

It's their weakness and their strength.

Quayl taught Ignis to know himself, to own both the faults and strengths of Ignis's nature.

And harness them...eventually.

Vitae had treated the whole Shield badly—especially Quayla, then blamed all of his action on tainted essence.

As if he wasn't already bossy and overbearing.

Ignis couldn't fault Vitae for being reborn in tainted blood in the height of combat. Both had happened in the same room as his nest, but afterward the life phoenix should have recognized the taint in his basin sooner.

Maybe he did. He just enjoyed having a ready excuse to show his true colors.

Atlanta's Shieldheart had danced a dual game for centuries, exercising power in the name of his title while complaining that they forced him into virtual exile except when he was required to clean up after one of them.

Ignis slashed through the room like a fiery zephyr.

He stopped, jaw tight with anger at his lapsed control. Moments of stillness and slow breathing wrangled the fury's sudden rampage.

Vitae had played the apology card like a lifelong abuser. Contrite and ashamed, he'd still turned all responsibility for their failure to locate the stolen eggs on the other four shields rather than himself.

And I'd stormed out like a hatchling with something to prove. I don't work for Vitae or his pleasure.

Nonetheless the search hadn't gone well. Mounting frustration exasperated Ignis's rising temper. He'd searched high and low. Every time he thought he was close, another pair of incursions called him away only to return too late and find his clues departed.

Pairs, always in pairs and I can't figure out why the change.

Seelie and Unseelie courts barely bothered to cloak their fighting. Between sudden skirmishes and the Wyldfae taking advantage of the chaos for their own mischief, his Shield had been run ragged. Ever the martyr, Vitae had sacrificed his precious time to fill in for Quayla.

She owned some fault originally, but she'd pushed harder than she ever should have to get back into the action. Some of her reasons had been selfish ones, but the results were the same.

And once she was acting, Vitae should have eased off his high horse and lent his skills to help her recover. We need all six of us out here.

Several quick strikes proclaimed Ignis's attempts to calm himself and think an abject failure. He'd hoped taking the time during the short respite would unlock an idea that would prove their solution.

It's not working. Might as well return to the hunt.

Removing his hearing protection replaced heartbeat with a teakettle whistle. He opened his eyes to scan the floor, only to find the room dark. Several sections of glowing piping leaked steam where they'd melted beneath his feet. The small turbines along one wall rattled under the stress of converting his anger into electrical energy. Quayla's spare Johammer batteries read full, as did the Shield's other battery packs, with the surplus energy lowering electric bills for the building's residents.

When I don't overload the breakers.

A wry chuckle escaped his lips. In the early days, Ignis's building would've had more hot water than it could use, even complained that the boiler needed turned down. The little thermal power plant was a better solution.

Pity Caelum doesn't have a laser weapon, I could probably keep the trigger-happy air phoenix up to his eyes in ammunition.

Ignis let a nimbus of flame shroud his skin, providing golden flickering light enough to navigate to his bathroom. Someone restored building power by the time Ignis finished showering. His bar of soap slipped as he returned it to the dish. He caught the slippery little object before it hit the ground.

An idea spread a grin across Ignis's face as he rinsed the slimy residue off of his fingers.

Caelum

Caelum stared at the monitor, trying for the fourth time to read a project summary for Circlestone's next medical research benefit. Despite his true nature, no wind remained in his sails.

Seelie and Unseelie forces had everyone but Quayla running all over town—none more so than poor Summus. They'd breech, fight, destroy mortal sanities or sections of city and then retreat beyond the Shield's jurisdiction.

Not that they all escape.

Caelum reached for his coffee cup to find it empty. He shook three more to-go cups, all but the last drained as dry as Vitae's sense of humor. The last coffee offered a swallow of cold dregs of unknown age. His assistant couldn't fetch a replacement fast enough to save him from keyboard prints on his forehead.

He swallowed the last dregs, regretting yet one more sacrifice his shield duties required. None of the captured Sidhe had confessed knowledge of their stolen eggs. If they'd spoken at all, they'd demanded release into the custody of the Sidhe Courts.

It's a good thing Vitae volunteered to handle that part. I might've just killed them and good riddance.

He rose, muscles protesting in mournful groans like a long disused door. He rumpled his hair to match the rest of him and trudged out of his office.

Brianna brightened. "Can I get something for you, Mister Kite?"

Caelum did his best to offer a smile. "Probably best if I get the coffee myself if I want to be awake to drink it. Can I get you anything?"

"Sure."

Caelum walked away three steps, then turned back. "I know how you like your coffee is somewhere in my brain, but—"

"Soy mocha latte, two shots of peppermint."

"Right." Caelum turned and made the Mount Everest-esque trek to the elevator. It opened just as his finger reached the call button.

Viviane stood in the car dressed in a midnight blue skirt suit almost as dark as her wavy hair. Coral pink lips a shade too light for most women curved into a smile that dazzled against her light skin. "Glad I caught you. Mister Heffernan wants to see you."

Caelum nodded and stepped into the car with her.

She flashed him a meaningful smile. "Rough night?"

Caelum grunted.

She stepped closer to him, eyes narrowed.

"I'm not on anything if that's what you're worried about," Caelum said. "Not even coffee."

She licked her thumb and forefinger, extending them to his ear. She rubbed his lobe and brought back fingers with saliva wetted violet Sidhe blood.

"You had some paint on your ear." She cleaned her fingers with a Kleenex.

"Thanks."

She smiled. "Wouldn't want to give Dunham any reason to let you go."

"Yeah." He sighed. "That would suck."

The elevator opened. They crossed a short hall, through a pair of double doors and into a lavish recaption area dotted with free-standing glass islands displaying Celtic, Norse or Pict artwork. More art rested beneath the glass tabletops that separated comfortable-looking furniture. A long mahogany desk dominated one wall beneath the Circlestone logo. A busty blonde that liked to giggle during orgasm glanced up, beaming when she saw him.

Viviane led Caelum through the double doors into an expansive office filled with art and décor to make the outer office seem a trailer park cousin.

"He'll be with you in a few minutes."

Caelum wandered across the office to the new artifacts. It took sluggish brain cells a minute to realize the new arrangement wasn't as new as it first appeared. Instead of being lined up along a wall, the five standing stones had been repositioned into a loose circle around a new stone.

He circled the five standing stones. No longer up against a wall, each resembled an ogre's thigh-high boot.

Or pant leg and a shoe.

Seams separated each standing stone from an oddly-shaped, oblong base—Caelum's 'shoe'. A long, low tongue cradled the taller stone, extending and widening into a circle one pace in diameter and two hands in height. A foreshortened big toe with a beveled face ended the base stone. Each bevel's face housed an empty socket that reminded Caelum uncomfortably of their failed search.

No doubt robbed of precious stones by some wafer.

Old runes encircled the base stones. Two columns of runic marks climbed the standing stone from where the basin met rising rock. A bowl descended in their center in uneven, rune inscribed stair steps. Two fingers of stone depression surrounded a wider step down a hand's breadth wide. Several more two-finger circles descended to a small hole deeper into the base.

Behind the stone boots, a new disk spanned two and a half paces. Sigils Caelum couldn't quite place carved two lines around a raised edge. The central stone's color seemed off. Unlike the smaller circles, the inner circle had been carved into a shallower bowl without a hole in the center.

"Mister Kite," Dunham called from the other end of the room.

"Morning, sir." Caelum said. "Just admiring your new display. The new stone doesn't seem like it goes with the others."

"Once more, you're correct. I got my hands on a new fragment that added enough details to the ongoing puzzle that I was able to have that center made."

"Rich as you are, I would think you could find a whole one."

"Center stones are rarer than intact dinosaur fossils."

Caelum cursed.

"This will serve for now," Dunham clapped his hands together. "Now, we agreed to come back together about the prospects of working more closely together. Have you come up with any ideas for making this happen?"

I wish. I'm lucky a breech hasn't called me out of here already.

"No, sir. I'm afraid things are getting worse at home."

"Not too bad, I hope. I'd hate to lose you."

"I'm trying to avoid that, but some things aren't in my control."

Dunham frowned. "How can I help, Caelum? What about a private nurse to see to your...relative?"

"To be honest, Mister Heffernan—"

"Dunham."

"The way things look, Dunham, I'm going to have to take a leave of absence to take care of things until they improve."

"I've got a lot of important projects in flight." Dunham frowned. "I'm not sure they'll succeed without your help."

"Don't get me wrong, I'd rather there was another way."

Dunham dropped his eyes to the floor. "Me too."

"I'm not gone yet," Caelum said.

By some miracle.

"How about this?" Dunham asked. "Can we hold off any major decisions until after the Labor Day picnic?"

"I'll do my best," Caelum said.

"Do that, and I'll work on ways that make it impossible for you to leave," Dunham said. "Nobody can do for me what you can, and I'm not willing to let you go for anything short of death or Armageddon."

Chapter Eight

Vulgar Fairies

Judith

Judith woke, sore and satisfied. She stretched out on the bed, her movement pulling the shirt until the collar tightened enough to choke her. Her eyes flashed open. She lay fully dressed in a strange bedroom surrounded by a horde of short, unbathed midgets straight from a Medieval Times show.

Oh, God. Oh, God.

She sat up, backing against the headboard and snatching a lamp from the nearest bedside table. She brandished the light, trying to remember where she was and how she had gotten there.

The bedroom door opened to admit the hairiest, ugliest mostly-naked man Judith had ever seen. He had to be a head taller than the others. He stunk of rot and something coppery and he hadn't brushed his pointy teeth in at least three meals.

A snide voice called from the other room. "I told you to get dressed first."

The ugly man turned away and trudged out the door.

Judith sprang up onto her feet, leapt over the midgets and out the door. Pain shot up her leg. Strong fingers jerked her back by one leg. She hit the floor face first, looking down to find long bloody furrows along the calf in the ugly man's hands.

The snide voice belonged to a handsome man stirring coffee on the opposite side of Quayla's breakfast bar. "Forget it. The law keeper's ready, just glamour yourself and go."

"Help me, please?" Judith begged.

"Sorry, love, not much I can do for you."

"Just let me go. I won't say anything about...anything."

He shook his head, adding honey to the steaming drink. "No can do. The bait never gets to go home."

Snickers floated into the room from the clogged bedroom door.

I have to get out of here.

Judith kicked ugly in the balls. She bolted for the door, agony blinding her every time she put the slightest weight on her sliced leg. She managed the door as several strong hands jerked her back inside.

Ugly slammed the door. "Can't we knock her out?"

"No," the man sipped his drink and added more honey. "She needs to motivate the law keeper."

Someone pounded on the door.

Judith fought them.

She kicked.

She screamed for help.

Despite their size, she couldn't free herself from their incredible strength.

Mrs. Cox

Hadley crested the second-floor stairwell. Another scream and series of thumps drew her toward Quayla's apartment. The door opened. In the blink of an eye, Quayla's assistant from the flower shop appeared and was then jerked backward.

The door slammed shut.

My door.

Hadley knocked as hard as she could.

The door sprang back open. An ugly naked thing appeared in the doorway. He inhaled several times, face contorting. Horrid yellow eyes narrowed, pupils blazing with hatred. He spat in Hadley's face. "Get lost, granny, you're not invited."

He slammed the door once more.

She glowered at the door.

No one—naked or otherwise—slams my door in my face. Oh no, they certainly do not do such a thing and get away with it.

Hadley marched back down the stairs and into her apartment. She jerked the phone off the table beside her rocking chair and dialed Quayla's number from memory. She paced while it rang, inadvertently getting tangled in its cord.

The call went to voicemail.

"Quayla, dear, this is Hadley Cox. I think your little helper from the flower shop just got abducted into some sort of free love shenanigans going on in your apartment. You know how I feel about shenanigans, young lady. I expect you to come set this right...oh, and I do hope you're feeling better. Miss you, dear."

Hadley hung up.

If you want something done right.

She crossed to an old trunk, pushed the afghan off of its top, unlocked it and opened the lid to expose a massive, ancient book. The tome opened to the page she'd wanted. She ran a finger down the handwriting, glancing twice at the artwork before gently closing the book and settling it back in the trunk.

She marched to her greenhouse in the backyard. She snatched up a sickle and garden sheers, going to work on an unharvested elderberry bush. She took the fresh berries back into the building and up the stairs. She stopped once more on the second landing, frowning up at Quayla's door.

Couldn't hurt to try it.

She returned to her apartment and unfolded the flaps of a

cardboard box at the bottom of one closet. She dug out some clothes abandoned by a long-gone renter, hanging a pair of pants and a shirt over one shoulder.

Hadley climbed upstairs once more. She laid out elderberries across the third-floor landing from Quayla's door to the top of the stairs. She checked her gardening tools tucked behind her back and knocked.

The nasty naked man poked his head out the door. "What do you want, old bag?"

"Oh, dearie me, I just wanted to ask you if you'd clean up these elderberries. Someone might slip on them and fall down the stairs."

He blinked at her.

Several goblins pressed past him, fighting to get to the berries.

She followed. "No need to fight. Here, let me help."

Hadley shoved them down the stairs, glaring after them. "I don't abide shenanigans!"

A hand spun her around. The hobgoblin bared its teeth and raised a claw to strike her. She ripped the clothes from over her shoulder and shoved them into its arms.

He blinked down at them, then her.

She frowned. "In folklore, giving a hobgoblin clothes makes it leave."

"Crazy old bat!" He reared back to strike her.

Her sickle impaled its forehead. "I told Nana that folktale was poppycock."

Judith screamed through her gag.

Hadley yanked the sickle from its head and waved it at the goblins surrounding the young florist. "Release that young woman. I will not put up with no-good goblins abducting people from my apartment building."

They picked up an arm chair and ran it at her like a ram.

Hadley sidestepped in front of apartment 3D.

The goblins lost momentum turning their charge, but pushed her back against the other apartment door in the narrow stairwell.

The others swarmed behind the makeshift blockade and down the stairs, suspending Judith atop their shoulders.

The glass in the ground floor entry rattled shut a moment later.

"Well, poop."

Detective Foxner

Sabrina blinked.

Her body ached.

The scent of recent sex filled her car.

The last thing she remembered was dragging the good-for-nothing purse snatcher into the doors of her precinct. Her phone verified it was still the same day, but she'd lost several hours.

Her frown deepened.

She was fully dressed. True, her muscles glowed the way they did after a wonderful night's sex, but that wasn't possible. Her body hurt too, like she'd overdone things at the gym or three days of—she pushed away the thought and tried to remember how she had ended up in her car parked near Quayla Buckler's apartment.

She hadn't felt as contented and wrung out for some time.

Not since before I told Mary...

A burst of activity saved her from dark memories. A horde of small, dirty-looking men in some sort of theater costume exploded down the front steps of the apartment building. The junior florist from Ponds De Leon Flowers thrashed atop their shoulders. She worked her gag free and screamed.

They hurried across the street and shoved the woman into a windowless panel van.

Sabrina turned on her light, blipped her siren and stepped out of her car. "Stop where you are."

One of the little men turned toward her. He flipped her the bird. Her vision swam, resolving into a wall of white.

Doors slammed.

Sabrina stumbled forward. White eased away enough for her to see them pull away down the street.

She hurried back into her car, wiping her eyes but unable to hurry away the fog across her vision. She followed anyway, siren blaring to help keep cars from her path.

The van turned left. The rapid direction change cost the van's back tires traction. They slid into a parked car with a crunch.

Kidnapping, hit and run, speeding.

She took the turn too fast too, but managed to avoid hitting the blurry parked cars and swerve around a car blaring its horn at the van. Their two vehicles wove left and right. It took all of Sabrina's training and no small amount of luck to keep up with the escaping vehicle.

I've never seen a van move like this.

"Dispatch, this is Detective Foxner," She rattled off her badge number, "I'm in pursuit of a suspected kidnapping and requesting backup."

"This is dispatch, we have your locator, Detective. Sending available units to assist in pursuit. Please provide regular pursuit updates."

The van raced deeper into Atlanta, leaving behind the older Marietta neighborhoods of Buckler's apartment building.

Come on, come on.

She tapped her left foot on the floorboards.

They turned onto North Cobb Parkway, weaving through traffic. They turned hard left, nearly ending up on two wheels as they cut off a pair of young bicyclists in their hurry to round the corner in front of the Big Chicken.

She looked over the frightened kids as she followed, ensuring them nothing more than shaken. The van headed for a far overpass.

Bet they don't know this one has no highway access.

She floored the accelerator, trying to catch up on the long straightaway. Her car proved its muscle, nearly catching the van.

They turned hard right, vaulting into the Whole Foods parking lot. They cut off an old gremlin covered on all sides by pagan coexist stickers—its driver flipping them off.

The van swerved hard twice, rocketing into the truck loading area behind the shopping strip.

Gotcha.

Sabrina radioed in their location and pushed her skills for all they were worth. One loading semi and she'd be able to box them in even without backup.

She slid around the corner with a squeal of tires.

She cheered her good fortune.

The van barreled toward the semi-truck trying to line its trailer up with a loading zone.

Sabrina accelerated.

So did the van.

She spied a small gap between the truck's cab and a retention wall. The van didn't veer toward it, but rather charged straight at the trailer.

Sabrina's heart leapt into her throat.

They're going to kill themselves and Buckler's helper.

The van shrank, squished downward on widening tires by some unseen hand.

Sabrina blinked again and again, unable to believe what her eyes told her as the van drove under the trailer. Shock grabbed her and held on, nearly causing her to collide with the tractor trailer. A hard right then left cost her traction, but she squeezed between the semi and the wall, only losing her passenger side mirror.

The van came back into view, returned to its former dimensions.

She floored the accelerator once more.

The van's back doors flew open. Two of the kidnappers played one-handed patty cake in the opening. Their game ceased, ending in twin rude gestures.

An enormous brick wall rose out of the ground, spanning the entire loading area.

She slammed on her brakes, and turned away to minimize impact inertia. She braced herself for a crash and subsequent side and front air bag impacts.

Her car stopped.

She opened her eyes.

Graffiti painted the brick wall in garish colors. "Screw off, pig. Huff and Puff somewhere else!"

"Dispatch, I lost them due...to a sudden obstruction. Have any of the other units got them?"

"One moment, Detective."

Sabrina took long deep breaths.

I can't have seen what I think I saw. It's not possible.

"Negative, Detective, none of the units moving to assist have eyes on your suspects."

Sabrina cursed. "Thank you, dispatch."

I sure as hell hope the cameras got all that.

Chapter Nine

Stolen Treasures

Quayla

I turned the old vellum page with care. Despite the library's lack of novels, it remained a peaceful place to rest between essence transfers when I grew stir crazy or sleep refused to come.

Even days later, the events of our last meeting left me unsettled.

I've never seen Ignis like that.

Vitae entered.

He visited the library often, preferring to read in his study and thus offered only a temporary nuisance. His shadow fell over me. I ignored him, hoping the dark cloud would blow away.

It didn't.

I raised my eyes from the pages of: *Primal Battle, A Primer on Essence Warfare*.

"You have a guest," Vitae said

"Quayla?" Dylan stood at the library's entrance.

I dropped the book and leapt out of my chair. I hit him like a runaway trolley, evoking a grunt.

"Good thing I decided to forgi—"

I pressed my lips into his, already tasting the salt of tears escaping my eyes. I poured myself into the kiss, trying to fill him with every bit of my love. Dylan answered back. His warmth filled me in return, swelling my heart until the overflow added to our passion.

Vitae stepped around us. The library door closed with a click.

"Shield Quayla...," Anima said.

Oh, God, don't let there be a breech.

"Your paramour's vitals indicate a need for oxygen," Anima said.

I eased away, cheeks burning with embarrassment. "I'm sorry."

Dylan's lips quirked. "Pretty much how every man wants to die."

I flashed a mischievous look. "Every man wants to suffocate with my tongue down their throat?"

"You know, there's really no good answer here."

Warmth shot through me. I'd missed him and his sense of humor more than I'd even realized.

"Is it my imagination or are you even smaller than before?"

"I died," I said.

"Way Vitae told it, you saved him and the whole Shield." Dylan ran fingers through my chin-length hair. "There's a shimmer of blue in your hair now."

"At least it isn't frizzy."

His eyes caressed me top to bottom.

"You're not going to freak out, are you? It was a bad situation, I only did what I had to do."

His brows rose. "Do I get to go exploring again?"

I rolled my eyes and batted at him. "I can't believe you're here or that Vitae let you in."

Dylan raised a card. "I have my own access."

I gaped, words log-jammed in my head.

"So, I'm supposed to evaluate your computer system for upgrades."

"Dylan meet Ani, Ani—don't steal my boyfriend."

"It is a pleasure to make your acquaintance, Dylan," Anima said. "Despite any desire I might have to experience your racing heartrate and the endorphins shooting through your body, Quayla, Dylan and I are not compatible."

"You've got an AI capable of humor and you expect me to upgrade your system?" Dylan asked.

"Shield Caelum has made minor upgrades, but the sanctuary's systems are in need of upgrades," Anima said. "Our Praefectus has several enhancement items in mind."

Dylan laughed, head shaking as he pulled out a new cell phone. "Here, you better take this before this charming young lady steals all of my attention. It's from Vitae."

"Did Vitae apologize to you?" I asked.

"He did, and he paid me to get you a phone that you'd like."

Maybe Vitae isn't so bad after all. Maybe he was just a victim after all.

"I ported over your number," Dylan said. "I hope you don't mind."

I kissed him again, joy flowing through me like an endless spring.

"Feel like a little exploration?" I asked.

His heated expression made my insides melt.

"Before that, Ani, where is Vitae? I owe him an apology."

"Vitae left a few minutes ago. You and Dylan are the only ones in headquarters," Anima said.

That was awfully accommodating of him, which doesn't feel right.

"Was there a breech you didn't tell me about?"

"No, Shield Quayla."

Why would the Shieldheart leave his nest of comforts without a breech to compel him?

I frowned. "It seems odd that he'd leave without a breech. Is it normal for a Vitae to leave the sanctum like that?"

"No. It's generally accepted for a shield to remain in residence, in most cases the Shieldheart."

"But I'm here, so he's got to go cover for me."

"Vitae has had to function as replacement in your convalescence. It is his honor to do so."

I'm sure he thinks so.

I stopped myself.

I have to give him more credit. He was tainted, essentially sickened out of his right mind.

"Are there any active breeches?"

"Not at this time," Anima said.

I grabbed Dylan's hand. "Come on, you can work with Ani once we're done."

"Is there a restroom I can visit first?"

I led Dylan to the bathroom, itching for him to hurry. I busied myself by opening the new phone. Dylan had already set the password to match my last one.

A notification suggested I'd need to charge the phone or it would run out of battery in three hours and nineteen minutes.

Might as well charge it while we play, but I don't have one for this model.

"Ani, do we have any phone chargers?"

"I believe Shield Caelum keeps several in his chambers."

I smiled. "Thank you, Caelum."

I hurried to fetch a charger before Dylan finished.

Caelum's room was an eyesore—a modern, art deco island in Vitae's turn of the previous century manor.

Looks like he updated all his electronics recently in case Vitae forced him to relocate. Is that a satellite internet node?

A brushed aluminum and glass desk offered a selection of tidy wires flanking a charging pad. I collapsed into Caelum's extremely soft leather desk chair.

I'm totally stealing this.

One of his cables fit my phone perfectly. I started it charging and configured it to use his Wi-Fi with information taped to the bottom of Caelum's router so the phone could download updates.

"Dylan? Are you finished?"

"Your paramour is cleansing his genitals."

I arched a brow.

Is he now? Does that count as considerate or selfish?

Notifications popped up one by one, enumerating a long list of missed messages and voicemail. I recognized most of the numbers as Judith or the flower shop.

Yeah, I'll bet she cares now that she's doing all the work.

The latest voicemail displayed a number I didn't recognize. I was tempted to delete the call record as just another spam caller, but something made me tap it open instead.

"Quayla, dear, this is Hadley Cox. I think your little helper from the flower shop just got abducted…"

The hollow still lurking from purging so much essence out of my body swelled, sending my head into a whirlpool as the rest of the message played out. A lot of it didn't make sense—not that people in my apartment abducting Judith made any more.

I need to talk to Mrs. Cox.

I dialed the unknown number.

It rang.

A thousand dark scenarios played through my imagination.

It rang again and again.

Images of poor, sweet Mrs. Cox trying to help Judith and falling afoul of whatever was going on knotted my gut. Lead lined my hollow core. I threw myself out of Caelum's chair—completely forgetting to steal it—and rushed to my room.

I snatched up both hilts.

They're in trouble. I need to help them. Dear, Creator, if something's happened to them…

"Dylan?"

"Almost done," he said.

"I have to go."

Alarm filled his voice. "What? Why?"

"Mrs. Cox and Judith are in trouble."

"You're too weak to leave," Anima said.

"Are my door privileges restored?"

"Not as of yet," Anima said.

I cursed. "Why not?"

"Your body remains too weak for field duty."

I dropped next to my nest and shoved both hands into the essence. Replacing it later would hurt, but if that was what saving Mrs. Cox or even Judith cost, I'd pay it. Essence rushed into my body until only two rebirths worth remained. Restored essence filled me with vim and verve, even if my reflection resembled a zombie movie extra.

"Now you can let me out," I said.

"I'm sorry, Quayla. I cannot. Perhaps if we contacted one of the others?"

"And what? Tell them they have to take care of my friends for me? That I am too weak? Give Vitae an excuse to forbid me friends outside the Shield?"

"Peace, Shield Quayla, your excitation is frightening me."

"Let me out, Anima."

"I am truly sorry."

"Me too." I snatched up a bedside table and threw it through the closest window. A moment later, I dove headlong after my furniture. Wind rushed past me, lashing my hair like a thousand whips. I reached into my core, willing my essence to compact into a tight egg of energy.

It built slowly.

Floors sped by.

I pushed harder.

Have to transmog high enough to avoid being seen.

The ground rushed toward me.

The power of my gathered essence swelled. I willed the transmogrification. The ground threatened to cost me one of the two lives in my nest.

I'm not going to make it in time—if at all.

I cursed, concentrating with all my will.

Pavement came into focus like some movie's slow-motion

action scene.

Please, change. Now. It has to be now, for...

I transmogrified, but neither far enough up to go unseen nor pull completely out of my fall. I flashed into my true form, wings snapping outward to stop most of my momentum. I shifted my body, restoring clothes and possessions while not shifting back my wings. I consumed my wings and shot all of that essence downward with as much force as I could muster. The counter force of the downward waterspout slowed me to a hard crash that luckily only shattered my legs.

I shrieked, drawing onlookers.

A man in business garb rushed up to me. "Are you all right, Miss? What happened?"

I put a hand down in the puddle, soaking up the essence to repair my legs. Knitting bones back together hurt—particularly shifting bone fragments through muscle into place. I restrained the cry behind my lips even though I lost the fight against shedding tears.

"I slipped and broke a heel," I said.

He smiled. "Unfortunate, but not worth making a pretty girl cry. May I help you up?"

"That would be most gallant of you."

His brows rose. "Gallant?"

"Sorry, been studying a lot of old books lately." I held out my hands as the last of my bones reknit.

He helped me to my feet, frowning at the ground. "You slipped because the sidewalk was wet, didn't you?"

"Uh, I thought so. Maybe my pants soaked up all the water."

"That's so strange. You'd think the pavement would at least still be damp."

"Thank you so much for your help." I kissed him full on the mouth.

And thank you Primal Battle.

He blinked at me, cheeks reddening and lifted a hand into view. "Um, thank you, Miss, but I'm married."

I gave him my best smile. "Just thanking you for your help."

A nervous chuckle escaped him. "Consider me thanked."

I aborted another round of thanks to flag down a passing taxi. The concerned man helped me into the back seat and disappeared on his way as I gave the cabbie my address.

Quayla

I pulled up to my apartment, tipped the cabbie and slammed the door in my headlong rush inside. Had the cab been something like a Prius, I'd have apologized, but the fossil-fuel guzzling sedan didn't deserve that kind of consideration.

I took the front steps two at a time. Despite drawing enough essence back into my body to fill it out, my knees buckled as I hit the landing. I grabbed the doors, barely keeping myself upright.

I used too much to heal the breaks. I need to rebalance again and build up my leg muscles.

Mrs. Cox appeared on the other side of the glass ovals. "Gracious, child, are you all—" Mrs. Cox opened the door. "Quayla, what on earth have you done to yourself?"

"Later," I said. "I got your message. What happened? Are you all right? Where's Judith?"

Mrs. Cox pursed her lips. "Come inside, child, let's get you some tea."

"I don't need tea!"

Mrs. Cox folded her arms. "You need to settle your nerves. If you saw the bodies in this state you might collapse all together."

Bodies?

I took Mrs. Cox's arm. "Bodies?"

Mrs. Cox led me into 1A and settled me into her rocking chair. I lurched back to my feet, but a dark look put my butt back in the seat. "There was some sort of hootenanny in your apartment. You know I don't—"

"It wasn't me. I was under medical care."

Mrs. Cox scowled. "Not your Dylan?"

"No. He's not like that."

Mrs. Cox gave me a piece of pound cake and a tall glass of milk. "I thought as much, elsewise I wouldn't have killed them."

I choked, spluttering milk all over the carpet. "You what?"

Mrs. Cox gestured dismissively. "They weren't regular people in any case, faeries of some kind."

The glass of milk clattered to the ground, spilling its contents every direction.

"Oh, dear," Mrs. Cox produced a towel and bent to clean up.

I took the cloth from her even though I wasn't much steadier than the old lady. I bent over the mess while Mrs. Cox clucked her tongue. "You need to be more careful, dear."

"T-tell me about the faeries."

Mrs. Cox folded her arms. "You don't believe me. You youngsters all just *know* there's no such thing as the faerie."

"I do believe you. I...I've seen the faerie."

Mrs. Cox patted my head. "Knew you were a smart girl. Have you experienced second sight too?"

"No."

She frowned. "I think Nana did. That's how she knew."

"So, you've seen faeries."

"Didn't I just tell you I killed some, dear?" Mrs. Cox took the glass into the kitchen and ran it under water. "You think I go around impaling random peoples' heads with garden tools?"

"What happened to the bodies?"

Mrs. Cox pushed a refilled glass into my hand.

"Mrs. Cox, you have to tell me what happened to Judith. You have to tell me what you did with the bodies. You could be in real danger."

Mrs. Cox gestured to the windows. "Elderberry sprigs wrapped in silver and salt on the sills. No mischievous Faerie Folk are going to invade my home."

"Some of the Folk come back from the dead."

Mrs. Cox blinked. "Really? Nana never said anything about that. Just as well I dragged them into your apartment and stabbed them in the head with my sheers for good measure then."

I downed the milk, earning brain freeze in my rush. Rubbing my tongue against the roof of my mouth to warm my palette garbled my question. "What happened to Judith?"

"I heard screaming and a commotion. Well, I run a quiet building, so I went up to have a word with the culprit. As I got there, she was snatched back into your apartment by a horde of goblins. A naked hobgoblin answered your door when I knocked. He not only slammed my door in my face, but he spat on me. Well, I wasn't going to put up with that kind of nonsense as you can understand."

"How do you know what a hobgoblin looks like?" I asked.

"Pictures—of course the pictures had clothes on them, not like this cheeky little bugger. Didn't really have that much to show off if you—" Mrs. Cox blushed. "I'm sorry, child, I shouldn't be saying such things in front of an unmarried girl.

"Anyway, dear, when I couldn't reach you, I checked my book then went out to the greenhouse to see about luring them with some elderberries—you know how Faerie Folk are obsessed with those."

My mind swam. "Book?"

"Don't interrupt, dear, I'll lose my place. One of the reasons I grow elderberries is in case of Faerie Folk, though you have to be very careful to wash them thoroughly—the berries, not the faeries." She smirked. "That rhymed. Anyway, there are all sorts of bad things that can happen to you if you eat or drink elderberries that have faerie saliva on or in them."

My mind refused to stop circling. Little Mrs. Cox, calm quiet landlady was a damned walking faerie wiki.

"So, while I was getting the berries, I thought to myself, Hadley girl, might not hurt to take the sickle with you, just in case they can't all be lured away by the berries. On the way back up I remembered Nana told a story about getting rid of hobgoblins by presenting them clothes—probably where that Rowling girl got her house elf thing. Anyway, armed for faerie, I went up to your apartment to save—Judith you said?" Mrs. Cox scowled. "I do hope the others weren't your friends, particularly since I killed a few of them."

"They weren't my friends, Mrs. Cox."

"Oh, good, I'd hate to do something like that to you."

"I appreciate it."

"The clothes thing didn't work and the berries only let me shove a few of those little buggers down the stairs. So, I gave the foul-mouthed naked fiend what for and the remaining goblins tore out of here with your Judith."

"Where'd they go?" I asked.

"I don't know, but that Detective Foxner had been on the corner staking out your apartment when they left. She pursued their van. I hope she caught them—she seems very competent even if a bit rude—in which case your Judith should be safe and sound."

Okay, the detective from the humane society is staking out my apartment, which odd as it might seem to me ended up being a good thing. Even if she lost them, she might have a line on where they took Judith. Wait...

I turned to Mrs. Cox. "The goblins had a van? Why?"

Mrs. Cox looked suddenly offended. "How should I know? Do I look like the kind of person to break into people's houses and indulge in strange practices?"

I laughed, I couldn't help myself. "No, Mrs. Cox. I'm sorry you thought that was what I was suggesting."

"Eat your pound cake, dear. You look a death."

I ate the heavenly cake, asking for more milk and cake as I considered things. Mrs. Cox knew things she shouldn't but apparently, she'd been taught by her grandmother which either freed me from any need to call for a rewrite or made for one hell of a time edit. I gobbled the third piece of cake, much to Mrs. Cox's beaming approval.

"Wait, you never told me where you saw hobgoblin pictures."

Mrs. Cox crossed to an old trunk shaped much like a fantasy treasure chest. She pulled an old afghan from atop it and unlocked it from a key on her crowded ring. She pushed aside two more blankets—smaller and much softer-looking—and brought out a leather-bound book almost a foot thick.

My brows shot up.

Mrs. Cox's gentle care placing the book on the coffee table still resulted in a resounding thunk. She opened the ancient tome, easing pages over one by one until she found one filled with hand-drawn sketches of what were undoubtedly hobgoblins.

Writing accompanied the pictures, but I couldn't make heads or tails of it. "What is that? I can't read it."

"I should think not. Took me two years to learn," Mrs. Cox said. "Nana wasn't a patient woman either. She expected me to know it from the first glance, though I can't say why. I can tell you, I got a switching for each week I got some word wrong until I was blistered and bitterly determined to learn the damned thing."

"What language is it?"

Mrs. Cox glanced around, her hands flitting through some sort of peasant ward. "The Romani Cant."

"Romani Cant? As in a Gypsy thiev—"

Mrs. Cox scowled.

"Um, never mind. Can I see the bodies now?"

Caelum

Caelum froze in front of his apartment. A cloying stench wafted from beneath his door typical of Unseelie mixed with a lesser but fresher stench of Wyldfae. He unlocked the door, chambered a round into each pistol and eased the door open.

Outrushing taint nearly bowled him over.

He fought its affect, sliding into the spacious living room decorated in a wide spectrum of black, white and greys. His eyes swept the immaculate room. A tent of white beckoned from the grey marble breakfast bar.

He took the long way around the couch, eyeballing his undisturbed bedroom through the doorway before closing to the tent. A neat handwritten note informed him he was out of milk.

That's not right.

Caelum's skin prickled.

The apartment wasn't that bad. I should've had enough credit for at least two more normal cleanings.

He slid around the bar into the kitchen proper. A quick check showed his own milk reserves exhausted. Cream cheese, sour cream, ice cream and even coffee creamer were all absent too.

What the hell?

Caelum crept toward his bedroom. The Unseelie taint grew stronger the closer he got.

How did Unseelie enter directly into my bedroom? I'd have sensed an Arch.

He glanced at his walls, verifying the vibrant, airbrushed canvasses remained. His weapon wall—depleted by recent action—possessed no new gaps to wring his guts. He inhaled, trying to determine if trap or ambush waited a step across his bedroom's threshold.

Another white tent rested on his far bureau. Something about the room troubled him. Something felt missing, but he couldn't place it.

Sound, there's no wind blowing.

Caelum charged into his room, jerking weapons toward the privacy screen. He edged forward. He froze, squeezing his essence. A wind jerked the screen toward him. It fell in slow motion, exposing the corner in which a whirlwind of balloons should've swirled.

The corner gaped empty.

He leapt the screen in a rush.

The Unseelie hadn't emptied his nest. They'd taken it.

What the hell did they want with my nest? Unless Vitae...

Hair along Caelum's limbs stood as pressure built behind his eyes. He tightened his grip on the guns in equal measure to the clench of his jaw.

He crossed to the second note. It gave him a phone number. Inside it read: These guys can fix the ceiling. They come highly recommended.

Caelum's gaze shot upward to the underside of someone else's bed, easily visible through the missing ceiling and floor between the two apartments.

Chapter Ten

Bloodlust

Vitae

A waterspout of dark blood swirled up out of my nest. It fanned outward like spreading wings forming a new body. Blood drew long bones, painted them with sinew, ligaments and shrouded the whole in muscle. Lean fat layered next as cushion to lustrous, bronze skin.

I parted curtains of long ebony waves to reveal supple curves and full breasts. A pert smile curled the corner of full lips—not from the beauty of my gorgeous female body, but the tingling power glistening along every inch like a sheen of sweat.

This ratio is...intoxicating...powerful.

"You are beautiful in your might, Master, but...," the coyll's canid ears pressed to his head, "your gender has been corrupted. You do not wish to be—"

I lifted a leg like a crane and let blood drip back into my nest. I turned toward the knee-high Wyldfae. "A bitch? Trust me, I will be no one's bitch, Scurith, but seeming so may encourage others to underestimate me. This body is a weapon suited to controlling wafers and Sidhe alike. With it, I can ensure Atlanta's peace."

And perhaps force Dolumii's sword to release Mare.

"I-if you say so, M-Mistress," Scurith stammered.

"Master!"

"Y-yes, yes, apologies, M-Master, many apologies."

"Well, let's find out. Notify Thatch that I am coming."

I placed the mostly dry foot onto the warehouse concrete, careful not to set bloody toes on any of the markings defining the magical circle used to imprison and bleed my captives. I lifted the other foot, wriggling toes to help it drip faster.

Out of the corner of my eye, I caught motion near the door. The coyll's tan and grey fur let it blend into backgrounds far more readily than the strong colors of its gnoll cousins. "Stop!"

Power washed out of me.

The smaller humanoid froze, paw-like hand on the handle.

"How very legalistic of you, Scurith, but you know I did not intend you to leave this building."

He bowed his head, sandy brown tail tucking between his legs. "I merely wanted to serve your desire, Mist-Master."

A flick of one hand lashed a line of fire across the distance and across the coyll's grey muzzle with a sizzle. Cooked dog fur fouled the air. "A message serves my desire, not an absent messenger."

"But the protocols, Master. Royal members of the Courts must be notified in person."

"Thatch is a filthy little goblin," I said. "He will accept a whispering wind and be glad to receive me."

Scurith bowed away from the door, ears flicking forward then against his head in turns. He scurried into the small office.

I examined my body once more. None of the clothing stored in the warehouse could cover my body in a manner suited to its new splendor. I turned to the rearmost area of the warehouse, the sway of my hips throwing off my balance.

I'd expanded my jail area, adding even more cages designed to hold Seelie and Unseelie of differing types and sizes. The more my Shield captured alive, the more cages I needed.

A dwarf threw himself at a cage door. "Release me! Holding me is a violation of the Articles of Ararat."

"I told you before, you'll be released once you confess to crimes against Creation and provide the location of our stolen eggs."

"I don't know where your damned eggs are."

I thrust out one hip and rested a hand on it. "Pity."

I scoured the cages, coming at last to an elven warrior in ornate armor. I circled her, weighing my options.

She glowered at me. "You might look like an elf, but you stomp around like a pregnant yak."

My lip curled. "Strip."

"You need real perfection to mimic?"

"I need your clothes, preferably unbloodied," I said.

"No."

I stepped closer to the bars, feeling a rising surge of magic. I fixed her with my gaze and pushed the magic into my voice as I took hold of the bars between us. Pain burned my palms and nausea washed up my arms.

I stepped back, seizing my midsection. Summoned magic fled to make room for sudden convulsions. My legs folded. I hit the ground writhing.

"First taste of iron is always the worst—not that subsequent tastes are much better." The elf sneered. "Looks like you got some weakness when you stole our strength. Serves you right."

It took several minutes for the sickness to fade and more to master myself. Anger replaced the heat stolen by the cement floor. Magic rocketed to my furious call and shot across the distance between my gaze and hers. "Strip and hand me your clothes."

A swooping sensation filled the sudden absence of magic, but vanished as my faerie blood restored the used power. The elf warrior handed out her clothes, taking the utmost care to avoid the iron bars.

I sauntered back into the main warehouse. "Scurith?"

The little coyll appeared.

Smaller than their larger cousins, coyll made up for their weakness with better magic skill. It was for that reason that I'd spared Scurith and pressed him into service. "Teach me to bespell these clothes to suit my tastes."

"Yes, Master. At once."

Once I had repaired and enchanted the armor into a resplendent mix of rich, verdant greens, silver and gold, I drove my Mercedes across town to the Central Presbyterian Church.

A block away, an Atlanta police cruiser flashed its lights at me. It took all of my will not to blind the wafer and leave him behind to park or crash. Still, I was a life phoenix. Protecting the interrupting wafer was my duty, even if I was protecting the mortal shield from his own impertinence.

The chirp of his siren almost prompted me to reconsider.

He took his sweet time sidling up to the car window. "License and registration?" He scanned my face, eyes sliding down my armored dress as he licked his lips. "On second thought, step out of the car please."

I caught the man's hungry gaze.

Normally, I'd have had The Isaac replace identity papers after a death, but I'd died a dozen times without contacting him. No one needed to know my business. I was a Shieldheart protecting my Shield. That was all that mattered.

"Ma'am?"

I pushed power out between my lips. "Truth is, there's no need for this, constable."

"Yes, ma'am, there is. You were speeding, and now I intend to make you bend over so I can ogle you."

"No. God created woman to be a helpmate, an equal partner. Your attitude disgraces His Creation." I pushed more power into my voice. "Women are not objects. You will not treat them or think of them in that manner, do you understand?"

He whimpered.

"Answer!"

"I will no longer treat or think of women as objects."

"Correct. As for speeding, you now realize the vehicle you

thought was mine was actually another. You made a mistake. You'll do better next time. Now let me go with an apology."

"I...I think I made a mistake, ma'am," the officer said. "You're free to go with my apologies."

"Thank you," I said. "Mark down in your logs that you gave me a warning and then forget the whole incident."

"Yes, ma'am."

"Tell me I can go."

"You may go."

I sped away without waiting on the officer to step away from the Mercedes' door. I parked at the church and strode across the lawn around the side.

A little old lady glared at me. "This is God's house, not some pagan hostel for harlots and deviants."

I stopped, turning slowly to the grey-haired harridan and her bony, brandished finger. Essence welled into my narrowed eyes. "I think you will find this is God's yard. That's His house, and since I see none of His light in you, what gives you any right to hurl judgement at a servant of His Undying Light?"

She snorted.

Magic frothed and fizzed in my center, shooting through my core and down one arm like foam made by warm root beer poured on ice cream.

Her eyes locked on my fingers as she shrank away from me.

I followed her gaze to emerald flame licking my fingers. "If I were you, I'd divest myself of self-importance, go in there and humble yourself to your Maker—before He has His anointed send you to meet Him in person."

I turned my back and marched around a trestle arch. Too-dry vine roses wove through the latticework. I dug an acorn and a small pinecone from a belt pouch, but hesitated.

This is no way to represent the Undying Light.

Transferring everything to my off hand, I squeezed my center and caressed the vines with the life energy pulsing in my hand. Ruby essence streaked with evergreen and violet spread up and down the plant. Buds and leaves exploded from hydrated, healthy stems. Crimsons blossom clusters flowered. Beneath the thick foliage, thorns lengthened and their tips darkened to violet.

Better. A crown of glory for the Most High.

I articulated and intoned the opening incantation with easy precision, filling the archway with swirls of summoned magic.

And without angering the heavens...unlike a certain greenhorn.

A wide, cobbled path led me up a rise under a star-filled night. Dark trees grew up to the path's edge, allowing me to see the sky through winter-stripped branches. Shapes moved in the distance, eyes gleaming yellow without light to reflect.

I drew Dolumii's sword. The hilt writhed beneath my fingers until it reformed into a perfect fit. The hilt bent around my slender fist, the violet glow along the dark blade casting long shadows on tormented faces mouthing silent horrors. I drew Gherrian's sword with similar results, save the pumpkin orange hilt where eyes narrowed but no mouths moaned.

"Your knights couldn't best me, but try me if you lust for death."

None did.

I reached the hollow. Cracked, blood-darkened mud replaced the former cobbles. Camp stools replaced cushioned chairs around a new table shaped by hard angles into a jagged M.

To the left beneath tall pines, a stone tower with lowered portcullis replaced the former silk tent—though ice blue and dark raspberry, evergreen and white still colored its exterior. Right mirrored left, daffodil and crimson, gold and orange failing to soften the tower's sinister feel.

A single figure guarded each—cloaked and hooded, but unmoved by the swords still in my grip.

I called out to the only unchanged feature. "Thatch!"

A rotund goblin in an Edwardian suit coat and vestment scrambled out of the tiny tent on the far side of the hollow. Long narrow ears extended a middle distance between that of a dark, greasy, ponytail and a nose twice as long. He bowed his head repeatedly, black brow bobbing as he hurried forward on patent leather clown shoes.

He eyed the cloaked figures. "You summoned me, Shieldhe—"

I sheathed a single sword to plant the hand on one hip. "Is there a problem, Thatch?"

"Um, n-no, no problem, Shield Vitae—are you still called Vitae?" Thatch asked, eyes taking in my new form.

"I am always Vitae, the vessel is no matter."

A rich European accent dried by scorn emerged from my left, "I disagree."

The guard's deep violet, velvet cloak dropped away from his shoulders. Ebony quicksilver framed thin angled features of silver-powdered Mediterranean olive. Armor more ornate than my stolen garb covered the Unseelie Knight in raspberry, midnight and silver filigree. Scaled gloves tucked into his belt by their thumbs.

The second elf threw off his cloak and bowed with a flourish that swept loose chestnut waves forward to curtain his face. He rose once more, a smirk lifting a corner of his thin lips up a bronze cheek. He too wore ornate armor, though pumpkin orange, scarlet and gold. "I must agree with Knight Dolumii, Lady Shield, though it grieves my sensibilities."

"Strange days, Knight Gherrian," Dolumii said.

"I must agree once more," Gherrian said.

Cold swallowed me, held back by burning magic reaching for my fingers. "I killed you both."

"While you fought well," Gherrian said. "Shield Aquaylae gets credit for our slaying."

"A deft kill," Dolumii said. "More the splendid for slaying all three of us by daring what you feared do."

"Reckless." I seethed. "Not daring."

"Whatever slays your enemy," Dolumii said.

"As long as the act is honorable," Gherrian said.

Dolumii snorted.

"You admit you were slain," I said.

"And assigned to guard an unused gate as punished for my failure," Dolumii darkened. "Still, I can now reclaim my blade."

"I shall take mine too, if you would be so kind," Gherrian said.

My eyes flitted from Dolumii to Gherrian to Thatch. "Explain how this is possible."

"Surrender my Champion blade, bird," Dolumii said.

"No," I drew my second blade and tightened my grip. "They are mine by right of conquest."

"Then I'm afraid we shall take them," Dolumii said.

"And you shall get no answer," Gherrian added.

They rushed me.

I pressed down on my essence, compacting it into a tight core.

Released in the transmogrification, the additional power I'd granted myself through experimentations exploded alongside my essence. Great black-edged crimson wings spread wider than they'd ever extended before. Enchanted elven armor and the Knights' blades changed with me, plating my phoenix form and wrapping my talons in razor gauntlets—one golden and one blueish silver. Magic crackled along my wingtips, arching from pinion to pinion.

Thatch gasped. "By the Pit."

Both Knights hesitated.

I didn't.

Dolumii drew a sword and summoned a handful of magic as he leapt clear of my talons. His defensive slash scored the armor protecting one of my wings.

I battered him with the opposite and thrust my beak at the elf's throat. A camp stool slammed into my back, driving my body forward to miss Dolumii's throat. I whirled around, slamming wings together. A wave of magical force aborted Gherrian's charge.

"Shield Vitae, you cannot attack Knights of the Sidhe Court

without cause!" Thatch yelled. "If you slay them with the Champion blades the consequences would be beyond dire."

Dolumii rolled to his feet and slashed.

I deflected the cut with the talon armored by Dolumii's transmogrified sword and struck with the other talon.

Gherrian tripped Dolumii with another stool and deflected my blow. My wing slammed into Gherrian. I snapped my beak after the fallen elf.

Dolumii stabbed up into my descending body.

Armor deflected his blow, but I released my anger in a roar. Dolumii threw his sword straight into my face. A wingtip's twitch slid me to the side as the blade cut across the side of my head.

Dolumii's victorious cheer turned to gurgling screams as my hooked beak tore his entrails from his torso. Gherrian leapt off the table onto my back. He hooked his sword around my throat and yanked backward. The blade cut into me. Blood sprayed cut feathers over Dolumii.

Gherrian's blade jerked backward through my throat as I transmogrified. He fell backward, striking his head.

I whipped back around, slamming armored wings through Gherrian's neck like scissors. Emerald light blazed from my eyes. "Come back from that."

"They will," Thatch said.

I rounded on him. "How? I've slain faerie for two millennium and never had one return."

"You've never killed the anointed Knight of a Principa—um, leader of one of the Courts," Thatch said. "They're lives are bolstered by their liege."

I seethed. "Tell me where to find their nests. I'll finish this once and for all."

"That's not how this works."

"No," I said. "If their deaths drew energy off Vusolaryn or Mariena to bring them back, then they would've known of the deaths before we informed them."

"They did," Thatch said. "Vusolaryn and Mariena....um, meant to play you."

"So, the only way to rid myself of these two is to slay Vusolaryn and Mariena?"

Thatch blanched. "You cannot. They are powers beyond anything you could muster. Attacking them would be like declaring—"

"War?" I sneered. "We're already at war."

"No," Thatch said. "Armageddon. You must not even speak of threatening them."

"Why not?"

"Slaying Gherrian and Dolumii in your world was bad enough they want your Aqua's blood. Slaying them here in the Courts will bring every Seelie and Unseelie calling for your blood. They will stop at nothing to avenge these deaths. I cannot even imagine the outcry for a worse offense."

I wrung the hilts gripped in my hands. "Let them come. I will decorate my kingdom with their skins."

"Kingdom, Shieldheart? Do you not mean Shield?"

"Whatever," I said. "I would hear what you have learned regarding our eggs."

"No one is speaking, Shield Vitae." Thatch gestured at the corpses. "Now, no word will escape their lips save the cry for your True Death."

Chapter Eleven

Calling the Cops

Quayla

I followed Mrs. Cox upstairs. My best efforts failed to rush the woman even though I needed to find Judith. In a way, she was right. She'd left the message on my phone hours ago. Judith was either safe or not no matter how much we hurried.

Taint on the air thickened with each step, pressing against my skin despite overpowering odors of chemical pine and copious white sage burning in the stairwell. The combination left me nauseous and light headed.

"Goblin blood really is noxious stuff," Mrs. Cox said. "Nana swore by lye, but I read somewhere that things from fairy land are supposed to dissolve into goo after they're killed."

I wrinkled my nose, trying to hold off a sneeze. "I know the book you mean. That's not how it works."

Mrs. Cox gave me a sidelong look.

An imperfectly removed blood stain marked where a goblin body had fallen only to be killed by the sweet little old lady.

I'm going to have to call Summus.

We crested the landing.

I slipped around Mrs. Cox, interposing myself between

possible danger and the old landlady. More stains that nothing on the planet could remove marked the carpet.

Nothing mortal anyway.

"I already killed them, dear."

"I don't smell one, but they could have an Arch inside my apartment."

"You're not human then?" Mrs. Cox asked.

I shook my head absently, focused on my senses as I eased open my apartment door. I choked back a gag and a sob at the same time. A tarp covered a mostly cleared space in the center of what had once been my living room. Rotting faerie bodies lay upon a plastic square amid the ruin. Barb maggots undulated atop the corpses like pallid seagrass. Tiny, high-pitched moans of zombie sopranos created an eerie chorus, the song interrupted slightly whenever the larvae bent double to gouge out a mouthful of flesh.

Old china plates circled the rotting goblins, ashes and a few unburnt chunks of white sage on their blackened surface.

Mrs. Cox scowled. "Those things weren't here before."

I pushed Mrs. Cox back toward the door, eyes flitting around the unlit room. Goblins had marred every inch of my walls. They'd cobbled together broken furniture into a hybrid easel and crucifix.

For torturing me or...oh, thank God Dylan never came back.

"Dear, they're only maggots."

"No, they're barb maggots, and where they are, damsel sprites aren't far behind."

"That doesn't sound so bad," Mrs. Cox said.

"They're like flying piranha the size of your pinky, they'll eat anything they can get their teeth around."

"Should I get more white sage?"

"Won't help. Sage won't affect the maggots and since they become the damsel sprites, there's nothing for the sage to ward away from entering."

"How do I get rid of them?"

I shook my head. "This isn't something that a wafer can take care of, Mrs. Cox."

"Now see here, missy." Mrs. Cox planted hands on her hips. "I can handle anything you can, and I'll thank you not to call me a wafer—whatever that means."

"A mortal, a normal, nonmagical being—plain as a vanilla wafer." I drew a silvered feather from my neckline.

"I'm not a woman to waste energy taking offense, but I don't like that one bit. It's degrading."

"I'm sorry, but it won't bother you long." I raised the feather to my lips.

A quiet croak halted the call before it escaped my lips. "Quayla?"

I scanned my apartment, all too aware that damsel sprites could cost me another life. A shift of movement drew my eye to the kitchen cabinets. A tiny hand flopped weakly in a crack between door and frame.

"Stay here." I rushed across the room, drawing the attention of the barb maggots like I was some kind of snake charmer. I threw open my cabinet to find Grynnberry laying in a puddle of his own blood. "Grynn?"

"I-I tried to stop them."

I eased fingers carefully under the little nymph. Using a plastic plate, I shifted Grynnberry over onto his stomach. Half of his dragonfly wings had been badly broken. A wing on his other side bent to a lesser extent.

There's no way he could fly.

I had to get him out of my apartment. Damsel sprites were a real danger to Mrs. Cox and myself, but they'd eat Grynnberry alive—literally.

"What happened?"

"I heard the goblins talking about it. They followed that woman from your flower shop. I unlatched the door when I heard her knock, hoping she'd know what had happened to you," He coughed, spitting green. "I was worried about you."

I eased us around the piled bodies, eyes scanning and ears straining for any hint of a damsel sprite.

"She came in, freaking out about the blood and ran for the door. Their hobgoblin was waiting for her." he gestured at the crucifix. "The rest was pain, vile Unseelie."

"Who's this little fellow?" Mrs. Cox asked.

"Grynnberry, he's a...friend. Hold him while I summon help?"

Mrs. Cox took the plate.

Grynnberry tensed. "If you're going to summon a divine, I need to leave first."

"You can't fly, Grynn, and I can't wait and risk damsel sprites getting lose in Creation."

She frowned. "What is he? He doesn't match anything I've seen before."

"He's pretty badly beat up, or maybe you just don't remember." I withdrew the silvered feather pendent from my neckline. "Summuseraphi, Summuseraphi, Summuseraphi."

"My mind is sharp as a tack, young lady."

Summus appeared in a blinding flash of life. "She's not just boasting. Good day, Hadley."

"That's Mrs. Cox—widowed, not divorced, young man, and I do not socialize with naked men."

Summus offered me a longsuffering smile.

"I need to go after the other goblins," I said.

"I'll take care of things here. Do your duty, shield," Summus said.

I took one last look at my apartment, swallowing the sob desperate to escape and bolted down the stairs. I hopped onto my Johammer and addressed the bronze angel.

"Ani, I need to find that Detective Foxner."

"Pardon me for saying, Shield Quayla, but seeking the police detective trying to arrest your body from two rebirths ago seems an ill-conceived plan."

"Can you do it?"

"I cannot, but I will contact the Isaac."

"Has Dylan already gotten your systems hooked into cellular communications?"

Please say yes, I'd rather call than talk over the open angel network.

Anima didn't answer. She went quiet for several minutes.

I tapped my thumbs against the electric motorcycle's handlebars, double-checking its remaining battery levels.

"Apparently the goblins eluded her," Anima said.

"Did you get her location?"

"I did."

"Where is she?"

"If she doesn't know where the goblins are, there is no need to risk a meeting with her," Anima said.

"Damn it, Anima. I'm a full shield just like the others. Stop questioning me and just give me what I requested."

Guilt swept in on me like a sea breeze. I rationalized it away, keeping in mind that Anima was just a computer AI.

No, that's not right. She's something else, and I owe her an apology.

Anima's wooden reply cut even deeper than the guilt had. "Detective Foxner is en route to her precinct. If there isn't anything else, I have duties to perform."

"I'm sorry, Ani. I shouldn't have snapped at you."

Silence.

"Anima?"

"Message received. Do you require anything more from me, Shield Aquaylae?"

The trip to Foxner's precinct took less time than I expected despite traffic and the guilt dragged out the time so I could replay my conversation with Anima over and over. I'd hurt her feelings—emotions I could no longer dismiss as a quirk of programming like the others.

I parked in front of the precinct and went inside to ask the front desk for directions. Officers stopped me at the metal detector, examining my karambit hilts. Despite the lack of a blade, they forced me to leave them behind before entering the precinct.

The directions led me to a tidy desk with wolf figurines and a bronze nameplate for Detective Sabrina Foxner. The detective wasn't in evidence.

Now what?

"Can I help you, miss?"

I turned, neck craning up to a pleasant dark-skinned face with a soft smile. The plain clothes officer had at least a head and a half more height than me.

God, I'm short.

"I was looking for Detective Foxner."

"I figured that out for myself." He flashed a wider smile. "Insights like that are why they call me a detective."

I returned his smile. "Do those skills include knowing where she is or when she'll be back?"

He licked his finger and raised it into the air. With closed eyes, his wetted finger swayed back and forth.

"I sense...I sense...," He spun, his opposite palm sweeping toward a hallway. "She's in tech ops, through there, take a left and then down the stairs on your right."

I flashed him another smile and sped down the indicated hall. A door at the bottom of the stairs bore only a T and a partial E. I eased the door open.

A wall of video screens displayed a white panel van as it distended and drove under a semi-truck trailer. The view jerked left then right.

A dash camera.

The van's backdoors flew open. Two goblins worked together to throw a hex. A brick wall sprang to life in front of the camera. The car's driver managed to stop just in time.

Foxner's rosebud mouth bent down in frustration. Snakes of dark brown hair escaped her normally restrained bun. Her athletic body was drawn taut, seemingly poised on the edge of violence. She slammed a fist into the desk and pointed. "It's right there on camera, Miri."

The other woman's dark curls framed thick, oversized spectacles. Her rumpled polo and loose jeans hid a modest figure visible only because bending over the console stole the shirt's slack. She blinked hazel eyes at Foxner. "But the wall is gone now?"

"The wall couldn't have been there before. Even if I had somehow not noticed it, the semi couldn't have pulled in to make a delivery with that there. Please tell me you have a rational explanation—preferably one that doesn't include blood cults."

Miri took off her glasses, wiping them with a cloth. "Some kind of wall of stone spell."

"A spell," Foxner said.

"As in magic, wizards, that sort of thing," Miri said.

Foxner ran a hand down her face. "Please don't mention Dungeons and Dragons."

"*You* are familiar with Dungeons and Dragons?" Hope brought Miri's voice up a few notes. "Do you play?"

Foxner groaned into her hand. "I asked you not to mention it."

"All right," Miri said. "If you prefer."

I debated.

The video offered some of what I needed to track down Judith, but I didn't recognize the location. Going through Atlanta checking behind grocery stores for a portal to another world wasn't fast enough to save Judith.

I'll just have to get her a rewrite later.

"That's a hex, not a creation spell," I said.

The other two jerked around to face the door.

"They layered a glamour spell in front of you with a nasty curse on it in case you drove through," I said.

Foxner's eyes narrowed, running up and down me—and not in a good way. "Buckler."

"You've lost mass," Miri said.

"It's been a rough month," I said.

Foxner took three rushed steps around intervening work-benches.

I backed away, hands up. "I'm here to help you, Detective."

"That would be a first."

"I need your help in return," I said. "We need to find the goblins that took Judith."

Miri's brow rose. "Would you please repeat that?"

Foxner closed until her body pinned me against the door-frame, but I didn't flee. Her gaze drove into me like a laser drill. Foxner's hands clenched and released, but she didn't strike.

I glanced over Foxner's shoulder at the other woman. "The word you want repeated is goblin. Is this room under surveillance?"

"Of course," Miri said. "She cannot accost you."

"Could you please turn it off?" I said. "Please."

Miri's other brow joined the first.

"I'm not your enemy, in fact we're very simila—"

"You and I are not the same," Foxner snapped. "You're a criminal. I don't know how you change your body, but you're guilty."

I need her help, and I don't have time to waste.

"I'm not human. I'm actually a phoenix." I squeezed my essence, compacting magical energy into a tight ball under pressure as I slid around Foxner into the room's center. "You should step back."

Foxner's lips pressed into a harder line.

Your choice.

I released my core. A starburst of power exploded outward. Magic rushed over my every cell, seizing each and rearranging it. I leapt upward a moment before my legs dissolved.

Foxner backpedaled into the door frame, rattling the glass of the thankfully-closed door. She hit the ground hard, but still managed to draw her weapon.

My wing slapped the gun from her hand just before she pulled the trigger.

Foxner seized her hand, blood running down her knuckles

from where my pinion had scratched her. She scrambled after the weapon.

On the opposite side of the room, Miri let out a startled squeak and fell out of her chair. She lifted her glasses to her forehead and blinked up at me from the floor. "Th-that's not possible."

I floated above them. Gentle strokes of my wings kept me floating and managed my position just below the ceiling.

"Then I'm not the only one seeing this?" Foxner asked.

"I-I believe I see what you see. Maybe, I hope so...kinda," Miri said. "Are you seeing a large bird which seems to be made out of water?"

"Y-yes." Foxner snapped up the gun. "Could it be a hallucination of some sort?"

"If it is, do you intend to shoot it?" Miri asked.

"Shooting things makes me feel better."

"It's made of water."

Sabrina held up her hand. "It's physical enough."

"You cannot possibly be a phoenix. You're made of water."

"A woman just changed into a bird floating in the room and you're being picky?"

"I'm trying to be rational."

Foxner gestured. "Rational? About that?"

"I can either apply logic or let the tiny shrieking voice in my gut focus on the giant bird of prey floating over both of us." Miri climbed with exaggerated slowness back into her chair and righted her glasses. "Phoenix, um, Quayla...Quayla? As in short for Aquaylae?"

I nodded.

"What are you talking about?" Foxner demanded.

"Latin for water. Never mind. Quayla, there are several things that trouble me."

"Why are you talking to her?"

"Hush, I'm trying to understand and not scream."

"She's a bird."

"A bird that was human a few moment ago." Miri addressed me. "You did nod, yes? You can understand us?"

I nodded my head.

"Can you speak?" Miri asked.

I shook my head.

Miri cursed.

"What are you doing?" Foxner asked.

"Learning."

Foxner's tone rose in pitch. "You're just going to stand there and calmly ask this killer questions?"

"You should holster your weapon, Sabrina."

"Are you nuts?

"Considering her talons and beak, I have no doubt if she wished you dead, you would already be so. Additionally, while I am baffled by the existence of a phoenix not formed of fire, I seriously doubt your bullets would affect what appears to be a body composed of glowing water."

I squeezed my essence once more, wishing not for the first time that I could transmog into a hybrid form like the divine phoenixes did. I focused on the little details and released a wave of essence to rewrite my form while restoring clothing and possessions.

"I am indeed Aquaylae, Shield of the Undying Light, protector of Atlanta," I addressed Foxner. "I was at the Humane Society trying to save the animals and stop a Sidhe incursion."

Miri brightened for a heartbeat before all color drained away from her skin. "Sidhe, actual beings from the Seelie and Unseelie races of the Fae?"

"Yes, I died attempting to seal a breach in the Veil between this world and the world of Faery."

"Fascinating," Miri picked up a yellow legal pad and a pen. "You said you died, but how were you reborn? Do you ignite when slain?"

"Miri?" Foxner asked.

Miri shushed the detective.

"No, I'm a water phoenix." I said.

"You aren't reborn from ashes then?" Miri asked.

"Miri!"

"No," I said. "I only told you these things because we must find those goblins and rescue Judith. If you'll tell me where the goblins vanished, I'll take it from there."

"The hell you will," Foxner said. "There's no way I'd let a person of interest go off hunting anything in my jurisdiction. Besides, you just confessed to breaking and entering."

The noise escaping me was one part sigh and two parts growl. "What are you going to do, Detective? If you try to apprehend me, I will have no choice but to resist so I can go after Judith. You can't hold me here."

Foxner jiggled her gun. "You don't think so?"

"I imagine that if you killed her," Miri said. "Her rebirth wouldn't happen here."

"I'd rather not die again," I said. "It's a huge pain in the ass. Just the same, I will surrender my life to save Judith."

Foxner frowned, gears running full speed behind her eyes.

"What's it going to be, Detective? Find a mop or help me save a mortal life?"

Foxner's calculations ran a few moments more. I tensed to force the issue, wishing what came next didn't necessitate replacing my karambit hilts once more.

"Fine, let's go," Foxner said.

"I do not believe the phoenix intended for you to accompany her," Miri said.

"She's correct, it wouldn't be safe for you to accompany me."

Foxner bristled. "I can take anything you can."

Miri cleared her throat. "Even returning from the dead?"

"You're not helping," Foxner snapped.

Miri shrugged. "Reason or gibbering."

I knew the expression on Foxner's face. It didn't leave any budge room, but the longer we argued, the longer Judith remained in faerie clutches.

I'll have her rewritten as soon as she gives me the information. Vitae's going to kill me when he finds out.

"Fine, but this is my jurisdiction. You'll follow my lead."

Foxner snorted.

"If we're going, get what you need," I said. "I'll wait here with your friend."

"Excellent, I have more questions," Miri said.

Foxner eyed me with suspicion.

"You haven't told me where to find the goblins," I said. "I'm not leaving until I know."

The detective scrutinized me for another four count. "Watch her, Miri. I'll be right back."

Miri offered a serene smile. "Gladly. Take your time."

"No," I snapped. "You need to hurry so we can help Judith."

Foxner rushed out the door.

"So," Miri said. "About my questions."

"I know the perfect person to answer them." I extracted my pendant. "Summuseraphi, Summuseraphi, Summuseraphi."

"Supreme seraphim?" Miri's eyes widened at Summus's appearance, pink creeping into her cheeks.

"Again? Really Quayla?" Summus asked.

"I'm sorry, but I'm trying to save Judith."

Summus pressed his lips together and turned toward Miri. She raised her yellow pad. "The water phoenix indicated you could answer my questions. What kind of phoenix are—"

Summus slapped his hands together. "Let's get this over with."

"The detective that chased the goblins will be back in a moment. Once she tells me where she lost them, she'll need rewritten."

"You do realize rewriting is not as easy as it looks, right?"

"How could I?" I asked.

"Okay, good point," Summus said. "It's exhausting, all right?"

"All right. I wouldn't ask you if I could do it," I said.

Summus went to work on Miri's memories. At first, I

watched, but looking directly at reality being rewritten made me sicker than I'd ever been. I paced the room, waiting for Foxner and hoping Summus finished before she arrived.

Summus's head snapped up. He swore then apologized heavenward. The changes around Miri sped up, culminating in a wave of power that left my skin tingling.

"Sorry, your detective will have to wait." Summus vanished.

I cursed and stepped out into the hall.

Chapter Twelve

Bending the Rules

Ignis

Ignis pulled his Camaro into a parking space along the bus line he'd taken back to the church after his death. His fury over the theft of his heart by the arrogant elf knight Dolumii had been enough to transform the natural gas fueled bus into a warm and cozy fireball.

Bastard died before I could pay him back and reclaim my heart.

Ignis took a deep breath before he melted his beloved car. His idea had calmed lingering anger and given him a new way to search for their missing eggs. Letting temper interfere meant losing the opportunity to shove their eggs under Vitae's snooty nose.

Can't wait to see his expression.

He stepped from the blistering car interior into a pleasant, hundred-degree Atlanta day. A few people without other options trudged through the heat, sweat damping their clothes before they'd taken a few steps outdoors.

Ignis drew in the heat. He had no issues with glorious southern summers—except maybe the humidity. Unlike Quayla, he couldn't do anything about the damp, sticky air. He'd tried warming his skin to burn it off, but the ever-present, pervasive humidity refused to be burned away, leaving him soiled and irritable.

Got to envy the Aquas. Caelum too for his ability to produce a drying breeze.

He inhaled through his nose, seeking faerie taint. Sulphur and marsh hid beneath sweaty pedestrians, overdoses of perfume and someone's garlic onion toast.

Ignis spun slowly, taking a few steps first one way and then another. Taint didn't draw him one way or another.

I miss Mare. She could've wrapped a necklace of essence beads around her throat and felt which pearl tainted fastest. My essence would only burn the taint away, besides I can't pull off the pearls.

He opened the Camaro's passenger door and dropped onto the seat. "Anima?"

"How can I assist you, Shield Ignis?"

"Anima, with as long as we've known each other, there's no need to be formal."

"Shield Vitae has reprimanded me for being too informal. Besides, did you not just call me by my full name?"

"You're right. Thank you for pointing out my hypocrisy. I meant no offense."

"None taken, Ignis. Forgive me, I just had a most disagreeable conversation with Quayla. How may I serve?"

"I need your help. I'm trying to track down a faerie who dwells in the general area of this bus stop. Can you measure the taint levels around all of the surrounding seeds and extrapolate a location or at least a path of pursuit?"

"Faerie aren't supposed to live in the mortal world," Anima said.

"One reason I'm tracking him down, Ani. Can you help?"

"One moment please."

Ignis waited.

"Ignis, I have an alert—oh, never mind."

"Ani?"

"I am sorry. It was only a 'hot and now' event near you."

Caelum.

Ignis shook his head. "It's fine. I thought Vitae purged those sensors from the net?"

"Caelum reprogrammed them with specialized logic which prevents them from displaying while Vitae is present."

"Too smart for his own good. He'd be a force to be reckoned with if he put that much energy into dealing with the Sidhe." Ignis's stomach grumbled. "Ani? While you're working on my search, where was that event?"

"I'm afraid I have already finished, and you must head north and a little west—away from the donut shop."

"North it is. Thanks."

Ignis caught a stronger scent five blocks north. It led west and north in a zigzag that seemed to work its way past a maximum number of smoke shops, bars and pizza joints.

Ignis turned a corner and slammed into a young man with a sweat-stained dress shirt, wild red hair, large ears and an attempted mustache more fuzz than fur.

"Sorry," Ignis stepped around him. "Excuse me."

An itch grew between Ignis's shoulder blades. He turned back to find the man he'd bumped staring at a weird device and Ignis in turns.

"You're yellow!"

Ignis's brows shot up. "Excuse me?"

The red head rushed forward several steps, one hand held up. "I didn't mean you're a coward or anything." He beamed down at the cobbled remote. "You're the yellow magic, one of the ones fighting the blue and red. Nice to meet you, I'm Bradley."

Ignis narrowed his eyes, dropping them to the device. One of the glass spheres glowed a swirling yellow. "What is that?"

"It detects magic," his smile widened. "I made it myself."

Ignis grabbed Bradley by his shirt. "Are you Fae Kissed?"

"What?"

"Have you made a deal with the faeries.'

"I didn't know that was an option," Bradley said. "Are they yellow too? Red? Blue? How would I get in contact with them?"

Ignis jerked Bradley closer, inhaling deeply. An odd taint lingered on him, but from casual contact rather than the reek of an infernal mark. "You don't if you know what's good for you."

Bradley titled his head, pensive expression vanishing behind a quick grin. "All right. You're the gold here, not me."

"Show me how this device of yours works." Ignis knelt to one side out of the direct path of the weird object. "Extend it forward?"

"Sure, anything for you guys. I want to help."

Bradley pushed the heavy device forward. As it moved past Ignis, the yellow glow softened, making it easier to see a slight blue glow in one of the other globes.

Ignis took the device and waved it at Bradley. All three globes lit ever so slightly, confirming Ignis's suspicion the man had been in contact with magic but wasn't bearing a source. He handed the detector back and drew out an ornate golden pocket watch. He opened the ornately-inscribed cover depicting an angel to reveal a glowing white feather instead of timepiece and clockwork.

Bradley pointed the detector at the feather. The golden globe flared to life like burning phosphorous. Awe dropped Bradley's exclamation to a whisper. "Great Gygax!"

"Summuseraphi, summuseraphi—"

Bradley frowned, cocking his head. "Prime seraphim?"

"Summuseraphi," Ignis finished.

A blinding light filled the side alley.

"Holy shit, a real archangel!" Bradley said.

Both Summus's wings and shoulders slumped. He took a deep breath, raising his head and throwing golden hair off of his face. He took one look at and Bradley and cradled his face. "You again?"

"Have we met?" Bradley asked.

Ignis took the device from Bradley's hand. "We need a rewrite, seems he's been tracking the faeries with this device. I'm pretty sure he isn't Fae Kissed."

"He's not," Summus said. "We've met before."

"I think I'd remember that," Bradley objected.

"You filmed it," Summus said.

Bradley reached for his phone.

"I've already erased the recording."

Bradley's face fell.

"Curious though about how you're aware again and so soon," Summus said.

Ignis turned his attention to Bradley. "Summuseraphi will take care of you."

Bradley stepped backward, taking his detector out of reach. "He's going to erase my memory, isn't he? That's why I can't remember meeting him from before. You know I'm only trying to help you."

"I need your detector," Ignis said. "You could help by handing it over."

Bradley's mouth quirked into a thoughtful half frown. He brightened. "Sure, anything you need."

Ignis took the offered device.

Bradley held up a forestalling hand before Summus. "It runs through batteries pretty quickly, and I think the gases in the globes are at least half burned out."

"Thank you," Ignis said.

"If you erase my memory, how are you going to get them refilled?" Bradley asked.

That's a good question. If this device proves useful, it might be best to minimize how much of his reality Summus changes.

Ignis looked over at the divine phoenix.

"I know that look," Summus said. "Our terra used to give me the same look before he got me to do something that caused trouble."

"It might be best to limit his rewrite to the last hour," Ignis offered what he hoped was a reassuring smile. "Besides, a smaller re-write will be less draining."

Summus's expression mirrored Bradley's previous frown. "I don't know."

Ignis turned to Bradley. "What's your name again?"

"Bradley Sky, junior assistant medical examiner."

Ignis gestured with one hand. "We know where to find him later if we need to finish the rewrite."

"The longer he keeps the memories, the harder it is to rewrite him."

"Oh, don't worry about me," Bradley said. "The people we work for figured Gus was nuts, and I'm not far behind him. Nobody would believe this even if I told them—and I'm smart enough not to say a word."

Ignis shrugged.

"All right," Summuseraphi said. "Just don't mention this to Vilicangelus."

Ignis clapped Summus's shoulder and returned to his search. Heeding Bradley's warning, he hunted by nose until he reached a multi-building high-rise apartment complex. His search took far too long, but less time than if he'd had to go through the taint-saturated complex door to door.

Three heavy raps on the door brought a grizzled, middle-aged man to the door. He rolled his eyes the moment he cracked it open.

"What do you want, bird?" Cember asked. "I'm not violating any of the Articles of Ararat."

"Except living in the mortal world."

"Give me a break," Cember said. "I'm not breaking any mortal laws. I'm not harming anyone—unless you call photographing evidence for my clients' court cases harmful. I even found a missing person for someone this week."

"Let me in, and we'll discuss it."

Cember eyed him. "All right, do you swear to abide in peace in accordance with the Laws of Hospitality?"

"I so swear to enter and leave in peace, causing no harm to any within the domain of your dwelling."

"Enter in peace, Shield Ignis of the Atlanta Protectorate," Cember stepped back, opening the door with an inviting sweep of his hand.

Ignis scanned his surroundings as he stepped inside. Cember's apartment seemed modestly furnished with an open floor plan and three doors leading off the main area. As soon as the door shut, the illusion of a grizzled old detective vanished.

The old pixie shoved a cigar between his lips, smoke trailing away from a salt and pepper beard. His patched simple tunic had seen better days, but it was clean and in good repair. He ran a hand along a buzz cut, faded wings twitching before they sped up to a blurred thrum. Cember flitted across the breakfast bar and dragged open the refrigerator. "Do you want a beer?"

"Thank you, no," Ignis said.

The pixie's strained flight hit the breakfast bar a bit harder than necessary. He darted back to the fridge, taking down a red plastic opener designed for children to open pop-top cans. He snagged a bendy straw on his return flight, popped open the can of imported German beer and inserted a straw.

"All right, bird, what do you want?"

"I want to hire you," Ignis said.

Cember spewed beer all over the counter. "You what?"

"Our eggs were stolen," Ignis said. "I'd like to hire you to track down the thief."

Gears spun so fast behind the pixie's eyes, Ignis smelled them burn under the friction. Even so, he answered fast. "Let's talk payment."

"What's the going rate?" Ignis asked.

"Normally, a per diem and expenses, but you're not a wafer."

"Which means what?" Ignis asked.

"Your fee will be special."

"I won't surrender any essence."

Cember waved the suggestion away. "I'm already something

of an outcast, but if the Courts are behind this and they find out that I helped you, I'm persona non grata, you know what I mean?"

Ignis gestured for Cember to continue.

"I want a work residency visa," Cember brightened. "Expenses too—even if they're Faery expenses."

Ignis scrutinized the little faerie. He'd tracked the little jerk down because he'd claimed to be a detective who obviously had contacts in the Courts as well as Atlanta. It was a long shot, but if it added one more resource to their search, it seemed worth a shot.

A work visa though, that's setting a dangerous precedent.

Terrance had a contact in the Wyld Wastes, but Yarque didn't live in the mortal world. The same was true of Caelum and Quayla's contacts. Ignis's own faerie contacts had closed down when he'd sought them out, yet this pixie was willing to help in exchange for staying in the mortal world.

I've already convinced Summus to go out on a limb, I doubt I can get him to back this. Vitae will never agree. Vilicangelus might consider it, if I could get ahold of him, but calling Vili will only get me Summus.

"Atlanta only," Ignis said. "And only for so long as you don't violate any of the Articles of Ararat."

"I hate be legalistic and all, but I'll need this in writing," Cember said. "Got to cover my own ass, you understand."

"Do you have any stone?"

Cember grinned. "I have just the thing. Come on."

Ignis followed into a small bedroom, a new octave of taint slamming into him the moment the door opened. The faerie glade contained within the room was and was not in the mortal realm. An old, winter-deadened stump dominated one quarter of the room. Slate stones circled a cold but not frozen pond, edged by evergreens and winter blooms.

Cember stopped on the largest of the paving stones and tapped it with a foot. "This should work."

That it should.

Ignis bent over the stone and summoned his essence. He stopped, raising his eyes to the faerie. "Don't make me regret this, Cember."

"You're doing me a huge favor, bird. I wouldn't dream of double-crossing you."

"Better hope not," Ignis's finger lit like an acetylene torch. "I have temper issues."

Ignis carved the visa into the stone, infusing the letters with his own essence to guarantee authenticity. Cember watched over his shoulder, a smile wider than his face trying to spread even further.

Chapter Thirteen

Uneasy Partners

Quayla

Rather than waste breath persuading Detective Foxner not to look in on Miri, I simply marched away, letting the detective's prey response drag her along my wake. She eyed my hilts when I reclaimed them from security, but didn't comment. She refused my suggestion to take separate vehicles—probably to strand me on foot and limit my escape options as if I couldn't transmog and fly away.

Foxner drove us through Atlanta in a tense silence. Unlike her friend, she didn't ask questions. She glowered out the window with the supple lines of her jaw hardened to near razor edges. When she did loosen her scowl, it was to grumble low enough she assumed I couldn't hear. "Driving criminals around... wouldn't do this if a life wasn't on the line... should be cuffed not in my passenger seat..."

"And I wouldn't have read you in if Judith weren't in danger."

We turned north on Cobb Parkway.

"What deludes you into thinking this is your jurisdiction?" Foxner asked. "You're not even a cop."

"I'm a shield, same as you, difference is our Praefecture

extends well beyond Atlanta's city limits." I gave her a frank look. "Besides, we're dealing with supernatural baddies definitely out of your league."

Foxner snorted through her pert little nose.

The car turned right at the Big Chicken, drove under an overpass and then pulled into a side alley leading back to a shopping center. Foxner drove behind the buildings into the loading area. She came to a stop just past the loading ramp where the wall had appeared.

I drew my necklace as I exited the vehicle. I whispered into it, trying not to sneeze on taint and faerie magic. "Summuseraphi, Summuseraphi, Summuseraphi."

"Well?" Foxner barked.

"Well what?"

"This is where they vanished, let's see your skills."

I looked around, but no divine phoenixes appeared. I kept walking, the scent of magic lessening the further I went. Taint levels dropped around where the goblins probably closed the back of the van. A sudden uptick of magic made me sneeze.

"Bless you," Foxner said.

We repeated the process two more times.

"Thanks. Walk me through what happened," I said.

"I'm the detective," Foxner said.

I shot Foxner a flat look over folded arms. "Grow up."

"I'm older than you," Foxner said.

"No, you're not, though you look it."

"You were only just born," Foxner said.

"If you want to take that tack, you're older than this body, but not me," I shot back. "Now, are you going to walk me through what happened or not?"

Foxner grudgingly related her encounter with the goblins and the particulars of their escape. I asked a few questions to pluck details out from points that Foxner brushed over.

"All right, I think I have the picture."

"Fine. Where did they go?"

"I don't know. I'm going to have to track them."

"How are you going to track them? They just vanished." Foxner narrowed her eyes. "You just going to fly around until you spot them?"

"Don't be ridiculous. I'm not using my true form in broad daylight unless I have no other choice."

"Then how—"

I held up a hand.

"Did you hear something?" Foxner asked.

"No, I just want you to shut up."

Foxner drew her gun. "That's it. I've had enough of this farce. You're under arrest."

"How do you expect that to work?"

"Get on your knees, hands behind your back."

"Or what? You'll shoot me?" I asked.

Foxner opened her mouth, hesitated, and then closed it.

"Exactly. Shooting me won't win you anything."

"I'll feel better."

"While I've been there, it still won't help."

Foxner holstered her weapon and marched forward. "Then we'll do this the hard way."

I laughed. "Got a bucket?"

"Huh?"

"How are you going to apprehend water?"

Foxner hesitated again.

I rolled my eyes and vindictively turned my back on Foxner. I sank into my essence before the sound of the woman's loafers reached me.

I traded flesh for liquid in a painful rush. In my hurry, I forgot to account for my clothing.

Foxner tackled me, diving straight through with only my shirt and bra to show for it.

I marched over to her, drawing in lost essence and snatching the clothes away. "Damn it, you got my shirt dirty."

I clipped the bra on, rotated it around and pulled the straps over my watery shoulders then pulled the shirt over my head.

"You're a walking washing machine. Deal with it."

This woman makes me want to scream...or punch things...or scream while punching things...like her face.

I sighed.

But I won't. She's pig-headed but only trying to do her job. I'd leave her, but I have to keep track of her until Summus wipes her memory.

I solidified, inhaling deeply through my nose. It itched, but I pinched it together to prevent another sneeze. "Come on, let's go."

"You're under arrest, you can't just go."

"I'm not," I said. "I'm tracking the goblins like we agreed."

"How?"

"The glamour they used to disappear. Can't you smell that?"

Foxner took a few exploratory sniffs.

I laughed.

I meant that as a joke, I didn't expect her to actually try.

"I've had about enough of you," Foxner growled.

I ignored her, focusing on the problem at hand.

The glamour used to disguise the goblin's van left a line of taint in its wake. Tracking the scent wouldn't be as simple as riding in Foxner's car with my nose out the window. Taint aroma faded with time even before taking surface winds into account.

Walking the taint path was just as likely to fail on foot, and the longer goblins had Judith, the higher chance they'd do something she would care about.

I closed my eyes and reached out to my seeds.

Foxner slapped a cuff around one wrist, the metal closing around my arm with an angry ratchetting sound. I ignored the annoying officer, trying to sense glamour's taint as it passed by my seeds. Unfortunately, the sentry net was composed of not just my seeds but those of the others which I had no way to feel.

Foxner wrenched my other arm around and into her cuffs.

Despite my bravado, I'd never been forced to test essence shaping outside a rebalance. Having a bullet or sword force its way through my essences was painful but not difficult. Holding my form while an angry detective dove through me was like rebalancing while trying to resist a desperate need to pee during a powerful sneeze.

"I knew you were bluffing."

I shifted into water and focused on my hands. Will thinned and stretched fingers. My hand bones narrowed until the cuffs slipped off my wrists.

Foxner cursed. Her grabbing hand splashed through my shoulder, sending ripples that interrupted my concentration and removed my shirt once more.

My eyes snapped open and bored into the human shield. "Do you mind?"

"You're under arrest."

"I'm trying to track the goblins, and you're interrupting my concentration. A woman's life is at stake here you know."

"I know that," Foxner said. "Which is why I'm taking you in for answers if I have to call for backup and a shitload of sponges."

I gave Foxner a disgusted look. "You're being unreasonable."

"Unreasonable is letting a confessed criminal waltz around free."

"Like you've never entered premises on probable cause alone."

Foxner opened her mouth, hesitated, then forged on. "That's different. I'm a cop."

I closed the distance between us until my vision narrowed to only her flashing blue eyes. "For all intents and purposes, so am I."

"No. Did you graduate the academy at the top of your class? Did you work your way up in a misogynistic career forced to prove yourself every day? Have you sacrificed everything to be the best cop in Atlanta only to..." She trailed off.

I softened my voice. "No. At least, not like that. I was created to do this job, but unlike you, I'm not allowed to be anything else."

Her expression wavered.

"You may feel trapped, but I'm chained to my job under constant supervision by a bunch of angels disgruntled because—" A thought froze the words in my mouth.

"Because why?"

Anima isn't an AI, she's something else, and she's tied into the angel network. Does that mean my divine token too?

I brought up the feather amulet, not having to bother easing it out of the shirt in Foxner's hand. "Ani? Can you hear me?"

"This is most unusual, Shield Quayla. I don't know how Vilicangelus will react to abusing his token to contact me this way."

Foxner's eyes narrowed. She tilted her head to hear better.

"I'm tracking a glamour through the...sentry net but I can't," I eyed Foxner, making a decision, "I can't access all of the...nodes."

"Why did you not contact me from your vehicle?" Anima asked.

"Police Detective Foxner and I are using her vehicle."

"I see. Has Summuseraphi been notified?" Anima asked.

"Yes, but he was called away before he could...be introduced to the detective," I said.

"Understood. Give me a moment."

Foxner opened her mouth to ask a question, but Anima replied before the words escaped the mortal's lips.

"I have traced taint fluctuations from your location through the seeds. There are a few variances, but I have an approximate location that I believe presents at least a seventy percent success probability."

"Damn," Foxner mumbled. "That was fast."

"Thank you, Detective," Anima said.

Foxner started.

I didn't hide my amusement, but I did snatch my shirt back. I donned my top on the way back to Foxner's car. "Where are we going, Ani?"

The area Anima provided couldn't be narrowed down enough for an actual address. Foxner headed downtown and through student housing around Georgia Institute of Technology. We cruised westward into progressively dilapidating neighborhoods.

I caught sight of a similar van down a side street. "There."

"We'll see," Foxner turned, driving without hurry until the license plate came into her view. She gave me a sideline glance. "Guess so."

"Phoenix eyes were the model for eagles."

"I'm sure they were," Foxner said.

"Ani, we've found the van."

"Do you require backup?" Anima asked.

"I don't think my current partner will wait."

Foxner's expression confirmed the statement with unspoken vulgarities. She parked, checked her weapon and got out of the car.

I drew my hilts and marched toward the foul building with my nose lifted and nostrils flared. I pushed open a graffitied door, entering without a pause.

Foxner's harsh whispered followed from the detective's cover position in the doorway. "Hey, slow down and check your corners. Are you some kind of rookie?"

I bristled. "No. I'm a full shield."

"Sloppiness and inattention will get you killed."

I turned, planting a hand on one hip. "So?"

Foxner was correct in a lot of ways. I only had two rebirths in my nest, and I'd suffered a lot of agony supplying those. Still, the detective irritated me. I had the goblins' trail even over the stench of garbage and marijuana smoke. I knew they were housed up two floors, and I really wanted to prove to the arrogant wafer which of us was the better shield.

I continued my march toward the elevator.

A backward glance found Foxner still at the entry door. I reached out to press the elevator door, but froze at the sudden wash of nausea radiating up through my finger. A spider web of runes glowed into view around the button in anticipation of activation.

The stairwell door exploded outward. Two goblins with serrated short swords leapt at me. Their eyes widened to lock on the shimmering karambit blades extended from my hilts.

"Freeze, hands on your heads!"

One of the goblins turned, his off hand reaching for his belt.

I sprang down the hall, sickness washing up my arms as karambit blades cut downward through both goblin skulls.

"What the fuck!?" Foxner said as the tops of their heads slid away to fall on the filthy, pitted linoleum. A goblin throwing knife clattered across the floor with a gentle spin.

"You're welcome," I retracted my essence and slid the hilts into my jean's belt loops.

Blighted hells, I didn't even sense them.

"You killed our suspects."

"One of them was about to bury that knife in your face, detective."

"Aren't you supposed to be some kind of cop? You didn't even warn him."

"I don't have to warn them," I snapped.

"So, you're what? Judge, jury and executioner?"

"If they're threatening a mortal, I am His justice."

Assuming I can get away without leaving any witnesses.

"God said you could kill them?"

"That's right."

"That sounds a lot like the same crap people use to rationalize holy wars."

I marched across the distance, ignoring how Foxner raised her pistol. "Except I've actually heard His voice. I'm a Shield of the Undying Light. He created me and my kind to defend wafers like you from the Sidhe."

"I wasn't the one about to be jumped," Foxner retorted.

"I knew they were there."

"Bullshit."

"Whatever, you're welcome, wafer."

"I'm not a wafer, whatever they are."

I stabbed a finger at Foxner.

She leapt back and put two bullets into my torso.

Pain flashed through me like twin lightning strikes. Neither bullet struck a mortal target. Before reading *Primal Battle*, I'd have been in poor shape even though I wouldn't have died.

I pushed essence into the holes and growled. Fury raged through me, roaring like river rapids careening through a narrow canyon. "You're a blind, arrogant mortal, a plain vanilla wafer without the sense He gave your kind. You've given us away, ruined my blouse and pissed me off, so I suggest you go back to your car."

"Or what?" Foxner backed away with her gun lowered until she had enough space to snap a shot at my head. "If you're supposed to protect humans, I seriously doubt you can just kill me."

"Accidents happen," I whispered.

Before I did something I'd regret, I threw open the stairwell door and jogged up the steps hoping for more goblins.

"What about the bodies? We have to call in a shooting."

"Not my problem. Besides, how are you going to explain goblins?" I pushed open the second-floor stairwell door and inhaled a deep breath. I'd been sure there were no goblins on the first floor, sure they were all on three—and I'd been wrong.

I shouldn't have missed them. I was careless. I won't let that happen again.

I jogged up the next flight ahead of the detective, whispering into my feather amulet to have Anima send putti out to clean up and removed the trap spell from the elevator.

On the switchback between second and third floors, a beautifully-rendered angel looked down upon me. Evergreen and violet spray paint tagged vulgarities across the exquisite graffiti. The faerie vandalism marred Caelum's seed, rendering it inert. Even so I paused to look at his art, so much more than my simple fountains.

Wow, Caelum, just wow.

I stopped on the third-floor landing, glancing back at Foxner. "Oh, and have them fix a couple new bullet holes and make the detective replacement rounds."

"Did she try to shoot the goblins?" Anima asked.

"No. She shot me. The faster Summuseraphi can get to us the better."

"Who's Summuseraphi?" Foxner asked. "That's the second time you've mentioned him,"

"My sergeant," I eased into the hall so I wouldn't have to answer any more questions.

The first floor was grungy, but the third was falling apart. The hall reeked in so many ways I couldn't separate them. Carpet and wallpaper had fed countless insects and several mold colonies. Shoes of all kinds had worn the cheap carpeting shiny, and clawed goblin feet had torn holes to help start the moths.

I readied my blades, following my growing nausea down the hall. I stopped at a door, gesturing at it with my glowing knives. Once Foxner got into position, I kicked in the door. "By the Undying Light, I command your surr—hells!"

Machine gun fire exploded out of the wall, obliterating the dry wall and filling the hall with asbestos dust. I grabbed Foxner, turned my back to the attack in the hope that my body's bulk might shield her and drove us through the opposite apartment door. We hit the ground, sliding into a shredded mattress converted into a rat nest.

Foxner's grunts were lost beneath gunfire, disgruntled squeaking, and the screaming pain riddling me. It was sheerest luck that I wasn't already back at headquarters in a new body. I cobbled together all the concentration I could manage, transmogrifying my body into water and rebalancing my essence.

Part of me wanted to complete the transmog and treat the gunmen to my talons, but I had no idea who was behind the Swiss-cheesed apartment wall.

Foxner grabbed my arm, trying to keep me down. She only

managed to remove my blouse. I smirked, converting the rest of my clothes into liquid. "What is it with you and taking off my clothes?"

"Stay down. I'll call for backup."

I fixed her with a hard smile and stood. "I don't need backup. Stay safe, Detective. I'll be right back."

I strode back into the hallway. I heard the detective moving behind me, but kept my focus forward. Another round of machine gun fire ate away at what remained of the wall, exposing a group of mortal thugs with uncertain expressions.

Bullets splashed through me, dragging trails of essence from my body. "By the Undying Light, I command you to lay down your arms and get on your knees."

"We gave you what you desired, stop her!" A goblin darted through a freestanding Arch behind the mortals.

Fae Kissed. Well, that makes things easier.

My failure with Emma and Bootsie flashed through my thoughts on a magic carpet woven of purest guilt. I'd been unable to kill her, even though she'd clearly been Fae Kissed. I considered not offering the gunmen a chance to repent, mostly because they shot at me, but also because I had every right to execute them outright for threatening a mortal life.

Not good enough. I have a duty.

"In His name, you will surrender boons provided by the faeries and repent your sins."

"Repent this, bitch."

A shotgun blast tore through my torso from one side, staggering me. The amount of mass displaced sent me off balance, tripping on an ammunition box of some sort. I flicked one karambit as I fell, whipping the blade through the bridge of the shooter's nose.

I extruded another knife simultaneous with drawing in my now filthy essence from the floor around me. "On your knees, weapons down or die."

They opened fire.

One of the thugs lurched backward in a spray of blood. A moment later, a second took two slugs to his center mass. The Fae Kissed turned their attention to Foxner as she reloaded.

I launched myself at them, my scream becoming a shriek as I transmog'd into my native form. I offered no mercy. I'd done my duty. I'd offered them absolution, but I was not going to let them harm the detective no matter how big a pain in the ass she was.

In such close quarters, my beak and talons took no time to end the threat. I whipped back around, returning to my human body. "Are you all right? Were you injured?"

"I'm not the one who got treated like a range dummy."

"Detective, are you shot?"

"No."

My tension vanished. "Thank God. You shouldn't have interfered. They could've hurt you."

Foxner scrutinized me, her lips pressed together.

I followed her gaze to the men she'd shot. I bent over the closest, one of the few bodies still in a single piece. I turned him over, ripping off his stained, bloody wifebeater tank top.

"What are you doing, this is a crime scene."

"I'm looking for...yes, that," I pointed to a violet tattoo marking him a thrall of the Unseelie Court.

"What does it mean?" Foxner moved until she stood over us.

"It means he's traded servitude for some boon from the Winter Court of Faery."

"I'm not sure I understand."

"It's complicated." I dusted myself off and turned to the Arch.

The interior walls of the apartment had been knocked down to make space for a huge Arch. Drywall, wood and plaster climbed bent rebar to form a jagged gateway filled with deepest two-dimensional black. Runes pulsed along the outer walls, inlaid on graffiti medallions along the painted barbed wire.

I drew up my amulet. "Anima, I've got a permanent Arch with a cloaking circle. Is anyone else available?"

"None of the others are available at this time," Anima said.

"All right, when the putti come to do the other job send them up to the third floor. I need them to clean up the weapons and the Fae Kissed but leave the Arch."

I crossed to the outer wall and raised my blade to slash through the cloaking circle. I held my strike at the last moment.

No, that's foolish. I'll let the putti handle this too.

"Shield Quayla, that is not in line with procedure."

"If they remove the Arch, I might not be able to return."

"Wait one," Anima said.

"What's going to happen to them?" Foxner asked.

"Bodies will be destroyed and all the damage repaired," I said.

"I discharged my weapon, if you disappear the bodies, I won't be able to explain the discharged rounds."

"Don't worry, the rounds will be remade. There will be no evidence you fired...thanks for your help, by the way. You shouldn't have risked yourself, but thank you anyway."

Foxner opened her mouth, but Anima spoke first. "Vitae requires me to tell you that you are not allowed to enter Faery under any circumstances, Shield Quayla."

"Is he on his way?" I asked.

"He and the others are occupied, but instructs you to hold the Arch. You are to await orders and reinforcements."

"Who's Vitae?" Foxner asked.

I glowered at the silver feather. "Vitae is my equal. He is not the boss of me. Stay here."

"Where are you going?"

I gave her a flat look.

"Shield Quayla, what is going on?" Anima asked.

"What do I do if something comes out of that?" Foxner asked.

"If it's human, use your best judgement. Otherwise shoot it in the head," I marched through the Arch into Faery.

Chapter Fourteen

Discoveries in Defeat

Caelum

Caelum jerked open his ammunition drawers to find them emptied. His eyes flashed up to the wall of weapons. With growing unease, he reached out toward the assault rifle closest at hand. A single touch dissolved the solid-looking weapon into violet smoke.

Caelum cursed.

Firearms weren't as hard to procure as specialty weapons like Quayla's dagger hilts, but school shootings perpetrated by Fae Kissed mortals had made purchasing guns harder.

Pity Vitae won't let me raid a drug den for replacements.

He turned back to the corner, eyes tracing the indentations in his carpet where the stone basin holding his essence had rested. One of the courts, Unseelie by the smell, had stolen his nest and his guns. He'd been ready to arm up and hunt them the fun way, but without an arsenal to give any action star a wet dream, he was reduced to what little he had on him.

Damn faeries have depleted my caches. Guess I could visit my safety deposit box.

He laughed.

Just imagine the reception I'd get entering Faery with storied battle fans—tantamount to walking around with Champion blades.

He raced to the elevator, pushing the gifts from his first mentor out of his thoughts. He'd used the weapons only once before deciding they were too precious—and too difficult to clean—for everyday combat.

Caelum opened his mouth the moment his motorcycle roared to life. "Ani? I—"

"Shield Caelum?" Anima asked.

If he told Vitae that his nest had been stolen, the stuck-up life phoenix would demand he move back into headquarters.

If I can get it back without him any the wiser, no harm no foul.

"Ani, I'm going to visi—"

I can just hear what Vitae will say if he learns I'm going into the Goblin Market, and I can't explain why I need to question Oshyn's brownies without telling him I lost my nest.

"Caelum?" Anima asked.

"I'm heading out to replace some of my seeds, so I'll be out of touch a while."

"Understood," Anima said. "With all the incursions, I'd appreciate it if you checked in often between paintings."

"I wouldn't go so far as to call my feeble tagging a painting, but how can you appreciate anything if you have no emotions?"

Her response sounded short and clipped. "You are correct. An unfeeling AI is unable to feel emotions such as appreciation."

"Anima? Is everything all right? You sound...hurt."

"An AI cannot be hurt."

Caelum drew out the word. "Right?"

"Do you require anything else, Shield Caelum?"

"No...no."

Maybe I should email her a picture of flowers just in case.

He roared across town to the Russian market. Without a trunk, he was forced to limit how much he collected. The thrice and thrice again penalty from Quayla's rampage would prevent the supply from going far, but he wouldn't be in the Market long.

This trip is for info, not shopping.

The gruff billy goat fey eyed Caelum's backtrail as he entered. Once they confirmed Quayla wasn't with him, they demanded their inflated bribe of candy bars. He paid them off and moved to one side, unfolding his silk carpet.

Festival music he didn't realize had stopped when he'd requested entry filled the Market. Streamers and chained sprites draped from every surface of the twilight-lit market. A little girl skipped by, forcing Caelum to do a doubletake. Dragonfly wings quivered in excitement. Blonde pigtails coiled around the base of her antennae then draped down along her cheeks to the top of a dress designed to look suitable for grade school—if Caelum ignored the shear material and her exposed breasts.

"Hey, what's the party dress for?"

She stopped, scrunching up her nose. "DragonCon, duh!"

"Won't being at war limit faerie activities? Are nymphs exempt?"

She rolled her eyes. "No and no, in fact, this DragonCon is supposed to be the most—"

The smallest billy goat spoke over her. "—relaxed DragonCon in history, what with the armistice requiring us to stay in our individual Courts for a private jubilee."

"That's not ri—"

The billy goat slapped a hand over the young nymph's mouth and gave Caelum an unsteady grin. "Market's closing soon, might want to see to your business."

Caelum scrutinized the door guard. Something wasn't adding up, but he doubted he could've pried it out of the old goat even at the height of his popularity.

He glanced up into the Market to catch two elves on the third tier sneering at one another. Seeing Seelie and Unseelie in each other's faces wasn't unusual, but seeing them stand so close without fighting was. Just beyond them a coyll opened up a trench coat, exposing a dozen kittens hung from loops sewn into the lining.

Caelum's heart leapt. He whistled a quick burst, pushing his carpet to rocket straight up. The coyll caught sight of him. His furred muzzle curled in a snarl a moment before he snapped his coat shut and darted deeper into the Market.

Pursuing on a carpet limited Caelum's options. He couldn't keep up with the coyll's ability to hop and dart on small silkways or stalls, through narrow paths or between close branches.

His pursuit brought Caelum to a small wooden building hidden in the low branches of the Market's tree. A blue-skinned ogre painted with tribal markings glowered up at Caelum, the small tiger-striped dragons on either side baring their teeth.

Shit. Thanks to Quayla, I have to let him go, but it's a clue.

Caelum offered the ogre mage a respectful head nod before turning his carpet away. A series of whistles floated him downward toward Oshyn's booth.

The half elf stammered at Caelum's arrival. "S-shield Caelum, you d-didn't need to come. We could've collected the rest of your fee."

"I want to know why cleaning my apartment was so expensive," Caelum shifted all of the milk and candy he had left onto Oshyn's counter. "And I want to question the brownies that did the cleaning."

Oshyn fidgeted. "Well, faerie blood is very difficult—"

"That was headquarters, Oshyn."

"No," a brownie squeaked. "Unseelie blood ma—"

Oshyn's growl silenced the little hairy creature.

Caelum turned to the brownie. "I didn't scent any Seelie taint, so unless you and the rest of the brownies cleaning my apartment jumped the Unseelie that took my nest, there wouldn't have been any Unseelie blood."

"Yes!" Oshyn thundered. "That's why the extra charge. They valiantly tried to defend your nest, Shield Caelum, but there were more Seelie than they could handle."

"Unseelie," Caelum corrected.

"Yes, of course, I meant Unseelie. The blood, oh the blood, Shield Caelum. It flew everywhere as my brownies fought."

"My nest still got stolen," Caelum eyed the organized shelves full of brownies. "How is it you fought a pitch battle that spread so much Unseelie blood, lost the fight to protect my nest and yet none of you were slain?"

"They retreated," Oshyn said. "Then returned to clean up the mess and honor our contract."

Caelum's expression hardened. He hadn't been happy to let the coyll escape, and a growing certainty insisted that Oshyn was lying to him—which shouldn't have been possible. "I want to know who took my nest, and I want to know now."

Oshyn's head fell forward. After a moment, he looked up at Caelum through long lashes. "Very well, Shield Caelum. We stole your nest."

"What? Why?"

"We were ordered to do so," Oshyn flicked a finger at Caelum. "Just as we were ordered to slay you."

Little brown hands appeared, parting their hair. Each held a tiny, bronze straight razor in all four hands. They whirled off of the shelf, spinning across counters onto Caelum's carpet and into him from all sides.

"Take care not to damage Shield Caelum's security card."

Caelum yanked his pistols and started firing.

Savage living blenders attacked him from all sides. Blood and essence flew in every direction. He tried to compress his essence and transmogrify, but the tide of sharp edges engulfed him.

Oshyn watched through his fingers, head shaking and a soft voice barely reaching Caelum's ears. "Thank you for your business, Shield Caelum."

Bradley

The slammed drawer echoed inside the wall, the corpseless space empty like Bradley's memory. Whiskers snarled an echo of his irritation. He'd looked everywhere, but he couldn't find his rattler.

Bradley lost things all the time. Fascinating things drew his attention away from less important concerns all the time. Wallet or car key, his lunch or pants couldn't compete with the kinds of neat discoveries he'd made in recent days.

Nothing's more important than that detector...well almost nothing.

The only thing more demanding of his attention was Whiskers, and only because of her claws. Bradley couldn't lose the detector. He'd spent hours and huge chunks of paycheck to scrounge, experiment and develop the magic-o-meter. He'd just filled up the detection globes with gas.

Damn. Damn. Damn.

He'd run out of Whiskers' food—or more accurately the mutated cat had gone through more than ever before. Bradley hoped it was just a hollow day like he sometimes got rather than the cat getting another growth spurt.

I can barely keep her caged now.

He opened and slammed yet another drawer containing nothing but a mid-forties man who should've said no to supersizing. Whiskers had been getting more and more irritable for hours. The plan had been simple. Take the cat's carrier and the rattler out on the town, find the bad guys and let her eat her fill.

A low growl went past menacing into the feed-me-or-be-food range. The noise left Bradley no good choices.

This must be how Rick Moranis felt.

Bradley dug out the first portable prototype, eyeing the globes.

Whiskers hissed.

"I should've named you Audrey. Once I recharge this, we'll find you some food, okay?"

The cat settled onto its scaled belly, licking sharp claws under glowing green eyes.

He retrieved the canisters from the rear most slab, grabbed his medical bag and set up a workspace on an empty gurney. Tools emerged from his bag that had nothing to do with actual medicine. A hand pump bridged the gas cannisters to a receptacle valve on his globes. Delicate work done, he donned an x-ray apron and lead-lined gloves.

Whiskers objected to the time it took, but Bradley charged the magic-o-meter and swapped out the cube of AA batteries duct-taped together. A quick wave in Whiskers' direction confirmed the device ready. He took both out to his old car, sidelining through a Popeye's drive thru to ease Whiskers' hunger on their way west in search of the bad guys.

Glowing lights out of a dark alley caught Bradley's attention before the early model detector lit every bulb. He pulled the car to a stop at the mouth and gaped.

Holy shit, this is just like in Highlander.

A man in out of date clothes with an elaborate sword in each hand faced off against two distinct groups. Ogres and goblins, elves and blueberry things Bradley didn't recognize shoved each other out of the way or into the swordsman's reach. All of them wore fantasy armor from simple on the ogre to highly ornate on the elves.

Bradley suppressed an urge to giggle. He wrenched around to look into the back seat. "This is our chance, Whiskers. It's time to make a difference."

Whiskers crouched, spines raised and a low growl bubbling out of her throat.

He raced around the car and jerked open his back door. A flash of light yanked his attention back to the alley.

An elf in blues and purples held a crackling globe of violet lightning between two hands. Bolts lanced out of the sphere. A golden-garbed elf drove at the strange defender with twin curved short swords.

The heroic man who had to be the source of the golden magic reflected a lightning strike off his dark blade and into the golden elf. He sidestepped a thrust, slashing his other blade to stop a sudden blueberry rush.

Dark blood oozed out of the cut.

Bradley recognized it at once. "So that's what those things look like whole."

Whiskers threw herself at the cage.

"Oh, right." He unlocked the cage, trying to open the door and get out of the way before Whiskers sprang to the rescue.

He wasn't fast enough.

Whiskers slammed into him, knocking him back onto the sidewalk with a smack. Claws dug furrows in Bradley's chest as Whiskers shot forward. Pain burned to supernova intensity in a moment, but he'd come prepared. He patted his pockets, digging out a tube of ointment prepared to neutralize the toxins on Whisker's nails and deaden the pain.

Bradley wanted to watch, but he knew he had to focus on deactivating the poison. Even so, he chanced a quick glance.

Whiskers rode the hero's back, snarling like a rabid tiger and clawing through the old trench coat.

"No!" Bradley shouted. "The others. Attack the others!"

The bad guys looked at him, the ogre licking his lips.

Bradley cursed and smeared ointment into still-searing cuts. He finished and managed his feet as the most incredible scenario he'd ever imagined got punked like a little girl.

The hero leapt into the air in the midst of what had to be faerie creatures. He flipped, throwing Whiskers into nearby brick. His entire body wavered an instant before exploding into an armored eagle with black-edged red feathers.

The eagle's wings filled the alley. Gold and silver talons slashed at the faeries. Hero and faerie lit into each other with a savagery apparently born of mutual grudge.

The eagle's body turned liquid around wounds, filling in and solidifying once more. Wings buffeted elves and talons tore into goblins. The eagle's beak—no, not eagle, the phoenix's beak drove into the ogre's chest and jerked back trailing blood.

Whiskers ran up a brick wall, claws leaving divots in the side and sprang onto the phoenix's back.

Bradley raced forward. He snatched up a trash can lid and swept it across the phoenix's back to clear the cat.

The cat bounded over the blow, leaving it to hit the phoenix.

The giant bird of prey whirled midair, glowing green eyes boring into him. Somewhere deep in Bradley's marrow, the eyes triggered a primeval prey response.

Bradley stumbled backward to the alley fear. "I-I-I, uh, h-hel-helping?"

The answering shriek froze Bradley in the certainty of being phoenix chow. A hot trickle ran down one leg.

Whiskers pounced on Bradley, tearing more holes in his clothes. Before he could raise hands in defense, the phoenix's beak snatched the cat into the air, opening again to snap Whisker's body from his head and swallow it down.

The phoenix turned back to the faerie while Bradley stared at Whisker's glowering head.

He's going to regrow that body.

Another thought struck him.

Do phoenixes regurgitate like owls? Is there going to be enough left of Whiskers to grow another Whiskers?

Whiskers tried to snarl without vocal cords.

I may not have thought far enough through the ramifications of making a troll cat yet.

Bradley flipped over the head, certain it had tried to bite him. He drew a butane torch from a pocket and set to cauterizing the thing's neck to prevent regrowing.

I'll work everything out before I raise the next one.

Quiet settled on the alley.

Bradley turned to find the phoenix back in human shape, standing with a foot on each of two elves' chests. He held blades to their throats, but his seething glower locked on Bradley.

"What are *you* doing here?"

"Have we met?" Bradley asked.

The phoenix man's eyes blazed with light that swallowed Bradley in an instant. "Tell me why you are here."

Words tumbled out of Bradley's lips, starting slow and rapidly growing in haste. He explained the things he saw in the morgue, his identification of troll bone marrow and his idea to reanimate Whiskers. He moved from there to his magic detector and his intent to—like batman—use his incredible, if not totally humble, genius to help the heroes wielding golden magic against the vile blue and red.

Bradley rubbed his tongue against the roof of his mouth. "Did I say all that in one go? Do you have a bottled water or—"

"You made that little abomination?"

"Cat."

"There is a difference?"

Bradley shrugged.

"You combined roadkill with troll marrow to attack me?"

"No, I wanted Whiskers to attack the others, but it didn't listen—not that you can ever count on a cat to listen. Maybe I should have tried with a stray dog instead, I mean—"

"Silence!"

Tingles washed over Bradley's skin. When he opened his mouth to speak, the tingles grew teeth. The moment he changed his intent to obedience, warm pleasure welled up throughout his body.

Bradley pressed his lips together to hold back the tide of words waiting to deluge the phoenix.

"Do a lot of unidentified bodies come into your morgue?"

Bradley tilted his head one way then the other.

"Answer me."

"You said to be silent."

The phoenix shifted one dress shoe onto an elf's throat and brought up his corresponding sword. "Answer the question, wafer."

The tingling redoubled.

"It's not one a day, and it varies greatly, but we get some." Pleasure washed through Bradley. "Why?"

A smile edged its way across the phoenix's face. "You wanted to help me."

"Well, your kind. Assuming you're the gold magic." Bradley raised the detector. All three colors glowed at varying strengths.

Could be all the blood on him.

Bradley tilted the detector forward, sweeping it from elf to elf to verify his detector picked up no golden magic

A sudden flame blossomed across Bradley's face. "I'm talking to you. You will show the proper respect."

Bradley raised a hand, wiping blood from his cheek. "All right, but you didn't have to cut me, lady."

"Vitae, not lady!" Vitae screamed. "But you may address me as 'my lord'."

"My lord?" A wash of pleasure aborted Bradley's forming question. "Ooooh, it should rightly be milady, but My Lord is good...really good with me."

"Good. Now, my servant, help me bind these faeries and then you can see to my other needs. It's about time the wafers of this city served in their own defense."

Chapter Fifteen

Crayola Island

Quayla

The Arch dumped me onto a deserted island drawn by a six-year-old. I stepped forward, gaze sweeping the small mound of sand. My foot set down in a gap between thick crayon lines, falling enough to twist my ankle.

"Holy shit, where are we?" Foxner asked.

I jerked my foot free and whipped around to find the detective standing in front of two overlapped palm trees formed of brown and the occasional red scribble.

"Get back through the Arch," I snapped. "You don't belong here."

"Like it or not, I'm your backup."

I rushed her, shoving the mortal through the palm trees. Foxner's heel caught on an uneven scribble. She fell hard onto her tailbone, but didn't disappear back into the real world.

I cursed.

Foxner cursed right back, aiming her profanities at me.

"Anima?"

No response emanated from the silver feather.

No Arch, no exit in sight. We're trapped.

I cursed some more, scanning our surroundings.

Spirals of dark blue and green crayon surrounded us as far as the eye could see.

"Where are we?" Foxner said.

"Faery."

"What?"

"The Land of Faery, realm of the Sidhe. A place you absolutely don't belong."

"What's that over there?"

Little mounds of drawn sand trailed through waves identical to clouds except in color. At the end of the stepping stones, the smiling orange sun reflected off the glistening surface of what looked like actual water.

Before I could answer, Foxner marched out over the water on the little mounds. Her foot slipped.

I lunged forward to catch her.

Before I could, the detective's foot came down on a blue spiral and stopped. Foxner frowned, stomping on the scribbled blue swirls. "It's solid."

"Great, it's solid," I strode past the mortal toward the reflected sun. "Don't hit your head on a cloud."

I came to where the sun reflected off a wide rippling pool. Unlike the blue squiggles, transparent waves let me see through the surface along a descending staircase.

I squeezed my essence, pressing it until I couldn't compress my core any further. I glanced back at Foxner once more. "You should stay here. I mean it."

"I can go anywhere you can," Foxner said.

"Are you sure?" My body and possessions shifted back into water. I eased down onto the first step. Tepid water surrounded my leg with a strange hugging sensation. Undulations mimicked a giant esophagus trying to swallow me. Unease rippled my gut, but there didn't seem to be any taint in the water.

After several steps the stair turned in a lazy spiral. Halfway through my first downward turn, I spotted movement above. Foxner ducked her head in the water, cheeks puffed.

In a flash, two creatures that crossed seaweed-green octopi with a young woman seized Foxner and pushed her out of the water. I sprang upward through the water to rescue her, but dark blue squiggles closed over the pool, blocking out the smiling sun.

I attacked the squiggles with a karambit, but the blade didn't so much as scratch the crayon even when I reformed the blade with serrated teeth. The holes between the squiggles were far too small for me to squeeze between them. There didn't seem to be any way to get back and help Detective Foxner.

I'm trapped. Then again, I was probably trapped the moment I stepped foot onto Crayola Island.

With up not available, my only hope to help the detective and escape the trap seemed downward. I resumed my descent, but kept my karambit extended and ready for anything. I slipped my senses outward, feeling the strange water to allow for an early warning, but the water around me resisted infiltration.

At long last, my stair ended on the edge of a sunken mermaid grotto. Huge clams nestled in piled coins and sailor's casts offs. Ornate artifacts and even a cockeyed golden throne filled the expansive depression.

I scanned the seabed, looking for some indication whether or not I was meant to keep going or enter yet another trap.

If I can't move through this unless it lets me, I may never be able to return to the surface.

I eyed my knife.

I won't be imprisoned here.

Doubt crept in behind thoughts of violence to undermine my determination. If the surrounding water kept me from moving, I'd be hard pressed to end my current life.

One giant clam opened. A cascade of bubbles shot out of its mouth. They spread across the grotto beneath my feet like a carpet. Bubbles popped against one another, transforming froth into a widening bubble of air.

A pale woman stepped out of a passage at the back of the clam's throat. Her dark, damp hair floated in the gentle turmoil. A silver circlet bound hair against the crown of her head. The tiara featured a disk of mother-of-pearl on her forehead with a teardrop sapphire embedded in its center.

Her melancholy smile rose to meet my eye. Wordless gestures beckoned me to the canted throne.

I hesitated.

If I was trapped, stepping down into the grotto couldn't worsen my situation. I scanned my surroundings once more and stepped onto the bubble carpet.

The first step dropped me enough to force my stomach into a short freefall. I hit water once more, but cool, loose water unlike the tepid esophagus that had swallowed me whole.

I righted myself and turned to face the woman with a karambit ready. The woman raised her hands. Her placating gesture dragged the hems of her sapphire and silk skirt up by loops tied around her fingers.

The ceiling of air plunged downward into the grotto, whirling around me as it pushed the water against the grotto's walls.

"Would you care to sit, Aquaylae?" Magic underlay the dry woman's dulcet voice. The notes caressed my ears with soft touches of carefully-wielded steel.

"Where is Judith?"

With a gesture, a still submerged giant clam opened. Bubbles streamed out between the shell's curved lip, but a single large bubble clung onto the bed of mollusk flesh like a pearl.

Judith knelt within the bubble, eyes widening as she recognized me even in my watery form. I crossed the distance and thrust my arm into the watery wall to grab Judith. A hard current knocked my hand away.

"In the name of the Undying Light, I command you to let her go at once."

Pale, coral lips curled. "All things in due time. First, you owe me your thanks and the debt that comes along with them."

I raised my knives. "How do you figure that, Sidhe?"

Judith's sudden yell cut off with a gurgle.

I whipped around.

Water poured into the bubble, submerging Judith.

"I like you, Aquaylae, but I do not tolerate rudeness."

I reached out into the water, willing an air passage through the wall to Judith. The water refused me. I tried harder, putting all of my will behind the effort.

"Return her air."

"Say please."

Judith held her mouth and nose below bulging eyes.

"Please," I blurted. I softened my voice in response to the woman's hard expression. "Please let Judith breathe."

A corner of the other woman's mouth curled. "She can breathe if she wants, just not air."

Frustration wracked me.

Judith's cheeks puffed out trying to hold in her breath.

"Please take the water away and let Judith breathe air."

Bubbles filed the clamshell, joining into a single sphere big enough for Judith. She held her neck, choking and gaping against the clam's fleshy foot. Before I could thank the other woman, the clam shell closed, forcing Judith to crouch prone.

"Now that I have your attention, I will accept your thanks."

"Who the hell are you?" I demanded.

"Interesting choice of words."

"What do you expect me to thank you for?"

The woman held up a sapphire and celestial silver shard.

That's a piece of shell from my egg!

"How did you get that?" I asked.

"I'm the one that shattered your egg, dear. If I hadn't intervened, he would have used it to kill you before delivering them all to me."

"He who?"

"A seventh son of a seventh son, drowned by terrified, ignorant wafers because of a 'witch' who escaped their pyre in the form of a giant watery bird."

I recoiled.

My heel caught on a conch shell, but I caught myself. Even without falling on my tail, my mind reeled. The attack on my Shield, the stolen eggs, everything going on was retribution against me.

My choice, my failings, I brought all this onto us.

My arms wrapped around my chest by reflex, but I returned them to fighting positions. "Give me Judith and the eggs, now."

"Oh, dear, you should never threaten someone stronger than you. Especially, if you don't have all the facts." She tapped a finger against her smile. "Still, I like your spirit."

I sprang at her.

Waves from either side of the grotto crisscrossed to slam into me. Watery fingers held me like a toy in toddler's hands.

The woman shook her head, tsking sounds escaping her lips. "Aquaylae, Aquaylae, this is getting us nowhere."

"Fine," I snapped. "Who are you? What do you want from me?"

"I've been called many things: rebel; principality; sword maiden; and lover. You're going to help me reclaim all that I lost as punishment for saving a seventh son you tried to murder—when your cowardice bestowed my newest name: The Exiled Lady."

"I'm your prisoner, at least let Judith go," I said.

"What would keep you from just killing yourself?"

I opened my mouth to give my oath not to commit suicide.

"Oh, right," the Lady snapped her fingers with a smile. "It really doesn't matter if you die. By now, he's taken your nest and employed your essence."

Employed my essence?

Cold washed through me. "Then you don't need to imprison Judith."

"A very good point."

The clam holding Judith opened. The Asian woman's eyes locked onto me. The bubble around her disintegrated into a thousand tiny bubbles.

"What're you doing?" I struggled against the hands imprisoning me.

"I'm curious," the Lady said. "How many atmospheres can Judith's body take before she'll admit to caring?"

Judith's gurgled shrieks knifed into me—a quick, deep stab gone in a moment. Blood seeped out of her mouth as her lifeless body settled onto the clam and the shell closed over her.

The Lady sighed. "I thought twenty atmospheres would crush her like a soda can, not just collapse her ribs into her lungs for a few moments of excruciating pain."

I turned away from Judith, icy fury focused on the beautiful woman before me.

Just you wait.

Detective Foxner

Sabrina put another round into the closest octopus woman. The creature bared lily-pad-green teeth and hissed. In the water both their tentacles combined with their prehensile hair offered the creatures rapid propulsion. Escaping the water onto the crayon squiggles meant to be water hadn't provided safety until Sabrina retreated from water's edge.

Mint faces contorted in hatred as their evergreen lips parted to hiss. The crayon landscape seemed to give them trouble. They scuttled across the sea in fits and starts, noises burbling from them in sounds vaguely reminiscent of 'genie' over and over.

They spread out around her, forcing Sabrina to retreat. She picked her shots, but so far bullets between their eyes had only encouraged temporary retreats and more hisses.

One to Sabrina's right scuttled forward, waving braids striking like a snake. A knot of braid thrust with a short knife of sharp stone too grey to be obsidian.

It sliced across Sabrina's shin. Ferocious agony shot up her leg, then died just as suddenly. The injured leg folded under her.

Some kind of paralytic. Think.

Sabrina shot the thing to give her more time. In groups to surround and armed with some kind of toxin to hobble their prey, the things could've easily subdued her and dragged her under water to drown or dismember. The confusing part was that they didn't seem intent to seize her.

She scrabbled away from them without the use of one leg.

Blue squiggles gave way to long, tan strokes.

A glance oriented Sabrina. A squiggle of grey and white hung low over one of the palm trees. Normally, the green frond never could have supported her, but normally she'd never have considered escape by climbing atop a cloud.

She pointed her retreat around the trees, hoping to use them as cover as she climbed the rearmost.

Faeries on either side darted forward in a cartwheel of tentacles. They boxed her in, but the third held back.

Sabrina shot the one on her left and rushed to take advantage of its retreat—except it didn't retreat. It rushed in, whipping armed braids at Sabrina.

The sudden onslaught drove Sabrina onto her knees in a rushed crawl toward the trees. Sabrina's heart rose to fill her throat. Neither the thing on her left nor the third leapt in to ambush her. They closed, keeping on the pressure but didn't take advantage of her vulnerability.

They should've jumped me. What gives?

The hair along her arms rose, performing the Wave up her limbs and onto the back of her neck. She looked up, realigning her escape climb. A flat blackness filled the space between the trees.

They're not trying to capture me. I'm being shown the door.

Sabrina's eyes flit to the water where Quayla had descended. If she let the creatures herd her back into the real world, she'd be safe, but the phoenix would be alone.

Like her or not, I've never abandoned a partner before. I'm not starting now.

The octopi women could kill her, but they didn't. If someone's orders kept them at bay, it was possible she could get back to the water if she got past them.

Sabrina shot the one in front of her and threw herself to her feet, intent to rush past it. The bleeding leg held—about as stable as the legs of a newborn foal. She dropped her magazine, losing it between the squiggles and replacing it with her last. An octopus woman rose up in a wide, almost spider web, splaying of tentacles, hissing teeth and sharp hair, cutting Sabrina's rush short.

The thing on her right darted in, slicing the calf of the already injured leg. She felt the cut, though not to the same degree as she had the first. The leg folded once more.

All three hissed at her in unison.

They're not letting me by. I'll have to come back.

Another thought cut in as Sabrina backed toward the flat emptiness.

If she dies down there, she'll just come back somewhere else, right?

Sabrina cursed.

She didn't know, and she doubted Google had anything on modern phoenix rebirths from fairy land.

But the boy toy might know, or the old woman.

Sabrina retreated into the darkness with a new plan. She reappeared in the dilapidated apartment once more. To her relief the darkness housed in the arch hadn't vanished like it had between the crayon trees. A pristine white card drew her attention to a line of bullets.

Sabrina picked up the card labeled with her last name, reading the note inside: Have a blessed damned day, copper.

Can angels say damned?

She glanced around for more notes only to realize that none

of the dead thugs' bodies remained. She scooped up the replacement rounds and brought up her radio. "Dispatch, this is Detective Foxner."

"This is Dispatch, are you saying you found Detective Foxner?"

"Found? No, I *am* Foxner."

"Are you all right, detective? Do you need medical assistance? Should we send an ambulance to your location?"

"Why would I need a bus?" Sabrina asked.

"Your tracker went totally offline at the address of a shots fired six days ago."

Cold worse than the fairyland water swallowed her. "I'm sorry, did you say six days?"

"Affirmative, Detective. You've been MIA for six days." The dispatcher hesitated a moment. "I've got units en route from GT's campus."

Six days?

She pulled up her cell phone home screen. The date matched the same day she'd entered the complex with Quayla.

This is some kind of elaborate joke, but why? They don't know I went—

The phone's date increased by six days.

She swallowed.

Six days.

"Detective?" the dispatcher called.

"Right, I'll, uh, meet them outside."

That isn't possible.

Sabrina's mind whirled while she waited for the other unit. Its proximity proved a saving grace, forcing the detective to turn her focus away from the impossible claims her cell phone confirmed.

Campus police were a part of the overall Atlanta PD, but they took a lot of grief for being glorified babysitters. The officer who got out of his car and insisted on putting her through a thorough check took no end of glee from ordering Sabrina around.

She let him.

It didn't matter how many times he shined a pen light in her face or peered deep into her eyes or asked her to blow on the breathalyzer. She'd lost six days in less than an hour.

Six days I have to explain away...and I still need to go back into Faery.

Chapter Sixteen

Sanctum Assault

Detective Foxner

Sabrina raised a fist to pound on the apartment door. She hesitated. The interrogation she'd suffered for the missed days had grated on her nerves. She was a good cop and had the reputation to go with it. They'd dragged her into the precinct after the EMT's cleared her, made her urinate in a cup and then put her in an interrogation room like a common criminal.

Every minute being grilled about her whereabouts had sawed her very last nerve. Two women—well, a woman and a supernatural being—were in danger and every second counted.

Not that anything I could say would be sufficient explanation.

The time probably wasn't as important as it felt either. An hour on crazy Crayola Island had equated to six days. That should've meant that during the hours of red tape and questions, Quayla and Judith had only been in danger for minutes.

But I can't shake the feeling those minutes are crucial.

Sabrina had managed to talk Miri into checking Quayla's apartment for Terrance Wall. She'd apparently found a lot to fascinate her in the apartment and in the person of Hadley Cox.

Unfortunately, that distraction had prevented Miri from going out to Wall's address or even remembering Quayla.

Sabrina had gone out to the Dallas home herself to find it quiet, empty and with no probable cause to force entry. With no other idea how to reach Quayla's stuffy boss, she'd chosen Dylan Snyder as the next best option.

Three solid, authoritative knocks filled the hall with sound.

Considering the discussion she was about to initiate, she hoped the boyfriend had been read in on all the supernatural goings on. With the scrutiny already on her, she definitely didn't need Snyder filing a harassment complaint and swearing under oath he'd been asked about faeries and phoenixes.

Shouldn't there be some sort of way to erase questions? I sure as hell need some way to explain my absence.

The door opened.

Snyder stood in the door wearing blue jeans and an untucked dress shirt. "Something I can do for you Detective Foxner?"

Sabrina tried to keep the desperation out of her voice. "Please tell me you know your girlfriend isn't human."

His eyes narrowed. "What are you talking about? What else would she be?"

"A phoenix?"

All color drained from him.

"Are you one of them?" Sabrina asked.

He set his shoulders. "Come insid—"

"Dylan, dear?" Mrs. Cox's voice reached Sabrina from up the hall.

Sabrina opened her mouth, but didn't for the life of her know what to say. The old woman was sharp as a Masamune blade, but there was no way to tell what she did and didn't know.

The more people I bring into this, the greater the risk.

"Mrs. Cox?" Snyder asked. "What can I do for you?"

The old woman held up a slip of paper. "I have a reminder here. It's in my handwriting and it says I need to call you about dead bodies in Quayla's apartment."

Sabrina's instincts lit up like a pinball machine.

Mrs. Cox furrowed her brows. "I don't remember writing this, and I checked. Quayla's apartment is clean—though it doesn't look like she's been home in weeks. Did I call you about...bodies?"

"No, Mrs. Cox, but why don't you come inside?" He eyed the hallway. "Seems both of you want to talk about things probably best discussed in private."

Snyder ushered them into his apartment. Socks and work shoes seemed to have been discarded at random in front of the couch, but otherwise the living area seemed just as tidy as Sabrina's last visit.

"Can I get you anything," Snyder asked.

Mrs. Cox patted his hand. "Such a good boy, you really should pop the question, dear."

"I already did." Snyder hesitated. "It's complicated."

"Please tell me that girl didn't turn down a fine catch like you."

Snyder glanced at Sabrina. "Like I said, complicated."

"Tea?"

"Mrs. Cox?" Snyder asked.

"You offered us something to drink. Do you have any tea?"

"Oh, right. Yes."

Snyder wound around an island separating the kitchen and living room. He emptied and refilled a kettle before setting it on the stove. "Detective?"

"No." Sabrina stopped herself on the opposite side of the bar. She gave Cox a sidelong glance. "Look, Quayla's in trouble. I hoped if you were the same thing she is—"

"Thing?!" Mrs. Cox said. "Detective, there is no call to be insulting."

Warmth prickled the underside of Sabrina's forearms. "I wanted to know if Snyder was a phoenix like Quayla."

Mrs. Cox's brows furrowed. "Pardon?"

"No," Snyder said. "Where's Quayla. What's happened?"

"We were chasing the...," Sabrina licked at her lips, glancing again at Mrs. Cox. "goblins that kidnapped her friend Judith. We followed them through an arch into...a crayon drawing of a desert island."

I can't believe these things are coming out of my mouth.

When no questions followed Sabrina's ludicrous statement, she forged on. "I was forced out of wherever that place was by a bunch of green...octopus...heads."

Snyder's fingers tightened on the breakfast bar's counter. "What about Quayla?"

"She didn't...come back out of the water," Sabrina said.

"You let her drown?" Mrs. Cox's accusation stung Sabrina.

"Of course not...she was...made of water at the time."

Mrs. Cox tottered around the counter to the whistling kettle no one seemed to have heard. "When was your last day off, Detective?"

"I'm not over wo—I didn't halluc—you know what? I have no idea what I am or am not anymore."

Snyder crossed to his side table and drew out a locked zipper pouch. "Can you take me back there?"

"When did you get a gun?" Sabrina asked.

"After that ogre attacked her," Snyder said. "I just needed to be able to protect her."

Mrs. Cox set out three cups, pouring hot water into the cups. "You're such a dear, but one hooligan shouldn't make you feel like you need to buy a gun."

"Do you even know how to use it?" Sabrina asked.

"I've taken it to a range a few times." He turned back to the old woman. "That wasn't just some hooligan, Mrs. Cox. That was an honest to god ogre that...right. You don't remember."

"I remember just fine, young man. You're blowing things out of proportion. Now, sit down and let me make you some tea. Everything's always better after some tea."

"I'm fine, Mrs. Cox, well, not fine, but fine. Quayla isn't human."

"She's a florist, dear."

"She's a phoenix," Sabrina insisted.

"You just said she turned into water," Mrs. Cox said. "Phoenixes are made of fire."

"No. Not every phoenix is reborn from ashes, Mrs. Cox. Quayla is one of a team of phoenixes protecting us from…faeries," Snyder finished lamely.

Mrs. Cox shifted her gaze from Sabrina to Snyder and back. She rolled her eyes. "Why didn't you tell me those rascals were involved? We'll need to stop by my apartment on the way."

Sabrina gaped at her.

"Mrs. Cox, you wouldn't be safe going to—"

Mrs. Cox jabbed a crooked finger into his chest. "Faery land? Now see here, young man. I am probably better prepared than either of you to face a bunch of faeries. I can't say Nana ever said anything about phoenixes—especially ones that aren't all fiery—but she did tell a lot of stories which ended with great birds doing in faeries."

"You can't come with us," Sabrina said.

Mrs. Cox patted her hand. "That's nice, dear. Drink your tea before we go."

Snyder glanced at Sabrina. "I have a key card for their HQ."

Hope swelled in Sabrina's chest. Snyder knew where to find the other phoenixes. "Great, Mrs. Cox can return to her apartment, while we—"

Mrs. Cox waggled a finger. "Now look here, missy, you're not getting rid of me that easily. I'm going home to gear up, not nap."

"I understand that," Sabrina glanced at Snyder. "I'll give you an address—"

"To a nice hair salon, no doubt—maybe even with great senior rates to distract the senile old bat. Not a chance in H E double hockey sticks, not when my sweet little Quayla is in jeopardy," Mrs. Cox said. "I'm going where you go. Besides, the Roma slip the cops, not the other way around."

Despite every argument to the contrary, nothing short of illegally handcuffing Mrs. Cox seemed enough to dissuade her. Sabrina stood in the doorway to apartment 1A as the old woman tottered around stuffing things into a huge carpet bag.

Drawers and cupboards slammed.

Dishes, pots and pans clattered.

But all Sabrina could do was shake her head and marvel.

Snyder sidled closer, lowering his voice. "Do you think we should try to slip away?"

"It's not nice to talk about people behind their backs, dear."

Sabrina gestured. "She's a force of nature. Do you think we could get away or that she'd stay behind now even if we do manage to find help?"

Snyder looked at the old woman. "Not a chance in he—"

"Dylan," Mrs. Cox scolded.

"Double hockey sticks," Snyder said.

Sabrina laughed.

At long last, Mrs. Cox latched a bulging bag and patted it on the side. "All right, I'm armed for faerie. Let's go kick some baby stealing, fairy dust trailing, Grimm's tale butts."

Sabrina raised her brows.

Jesus, I'm stuck in a real-life Stop! Or My Mom Will Shoot. Why couldn't this have been a simple hostage situation with a negotiator, a suicidal scumbag and SWAT rather than Annie Schwarzen-landlady?

"Oh, I almost forgot." Mrs. Cox opened an old trunk and drew out a bundle of fabric. She unfolded an age-faded shawl lined with small coins and wrapped it around her shoulders. Several sections showed newer colors where holes had been mended, but the coins all suffered under years of tarnish. "Can't forget Nana's shawl."

Snyder directed them to a high-rise building. They parked in a garage and Quayla's boyfriend got out of the car the moment it was stopped. Sabrina shut off the engine and followed him to an elevator. The clinking of Mrs. Cox's shawl followed a moment later.

"You might not be welcome up there," Snyder held up a security keycard. "You wouldn't believe what it took to get this."

"We stick together," Sabrina said. "Besides, I'm the pol—shield here, not you."

Mrs. Cox patted Sabrina's back. "I'm sure your badge will make barging into a nest full of supernatural birds of prey just fine."

Sabrina turned to find a mischievous smile playing at the edges of the old woman's lips.

Sarcastic old bag.

Anima

A phoenix's dying cry pierced Anima's heart.

Dear Creator, let it not be Quayla once more.

As their caretaker, Anima loved all of her shields with His heart, but Quayla had suffered too much in recent days. She'd taken a mortal into what could only be a trap laid for Quayla within Faery.

A whisper of fear crowded Anima's heart.

If either mortal dies, Vitae will demand Vilicangelus destroy her.

She shook off her fear and touched a finger onto the sapphire eye embedded in her forehead, opening herself to Quayla's essence and peering within.

No sense of Quayla herself reached Anima, but the essence within Quayla's nest and seeds remained the same as it had when last touched.

Anima let out a relieved breath.

Before she could open herself to another shield, a sudden surge of Wyldfae magic stole Anima's breath.

Wings spun her around, oriented within a storm's eye of mist and magic, Creation and Infinity. The phantom, spirit-world soul of Atlanta surrounded her in translucent echoes, mired in an ever-darkening fog of taint and the floating constellations of her Shield's seeds.

Taint of the fallen Sidhe swallowed her in its strength, but unlike her shields couldn't cause Anima's incorruptible form illness.

She scoured her world with narrowed eyes, searching every mote in her little corner of infinity. Had she chosen, she could've looked beyond swirling nebulae filled with mirror pools of Eden-born spring water to other such islands and her fellow Watchers.

She redoubled the search of her shire, pinning a lip beneath teeth in a learned habit that infuriated The Isaac.

An instant of self-loathing washed over her, heralding a twinge of doubt. She granted them no time to settle, sweeping her hands outward to unleash her inner fire to incinerate the dark spirts attempting the delivery.

Another sweep of wings pitched her forward enough to confirm the taint source directly below her—at the foot of her Shield's tower. Pools around her rippled within the rainbow clouds framing them, resolving into reflections of the Shield's hallways seen through technological eyes.

A temporary arch darkened the tower's foyer. A small army of brownies poured out of the breach and toward the elevator bank.

Caelum did not tell me the brownies were returning to clean once more.

She touched the yellow topaz eye within her forehead, peering into the wild but charming essence that so epitomized Caelum.

He's not in Creation eith---wait, he is, but I can barely feel him.

The weak connection didn't make any sense to her, but she had no time to dwell on it. Without Caelum to ask about the brownies, she needed to contact their Shieldheart.

He wasn't in the shield headquarters. None of her phoenixes were present to deal with the small army of brownies pouring into the tower's elevator.

She reached for the garnet in her forehead, only to stop short when a half elf entered the car and scanned Caelum's keycard.

She whispered down onto the tower. "You have not been invited here, Sidhe. Return to your realm."

Oshyn made a rude gesture at the elevator's camera. "Get stuffed."

She raised her voice. "I said begone, ye foul perversion of Creation."

The Sidhe slapped hands over their ears. The brownies made a cheerleading pyramid, drew straight razors and severed both speaker and camera cables.

Anima reached into Vitae's essence. His nest remained full and undisturbed in his bedroom, but she couldn't feel him within their shire either.

What am I going to do?

Heat rippled through her core. She released it once more, burning away the spirit of doubt sent against her.

Anima placed a finger on each of her five embedded eyes and peered into the world. Connection to all five of her shields bolstered her call. For a moment, she glimpsed Caelum and Vitae before something hid them away once more.

She placed her other hand on the pulsing sphere of Light embedded in the center of her chest and pushed with her will. "Shield Headquarters is under assault."

Her words reverberated through Ignis's essence. He hesitated an instant in the pitched battle he waged against a half dozen ogres, but the phoenix was too far to hear the words and too busy to give the sudden prickle in his essence more attention.

Terrance's stolid, baritone reached her. "I come. What can you tell me?"

Anima filled lungs yearning for another breath. "Brownies and the half-elf named Oshyn."

"Are they entering on Caelum's behalf, little oracle?"

"I don't think so, Shield Terrance, but I cannot reach Caelum to verify. I can't reach anyone."

The brownies swarmed into headquarters, spreading out in every direction. Several attacked the frame of Vitae's bedroom with razor blades like living buzz saws.

"They're assaulting Vitae's bedroom and the library."

Terrance's essence went still. "I will make haste."

The earth shield's vehicle stopped moving.

Anima was about to ask Terrance what had gone amiss when the emerald in her forehead blazed with power.

He has transmogrified. Oh, no, he may be seen.

Her fingers squeezed the light at her center. She debated summoning Summuseraphi or even reaching out to Vilicangelus.

I must trust my Shield and its warriors. Terrance will set all to rights.

A tiny bell drew Anima's attention back to the elevator.

Oh, Maker, no! Quayla's mortals. They cannot enter while we're under assault. I have to warn them away.

Detective Foxner

Mrs. Cox oohed in delight as the elevator doors opened onto a magnificent foyer. They stepped inside. To the left, double doors lay askew, their hinges somehow sawed from their frame.

"Anima?" Snyder asked.

A voice whispered from everywhere. "Oh, Creator, Dylan. You have to leave. It's not safe for you here."

"Quayla's been captured," Sabrina said. "We came here for help rescuing her."

"Leave," Anima squeaked. She repeated her warning in a harsh whisper. "You have to go."

Sabrina drew her pistol, holding it low in both hands and stepped further into the foyer.

"Detective, if the voice inside the lair of a supernatural creature tells you not to enter, it seems wise to at least consider their warning," Mrs. Cox said.

"I considered it," Sabrina said. "The police don't run away from a crime in progress."

"We don't even know that's what—"

A shin-high whirling car wash brush spun out from under the fallen doors with an ear-piercing trill. A second followed and a third. They stopped. Every one of them held a straight razor in each of their four hands. Five more of the junior Cousin Its followed, carrying a stone basin of some kind.

"That thing is filled with blood," Mrs. Cox made a warding gesture and dug into her bag.

Sabrina raised her gun. "Halt! Police!"

The lead three twisted toward each other. Twitters and chirps flew back and forth. The lead barked something, let out a battle cry several octaves too high and attacked like a furry Cuisinart.

Shots barked out of Sabrina's gun. Leading her target against the insanely fast rope mop cost her the first few rounds. One rang off a razor, knocking it free from the thing's grip. Her fifth shot stopped the mop cold and splattered blood and guts across the foyer floor.

The other two whirled into action.

Sabrina shot Snyder a quick glance. He held a humongous book open in front of the old lady as she flipped pages. "Are you going to use that gun or not, Snyder?"

"I left it in the car."

"Why in God's name did you do that?" She fired at one target then the other, backing away in a rush.

"We were coming to ask for help, not threaten them at gunpoint."

Sabrina managed to shoot another razor, but that left seven spinning toward her intent on removing her ankles.

A piercing whistle demanded attention. Mrs. Cox removed her finger and thumb from between her lips. She shimmied her shoulders, the whistling hand holding a small plastic lid.

The mops froze, shying away from the coin maraca.

Mrs. Cox shook a Tupperware cup and scowled. "Stop where you are or the milk spills."

A few of them whimpered.

"Now," Mrs. Cox said. "We're going to back into the elevator. When the door starts to close, I'll set the cup down for you. If you move before then, I'll spill it over the gap between car and shaft."

More whimpered.

"What the hell are you doing?" Sabrina demanded.

"Back into the elevator, Detective, unless you aren't fond of your feet. There's no way you can kill all of the brownies."

"There are only seven of them. I've got two spare magazines."

Snyder pointed. "Might want to count again."

Sabrina followed his gesture up a banister lined top to bottom with little, living mops.

"Dylan, dear, get the doors open. Detective, you first."

"You're not even armed," Sabrina said. "If they want the milk so badly, why don't they just rush us and take it?"

"That's not how the old ways work, Detective," Mrs. Cox stepped over the elevator threshold and lowered the cup with a less than steady hand. Milk sloshed over the top.

The collected brownies sucked in breath.

Two lines of milk ran down the outside of the cup. Mrs. Cox caught the runoff on the lid and tipped it back into the cup.

"Milk for letting us leave," Mrs. Cox said. "A fair exchange, yes?"

The army nodded slowly, attention never leaving the cup.

The elevator commenced its descent the moment the doors closed. Snyder exhaled a held breath. "I don't understand what just happened, but thank you."

"What now?" Sabrina asked.

"We save Quayla ourselves," Mrs. Cox said.

Terrance

Terrance folded his wings and dove out of the night.

He pulled up, threw his talons forward and back-winged hard at the last moment. He released his compressed essence. His body rippled, trading his native shape for a hybrid of his human form with pumice and obsidian wings.

With each step across the headquarters balcony, essence slid beneath his skin, solidifying the granite armoring him and flint bolstering his bones. Quartz pierced his skin, forming jagged spikes along the stone-armored cestus sheathing his arms.

Anima's voice boomed, amplified with anxiety and anger. "Terrance, they're stealing our nests."

Terrance threw open the balcony doors and did a little roaring of his own. "In the name of the Undying Light, I command you to surrender."

Brownies swarmed him, razor-edged Tasmanian devils hurling themselves at him to cut Terrance down.

Terrance drew back a fist and drove a brownie into the floor. He yanked the fist back, quartz spikes impaling those in the way of his back swing. His other fist sent two brownies through the air. They impacted against the wall, further shattering their bodies.

Broken razor blades crunched under his feet. Obsidian edges ridged his toes and fighting spurs barbed his feet. He kicked out, halving the first brownie and decapitating the next.

"Terrance, the elevator!"

These are the distraction.

The earth phoenix ignored the faeries climbing his body to break more blades on his neck. He backhanded several brownies, striding through them with stone-bladed kicks.

Even built for his form, it took time to thwart inertia enough to manage a full run. Stairs cracked and splinted under his weight as he descended several at a time.

Brownies threw themselves at him from every angle.

Most ended up against a wall broken by fists before they hit. Terrance's wings hurled many through the faerie-splintered banister to impact a far wall.

Oshyn's wide, frightened eyes shot between Terrance and the elevator button he rapidly punched with increasing desperation.

A concerted wave of brownies leapt from the upper floor as Terrance descended the last few steps. The assault swamped him, ratty dreadlocks blinding him.

Cestus slammed together, splattering the small, hairy faeries. Obsidian wingtips painted the stair in brownie blood.

The elevator door closed.

Brownie laughter taunted him a moment later.

Instead of turn to punish the unrepentant creations, Terrance pushed essence out his fingertips and solidified them into iron spikes. Rending metal squealed as he tore the elevator doors open.

Silence filled the foyer.

Terrance shot the cowering brownies a malicious grin, swiped his claws through the braided elevator cable and leapt into the shaft after the falling car.

Chapter Seventeen

Faerie Bane

Mrs. Cox

The police detective drove them onto northbound I-75. The woman refused to tell them where they were headed, so there was no way to offer helpful directions. Hadley wasn't fond of the woman after the shenanigans with Quayla's picture, but her actions at the phoenix headquarters proved her competent.

I'll give her a chance, but competent or not, I will not tolerate shenanigans.

Hadley watched Atlanta go by outside the window. So many things had changed over the years. Architects worried about beauty and grace surrendered to youngsters interested in glass and metal.

A shame, really, a city should feel alive—not like a hospital lobby.

She turned her attention to the coins hanging from Nana's shawl. The handmade scarf was made to hang around a woman's hips, rather than her shoulders. She'd inherited the shawl after snaring her Joshua—God rest his soul—never needing to dance provocatively before the fire with a declaration of her bride price around her hips.

Nana might have, even at my age she'd had an untamable streak.

Her Nana had fancied Hadley over all the other girls. She'd woken Hadley up late at night for stories and tea before sending her back to bed and nightmares. At first, it'd seemed Nana was just trying to make Hadley feel better after she experienced what doctors now called Night Horrors.

The others had made fun or just not believed me, but what I experienced hadn't been just my imagination or digestion issues. Nana had known that even when I wasn't sure myself.

Some of the stories had been too fanciful to believe, but Nana's serious expression never cracked in jest. If Hadley had questions Nana couldn't answer, she went to the Book.

She drew the Book out of her bag, turning the ancient thing over in wrinkled fingers. The cover and the thongs that tied the pages between were old leather, preserved from cracking though Hadley's painstaking care. The Book had passed directly to Hadley on Nana's death, not like the shawl which had come through Hadley's mother.

Momma couldn't read the cant anyway.

She'd been sure the little creatures invading Quayla's friend's place were brownies. Problem was, brownies weren't supposed to be scary. Folklore never painted them as anything other than helpful creatures—willing to clean for some nectar from a Mother's bosom. The differences left Hadley doubting herself.

Hadley fingered one of the old coins on the shawl.

They knew to fear these though, knew a Romani witch's never paid dowry carried a curse for any who looked upon it with intent to cheat a bargain.

The detective pulled off the interstate in sight of the old red V of the Varsity's sign. A lot of people swore by their food, but the wait staff were rude and the food gave Hadley wind.

Atlanta had rebuilt the area around Georgia Tech so that it wasn't as dangerous as it once had been, but only to replace desperate criminals with more unscrupulous men in need of a hot-iron gelding.

The detective instructed Quayla's Dylan in fire patterns and strategy as if bullets would make a difference in the coming rescue.

Hadley stroked the Book. Quayla's life depended on the old texts and the items hastily stuffed in her old carpetbag.

I only hope I grabbed everything we need.

The neighborhood worsened once more. The detective parked in front of an apartment complex probably better burned to the ground than occupied—even allowing the number of vermin the burning would push into the surrounding buildings.

"We're here," Foxner said.

Hadley slid the Book back into her bag and climbed out of the sedan. Her hip clicked in a minor pop that shot pain up her side, but she didn't give the youngsters any outward excuse to leave her behind.

Hadley Cox followed the detective and Quayla's Dylan into the building. The detective moved much like you'd expect watching cop shows.

Like the new one with that sexy boy—Nathan something.... He's so much prettier than Bill Shatner, and more believable as a cop— even in that show where he just hung out with the cops.

Entering the apartment building scandalized Hadley's nose. That any landlord would allow their premises to deteriorate so far appalled her. A little elbow grease, some soap and a bit of white sage could've put the place right. There was no point blaming the tenants. A self-respecting land lord didn't rent out to hooligans and certainly didn't tolerate any shenanigans.

"Mrs. Cox?" Dylan asked.

"Right behind you, dear."

"Detective Foxner says Quayla found a trap on the elevator, are you okay taking the stairs to the third floor?" he asked.

She patted his arm. "Stairs aren't any fret, dear."

The stairwell hosted graffiti painted by small minds with

limited vocabulary. The school systems were to blame—not the teachers so much as the absence of yard sticks and back bones.

A beautiful angelic image covered the back wall of the second floor. The art showed talent, enough that she felt guilty knowing the graffiti needed whitewashed away. A far cruder delinquent had destroyed the art with vulgarities.

They both need the hides tanned, that's for certain. Still, once that's dealt with, I'd love to introduce the artist to Larry.

Detective Foxner led them into the third-floor hall. She took in a slow breath and pushed upon an unlatched door. Hadley heard her relieved exhale.

"It's still here," Foxner said.

"Thank God," Dylan said.

Hadley entered the room, looking to the makeshift arch and its oddly two-dimensional darkness. Something about it nagged at her memory. She pulled the Book from her bag.

"Dylan, be a dear, won't you?"

He stepped over to her and extended his hands, taking the Book's weight with less surprise the second time.

Hadley flipped through the pages.

"What are you doing?" Foxner asked. "We need to go after them."

"We will, dear, in a minute."

"There isn't time for," Foxner gestured uncertainly, "for whatever it is you are doing."

Hadley tsked and turned more pages. She found what she was searching for just past the half way point, right after the description she didn't remember of a blue-looking faerie race that prized growing mold colonies on their skin.

A wicked-looking hand-drawn tree dominated the page with a wide blackness inside. In a two-dimensional drawing, there was no real way to differentiate the darkness from the tree, but the darkness in the construction material arch matched the description written in Romani cant.

Hadley sucked her teeth. "This is bad."

"Yeah," Foxner said. "This is where they're holding Quayla and Judith."

"No, dear, this is a door into Faery."

Foxner licked her lips. "I already know that."

"Do you also happen know how much innocent blood it takes to make a stable door into the world of the Fae?"

Foxner's expression changed. "What kind of innocent blood?"

"Elves are fond of stealing children," Hadley said. "Always blamed it on Nana's people."

"I'm sorry," Dylan said. "I don't claim to be an expert, but this hardly looks like elven architecture."

Hadley patted his arm once more. "This isn't the movies, dear."

"What are we talking about? Virgins? Kidnapped coeds?" Foxner's eyes narrowed. "Shelter animals?"

Dylan attention shot around to Foxner.

"I suppose animals could work," Hadley said. "Faerie magic wasn't something they taught us in school, Detective. No matter what though, it means whatever built this thing is mean and powerful."

Foxner patted her shotgun. "That's why we came armed."

Hadley shut the Book harder than she meant. "Oh, well then by all means, Detective. Sound the charge."

For a moment, Foxner looked on the edge of a scathing rebuttal. Instead, she narrowed her eyes at Dylan. "If you're coming, you need to take that gun out of the bag."

Dylan looked on the edge of vomiting, but his expression tightened. He removed the gun, shoved spare bullets into a pocket and dropped the case to the ground.

Foxner inclined her head, charged the darkness and vanished.

Dylan gave Hadley an uncertain look. "Mrs. Cox...it might be best—"

"After you, dear, our Quayla needs us."

Dylan fidgeted with the pistol, trying to figure out how to

hold it on the move. He squared his shoulders and stepped into the archway.

Hadley followed.

Horrid stench and dirty walls vanished, replaced by a thick scent of wax and a bright, sky blue squiggles.

Hadley lifted her brows. "It is a crayon drawing."

"And they know we're here," Foxner said.

A splash some way out in the drawn water drew Hadley's eyes to what Foxner had aptly described as green octopus heads.

Foxner directed Dylan where to stand and both readied their weapons. Hadley knelt, her knees creaking as she laid the Book on long tan strokes.

Gunfire erupted.

"What are you doing, Snyder?"

Hadley chanced a glance.

Quayla's Dylan stared at the oncoming creatures.

Foxner barked orders at him as she fired. "If you want to help your girlfriend, you need to get your head in the game."

He raised the pistol with an unsteady hand. "They're not real. This is a game. This isn't real."

One of the creatures charged him.

Foxner leapt from where she was, throwing him back and putting two bullets into the charging creature at close range as its hair sliced into her.

His fall put him in the path of an attack meant for the detective. He reacted, firing seven times even though the last two clicked against already discharged shells.

"I-I got one." Dylan said.

"More incoming," Foxner snapped.

Hadley returned to the book, flipping pages as respectfully as her hurried search allowed.

Foxner fired over a kneeling Dylan as he slid shells into his pistol's cylinders.

Three more heads reinforced the initial wave.

She flipped more pages. Something green caught her eye. She

turned pages the other way in a hurry, drawing a finger down the cant under a picture of their attackers.

Scribbles in the margin drew her eye away from her finger. She squinted, forced to fumble her glasses out of the bag and squint at Nana's horrid penmanship.

A chuckle escaped her lips.

Oxen plops! Ain't nothing better for sorting Jenny Greenteeth than a cast iron walloping 'til she gets the point.

Hadley was tempted to keep reading the rest of the passage, but Nana's notes had never proved wrong.

Besides, this sounds like fun.

She dug into the bag looking for her heavy Sunday Fried Chicken pan, grabbing onto a thick line of dark brown above her in the tree trunk. The handhold helped her regain her feet. She picked up the bag with one hand without letting go of the pan in her other.

She picked her steps across the treacherous drawn landscape as Foxner and Quayla's Dylan fired their guns. To either side, the nasty green heads spread out, trying to circle around them. One of the nasty green heads eyed Hadley a moment before rushing by on a headlong dash toward Quayla's Dylan.

Hadley brought out the pan in a smooth overhead swing.

Cast iron splattered the head against the drawn water, evergreen ick dripping down between the lines.

All of the Jennys froze, turning their attention toward Hadley.

Foxner gave her an incredulous look before shooting the still faeries.

"They sell single person versions at Bed, Bath, & Beyond," Hadley stalked toward the next nearest Jenny. "Not sure they'd be quite as effective as this old hand-me-down though."

"No, sh—shoot," Foxner said.

Hadley's cast iron pan smashed another Jenny like a week-old jack-o-lantern.

Foxner barked instructions and both of them rushed around behind Hadley, taking up protective positions to either side as she strode to each Jenny in turn. When only one remained, it retreated back into the water.

Hadley stopped short at the water's edge.

Dylan turned away from them, dropped to his knees and sprayed the squiggles with vomit.

"He'll be fine," Foxner said. "Please tell me that book has something that can help us with this."

"No," Hadley dug a small oxygen tank with a breathing mask from her bag. "This isn't a SCUBA tank and won't last three of us long, but it might serve long enough."

Dylan wiped his mouth and reached for the tank. "I'll go down there. You two—"

"Can you believe these two aren't married yet?" Hadley asked.

"They're not even the same species," Foxner said. "If anyone's going down there alone, it's me."

Hadley rolled her eyes, set the bag to one side, took a deep breath and descended the stairs. A line of pain lashed across her calf. Red blossomed in the water at her side. Hadley slammed the water near her leg with the pan.

"Let me by," Foxner said.

Instead, Hadley took several hurried steps downward, squatting a little once the water buoyed her weight. Pain flashed across her arm. She flinched, nearly dropping the oxygen tank into the water. She two more hurried steps, submerged her head and blinked rapidly until she could see.

A blob of green rushed toward her through the water.

Hadley extended the pan, her voice coming out strange to her ears. "Back off, missy, or you'll regret it."

Foxner shot downward in a line of bubbles, twisting in the water with flashlight and gun pointing wildly. She'd only gone a few feet below Hadley before bubbles erupted from the detective's lips like she'd been punched.

Hadley hurried down the spiral stair. She got as close as she could to the detective and extended the frying pan. "Grab on."

Foxner dropped her flashlight and grabbed the pan.

Hadley dragged her back onto the stairs and pushed the tank toward the detective.

She had to holster her gun to turn the tank on and fortunately had enough air left in her lungs to expel water from inside the mouthpiece.

She took a few deep breaths before handing it back. "Thanks."

Hadley pressed the breathing mask to her face, tipping it a bit to leave the bottom of the seal loose and exhaled the used air from her lungs. She pressed it tight against her face and took a long breath before handing it up to Dylan.

SCUBA mouthpiece would've been easier.

She turned her attention back to a rapid descent, but Foxner refused to surrender the lead. Luckily, the detective didn't dally, even while drawing her weapon.

Can that thing even fire under water?

Hadley kept an eye out for Jenny as they continued trading the tank all the way down to the bottom. About one flight up, she caught sight of some kind of grotto in a bubble.

She pointed.

Foxner leapt off the last few steps, careless that the pressure off the stairs had been so much greater when she'd jumped before.

Maybe she braced herself better this time.

It took only a moment to see Foxner was in distress. Cries bubbled from her mouth.

Hadley rushed the last few steps, then hesitated. She turned back, gesturing for Dylan to take the oxygen to the detective. As much as she hated to admit it to herself, she had to let Dylan take the risk. If the pressure was too bad, her older bones wouldn't take as much beating as his would. As long as she stayed on the stair, she could drag him back on and hopefully Foxner if he grabbed the detective.

Dylan fared no better than Foxner, losing the tank when the pressure hit him.

"Grab her and grab my hand," Hadley shouted into the water.

Quayla's Dylan clawed at his throat.

Hadley reached out, trying to hook him with her pan. He slipped off the rounded cast iron.

A flash of blinding blue light exploded through the water. Hadley nearly gasped as a majestic bird rocketed through the water like a water-spout-driven manta ray. It grabbed Foxner and Dylan in its talons, shoved them into the grotto and circled back to grab Hadley.

Despite being made of water, the talons pinching Hadley could've shredded or broken her like a titmouse. A shroud of darkness swallowed Hadley as Quayla jerked her off the stairs. It departed just as suddenly as Quayla set her down on soft sand. Foxner and Dylan choked on hands and knees to either side.

Woman Quayla bent next to Dylan, face taught with worry and eyes filled with daggers for the other woman present.

Hadley knelt next to Foxner, thankful for soft sand to cushion her knees. "Are you all right, dear?"

Foxner choked and nodded.

Hadley rose to face the other woman, extending her cast iron pan. "You're going to let Quayla go or there will be trouble, missy."

The Lady laughed.

Hadley shook the pan. "I mean it."

"I have no intention of surrendering my prize, Hadley Sage Cox—at least not to you," the Lady said

Hadley thumbed her shawl's coins. "It's a bargain then is it?"

The Lady laughed again. "I am not frightened by your forbear's bride coins or cast iron. You haven't anything worth the trade."

"My life," Hadley said.

"Mrs. Cox, no!" Quayla objected.

"Too old."

Dylan struggled to his feet, voice croaking. "Then take me."

In the blink of an eye, sweet Quayla became something dangerous. A harsh growl rasped from her throat. "Absolutely not. You shouldn't have come."

The Lady tilted her head to one side, a brow arched high on her pale forehead.

Foxner shot her.

The Lady reeled, blood bubbling from the chest wound. She tumbled on the edge of the clam's shell.

Foxner leapt to her feet and charged, training the gun on the prone woman. Before she took a second shot, water rushed into the grotto. The clam closed around the bleeding Lady a moment before Quayla wrapped around Hadley once more.

Darkness and motion delivered her, Dylan and Foxner to the top of the spiral stair, vanishing as Quayla dove back down to the grotto.

Dylan tried to force his way past them and back down the stairs, but Hadley grabbed him. Foxner muscled him above the water by his other arm.

"What are you doing," Dylan asked. "She needs us."

"We don't have any air," Foxner shot back.

"Out of the water, children," Hadley stepped out onto the blue squiggles. She checked her bag unpilfered, relief flooding as the Book she hadn't dared take underwater came into view.

Foxner fought Dylan onto what served as ground. She was smaller, but exploited the benefits of police training to get her way. Dylan relented, rubbing his shoulder after she released the arm lock she had him in.

Quayla walked out of the water a moment later, Judith's body cradled in her arms.

"Oh, no," Hadley said.

Terrance

Terrance jerked his truck's steering wheel, and shot into his driveway. He'd slammed through the roof of the elevator where emergency brakes had stopped it in the shaft. The car had been empty, Oshyn, his brownies and the stolen nests gone through an Arch into Faery.

He'd left no traffic law unbroken in his rush to reach his Dallas home. He barely avoided ripping the door off of his truck in his haste. Taint slammed into him the moment the door opened.

He summoned his cestus, rushing through the security system so fast he had to do so twice. He hurried into his trashed living room, eyes fixed on cracked and violet-smeared atrium glass.

He charged up the hallway, ignoring ripped open doors and trashed contents. The security door into the atrium had been ripped off its hinges by something enormous. The atrium itself was strewn with body after bloody, Unseelie body.

Under shredded edderkopp web, Yarque lay in the place where Terrance's nest belonged. The kobold's *tracht* was ripped and bloodied, golden blood staining white shirt and evergreen vest a similar brown.

Golden blood?

Terrance pushed the thought away and dropped next to Yarque. The old kobold's eyes flickered open, malicious delight sparkling.

"You're going to owe me big for this, boy."

"You want to tell me for what before I agree to an unbalanced payment?"

"They smashed my hat and ruined my clothes. You're going to offer me recompense, boy, and make no mistake, when you find the nasty scunners, you'll call Yarque for a reckoning," A coughing fit overtook Yarque. "They'll show a soldier of the Most High proper respect or by all that's precious I'll rip their legs off, shove them high and make them hop on their asses."

Terrance couldn't help a laugh. "Rest up, old man. You'll get your chance. Did they take my nest?"

"That they did, boy. Couldn't stop them."

Brows shifted up Terrance's forehead. "*You* couldn't stop them?"

Yarque shook his head, helped to a sitting position. "Three old nasty trolls, almost my age if you can believe it, and dozens of Unseelie whelps I broke in your honor."

"Why so many just for my nest?" Terrance asked.

"Take it as the compliment it is, boy. They came looking to war with you, and they did not spare the troops," Yarque laughed. "They didn't count on you honoring a truly old Power with a place in your garden."

"It's you who honor me, Yarque." Terrance brought him a wooden cup of spring water. "If you're well enough, I must step outside and contact my Shield."

Yarque took the cup, nodding as he drank so fast that water spilled out the corners of his mouth.

Chapter Eighteen

Facing the Music

Quayla

I stepped back into Creation with Judith still cradled in my arms. The space between crayon palm trees had seemed empty, but sweet Mrs. Cox shook her book at us and insisted the portal worked both ways if we could believe past the glamour.

Dylan and Foxner might've had a harder time with their weaker human wills, but Mrs. Cox disappearing through the empty space had made them believers too.

I assessed the tableau waiting for me.

Dylan stood in the open room, gills a little green, jaw tight in that line it got when he was working out a hard problem. His hand shook almost imperceptibly around the revolver he'd used to kill faeries while charging to my rescue. If it hadn't been for Judith's corpse in my arms, his masculinity might've stirred up desire.

Foxner stood guard near the doorframe, gun ready for trouble. Dirty and disheveled, she remained a solid warrior. A modern-day paladin—fierce, forbidding and hot in a way that gentle Dylan couldn't quite mimic even after his heroics.

Mrs. Cox sat atop an old box with a garish carpetbag on her

lap. Her eyes examined the room in much the same way as I did. A wary, piercing look spoke of a mortal that saw more than the others.

Too much more.

A muffled voice reached me from beneath my blouse. "Shield Quayla? I see you. Are you well? What has transpired?"

"Not now, Ani. I'm fine, and I'll report soon."

"Your nest has been stolen," Anima said.

The world wobbled on its axis. Before I knew it, Foxner was there catching Judith and reaching out a steadying hand.

"Did Anima say your nest was stolen?" Dylan's voice sounded too high in the empty ruin of an apartment. "But without an egg and a nest—"

"Not now, Dylan," I snapped.

Mrs. Cox got off her seat and sidled to his side. She drew him away, speaking to him in low tones.

I didn't have time for him at the moment. I could apologize later. The Lady had claimed my nest lost, but I hadn't fully believed the powerful faerie. I'd snapped at Dylan because he'd voiced my rising terror before it could solidify enough for me to get a grip on it.

"I'm sorry," I said to the room in general. "Just give me a minute."

Only moments before, I had been on the precipice of several horrible choices. The three mortals in the room had gone where they shouldn't, seen what they were forbidden to see, and endured things their brains weren't meant to contain.

I needed to call Summus for a rewrite. Only hands filled by Judith's body had shielded me from making that decision. I looked down at my empty hands and the body Foxner set down in the debris at my feet.

She's dead because of me—not because of my choices, I don't really have any, but because the faeries wanted to attack me.

My eyes rose to meet Dylan's concerned gaze. I dropped them to the gun in his fist.

I love you, Dylan, and I can't bear to lose you. Rewriting away this incident won't be enough to protect you. It might stuff Pandora's shadow back into an amphora, but you'll still be on the target list.

If I rewrote him back to before he'd seen the ogre, he'd be the same man I'd fallen in love with, but less armed for dealing with the stress of the world evolving around us. If I rewrote him completely out of my life, he'd be safer—probably—but I wouldn't have him to bolster my strength and make me feel sane when the world tried to break me.

The feeling of scrutiny drew my eyes to meet Foxner's. Shadows watched me from within the deep blue. I could almost feel the other woman's understanding, even her pity.

They all needed rewritten. That was the selfless decision. If their realities had never included the recent madness, they couldn't become leverage.

Even if it means surrendering people from my life that in many ways are more in my corner than my fellow shields.

I looked at Judith once more.

There was no rewrite for my friend. Her soul had gone to the Creator's arms. He would not relinquish her.

"Stay here, I have to talk to headquarters."

I strode to the door with all the certainty and purpose I could fake. I had to surrender them for their own protection. It was right, and doing right was why I was created.

I strode down the hall and into the stairwell. There was no reason to worry about cell signal for the call before me, so I tried to walk off the pain going up and down the stairs.

I drew the silvered feather from within my blouse and held it up to my mouth. "Summuseraphi. Summuseraphi."

"Quayla?" Foxner stood at the top of the stairwell, just above Caelum's marred painting of an angel. "What's going on?"

"Everything's fine, I jus—"

"Bullshit," Foxner marched down the stairs. "You look like you're about to call IA on your partner."

I closed my eyes, but my lids couldn't hold back the tears. "Judith's dead just because she worked with me."

"Judith's dead because whoever that bitch was that I killed, she was a sociopathic nutjob."

"Technically faeries are amoral rather than sociopathic."

"Same difference. What's going on?"

"I'm calling for someone to re-write you, essentially—"

"Erase our memories?" Foxner's expression shifted into the middle distance and her voice dropped to a mumble. "That's why Miri didn't understand what I was talking about."

I raised the pendant once more.

"Fuck that!" Foxner closed the distance and slapped away the feather. "I don't want you screwing with my brain."

"It doesn't really affect your brain. Look it's complicated and it's for the best. If you don't know, then you'll be—"

"Safer? Like Judith?"

Rising fury momentarily burned away my other emotions. "You have a really annoying habit of interrupting people."

"As opposed to brainwashing people?"

"Damn it, Foxner, this is the way it has to be. Wafers can't know about the supernatural world. Too much is at stake."

"I'm not a wafer. I'm a shield—like you."

"It's too big a risk," I said.

"You let your boy toy know what you were."

"And maybe that was a mistake. Humans are...awful," I held up a hand to forestall another interruption. "Yes, you have so much potential for good and giving, but too many of you are selfish beyond reason."

"What has that got to do with anything?"

"Imagine what would happen if I could grant you a wish, any wish in Creation."

Foxner's expression turned inward.

"Sure, if I grant that wish to an incorrupt saint, maybe that wish would benefit humanity."

"But even saints have ex-girlfriends, hurts they want righted," Foxner said. "They might wish wrong."

"Now imagine armies of wish granting amoral nutjobs handing them out to anyone and everyone willing to make a deal."

"Even the good wishes wouldn't be able to counter the global bloodbath that would ensue."

"That's assuming the nutjobs bothered offering wishes to the saints," I said. "We keep that in check—maybe not perfectly, but the best we can. If humanity learned about what the faeries could offer, it would be like shattering Pandora's amphora."

"Box."

"It wasn't a box."

"Whatever. Wouldn't you still be able to hold things together? Maybe work with human law enforcement?"

I shook my head. "We'd have failed. Maybe we'd simply be uncreated. Maybe we'd be replaced like we replaced the last heavenly host. Maybe we'd just stop being reborn."

"If you erase us, you'll be alone."

The tears escaped, but I shook my head. "I'm never alone. I am a Shield of five parts cradled in the hands of the Undying Light."

"Lot of good they did you today," Foxner said.

"We're at war," I said. "We're spread a bit thin, but they have my back. We're a family."

"Even that stiff douche bag?"

A chuckle escaped me. "Yeah, even Vitae."

"If you didn't erase me, you'd have backup when the rest of your Shield is too busy," Foxner said.

I yearned to say yes. The word struggled against my sternum, threatening to shatter ribs to escape if need be. Foxner was a shield, a warrior, but there was no way to tell if she was strong enough to go toe to toe with faeries day after day and not break or be seduced.

And she has none of the physiological enhancements we do to face off against them. Asking her to fight would be tantamount to feeding her to wolves myself.

I needed someone in my corner. If I had to sacrifice Dylan, at least having Foxner for help running down leads and accessing the human resources would mean I wasn't alone.

"I don't want to stop loving you," Dylan said.

My eyes shot upward.

Dear Maker, how long has he been there?

"Quayla, I love you. I proposed. I bought a gun and came to your rescue in a crayon drawing," Dylan said. "What more do you want to prove my love is the real thing?"

"Those are pretty solid credentials for a civvie," Foxner said.

"Dylan, please don't do this. I don't want to give you up, but I can't stand to lose you like I did Judith."

"Even knowing everything, I chose you, I chose our love." Dylan's lips pressed into a thin line. "Those are my choices. You do what you feel you have to do."

My voice broke. "You'd choose to die?"

"I'd trade my life for yours even if it meant only being able to love you for one more moment," he said.

I can't do this, I can't choose because no matter what, every choice is selfish.

I raised my eyes to the ceiling.

Lord Creator grant me wisdom.

Dylan gasped and Foxner drew her gun.

I whipped around.

The air fled my lungs.

An angel floated before me, there but not quite substantial. Four wings kept the child floating, two from her shoulders and two from her calves. There could be no question the being before me was angelic. The light escaping from the swirling fog of colors coming off of the hovering, vaguely feminine entity washed away age and wear from every surface it touched.

Energy surged into me, pushing away weariness and somehow filling me with wholeness.

She watched me in silence from eyes embedded in her wings and her hands, on the tips of her fingers and her face. Five gemstone eyes glowed in a rainbow along her forehead.

"Forgive me, Shield Quayla. I know this is a forbidden, but I did not wish to speak where others might hear."

"Ani?" I asked. "Dearest God, you're so beautiful."

The eyes in Anima's coloring cheeks flicked away and her head lowered so that none of her eyes met my gaze. "I am but a lowly cherubim, reflecting the Light of my creation."

"A little while ago I thought you were some kind of AI, how is this even possible?" I said.

"Maybe a better question would be, 'why is she here' if being here is forbidden?" Foxner asked.

"I heard your travail," Anima glanced around at things I couldn't see. "I must leave, but think on this. Any re-write to Hadley Sage Cox's reality would reveal your other mortals."

The stairwell shook with sudden thunder as Anima popped out of existence. The weight of her departing words pressed down on my heart. The cherubim spoke true. My choice was all or nothing no matter what I might personally want.

The grime Anima's presence cleansed didn't return, leaving Caelum's painted angel peering down into my very soul.

My thoughts flitted to the other shields, to Caelum's sport sex, to Ignis and Terrance's celibacy. I could reach out to them, seek their council, but nothing they said would lift the decision from my shoulders.

I climbed the stairs to Dylan, looking deep into his eyes. Warmth blossomed with his answering smile, curling my lips. I slid my fingers into the hair behind his head and drew him forward.

Three words escaped my caressing lips over and over. Tears ran my cheeks as his answer washed through me one last time.

He pulled away. "Quayla?"

"I love you," I whispered.

"I love you too."

I am not an individual. I am a shield of the Undying Light, created with the duty to protect Creation, not to endanger it for my own comfort.

A corner of my lips quirked up. "I love you more."

Too much to kill you by being selfish.

"I'm sorry," I whispered, pressing fingers against Dylan's mouth. "Goodbye, my love. Summuseraphi. Summuseraphi. Summuseraphi."

Summuseraphi

Summus looked through the thin veil of light separating them from the three still mortals. They weren't frozen in time so much as Quayla and he were held in a bubble stretching an instant out as long as he needed.

His shoulder muscles burned holding open his wings to shroud them in that moment. "Curse it, Quayla, I don't need this."

She refused to look at him. Tears he of all people knew she didn't have to shed rained to their feet.

He barely heard her reply. "I'm sorry."

"Rewriting reality takes essence. Essence I never had much chance to build up and you people seem to be going through in tidal waves."

She didn't throw his own complicity back at him. If he'd rewritten the detective when she'd asked, Sabrina Foxner wouldn't have ended up in Faery, wouldn't have dragged Hadley and Dylan in after her, and wouldn't have rescued Quayla.

He'd heard Quayla and Anima use Vilicangelus's feather. He'd known Quayla was in trouble, but had trusted her to persevere. She was water after all, in many ways—pride notwithstanding—the most capable of the five phoenixes where it came to adaptation or escape.

But I should've checked that she got at least the basics of the training I received. Why did Vilicangelus prize this Shield so much? It's a wreck. Their library has all the material, but their Shieldheart didn't teach her. It's almost like he wanted her to fail.

Summus took a deep breath, resigning himself to setting the Shield right once the crisis had passed. In the meantime, he had a triple re-write to perform.

"I'm sorry," Quayla whispered once more.

Summus drew up her chin and smiled at her. "You are brave, not sorry. After everything you told me, choosing to call me couldn't have been easy."

"It's right."

"Yes. You're needed elsewhere, and you really don't want to be around to see this."

Quayla opened her mouth.

He inclined his head. "I will rewrite things so the detective rescues your dead friend so that the time she lost isn't held against her."

"Will they remember me at all?"

"I will try to erase you completely, but if reality's flow doesn't allow you to be completely erased, I'll leave only fond memories of an acquaintance—a quiet, law-abiding, and very private girl who kept to herself."

Quayla looked at Dylan, choking back a sob.

If only I could rewrite her so that this didn't hurt so much.

"Now, get back to headquarters. We need to regroup and find those nests before whatever the faeries are planning comes to pass and we're forced to fight under threat of True Death."

Ignis

Ignis surveyed the Sidhe bodies strewn along the alley. The Seelie and Unseelie died before his arrival. Gnoll and coyll, goblin and grendling bodies lay where they'd fallen interspaced with more powerful fey—an elf, a half-ogre and a dwarf.

Left for the mortals to find.

Movement drew Ignis's eye to the alley across the street. A hunched figure bobbed a purplish head. Ignis strode toward the faerie, glancing both ways before crossing between cars.

"You, do not move."

The grendling's head shot up, blood painting his chin. It clutched the dog held in its hands closer to its chest and hissed.

"In the name of the Undying—"

The grendling bolted.

Ignis lifted his hilt, sending bright yellow essence out each end.

The grendling ran a serpentine retreat, ducking its head to rip free more dog entrails as it ran.

The tips of Ignis's bow glowed like stars, each casting a tine of light toward the other. He extruded a spark of essence from the thumbnail holding his hilt, stretching the mote back until the connecting shaft touched the line of starlight. Ignis pulled back both shaft and string together, the shaft's end blossoming feathers as the string reach its limit.

He loosed the arrow.

The firebolt splattered the grendling's head. The little fey sprawled forward, cranium smoking.

Ignis crossed to the distance, kicking the grendling over. The mutt beneath was long dead, most of its organ eaten by the grendling. A lump clogged Ignis's throat. He knelt, summoning essence to cremate the dog so that nothing else got the chance to chew on the stray.

Runes burnt into the leather strap around the dog's neck caught Ignis's attention. He removed the collar and turned it over in his hands until he'd deciphered the spell.

Null magic?

Ignis touched the dog then the grendling, pushing fire into

both. He returned to the first alley, still troubled by the collar. He incinerated the Sidhe bodies left behind.

How does this fit with what's going on? The collars that Fae Kissed made weren't anything like this.

He took the collar back to his car. Anima's voice drew his attention to the bronze angel on my Camaro's dashboard. "Ignis, I'm sensing an incursion in Buckhead."

"On my way." Ignis set the collar aside, put his emergency light onto the dashboard and sped to the nearest freeway onramp.

While en route, Anima provided an address to the incursion. Due to a recent fire, Ignis knew the Piedmont Road strip club.

He laughed.

"You sure Caelum isn't free for this one? It's definitely more his speed."

"Caelum informed me he would be out of touch replenishing seeds," Anima said.

Ignis whipped across traffic and into the strip club's parking lot. As he threw open his door, a gaping hole in the front wall allowed a shrill scream to escape. He drew his hilt and raced to the opening.

Cries, laughter and sobbing filled the dark interior. Taint overwhelmed the stink of cigarette haze and old alcohol. A dark shape loomed out of shadow. A massive hand seized Ignis, jerking him off the floor.

An adolescent ogre fifteen feet high sneered down. "Who are you?"

Flames sheathed Ignis in a crackling nimbus.

The ogre dropped him, sucking fingers into his mouth.

"In the name of the Undying Light, I command you to surrender."

Another large shape stepped into the orange and yellow light of Ignis's aura. A third appeared with a topless woman hanging unconscious in his hands. A fourth and fifth adolescent ogre entered the firelight from either side.

Ignis pushed a long, curved blade up through his hilt.

A sixth ogre filled the last opening in the semicircle, naked women struggling in his hands under his cheesy grin. "Nice sword. Hand it over or I shake their maracas."

Half a dozen ogres, even adolescents, presented a difficult challenge, worsened by the presence of hostages. Relinquishing his hilt weakened his arsenal, but under the circumstances it bought time without offering the ogres any advantage.

Ignis drew his essence out of the hilt and tossed it to the ground. "There. Now let the mortals go."

Six's grin widened. "Why?"

Ignis eyed the other ogres in turn. "I did as you asked. You have my hilt. Everything is still fine. Release the mortals and I will allow you to return peacefully to Faery in accordance with the Articles of Ararat."

Six licked his thick, cracked lips. "I like these girls. Maybe I'm not done playing with them yet."

The others chuckled.

Ignis softened his voice, filling it with menace. "Maybe if you don't release the mortals, I'll be forced to teach you boys proper respect for a lady."

Six lurched forward stomping Ignis's hilt. "With what?"

"Yeah, what're you going to do?" Five shoved Ignis. "You going to tickle us with your feathers, tiny?"

Ignis recovered his footing, transmogrified shirt unfolding into flaming wings as fire wreathed his fists. "If you insist."

"What do you know," Six laughed. "The buffet includes flame roasted chicken."

"Last warning," Ignis hardened his feathers.

"Pull him apart and make a wis—"

Ignis's pivoted left toward the first ogre, right wing whipping forward. A flaming pinion shot through the club, impaling Six between his eyes. He slammed both fists into One, ducked wild swing from Three and sidestepped a stomp from Two.

Discarded women scrambled away in tears.

Four seized Ignis. Ignis's wings scissored forward, burning

away both of the ogre's arms. One and Three grabbed a wing, pulling Ignis away from Four's screams.

Ignis drew in his wings, hit the ground with a roll and spun to face the ogres. Someone walked over Ignis's grave and a whisper of his name prickled his skin. The sprinkler system cut loose above them, flooding the club with old water.

Two grabbed a steaming Ignis, fingers crushing him until bones snapped like twisted bubble wrap. "So much for you, bug."

Ignis fought the pain, compressing his essence. "I'm not the cream filled kind."

He released his power, transmogrifying into pure flame and rebalancing his limbs whole. Two jerked his hands away, but not fast enough to escape the inferno Ignis sent up the ogre's limbs.

Two ran screaming. He tripped on a pleather couch and careened into the bar. Alcohol and cheap plywood burst into flame.

Three wrenched a pole out of the ceiling and slammed it into Ignis's back. The impact sent Ignis flying into a nearby wall. Fire licked up the wood paneling as if it was soaked in gasoline. Three tromped across the intervening space, pole raised for another blow.

Ignis rolled to one side, avoiding the strike. He put his left hand on the burning wall and extended his right toward the ogre. A stream of yellow-white fire roared from his palm, engulfing Three.

Ignis climbed to his feet. He strode across the club, will drawing the flames away from the paneled wall behind him. "I would've been satisfied to let you return to Faery."

He stopped next to the bar, turning to face uncertain-looking adolescents holding furniture at the ready. "Instead, you had to play the bully, picking on smaller mortals."

One and Five eyed each other.

"First lesson about playing with fire." The inferno washed into Ignis, adding to his essence until his height matched theirs. "You have to be careful you don't let it grow out of control."

Despite his calm facade, a firestorm of anger coursed through Ignis's veins, demanding to be unleashed.

Both ogres tossed away their makeshift weapons, speaking at the same time. "We surrender."

Ignis's voice escaped low and throaty like a snarling dragon. "What's wrong, don't want to pick on someone your own size?"

"We surrendered," One said. "You have to let us go."

"Why?"

They looked at one another.

Ignis unleashed all of his pent-up rage and frustration. He rode a wave of cold fire through the club. Thick, crystalized flame swallowed the ogres like hot cotton candy then filled room after room. When Ignis was certain all of the club's workers had fled to safety, he ignited the fibers. The club disintegrated in a firestorm.

Ignis strolled from pillar of flame, transmogrifying back to his mortal guise. He rolled his shoulders and dropped into the seat of his Camaro. "Anima? Did you try to summon me?"

Her voice escaped a slack-jawed bronze angel with a note of apprehension. "I did, but Shield Terrance has dealt with the incursion."

"Great. Can you order up a putti crew?"

Anima gasped.

"What? Is everything all right?" Ignis asked.

"Uh, yes. Of course, Shield Ignis, I just accessed a nearby traffic camera."

Ignis frowned at the still smoking ashes. "I may have lost my temper." He smiled. "But I'm feeling much better now."

"I'm glad?"

Ignis laughed. "If there's nothing else, I'm headed back to my apartment for a quick rest. I broke my hilt and had to use a lot of essence. I need to draw some from my nest."

"I sense your nest is full and still in your apartment."

"Of course, it is. Why wouldn't it be?" Ignis asked.

"Brownies assaulted headquarters. Shield Terrance slew most of them, but they got away with Vitae and Quayla's nests."

Cold flashed across Ignis's skin. "They stole our nests right out of headquarters? Why didn't you tell me?"

"You seem in need of a break. Shield Terrance arrived here with haste, but not quite soon enough to stop them. He is addressing the problem."

"How did they get in?"

"Caelum's keycard. At first, I thought they'd been hired to clean once more, but I could not reach Caelum to ask after his death."

Ignis cranked the Camaro to life with a roar. "Have you heard from him since?"

"No, Shield Ignis, and I cannot sense him, Vitae or Quayla."

Ignis turned on his flashing dash light and siren, pulling into traffic with all the horses available. "They're all missing?"

"Shield Quayla is out of reach, but not missing."

"What does that mean?"

"She entered Faery with a mortal shield intent to rescue the woman who works at her florist shop from abduction."

Ignis cursed and took a hard turn, back wheels sliding on the street. "I'm on my way to Caelum's. Any idea where I can search to find Vitae?"

"Should you not check on your nest first?"

"You said it was where it's supposed to be, besides, nests can be rebuilt. I want to make sure Caelum is safe. Where is Terrance?"

"He's just left headquarters to verify his nest," Anima said. "It is no longer in my sight."

Ignis cursed harder, whipping around traffic. After too long, he pulled into the parking garage for Caelum's apartment. Rather than wait for the elevator, he took the stairs at a run. He didn't bother trying to catch his voice to call out for Caelum, instead wrapped his hand around Caelum's lock.

Small flames licked up the door from where the metal casing melted, but Ignis refused the flames any further growth. He shouldered the door open to find Caelum's apartment undisturbed.

"Caelum? Anima?"

A quick search turned up no Caelum and no nest. Unease edged into Ignis's awareness.

The whole shield had tried everything to find the culprit responsible and reclaim their eggs. They'd called in every marker and shaken down if not every tree, at least several forest's worth. He'd lost count of the number of Seelie and Unseelie he'd handed over to Vitae for interrogation, and they still had no answers.

Vitae...could he have...no, Anima said his nest was taken too.

On the heels of that assault, their nests had been stolen.

"The faeries aren't acting to spec anymore either. We're not seeing something."

Faeries aren't the only things not acting right. Where is Vitae? Quayla is out of convalescence. He should be in the tower.

Ignis resisted the urge to transmogrify and fly across the city to his nest. He took the Camaro, and while the trip wasn't as fast as the crow flies, it wasn't much slower either.

Firetrucks blocked off the block around his apartment building. He threw his inspector plaque in the Camaro window and sprinted over to the man-in-charge.

"Inspector? What are you doing here?"

"I live just there. What's your status?"

"Some sort of boiler explosion. We shut off the gas and evacuated the building. Guys are just going in now."

"How'd you get the call?" Ignis asked.

"Strangest thing. They called 911, but the operator wasn't able to trace the call at all, and yet he identified himself as C. Lee Knight. When the dispatcher thanked him, he told her he had the heart of a fire inspector."

Ignis's flames damped.

"Inspector? Anything wrong?"

"N-nothing's wrong. Just suddenly thought I'd left my keys in the car. Let me check real quick."

"No problems. I get to a fire and everything but fighting it goes right out of my head."

Ignis inclined his head and jogged back to the Camaro. It took a lot of will to keep the jog from becoming a run. He reached out to his seeds. Taint overwhelmed the nearest spots of his essence.

"Anima? Can you still sense my nest?"

"No, Shield Ignis. I sensed an incursion in the basement of your building, taint flooded your nest and now nothing."

Ignis cursed. "Apologies, Anima. Have you gotten in touch with the others?"

"Terrance's nest has been stolen and Quayla called Summuseraphi for a rewrite of her mortals. Both are headed to headquarters."

"What about Vitae?"

"No contact yet."

Ignis growled. He weighed waiting to inspect his apartment versus joining the others at headquarters. Like it or not, the loss of his nest seemed a certainty. He returned to the man-in-charge.

"What's the word?"

"More strangeness, inspector. The boiler which blew wasn't connected to any gas lines, but it was connected to your apartment."

Ignis feigned shock. "What? How?"

"They haven't come back out with the film."

Ignis cursed inwardly. He'd only stayed to gather another hilt. "Any chance I can go inside and see for myself?"

"Sorry, no can-do inspector. We're checking the boiler for explosive residue and the local authorities are inbound. They'll probably want to talk to you."

"Makes sense. I'll wait by my car."

The man-in-charge seemed about to object when one of the firefighters that had gone in rushed up to him. "Sir, we just found another explosive on the second boiler."

Not going to get a better chance than this. So much for Ignis Kite, fire inspector.

Chapter Nineteen

Sinking in Quicksand

Caelum

Caelum's body struggled to reform. He could feel the new body, feel the essence in his nest, but the tornado that should've blown him back together remained only a light breeze.

Panic filled his soul-self.

Is this my egg? Is it too far away? Must be. I'm going to die for real.

He threw all his will into reforming. If he was going to face True Death, it wouldn't be with callous humor and a paltry effort. He would rage against anything that tried to separate him from the Undying Light.

His body assembled with agonizing slowness.

Silence struck him first, broken only by a faint hiss of air. The lack of scent struck next. His nose had always been more sensitive than the others, the air whispering things to him that the others couldn't hear.

Bright light blinded him, but not the Light of Vilicangelus or any other divine phoenix. Ridges dug into his feet.

He looked down. Golden hair fell across his face. He pushed it aside and shuffled backward to see beyond firm breasts and tones thighs.

His head knocked against glass with a dull ring.

Eyes flashed around at a double-layered bell jar encasing him like he was an enchanted rose. A mechanical arm of some sort stretched from atop his cylinder into a ceiling covered by a wide circle of runes and sigils. Below him, stair-stepped stone depressions descended like a Minecraft funnel to a small hole with some kind of valve that let in his essence in tiny amounts.

"Well, well, Caelum," Dunham's deep voice carried amusement and delight. "You're going to need a new security badge photo."

Caelum held his temper. Wild as the wind might be, too many things were wrong to rush. He gave his body another passing glance. His last body had been only a little taller and slightly less feminine. Caelum had worn more sultry bodies—particularly the voluptuous Asian beauty or the flame-tressed, thick, but pale-bodied Caucasian of Celtic stock that Shelby had loved.

He looked up through the double glass into Dunham's face. "Not bad, Caelum, but you needn't worry—men aren't that picky."

Roaring wind coursed through Caelum's veins, thundering in his ears. The insults didn't trouble him. All shields wore angelic beauty. Dunham's betrayal lit temper like lightning the skies. He took a calming breath which took too long because of the thin air in the chamber.

Dunham knocked on the glass. "Vacuum chamber. Nobody's used these stones in a very long time. I couldn't take the chance any of you would escape if the spell translations weren't right."

Caelum whirled, searching for the others. It hit Caelum like a winter zephyr. The light reflecting off the glass walls of his cage made it harder to see, but he recognized the standing stone at his back and the stone disk beneath his feet.

He crouched, running fingers along the glass parting him

from glowing runes. A toe of stone jutted out of the base stone under his bell jar.

I'm on one of the shoes.

The rest of Caelum's surroundings were foreign, but the walls, floors and ceilings matched those in Dunham's office. A pool table crowded one wall of a living area—unplayable shoved up against a wall.

These are the upper floors. Dunham's private chambers.

"I was concerned that your knowledge of history would clue you in to their purpose too soon, but they didn't."

"What do you want Dunham?" Caelum's voice pitched into the alto ranges.

At least it isn't any higher. Faeries don't respect orders being shouted by a helium-voiced woman.

Dunham bent, withdrawing a large ovum of yellow topaz and celestial silver. He held it up for Caelum to examine, his brows flicking up and down. When Caelum remained silent, Dunham blew a soft wind that sent gooseflesh running up and down Caelum's new body.

"These eggs are truly magnificent. Normally, I'd display such a treasure, but these might be too much for a thief to resist."

"Takes one to know one," Caelum seethed under his breath.

"What? I didn't hear you."

"Nothing."

A titan's hand squeezed Caelum. Cracking bones sent pain up and down Caelum's body, but his squeezed lungs couldn't draw in enough breath to scream.

"Did you know, that beyond their life-saving qualities, these eggs serve other purposes with the right spells?" Dunham bent, pushing the egg into the stone's toe socket.

The first time Caelum had examined the standing stones and their bases, the large empty socket hadn't seemed very large—certainly not large enough to fit Caelum's egg. The stone opened wide like a toddler trying to stuff too big a bite into their mouth.

As the stone closed around Caelum's egg, it felt as if a strait jacket closed around his entire body.

"You've got our eggs, no wonder we couldn't find them among the faerie," Caelum squeaked. He put more force behind his voice. "How did you stage the attack to make it look like they assaulted us?"

"Easy, I hired them to assault you."

"How do you even know about them, much less contact them?" Caelum asked. "Most Fae Kissed have an actual soul to exchange for power."

"You might be surprised."

"What do you want?"

"Oh, well, considering our long working relationship, I should tell you—nothing. Do I look like some cartoon villain to you? Have you no respect for me at all?"

"Less than I had this morning."

"I understand. A lot of your paradigms have changed in a short period. It will take time for you to adjust." Dunham smiled, stepping to the next stone base. He bent to work on something Dunham's body obstructed.

The cage around the next stone looked nothing like Caelum's own. Fine lines of string or glass ran top bottom just inside a thin plastic cylinder. Nothing about the cage looked particularly sturdy.

After a few moments, Dunham looked up. "For your Vitae. I know, it doesn't look that tough—particularly to hold a phoenix that can become liquid, but don't forget the magic holding you in —besides, these filaments are assembled from graphene nanotube and transport some of the nastiest poisons and weaponized pathogens I could buy."

Caelum squeezed his essence, using it to magnify the strings. None of them looked so much as damp, but up close they were a series of oblong and spherical shapes.

"The toxins travel through via capillary action. They stay

inside as long as the chains remain aligned, but," Dunham pushed on the thin plastic until it bent one of the strings.

Liquid oozed from all but invisible joints in the chain.

"Now, if I were you, I'd turn your attention to that small pressure bottle on the side there. I've already used a lot of your essence, and we wouldn't want your nest to be lacking the next time you die."

"I'm in a cage."

"For now, but while I won't fill you in on the plan, I can tell you that you and your shield brethren will be in a real danger." Dunham stood and met Caelum's eye with a gaze as cold as the ocean floor. "If any of you end up in your eggs, I'll shatter them."

Dread pressed down on Caelum. His eyes flicked down to find Dunham's toe pressing down on the jeweled egg.

"You're well aware of my zero-tolerance policy. True Death for failure seems zero tolerance to me." Dunham returned to the base of Vitae's future cage. "Best get started."

Caelum stared.

He'd liked, even admired Dunham. The mortal was smart, careful, and thorough. Caelum's gaze shot to the trap Dunham prepared for Vitae and then his own.

Too thorough. Vacuum for me. Fast-acting toxins for a life phoenix.

Caelum turned his back on Dunham. The nearest cage on the other side was a dark material Caelum didn't recognize with a top to bottom slider in place blocking who knew what. Without any clue as to its particulars, he tried to glimpse any changes made to the center stone.

The pentagonal stone hadn't been walled off, but glowing lines stretched out in an attempt to form a pentagram. Light seemed brightest from the two lines reaching out from where the base of Vitae's standing stone fit against the central stone.

Caelum couldn't bend enough to see the lines connecting to his own stone, but two other paired lines glowed brighter and brighter as they neared a gleaming intersection just under the back of the standing stones. Just above the intersection point, runes ascended the standing stone's back face. One set of runes glowed brighter than the others whereas one line above a dark intersection failed to glow at all.

He's using our essence to power some kind of summoning circle.

Caelum's cage wasn't comfortable, but Vitae wouldn't be in any immediate danger of poisoning himself once caught. The central stone stretched twice the diameter of the smaller stones.

Whatever he intends to summon is going to be huge if the stone's size is any judge, but the stone looks off, like it was cast in a mold made from pieces that didn't quite fit.

"Caelum, your work ethic is usually much better."

"You said you used my essence? For what?"

Dunham chuckled, crossing to a line of large packing crates. "Wild parties, various debaucheries, perhaps even some dead kittens."

"You're a real asshole," Caelum said.

"Just because I shared my good booze with you doesn't make us girlfriends," Dunham's voice hardened. "You phoenixes only have that 'sister' of yours to blame."

"What are you talking about?"

"Think about it while you gather essence for your next death."

"Something is wrong with one of your stones," Caelum said. "Bulb's burned out or something."

Dunham stopped what he was doing and closed to the other side of Caelum's cage. He dropped his voice enough it barely made it through the glass. "Stop fishing, Caelum. Fill that bottle. Now."

Bradley

Bradley wheeled another John Doe into the loading entrance of an old, condemned hotel. He leaned heavily against the gurney, using it to keep his tired legs under him. Goblins and something his master called grendlings—working in an obviously uneasy truce—lifted the gurney and headed for a rickety service elevator.

A gruff, slobbering grendling that reminded Bradley of the love child of Veruca Salt and Violet Beauregard shoved an empty gurney into his hands. "Move faster, wafer."

Wafer?

He froze, his mind circling the word in search of meaning. His stomach snarled.

God I'm hungry. When was the last time I ate?

Pain creased his face.

He looked down to find the ugly grendling perched on a box poised to strike him again. Excitement bubbled up inside Bradley. The creature in front of him was a faerie, an honest to god fantasy creature standing in Atlanta.

The grendling hit Bradley again. "Move!"

Bradley pushed the gurney toward the waiting ambulance. One hand reached up to his face, coming back covered in blood. Bradley stared at it, his tired mind trying to encompass the problem.

I'm bleeding. He hit me, broke the skin. I should bandage this. I have to stop the bleeding and add antibiotics to ensure there's no infection. God only...knows where...that...uh, faerie came from?

Bradley's pulse raced, grin widening to increase the pain in his cheek. He was surrounded by faeries.

"Wafer!"

Bradley whirled to look up at his sultry Master.

He's a she, shouldn't it be Mistress?

He bowed to one knee. It pleased her...him, and when he was pleased, pleasure seemed to wash through Bradley.

It's like an intense surge of dopamine shot—

"I am speaking to you."

"Yes, Mistress."

Vitae darkened.

Pain receptors throughout Bradley's body shrugged off the dopamine and fired off spikes of agony.

"Master, I meant Master."

"Better."

The pain faded and pleasure returned.

"How many more can you acquire?"

Bradley yawned and his stomach complained. "There is only one more waiting for pickup."

"They will wait, you have other things to do." Vitae strode toward the entrance, head high and a tantalizing sashay to his incredible ass. "Come with me."

Don't have to ask me twice.

Bradley giggled. He hadn't been this besotted since he'd latched eyes on that Dungeons & Dragons playing girl, Joanna, in the second Gamers movie.

Not that she was real exactly. Well the actress was, but not Joanna. Hell's I'm even babbling to myself. It's like I'm so exhausted I'm drunk.

Vitae strode out of the service areas into the hotel's old dining room. Motley construction crews of mixed faeries worked feverishly to repair the dilapidated room. If the gold and silver gilding and elaborate ornamentation emerging were any indication, his Master's throne room would be opulent in the extreme.

Bradley yawned.

They passed the mostly-finished throne to the main elevator bank. A hobgoblin in a bellhop uniform pushed open a rebuilt gate and gestured Vitae into the elevator.

Bradley trudged inside, stomach grumbling.

"Stop making those noises," Vitae snapped.

"Sorry, my lord."

"Your whole species is sorry," Vitae said.

The hobgoblin smirked, pushed the gate closed, took hold of the elevator control lever and wheeled it forward into the descend position. The car stuttered downward.

Oh my god, a hobgoblin is lowering us to a secret lab! My, no, Master's lab.

"How long will my first batch of enforcers take?" Vitae asked.

"I'm not sure," Bradley said. "Whiskers took several hours, but she had originally seemed geriatric. Still, a human body has quite a bit more mass for the troll marrow to regenerate."

"I need them immediately," Vitae said. "There's a war on. My domain must be secured before we conquer our enemies."

The old-style laundry was the only fully-rebuilt room outside Vitae's suites. Bright fluorescents reflected off of white tiles and shiny medical equipment. A lot of the equipment he'd procured himself, but once he'd collected a full set, the faeries had been sent out to acquire duplicates.

To Bradley's left, goblins and grendlings fought corpses into refrigerated drawers. At the far end of the room, security doors separated the lab from rooms Vitae forbad everyone to enter.

"I want your first batch ready by—"

"B-batch?" Bradley's squeak turned into a yawn. "With respect, my lord, I haven't tried this on humans yet. I should start with one, and—"

"You will start with five."

"Whiskers didn't exactly follow my orders. Sure, she was a cat, but I have no idea how well controlled human-troll hybrids will be. If something goes wrong, I might not be able to control—"

"Silence, wafer!"

Bradley's lips clamped shut.

"I cannot take any more of your sniveling," Vitae glowered.

Pain shot through Bradley. The emptiness in his stomach intensified the constant ache to something Jurassic. His limbs folded, collapsing him to the floor. He'd only been trying to explain the dangers involved, trying to protect his master from untested and unforeseen consequences.

"Control will not be a problem. Remain here."

Obeying Vitae eased off the pain. The pleasure crept back in to overlay it as Bradley stayed where he'd fallen.

Dopamine is known to create addictive side effects, and repeated exposure to dopamine in these doses is likely to force my body to build tolerances. How much longer before my world is only pain and not-pain?

Vitae returned carrying a tray of blood packs. The sight of him spiked the dopamine in Bradley's system and all that mattered was how much Bradley adored his master.

"Introduce this essence compound into the bloodstream as you animate my enforcers. They will obey without question." Vitae's nose wrinkled. "I included a small amount of your essence so you may command them in my stead so I needn't waste any more of my valuable time on such trifles."

"What do I do when this runs out?" Bradley asked.

"I will prepare more as the ingredients become available. This should suffice for your first batch. Now, get to work."

Chapter Twenty

Shared Intel

Quayla

I trudged into the sanctum. Its destruction registered somewhere in the back of my mind, but I lacked the energy to care.

"You did the right thing," Anima said.

I nodded, picking my way up shattered stairs.

A flash of light blinded me on the first landing. Power washed over me—fire and life, lightning and ice, mixed in a warm blanket of what I could only name palpable love. Arms followed the power and then wings.

The embrace echoed the moment of my birth, the hands that had lifted me from the shell fragments and cradled my first vulnerable moments in Creation.

Anima whispered into my ear. "You're not alone, Quayla."

I eased back from the embrace. Just as fast as I'd been wrapped in the strange power, it vanished, but in that last moment I'd glimpsed Anima once more.

Every eye on every part of her body was crying.

Dread rose with every step. I stopped at the landing, eye locked on my bedroom. I crossed to my door. There weren't any good reasons for Summus or Anima to lie about my nest going missing, but after all the work I'd done to refill it, I had to see for myself.

The door to my room hadn't been locked, but the faeries had torn it from the frame anyway. I picked my way through the refuse and stared at the place I'd killed myself to save Vitae.

I failed that too.

The Lady had warned me that someone who wanted me dead had stolen my nest. A quiet sound rose in my ears—a gentle river hastening toward a towering waterfall.

"Quayla?" Anima said. "They're waiting for you in the garden."

All that work. All my sacrifice.

"Shield Quayla?"

"I'll be right there."

We'd tried to find the faeries responsible for stealing our eggs. Ignis, Terrance, and even Vitae had searched and questioned and fought for those answers. The egg's value to a mortal would dwarf a king's ransom, but with faeries I'd been unable to discern a motive.

Taking the nests made even less sense.

It was insult atop injury.

I wasn't the reader Vitae was, but I'd learned enough to understand why the others couldn't replace their eggs. We could, however, simply construct new nests. *A Shieldheart's Guide to Nests* made replacing a nest sound like a tedious pain in the ass, and refilling a new nest would be worse, but losing our nests wasn't the crisis losing our eggs presented.

It's almost a good thing we haven't rebuilt my egg yet.

"Little Sister?" Terrance asked.

I turned to find both Terrance and Ignis in my doorway.

"Are you all right?" Ignis said. "Anima said you were crying."

"Yeah, sorry," I wiped away tears I hadn't realized had escaped. "The Lady told me, but I didn't want to believe her."

"What Lady?" Terrance asked.

Ignis extended a hand before I could answer. "Come along, we can discuss this in the garden."

I took his hand, happy for its warmth, and let him lead me into the garden. Sights and sounds in the greenhouse heartened me—probably as Ignis had known they would.

Summus slumped on the fountain's edge looking wan and pale. He flashed me a smile, lifting one hand high. "I'm fine, just need a short breather."

"Rest, Divine One," Terrance flashed me a smile. "Little sister is going to tell us a story."

"Where are Caelum and Vitae? Without my nest, we need to rebuild my egg."

"I cannot reach either of them," Anima said.

"Tell us about your Lady, little sister."

I took a deep breath and launched into my exploits, starting with the revelation of phoenixes to Detective Foxner and ending with the rewritten memories of every mortal I cared about.

Ignis's eyes focused on the middle distance, but he nodded grim-faced. Terrance looked old, launching into his encounter with the brownies and Yarque. Ignis's attention returned and he added his own encounters to the tale.

He included his encounter with Emma, eyes accusing me with every word. "Quayla's assertions proved correct. Emma accepted a Fae Kiss for the return of her cat. Originally, I thought she'd been innocent of anything but drawing the initial runes and a healthy case of denial. After she was cleansed, I found a work space used to add runes and faerie essence to animal collars. The runes weren't complete, so I am not sure of their purpose."

The revelation shocked me. I'd let Emma live, been convinced of her innocent ignorance. I almost couldn't face him, but I had to know. "The collars, could they have something to do with the abductions?"

"I found another runes collar in the remains of a battle ground. Different, but I think both are connected to your animal thefts." Ignis's voice hardened. "You should have destroyed her, Quayla. You never should have left a Fae Kissed alive and free."

Summus stiffened.

The world seemed to fall away beneath my feet. I'd tried to slay the sad little woman, but I hadn't been able to deliver the stroke. I'd even gone so far as to tell Ignis he didn't have to investigate.

But he did anyway, and he didn't fail in his duty.

"That choice isn't yours to make, Ignis," Summus said.

"She refused repeated offers for redemption. There was nothing left to do but slay her," Ignis said.

"You should've brought her to my attention so I could judge her," Summus said.

"Be at ease, Divine One," Terrance said. "What would you have done different? She was colluding with the Sidhe, doing their bidding. She couldn't be allowed to spread her knowledge of faeries or their offers."

"I know that," Summus snapped. "It still wasn't a choice for a shield to make without consulting us."

"I will not apologize for doing the right thing, Summuseraphi." Ignis folded his arms. "There was no reason to tax you emotionally or essence-wise when the solution was so obvious."

I barely dared utter my speculation. "I figured the cat was so old, it couldn't have lived much longer. I thought maybe after the thing died, Emma could've changed her mind. Repented and come back to the light."

"No, little sister. Even if she hadn't been crafting collars for the Sidhe, we couldn't have risked what someone she told might've chosen to do. I stand in accord with Ignis," Terrance inclined his head to Summus. "Neither you nor our Divine One have faced as many Fae Kissed as we have. We've seen how quickly a bad apple can spoil a bushel."

"Ignis still shouldn't have taken it on himself," Summus said.

"With respect," Anima said. "We have larger issues needing

your focus. I am unable to find Vitae or Caelum, The Isaac will need to prepare a new identity for Ignis, we don't know why your nests were stolen, and if Quayla's description of her encounter is accurate—meaning no suggestion that you fabricated any of it Shield Quayla—then one of the Dark Trinity may be behind much of the death and chaos spilling over into Atlanta's streets."

"Anima is correct," Terrance said. "Summus, can you locate our wayward shields?"

Summus went still. After a few moments, his head swung back and forth. "Caelum has not called for his Divine feather."

I swallowed. "Could he be in his egg?"

"Caelum died after entering the Goblin Market, and the brownies used his access card to invade our sanctum," Anima said.

I turned to the elder phoenixes. "Is there any way to tell if Caelum was reborn versus in the process of rehatching?"

"Not without his egg to examine," Ignis said. "Any luck locating Vitae, Summus?"

"None," Summus said.

"What about Vilicangelus? He and Vitae always seemed to share a connection."

"Vilicangelus was grievously injured," Summus said. "He cannot help in this case."

"You don't look to be in too good of shape either," I said. "You mentioned being low on essence?"

"Yes. Yours is not the only Shield I am watching, and the Sidhe war has increased the need for my attention ten-fold of what it should be."

"You need to recharge your essence," Terrance said.

"Yeah, but I haven't the time."

My thoughts flashed back to Summus's initial description of how he'd been elevated to Divine. "Terrance is right. You have to make resting a priority."

"I can't. I would be out of touch. There isn't anyone who could cover for me while I'm away."

"There are many Shields but few divine," Terrance said. "We will manage while you recuperate."

"I've only been Divine a little while. I can't just take a vacation."

"I think dying would be a worse sin," Ignis said. "We'll find the others and take care not to needlessly expose the truth to wafers."

"As is already your duty," Vitae strode into the garden, dark formal robes embroidered with crimson and gold replaced his suit.

"Where have you been?" Ignis demanded.

"Attending my duty," Vitae said. "Where is Caelum?"

"Missing," I said.

Vitae dismissed me with a look. "Anima, locate Caelum."

"Shield Quayla spoke true, Shieldheart."

His expression hardened. "I heard Shield Aquaylae, Anima, and I gave you an order."

I charged him, stopping just short of colliding nose to nose. "Leave her alone, Vitae. I already told you that Caelum is missing."

"*It,* not her," Vitae turned his back on me once more. "What news on the search for our eggs?"

I inhaled, a hint of taint underlying his spicy scent.

"We've already brought Summus up to date," Ignis said. "How about you inform the rest of us what you've accomplished?"

Vitae made a dismissive gesture. "My research hasn't yet born fruit, though it seems clear we must take the fight to the Sidhe, teach them our Shield is not their playground."

I lowered my voice. "Ani? Is something wrong with Vitae?"

Hurt undercut Anima's response. "There is a lot wrong with Vitae, Shield Quayla."

"Anima," Vitae scolded. "You will show the proper respect."

"Little sister?"

"Vitae doesn't smell right," I said.

"I got Sidhe blood on my robes." Vitae looked down his nose at me. "Since I've driven myself tirelessly in the search for our eggs, I haven't had time to give them proper laundering."

I frowned. "Where's the *Shieldheart's Guide to Nests*? It's not in the library."

Vitae hesitated. "Were you not the last to take it from the shelves?"

"You removed it from the sanctum, Vitae," Anima said.

"If that's so, I must have left it in the car. What do you need to know, perhaps I can answer your question," Vitae said.

"We need to make new nests to replace those that were stolen," Terrance said.

"Including yours," Ignis added.

"So, we need the rune diagrams for nest dominance," I said.

"Anima, please display the necessary runes," Vitae said.

"I cannot display that information within the greenhouse."

Vitae whirled toward me, face contorted. "What the hell did we hire your wafer for then? Get him back in here to finish the job."

I held myself still lest my grief show. "He's been rewritten. He won't be of any further assistance."

A smugness replaced Vitae's anger. "Good for you."

"But you still need to modernize this Shield," Summus said.

Vitae whirled, a rejoinder on his lips. A neutral mask fell over his features as he inclined his head. "As you direct, Divine One."

"We will need the guide, Vitae," Terrance said. "DragonCon began yesterday and as of now any death will send us into an egg."

"Except for me," I said.

"We will not let you suffer True Death," Ignis said.

"Exactly why I shouldn't go off to recuperate," Summus said.

Terrance scowled at Summus. "We can build new nests without you. You need to rest for when we or your other Shields have need of what only you can do."

Summus nodded at the floor. "To be gone as short a time as

possible, I'm going to have to try a deep slumber. I won't be reachable until I'm done."

"We will endure until you are fit to perform your duties, Praefectus," Vitae said.

Was that meant to be condescending? Us, sure, but would Vitae really treat a Divine One with open disdain?

Summus stiffened.

He heard it too.

Our Praefectus gave Vitae a hard look before vanishing in a flash of light.

Summuseraphi

Summus stood in Atlanta's Sanctum hidden behind a veil of light. He was exhausted, but he couldn't shed the feeling that Atlanta's Shieldheart was the heart of the Shield's internal troubles.

He drew on his essence, concentrating his core much as he had transmogrifying as a water phoenix. He pictured his mentor.

"Vilicangelus, Vilicangelus, Vilicangelus."

Summus clapped his hands together.

Light sped around him, streaking by as if he were driving through a blizzard.

The sound of Summus's clap faded.

He appeared in a vast hall. Ancient, glowing columns illuminated the room. A choir filled the background with dulcet harmony. Light and music enervated Summus.

Vilicangelus sat slumped over in a Roman-style u-shape chair. A jagged scar throbbed across Vilicangelus's breast. Burns charred his right arm, side and the stump of his leg.

He looked up, golden hair falling away to display a face burned almost to the bone.

Summus fell to the floor at Vilicangelus's feet. "Dearest Creator, I'm...I knew..."

<Be at peace, Summus, I will heal with time.>

Summus looked into Vilicangelus's one golden and one melted eye. He concentrated. *You cannot speak?*

Vilicangelus shook his head. *<You may speak if you prefer. What brings you here?>*

"Things are worse. I can barely keep up with the Shields you entrusted to me, and then there's Vitae—um, that is, Atlanta's—"

<I know which Vitae you mean. I would've known even if you hadn't projected the images in your mind along with your thoughts.>

"Is there anyone who can help oversee your old territory while I recover?"

Vilicangelus shook his head. *<No, Summus, we've lost three more Divine Ones.>*

"Totally lost? As in they had no chance to elevate anyone?"

<Destroyed. Their energies wiped from Creation or stolen outright.>

"How? Why?"

<The Dark Trinity are furious. This war of theirs isn't the game it was last time, not after Vitae slew Dolumii and Gherrian in Faery.>

"I know Vusolaryn and Mariena are powerful faeries, but—"

<No, Summus, I'm not talking about a prince or princess. The Lady of Fire herself nearly slew me.>

And the Lady of Water trapped Quayla.

Summus fell backward off his haunches. Righteous anger blossomed into a bonfire. "Vitae caused all this? Should I seek a replacement?"

<You must recuperate your strength.>

"What about Atlanta?"

<Trust Ignis and Terrance. They will keep the Shield together.>

"What about Quayla? They're all under a lot of pressure."

Vilicangelus smirked. *<You know the nice thing about water? No matter how much pressure you put water under, it's nearly impossible for anything to crush it.>*

Quayla

"That was rude, Vitae," Anima said. "You should not speak to Summuseraphi in that manner."

Vitae darkened. "Silence, automata. Shields are speaking."

I rounded on Vitae, shoving him backward to the edge of the fountain. "Ani is as much a part of this Shield as you are."

Vitae's eyes flashed dangerously, hands sweeping back his robes to reveal the two confiscated Champion blades.

Ignis and Terrence stepped between Vitae and me. I couldn't see their expressions, but their bodies held taut, fighting stances.

Terrance's deep voice filled the greenhouse. "It seems obvious that we are all so exhausted that we've forgotten both manners and that we are a family."

"Vitae's the one treating everyone like garbage," I said.

Vitae's light, liquid tone carried real menace beneath the silk. "You are lucky they intervened, Aquaylae, before you forced me to discipline you."

"Bring it on!" I extruded blades into the karambit in each hand. "I've faced down one of the Dark Trinity, you don't scare me."

"Quayla, that's enough," Ignis put his back to Terrance and Vitae. "We're all under a lot of strain, but we need to act in concert to overcome this threat."

"Don't tell me you aren't angry, Ignis. I can see it in your eyes."

"No doubt he is fed up with your tantrums," Vitae said.

Terrance's low growl mimicked an avalanche. "You will restrain your tongue, Shieldheart."

Tension ratchetted up. My hands tightened around both hilts. The others stiffened.

I readied myself for a defensive but decisive assault. Taint flooded my senses. The world spun. My hilts tumbled from my grip, essence shrinking back into me in response to a sudden wash of terror.

"We have a major incursion inside the Atlanta Marriott Marquis," Anima said. "The Isaac is sending over video feed."

Ignis stabilized me, holding me as I retrieved my hilts, He helped me into the command center.

Interior and exterior views filled the small room. Cosplaying wafers ran from a sudden forest of green spreading out of the hotel's entrances. A massive, humanoid tangle of kudzu towered at least ten stories from foot to thorn-crowned head. Forty feet of leafy arm swept across a balcony, sending wafers screaming through shattered railings.

Last in the room, no one barred my way when I spun and raced toward the sanctum's balcony, gathering essence as I ran.

"Stop!" Vitae commanded.

My limbs hesitated. I whirled around, rapids racing through my veins and a waterfall roaring in my ears. "What?"

"You mustn't expose us," Vitae said. "Even you must've grasped that by now."

I pointed at the monitor. "Cat's out of the bag, Vitae. People are dying. We'll worry about collateral damage once they're safe."

Vitae yanked his cigarette case from his robes. "I've enough of self-important children."

He withdrew a glowing white feather. "Vilicangelus. Vili—"

"Vilicangelus was injured," Ignis snapped. "We're all out of Divine backup, so check your ego, because Quayla's right."

Vitae shook his head. "Vilicangelus."

Terrance slapped the feather from the life phoenix's hands. "You are right about one thing, Vitae. We have had enough of self-important children."

Vitae opened his mouth, but Terrance's massive hand collided with his face. "Quayla is charging to rescue mortals without a nest or an egg, like Mare, so you will close your mouth, join with this team and do your duty, or by the Undying Light I'll put you in your egg to think about it for a century."

I didn't wait for them to settle things. I bolted outside and threw myself from the building's top. Essence exploded from the tiny star I held under pressure, rippling outward in tingling waves to form my wide wings and luxurious tail.

The exhilaration of falling, then diving through the sky like a peregrine pouncing on prey electrified me. Despite the pleasure of flight distracting me from the very real chance of dying a True Death, I adjusted pinions to sweep me back toward the clouds and climbed higher into the sky.

Had it been night, I might have worried more about the luminescence of my true form showing up against a dark sky. The sunshiny day would hide me better above the buildings, quite a bit better than blue sky would hide Ignis.

I threw energy into speeding my flight.

Saturday boasted the highest concentration of DragonCon attendees. Instead of taking advantage of the power boost from countless people inadvertently honoring them, the Sidhe were using that strength to openly attack the mortals.

They had to be stopped.

Before everything I sacrificed was for naught.

Chapter Twenty-One

Tangled Fates

Quayla

Hundreds of attendees surrounded the chaos pouring out of the Marriott. Most kept to a relatively safe gawking distance and many of them held cameras up to capture the event. Vines writhed out of the hotel's every opening, expanding onto the streets. Mortals struggled to escape their leafy captor, helped by cosplayers hacking the vines with formerly peace-tied swords.

Police cars screamed through the streets with their lights blazing, rushing to reinforce officers already working convention security. Firefighters joined the armed cosplayers, attacking the edges of the spreading foliage with axes or freeing people imprisoned in cars tangled in the spreading kudzu.

I circled high above.

The cat's definitely out of the bag. Still, no point making things worse. Think.

Not even Terrance could bull his way through the impenetrable wall of southern foliage. Whatever the faeries intended, they'd blockade themselves inside in a way that prevented all of us entry—except maybe Ignis.

I can't wait. People are dying.

Curses sealed my doomed intentions of a stealthy approach. Wings folded and talons outstretched, I dove. Floors flashed by almost too fast to count. With closed eyes and a pivot of feathers, I juked my dive into the side of the hotel, smashing through floor to ceiling windows into someone's room.

I snapped open my wings, back-winging as hard as I could. A talon caught bedclothes and suitcases, adding further disarray to the shattered glass and chaotic assortment of food wrappers and costumes littering the room.

I hit the wall between living area and bathroom too hard, a talon punching a hole in the drywall and evoking a scream from someone inside the bathroom.

Pain lanced up and down broken legs.

Shattered wings burned.

Pain didn't matter.

Only mortal lives mattered.

I'm a shield of the Undying Light and my charges are endangered.

Pushing essence into a tight ball at my core, I gathered will and desire for another transmogrification. Instead of restoring my former clothes, I chose to follow Terrance's example with the help of *Primal Battle*. Employing essence to form a thick leather body-suit left me resembling a skinny looking woman from one of the comic books—I couldn't remember which.

A pale, shocked face watched me through the hole in the bathroom wall.

I cringed and offered a little wave. "Hi. Sorry about the mess."

The wafer's eyes rolled back into her head. She vanished from sight, followed by a heavy thunk. I disentangled myself and rushed for the room's exit, pulling my amulet from where it was squeezed by the leather bustier.

"Anima, if you can hear me, we're going to need a lot of putti."

I reached the balcony overlooking the atrium. I'd misjudged

my descent, piercing the hotel at least a dozen floors higher than intended.

"Nice of you to make us an entrance, little sister."

"Yeah," a dark chuckle escaped Ignis. "You might've let the shield best designed as a battering ram handle that."

"I was in a hurry," I whipped around. Vitae's absence didn't surprise me. The sight of Ignis and the armored Terrance in winged human shapes left me gaping.

I thought only divine could do that.

Ignis smirked. "Nice outfit, by the way."

"How do we handle this?" I asked.

"I'll give the construct heart burn, Terrance will pull the weeds out by their roots and you can help by trimming the hedge when you're not too busy getting people clear."

"That plan sounds suspiciously formed to keep me from fighting. I'm a full shield, same as you guys."

"No one ever said you weren't, little sister, but you don't have two millennia of battle experience."

"Besides, the plan was formed to limit your risk," Ignis said. "You don't know if your stolen nest has any essence in it and we never got a chance to reform your egg."

Terrance laughed. "That's Ignis's dispassionate way of saying we love you and want you to stick around. You'd think a fire phoenix would have a little more personality."

"Some of us can rise above maternal tendencies, Mother Terra."

Desperate shrieks punctuated their banter. Ignis and Terrance threw themselves into the atrium's airspace.

So much for not drawing more attention.

I dove off too, transmogrifying once in the air. I tightened my essence into a compact star, preparing to transform back when a wall of vines slammed into me.

The blow sent me tumbling through an opening in an already-broken railing. Impact dazed me, causing me to slide down onto several supine bodies. Several blinks dismissed my disorientation so I could check the wafers. I cut a shirt away from an unconscious woman, wrapping the words 'Don't Panic' around another woman's head wound. I hurriedly moved them deeper into the hotel away from the kudzu elemental.

Where is Vitae when we need a life phoenix?

I did a quick circuit of the level, bandaging and moving injured further from harm's way.

Beyond the railing, Ignis fought like nothing I'd ever imagined. He shot through the kudzu creature like he was rocket-propelled. Wings one part inferno and a second part scythe sliced through the beast like Dylan's beloved lightsabers.

A wild blow missed Ignis by feathers. The flailing vines careened through a railing several stories above me. They impacted a costumed woman filming with her phone, hurling her into open air.

I dove, transmogrifying with less thought than it had ever taken before. I impacted the woman with bone-jarring force. We crashed down a debris-strewn hallway branching off from the balcony. I flipped beneath her as we bounced, cushioning her as best as I could.

A quick check confirmed the woman alive, unconscious and in serious need of paramedics. I pried the phone from her death grip and rammed a karambit blade through it.

Stupid wafer.

I hurried to rejoin the fight. The level—in easy reach of the beast—had been decimated, but debris and bodies had been mostly swept away.

A leafy fist rocketed toward me.

I dove sidelong, shifting to liquid to speed my slide before kicking off a door frame and shooting back the way I'd come. Karambit blades hacked away vines as fast as I could swing them.

The elemental's other hand slapped me against the first.

I bounced off one arm and against a wall. Vines unraveled from both beastly limbs and writhed around me. Grabbing my arms and legs, they forced me to strain against their impromptu drawing and halving.

Fire exploded the wrist holding my legs a moment before Ignis swept a flaming blade through the plant monster's opposite elbow.

The tension on my body fell away, but despite losing attachment to the rest of the creature, the vines snaked their way over me in an extremely convincing python imitation.

This thing is as bad as real kudzu. Leave even a little bit behind and it grows back twice as bad.

My karambit knives quickly proved insufficient for defense against the fierce flora. I transmogrified once more. The vines took a moment to adapt to my change in form. I leapt from their grasp, snapping open my wings and sweeping them down for a little extra height.

Rather than flee, I started a spin. Feathers fell from my wings and my body, orbiting me in glistening shades of sapphire. Unlike at the humane society, there was nothing living visible in the immediate area except the monster.

Feathers lost their form, their liquid joining with neighbors into a long spiral of water like a ribbon trailing from a spinning ballerina's fingers.

The severed vines reached up for me, climbing up a level and trying to encircle me for another attack.

I let them, hardening my will and spinning faster.

The vines closed the sphere.

I released the ribbon of razor-sharp water.

Shredded kudzu tumbled to the atrium floor as my spiral blade hacked into the main beast. Ignis drove his flaming blade into the incision I'd made, foliage wilting, shriveling and combusting near the blazing winged man.

I perched on a section of undamaged railing for a quick breath.

"This damned thing smells of you and Terrance," Ignis shouted on a close flyby.

Far below, it was hard to tell whether the monster or Terrance was doing the most damage. Both were getting as well as they were giving.

He needs help.

I glanced at Ignis.

Both of my elders fought like they wielded the fury of the Undying Light Himself. The full fury of their elemental wrath was terrifying and magnificent at the same time, but Ignis fared better by the sole virtue of his element.

I scanned for more mortals. The higher levels of the atrium were ringed with video-recording bystanders. A scream turned my attention to the floors below.

The plant elemental stumbled backward against one side of the atrium, a foot coming down through several floors.

Vitae stood in the hotel entrance surrounded by dying foliage. Vines writhed toward him from every angle only to shrivel away the moment they touched him. He held a Sidhe Champion blade in each hand, swinging them in a whirling pattern that made the blades scream as he tore into the kudzu elemental's nearest leg.

Vines whipped out from the leg, trying to wrap Vitae as they had me. The more vines touched him and shriveled away, the more Vitae's aura intensified.

His voice filled the atrium. "I command you in the name of the Undying Light to kneel, beast!"

Kneel?

The monster actually hesitated.

"Aquaylae," Terrance pointed. "Help those mortals."

I threw myself from my perch, eyes scouring the areas where the monster had crashed through more of the hotel. Sure enough, a woman in a Poison Ivy costume covered a cowering child, her skin pale and covered with blood the color of her hair.

I pivoted, turning sideways to slip between the monster's legs toward the fearful mortals.

The creature brought its legs together as the smoldering

stump of a new arm smashed down to ram me against their quickly-woven-together shins.

I threw my talons forward, reversing my wings so that their thinnest edges faced the elemental. I focused on the lead feathers like I had the ribbon, thinning them to an edge and trusting momentum to take me through the impromptu thicket.

I did everything perfectly—except notice the broken furniture the creature had gathered up as a makeshift spiked fortification just beyond its legs.

"Aquaylae!" Terrance careened into me, knocking my flight path askew as his flight rebounded down the same target path I'd intended. His bulk smashed through foliage, obsidian and iron tearing vines from his way. Even armored with granite, the force of his impact drove pieces of the barricade through his armor.

Terrance!

I changed flight paths, heading to his aid.

"See to the wafers!" Vitae commanded.

A life phoenix was far better equipped to help Terrance than I was. I hesitated for only a moment before leaving Terrance to Vitae's care.

Magic washed through the atrium like a tidal wave dumped down a well. I executed a barrel roll in time to see water falling from firehoses on a dozen levels form a fist.

I changed back as I landed, skidding to a stop only a few paces from the woman and child. My gaze shot up toward Ignis. His flaming blade sizzled a channel in the humongous water hand.

I exhaled a breath I hadn't realized I was holding.

At the last moment, tendrils snapped out from both water hemispheres, seized each other and slammed the sphere of water together around Ignis.

Lightning hit the sphere. The sky fire slammed Ignis's cage once, twice and again.

I launched myself airborne, reaching for the water encasing, and potentially drowning, Ignis. Taint filled me and nausea filled my stomach with barb maggots. I flew as hard as I could, reaching out to the water like I would my essence.

Foul water left sitting too long in the lines resisted my grip, but I refused to give up. None of us knew where the nests had gone. We had no idea if the nests still contained essence and even less idea whether or not the eggs remained to catch Ignis's spirit.

I'd left Terrance to Vitae, but someone had to help Ignis.

My grip solidified.

I wrenched the water away from him, drawing it—foul and tainted—into myself.

Another lightning strike thundered through the confined space. Without the watery sphere in its path, the bolt struck Ignis head on.

Ignis!

A kudzu fist met me midair. I hit the ground, bones shattering. Consciousness wavered, held back only by excruciating pain. I claimed the pain, and bent it to my will.

Pain is life.

I focused on my essence, forcing it into a star blazing at my core as brightly as the agony burned in my body and the sorrow that pierced my heart.

I transmogrified, climbed to my feet and faced the plant monster with trashcan-sized spheres of foul water at either hand.

"See to the injured wafer," Vitae said. "I can handle this beast."

"You take care of Ignis and Terrance," I ground my teeth. "This fucking thing is mine."

Will turned the globes into floating whirlpools. They flattened and distended, both forming into two larger serrated versions of the s-shaped blades joined into a free spinning X.

Vitae's Seelie blade slammed into the side of my face hilt first. "I gave you an order, Aquaylae!"

I wiped blood from my cheek. I wanted very few things as much as to turn and slam a fist into Vitae's guts, but destroying the kudzu elemental trumped even that not so small satisfaction.

I turned my attention back to reforming my blades. A kudzu foot came down to stomp me.

The spinning food processor blades split from two to four and flashed a crisscross that shredded the leg as it came down.

"Do as you're told." Vitae struck me with the pummel of his Unseelie blade. Energy washed out of me into the sword.

I whipped around, catching his blade with my karambit. I drew in essence from every direction, summoning the little motes I seeded throughout downtown. I absorbed strength from every seed I could reach. Bladed cross guards grew out of my hilt's ring, protecting my hands with its razor edge.

The snarl tore its way from my throat. "Help Ignis and Terrance!"

"You will see to the wafers. They're what you really care about. I will defeat this beast alone and then see to Atlanta's real shields."

I could kill Vitae in half a beat of my hammering heart. The four blades awaiting my command needed their current mass to deal with the kudzu creature, but they had more than enough mass to become eight and mulch the arrogant jackass giving me orders.

Terrance is right. Like as not, we're family and now is not the time.

I turned my back on Vitae and threw my hands forward toward the quickly-recovering monster.

The hair along the base of my neck prickled.

"You will obey your betters!"

I spun, jerking to a sudden sideways halt as Vitae's two glowing swords thrust where my back had been only moments before.

My huge, whirling blades quartered Vitae with a thought. The two Champion blades resisted a few strikes before the repeated impact sent them flying. I let Vitae fall where he may and turned my blood-covered blades on the monster.

Every pass through the creature added to the blades' weight.

They flashed in and out of the foliage like they were dancing in a strobe light. Leaves and vines rained down around the atrium like the Creator had rung a gong sounding sudden fall.

I stood in the leafy rain, pulse still roaring rapids in my ears and every instinct tingling. I needed to check Ignis and Terrance. I needed to see to the injured mortals, but I didn't dare lower my guard until I knew we were safe.

Above, countless cameras watched my gleaming blades and feats of aquakinesis. Phones and their wielders had witnessed us at our best and our worst. The ramifications of our exposure, of the carnage and death, loomed like a Sword of Damocles that I didn't have time to fear.

When nothing moved for several moments, I looked for Ignis. I didn't immediately see him. I checked for Terrance. A pile of dark soil sloughed up against the remainder of the bloody, furniture barricade.

He died to protect me.

Tears brimmed my eyes.

I blinked them away and rushed toward the railing overlooking a lower floor near where I'd last seen Ignis. His hilt lay a level below, rolled into a seat crack of a chair next to a table covered in ashes.

I drew the silvered feather from my bodice and marched toward the woman and child. "Ani, please tell me you can sense the others."

"I saw them fall, but there is no sense of them," Anima said.

I bent next to the cowering woman. I checked the child first, finding no pulse in his neck.

If I'd been faster, I might've been in time to save him.

I cursed, easing around the child to check the woman's neck. Her strong pulse allowed me a relieved sigh. "How badly are you hurt?"

"I don't know," the woman said.

"Let me move the boy and check you, all right?"

The woman's arm around the boy tightened.

"I'm sorry. He's gone." I lowered my voice. "Ani, can putti rewrite memories like they can buildings?"

"They cannot. I've contacted the Isaac, perhaps he can reach someone who can help contain this."

Loud, slow claps echoed behind me. I lifted my head to find Dunham standing in the middle of the atrium. He wasn't dressed in a business suit like I'd have expected. Instead, he was garbed in knee-length trousers, a long vest and a bandolier of colorful vials out of some medieval reenactment. Celtic markings covered almost all of his skin, the runes pulsing with a steady glow.

"You are truly impressive, Quayla," Dunham stopped well out of reach, lowering his hands to his sides. "Not that you beat my elemental. There just wasn't any point continuing when I'd already met all my goals. If I were honest, I'd have to admit that I expected you to run...that's what cowards do after all."

"You're behind all this? You work for the Lady?"

Dunham's smile grew wider. "Well, they say the faerie are treacherous in all their dealings. It seems that truism covers their most as well as their least. I'll deal with that later, but first I must thank you."

I tensed, pushing essence into my karambit in preparation to whip the blade toward him. "Why thank me?"

"It's a long list, but I think I'll start with your killing the Vitae. I've never heard of a phoenix with such powers. He was about to foil this whole trap."

"I don't know what powers you traded for your soul, but there's still a phoenix alive on this battlefield," I scanned the glowing marks and other tattoos, "druid."

He showed his teeth. "True, a water phoenix, a bleeding heart disgraced by her own cowardice and therefore moved to compensate by helping mortals."

"I'm a shield of the Undying Light," I said. "I care for all Creation. That doesn't make me a bleeding heart."

"This does," the injured woman jerked a knife out from under the dead boy and shoved it into my chest.

Chapter Twenty-Two

Painfully Desperate

Quayla

My body reformed with agonizing slowness. Killing myself to protect the Shield Sanctum when I hadn't been sure enough essence remained for rebirth had been hard. The struggle vexing my body as it tried to form felt a thousand times worse.

My essence stabilized.

I opened my eyes to find myself in a cramped glass container of some kind. Another similar container loomed to my left. A viscus liquid swirled between the thick outer layer and a dark inner layer of unknown thickness. An odd birdcage-shaped beaded curtain stood to my right and beyond it a glass bell jar containing a shapely blond woman. Instinct told me the unknown woman had to be Caelum.

"Caelum?"

The woman didn't respond.

I pounded on the glass. "Caelum?"

The cage around me was too short to afford me jumping up and down room, so I waved large, manly hands back and forth. A glance confirmed my chest covered by fine auburn curls rather than breasts and a matching collection of hair around my penis.

I crouched to examine the basin beneath my feet. A small rubber diaphragm capped the bottom of a squared, stone funnel. Runes glowed around me and my cage, emanating the same feel as the magic that had electrocuted Ignis.

Knowing Dunham had prepared the trap, it took me only a moment to recognize the standing stones I'd ogled in his office. A center stone had been placed between them on the opposite side of the standing stones from the basin beneath my feet.

A glowing pentagram of scintillating energy crisscrossed the center stone, points of its star at the back of each standing stone.

Essence?

I placed a hand near the diaphragm and extended my senses. Essence—my essence—lurked just beneath my feet.

Then why was rebirth so difficult?

The diaphragm seemed the obvious culprit. I glanced at Caelum to see if he'd noticed me yet, noting a small jar. A quick check confirmed my cage included one as well, though mine had a funnel attachment while Caelum's had some kind of valve.

Dunham's going to milk us for our essence?

I scanned the room beyond my glass enclosure. Mechanical arms served the obvious purpose of lifting my cage upward and probably the cages of the others. Markings surrounded the arrangement of stones, probably what blocked Anima from sensing Caelum and our nests.

I noted another stone not far away that matched the center stone. Glass beakers filled with glowing essence stood at the five corners of its pentagram, light brighter beneath them than anywhere else.

Druid magic too?

I turned back to face the center stone

If he's feeding that pentagram with essence, then these basins are somehow feeding the stone our essence while also allowing us to be reborn.

I looked up to find Caelum watching me. The air phoenix's

mouth moved, but I couldn't hear him. I pointed at my ear and shook my head.

Caelum deflated.

An idea played across his face. He squatted, holding a pantomime newspaper then rose, turned and depressed something. One hand twirled a finger in a wide spiral.

Ask to go to the bathroom?

Disgust wrinkled my face.

He wants me to pee?

Caelum hit a fist against his cage, not that I could hear the impact. He pointed at me and made a fist, then changed the fist to a horizontal hand making wave gestures before reorienting it vertical and making more rapid wave motions.

Rock, paper, fish? Fist, waves, wiggles?

Caelum seemed to recognize my confusion. He made the fist sign once more, then repositioned his body to look bulky. He followed by making waves, pointing to me, making squiggles and pointing to himself.

Earth, Water, and Air?

It hit me all at once. Caelum's charades represented the states of matter. When my expression cleared, he nodded and pointed down.

He wants me to turn into true liquid and go down the drain? If that would allow us escape, why hasn't he turned into gas and escaped already?

Caelum scanned the room before turning into a human built of essence like I had descending into the Lady's grotto. He bent, fingers trying to pry up something at the bottom of his basin. After a minute, he shrugged.

I frowned.

Why wouldn't he be able to open his diaphragm?

My eyes flashed to the valve I'd noticed on his small bottle.

Unless he has something different keeping him in.

I had turned my human body into water to help me under-water and to limit damage from bullet impacts. Outside of deforming my hands to escape Foxner's cuffs though, I'd never tried to be anything other than human or phoenix. Caelum was suggesting I somehow release all shape, become amorphous and escape down the drain.

Another idea occurred to me.

I transmogrified into water and formed a ribbon of water around me. With an effort of will, I rotated the ribbon faster and faster before pressing it against the glass of my cage.

I grinned and checked Caelum.

He rolled his eyes, head shaking back and forth as he held up his hands like they were pressed together in prayer. He parted them and sucked in a breath between them.

I frowned.

I wasn't sure what he was trying to tell me, but Caelum didn't seem to think I'd be able to cut my way free. I examined the basin.

I suppose it's possible.

Dunham had been downtown, but I had no way to tell when he would return.

Unless I ask Anima. I was reborn here, so this is my nest or at the very least my nest is under this basin.

I grabbed for the silvered feather, but it was gone. I tried the summoning chant, but the amulet didn't appear. I lowered myself to the basin, easing up the rubber diaphragm. "Anima?

No answer.

I glanced at Caelum.

He gestured for me to hurry.

I took in a deep breath and tried to relax. Being imprisoned after fighting for your life, killing your Vitae and being murdered proved a poor starting state for relaxation.

I need to loosen my hold on my shape like when I change between forms, then move like an inch worm where I can't just flow naturally.

I tried over and over, every moment ratchetting my tension that Dunham would return. He lived in the room where he'd caged us. Once he came home, there'd be no chance to escape until he left again.

The magic in the stone feels latent, like it's not active yet.

I compared the glow of my basin runes to Caelum's.

Definite difference.

I tried and failed again.

Maybe forget relaxing. I need to shape myself kind of like those creatures in that movie Dylan showed me—Abyss?

It took a few minutes of staring at my liquid finger to stretch it. A few minutes more and my index finger had become a sparkling licorice rope. I lifted the diaphragm with one hand and pushed my finger down into the basin. It encountered other essence almost immediately, but nowhere near as much as had been in my original nest.

Doesn't feel like enough for another rebirth either.

My finger felt its way through the mostly empty basin, eventually feeling its way to another small passage. The new passage felt rough against my—well, not skin, but skin. Rough stone scraped at my finger like jagged sandpaper as I pushed.

The tip stopped hurting, the scraping sensation falling away from more and more of my finger until the blue pseudopod appeared inside the circle of the center stone.

I glanced over to find Caelum's breasts bouncing up and down to his cheers. A kind of hybrid tingle and itch grew noticeable between my legs. I growled and forced my attention away, pushing more and more of my essence into the drain.

Damn new bodies and male wiring.

Pushing my essence through the rough passage was a long, torturous agony I'd have done anything but rewritten Dylan again to avoid. When all of me that had not been scraped away in the process stood inside the center stone, I mustered a tiny cheer and face planted against a magical barrier.

The sudden resistance knocked me onto my ass. All the effort, all the pain and I was still trapped. I wanted to cry, not overly concerned that people seeing my new body cry in public wouldn't approve.

Screw them.

I examined the center stone. Mismatched sections suggested concrete or similar had been poured into a mold of pieces that didn't quite match. I got as close as I could to the stone. It took forever to scrutinize every inch, but at last I found what water had sought down through the ages—a crack through which to flow.

Damn, this is going to hurt.

Hurt proved far too small a word.

Magic prevented me from opening Caelum's cage. Mechanical arms held Ignis's and Terrance's cages in place. I tried to access a console that seemed to control them, but couldn't bypass its security.

Every moment I remained increased the chances of being recaptured. My Shield needed me to rescue them.

Maybe Terrance will have an idea.

I circled the standing stones until I could see the face of a dark-skinned woman through a small transparent window in the swirling muck. The new Terrance smiled sadly, lifted his hands into my view, hooked his thumbs and flapped his fingers.

Fly away.

I cursed myself and fled.

Dunham

Dunham pushed through the doors to his office. Cleaning up the Atlanta Marriott Marquis and wafer memories had taken an eternity even with the army of faeries invested in the task. He'd been forced to trust some of the verification to Knight Dolumii and Knight Gherrian. Viviane assured him employing both on any task ensured success.

Their honor and their rivalry will force thoroughness.

A team of hackers in an Indian Circlestone office had purged the uploaded pictures and movies as they tried to go live. Having such a large staff waiting had been supremely expensive, but not as costly as paying out life insurance claims to the dependents of those same hackers that'd blown up with the building directly after.

Better to insure it all myself then have an insurance company I don't control running the investigation.

After so many decades waiting and sacrificing, planning and preparing, he'd done it. He'd made a Shield his own. Everything he'd strived for had finally fallen within arm's reach.

Now I will get my reckoning.

Viviane lounged in his chair with her feet on his desk.

He frowned, but didn't correct her. Their association came with certain benefits he was loathe to sacrifice over such a minor slight.

"I understand you had a *tête-à-tête* with our new water phoenix."

"And if I did?" she asked.

"That leads me to believe the loss of her egg was no accident."

"You have tunnel vision when it comes to Quayla. I assured you didn't waste an opportunity you worked so hard to achieve."

Dunham forced his voice to remain calm. "Was she meant to escape you?"

"Was she meant to escape you?" Viviane cocked her head.

Cold washed into him as if he were drowning in an icy lake. Her glib tone knotted his guts, but she'd been known to play with his emotions for her own amusement.

Either way, I have to be sure.

He pushed through the secret door into Viviane's office. The wall of retractable, soundproof doors gaped open, exposing her opulent apartments to view. Dunham turned aside, ascending a spiral stair two at a time.

The cages came into view. The air phoenix slept in a heap at the base of her bell jar.

Heat wavered the air around the view window in the cage built of hafnium carbide. The viewing glass and air capillaries twisted through layers of the heat resistant ceramic were the only weak points in his design—the glass was the only part susceptible to damage from temperatures over four thousand degrees Celsius.

The birdcage of toxin laden graphene nanotube stood empty as did the aquarium glass containment unit he'd designed to augment the magical barriers restraining the other phoenixes.

He whirled around. "How did the Vitae escape?"

A nonplus Viviane didn't even seem winded from the mad rush up to his chambers. "He never arrived."

"I saw her kill him."

Viviane shrugged. "No plan is perfect."

Dunham snapped up a nearby chair and hurled it at her.

She sidestepped without haste. "Temper, Dunham dear."

"I followed the grimoire's instructions to the letter. You swore that the stones were authentic and the containment spell matched one used successfully in the past."

"They were."

"I augmented the trap with custom cages designed from the most advanced materials available. This set up has cost years and billions."

"And?" Viviane studied her nails.

"And how the hell did she get out?"

Viviane shrugged. "She turned into water and exited through the feed lines for the pentagram."

"Fine, but she should still be caged in the summoning circle."

"She found a crack," Viviane shook her head. "If it's any consolation, escaping in that manner must have been beyond excruciating."

Dunham turned so that his back faced the phoenixes watching him as well as Viviane. Part of him wanted to rage, but he forced himself to calm. Haste and anger would forge mistakes. Not all was lost. He still had enough of Quayla's and Vitae's essence to perform the summoning ritual.

Dunham folded his hands behind his back and marched nearer the Pyri's cage. "By what name do you answer, fire phoenix?"

Unlike air, earth and water cages, the fire cage didn't have to be vacuum sealed. If the Pyri managed to generate enough heat to melt the view glass that allowed them to meet gazes and somehow managed to squeeze out the small rectangle, he still wouldn't be able to escape the magical barrier.

Eyes the color of glowing coals glared daggers at Dunham.

Dunham extended a hand.

Viviane fished a ruby, gold and silver egg from an inscribed bag resting on the billiard table. She walked it over with a casual seductiveness that she never seemed to shake.

Dunham took the egg from her and squeezed.

The edges of the Pyri's eyes tightened, but unlike Caelum, the fire phoenix gave no indication of the pain.

Dunham squeezed harder. "Answer me, shield."

Coal eyes blazed hotter. "Ignis."

"Good," Dunham cooed. "I don't believe we've been formally introduced, Ignis. My name is Dunham Heffernan. I'm an old friend of Quayla's—oh, and I'm also your new master."

"You are not our master. We serve the Undying Light."

"It would be disruptive and not a little juvenile to force you to hit yourself while telling you to stop just to prove you wrong." Dunham bent, sliding the fire egg into the basin socket designed to accept it. "As I told Caelum, you will need to produce essence for rebirth since you will be dying in my service. If you fail to do so and are reborn in your egg, I will smash it."

"Smash it, I'll take True Death over serving you," Ignis said.

"Fire." Dunham shook his head. "Viviane warned me you might be the hardest to control. Sure, stone is stubborn, but fire is too wild for its own good."

He stood back up, extending his hand once more. Viviane handed over another object without a word.

Dunham held up a flaming ruby. "That's why I took the precaution of securing your heart too."

Ignis threw himself at the cage, light and heat flaring behind the glass. In no time the fire burned the thick transparent material black enough to block all visibility.

"Thank you, Ignis," Dunham said. "That ceramic can take more heat than you can generate, but waste not want not. That's why I incorporated a sealed liquid sodium cooling system and heat exchanger. Your little tantrum just powered my building for a week.

"Now, you can continue helping my bottom line or you can tell me why your Vitae wasn't reborn here when he died."

"If I knew, I wouldn't—"

Dunham passed a hand over the heart and chanted.

Ignis shrieked and convulsed.

"Seems he doesn't know," Viviane said.

"Waste not, Ignis. Why didn't your Divine come to the Marriott and assist in clean up?"

Ignis's screams became maddened shrieks.

"You will answer," Dunham said. "Save yourself the pain."

"He's sequestered, healing injuries and regaining essence."

"For how long?"

"I don't kn—" Ignis screamed and convulsed.

"How long?"

"I don't know," Ignis growled.

"Inconvenient."

"We may be able to work it out," Viviane said.

"I do know that after I get my hands on you, you'll never play with fire again," Ignis spat.

"Perhaps the Terra will be more cooperative," Viviane said.

Dunham cast the second incantation over Ignis's heart. He considered keeping its purpose a secret, but decided he'd rather see the fire phoenix's expression. "That spell will cause you indescribable pain every time you feel the need to lie, threaten or otherwise disrespect me. You don't even have to act on those thoughts, your heart—"

Ignis disappeared with a scream, writhing in agony at the bottom of his cage.

"Yes, I think we should finish sealing in the Terra and chat with him while Ignis enjoys his reeducation."

Quayla

I stepped off the MARTA train at Peachtree Center station and bolted for the escalator. The clothes I'd grabbed from the rooms below Dunham's quarters hadn't fit right, but I'd transmogrified them into my true form then back with a few adjustments when I landed at the train station. In theory, I should've been able to clothe myself by just willing myself dressed when I transmogrified back to human. Building clothes from scratch required a lot of concentration and consumed essence.

Not really worth it.

A group of Cosplayers blocked my headlong rush up the escalator. I wanted to shove them out of the way, but doing so on the steep rising stairway risked injuring them.

"A movie? Really?" a costumed hero asked.

The vampire nodded. "That's what the Georgia Film Commission told the press."

"That film company's going to be paying out the ass for not properly posting signs, man," a wizard in marijuana leaf covered robes said.

"But I bet that'll be it," the hero said.

"Disgusting how companies like that get away with murder," the vampire added.

"Literally," the hero added.

The top of the escalator allowed me to dodge around the convention attendees. I raced into a food court packed with rabid, wall-to-wall fandom. Any other time, I might have leaned against a wall and enjoyed the weirdness, but I had to reclaim any essence I could get—Ignis's, Terrance's or mine.

And Vitae's too, I guess. Ass or not, he's a shield.

A grin played across my lips.

It's probably sinful to have enjoyed killing him, but he attacked me.

I reached the correct sky bridge and was forced to slow by heavy traffic and a group taking pictures of some elaborate costumes. I resisted an urge to scream.

Heart hammering my chest, I raced into the Marriott Marquis atrium to find it perfect. Every broken wall and shattered balcony looked as if it had never been damaged. People wandered around the hotel like nothing had ever happened.

I stopped a concierge. "Excuse me, someone said there was a disturbance of some kind here."

The woman pushed a stray hair out of her face. "Sorry, you missed it. After those people died, the studio packed up."

"People died?" I asked.

"Yeah, the studio hired a bunch of attendees as extras, but somewhere along the way a few people who weren't part of filming the scene ended up in the wrong place at the wrong time."

"Let me get this straight," I said. "That big plant monster was part of some movie shoot even though it destroyed half the hotel and killed a bunch of people?"

"Amazing what they can do with special effects these days," the woman said. "Is there anything else I can do to help you?"

I shook my head, disbelief stealing my powers of speech. I supposed the story made sense if Vilicangelus or Summuseraphi had arrived in time to do a mass rewrite, but there'd been people recording the fight—some of them no doubt streaming live.

How could they have covered everything up so completely?

Anima would know. The only way to get to Anima was to return to headquarters. I had to be quick. Dunham might set an ambush for me at the Shield Sanctum if he learned of my escape.

No, I can't risk it. How can I reach her? The angel on my Johammer? No, it and all the rest of our vehicles are parked beneath the sanctum.

I discounted my amulet next, the box was in my room in the sanctum. Caelum's box would be in his apartment, but his place seemed a likely ambush target too.

Ignis said his apartment had been lost. Creator! What do I do?

Costumed convention goers wove around me in a frenetic dance. Surrounded by tens of thousands, I was alone, truly alone without any place to go.

THE STORY CONTINUES…

Keep reading for a sneak peek from
Blood Phoenix Chronicles 3:
Vengeful are the Drowned

Thank you for reading *Ruled by Tainted Blood*.

Word of mouth recommendations and book reviews are insanely helpful, not just to other readers, but to an author's success. Moreover, we use these reviews to know what *you* want to read more of. Please consider leaving a short, honest review—nothing special required, just a sentence or two about how you felt about this book. I can't thank you enough.

If you loved this story and would like to stay up to date on the latest book releases, promotions, giveaways, and a free story, please be sure to become a member of the Delirious Scribbles Readers Group. [Your email address will never be shared, and you can opt out at any time.]

Begin your journey, just scan this image with your phone camera!

Keep reading for a sneak peek....

Sneak Peek:

Vengeful are the Drowned

Vitae

I swirled into existence, heart still thundering in my ears. Fury beat at the inside edges of my chest like a firestorm.

That ungrateful whore bitch killed me!

It didn't matter that I'd intended to punish her for disobeying. She needed to be taught her place, but instead of taking her lesson like an adult she'd turned around and…cold washed through me.

Dread froze the breath in my chest.

Distantly, my brain sought refuge in cataloged my reborn form. Breast size, hair color, height—none of it mattered as long as I had the advantages a female body offered as vehicle to my goals.

Rage overtook me, vibrating my whole body.

Dolumii's blade! Mare!

No matter how many times I argued with Vilicangelus over Aquaylae, he'd refused to recognize the threat she represented. He'd overlooked her disregard of duty. He'd discounted her laziness, her selfishness and her undisciplined attitude as youthful aspects.

And now, in disobeying my orders, she's cost Mare's freedom.

I stormed away from my nest through the security doors into my thrall's basement laboratory. A half-elf attendant—hybrid bastard of an elf and a Halfling—pushed replacement robes and fighting batons into my hands. I pointed with a baton at six hulks standing along one wall and pulled the robes over my head.

"I can dress myself, summon the car."

By time the robe's folds settled around my sultry hips, the six enforcers bracketed me in a semi-circle. Their constant growth prevented dressing the wafers reanimated with troll marrow in clothes suitable for a gentleman's entourage.

The thrall claimed their constant 'hulking' out of their clothes wasn't likely to stop as long as we continued exposing them to x-rays, but the obvious advantage of naturally armored muscles and spiked limbs compensated for their lack of decorum.

I'd ordered them painted. Despite the thrall's objections regarding clogging their pores, the troll DNA kept the head-to-toe black from killing them a second time.

And when I proved he was wrong he had the temerity to suggest we paint them green.

I stormed out of the basement for the front entrance, my temper heating further as I reviewed the travesty of the last few hours.

The young divine had summoned me—me—to a meeting to compare notes with the other shields.

As if I did not already know all I needed to know.

He'd shown his inexperience—nay incompetence—abandoning us with claims of overwork for some vacation frolic. When a major incursion had demanded our attention, my fellow elder shields had defended Aquaylae's complete disregard for secrecy. They'd threatened me.

I did my duty anyway.

Choosing an inconspicuous route, I'd trekked through downtown to the DragonCon hotels, even paying for parking that should have been mine by right as the city's defender. Irreverent crowds and would be photographers hampered my rescue mission, further endangering their fellow mortals. One mannerless cad had groped me rather than let me pass.

His hand won't be the only thing that rots away.

The instinctual use of life's antithesis on the naïve opened my eyes to a power I'd never considered. Employing my essence to draw life away from the barricading foliage allowed me to penetrate the hotel. Wielded against the kudzu beast, I'd been nigh invulnerable.

It was for that reason I instructed Aquaylae as to the ideal course of action while I thwarted some druid's elemental.

A goblin in a chauffer's hat met me outside the dilapidated and condemned hotel that served as my new residence. The little faerie opened the back door of my 1937 Mercedes Landaulet limousine.

One of my enforcers wedged himself into the front passenger seat of the vintage car. The other troll-kin squeezed into an armored SUV gifted me by an agent of wafer government I'd enthralled.

Pushing a copy of *Wuthering Heights* aside, I slid onto the luxurious seat and reached for a decanter of aged brandy. "Take us downtown to the Marriott Marquis."

"Lots of activity down there, Master. Many faeries."

"Did I give you permission to speak?"

"Yes, Master, when you tired of my gestures."

"Use it again to express an unsolicited opinion and I will revoke that permission."

"Yes, Master."

Good. Better than Aquaylae.

The water phoenix has ignored my orders outright. Instead of stepping aside to care for injured mortals, she'd insisted on hogging the glory of the kill. She'd even had the temerity to relegate me to a support role like some kind of battlefield midwife.

When I'd objected, she'd attacked and killed me.

That is the last time I'll allow her to cost our shield lives.

"Drive!"

"Yes, Master."

Bystanders gawked as my vehicle pulled out of the dilapidated hotel. Crews of enthralled faerie workers pressganged into renovating the interior of my new Shield Sanctum hadn't begun work on the old hotel's exterior. There was no need to hurry them until I decided whether or not the hotel's exterior condition served better as camouflage of our new headquarters.

The larger building offered solutions to our Shield's most significant problems. It removed us from our 'lofty heights' effectively eliminating any arguments about the other shields living outside the sanctum. It provided more room so younger shields who were worth sparing could train to a satisfactory level. It included space for servants to take over the insignificant details so we could focus on our duty.

Once Mare is returned and we're rid of Aquaylae, this new headquarters will enable us to build the greatest Shield ever assembled.

I turned on the television.

I abhorred the mindless teat used to pacify the gormless masses. Unfortunately, without Anima's control center, the local news had to serve my intelligence gathering needs. The new headquarters needed a control center but I was loathe to simply relocate the automata. Caelum's mucking about had altered the artificial intelligence so that it no longer knew its place.

I should rebuild the oracle we used before. At least then there wouldn't be any confusion—or any reason for that ignorant fledgling bitch to correct me.

My grip on the crystal tumbler tightened until brandy-coated shards dug into my hands.

Obviously, some problem afflicted our newest generation of phoenixes. Pollutants and toxins damaging Creation may have also damaged the development of young phoenixes. Such at least provided a rational excuse for Aquaylae, Caelum and the ignorant boob serving as Atlanta's Praefectus.

Vilicangelus and I will sort this out once he has a spare moment. Once we've replaced the dead weight and proved this Shield the most superior in Creation, he can see me elevated as a worthier successor.

With the power of faerie magic and the gifts of a Divine One, I'd reform the whole region until the other Praefectures adopted my training methods.

One task at a time.

A check out the window showed us moving too slowly. "We're in a hurry, goblin. Drive faster."

"I'm doing the best I can, Master, but DragonCon—"

"Be silent and drive!"

For a moment, I toyed with replacing the goblin with the enforcer, but the bulk of the former corpse would've made any attempt to operate the vehicle difficult.

I turned my attention to the news reporter staring blankly into the camera, oblivious to an off-camera woman repeating his name. My disgust rose until I reached for the device's power button. A finger's breadth from replacing wafer gibberish with classical opera, the picture changed to a studio anchor. It took only a few words for me to realize the off-camera voice belonged to the attractive Moor.

"Georgia film industry officials have confirmed that what was reported as some kind of supernatural event was in fact film work for a new fantasy movie."

She droned on and on about safety signs and security lapses, accidents and lawsuits. Her comeliness couldn't overcome the selfish entitlement—a recent wafer epidemic—escaping her lips.

Despite my disgust, the explanation fed to the media bore all of the hallmarks of a well-conceived story. The fiction offered a sufficiently plausible scenario to ensure the secrecy of Faery despite all of the witnesses involved.

That idiot Summus must've lied about Vilicangelus's condition. Didn't want Vili learning of his shortcomings. This whole generation is as bad as Aquaylae.

The limo slowed, crawling forward through crowds and cars

in fits and starts. The third stop exhausted my patience. I had to reclaim the Unseelie Champion sword without further delay.

"Stop. I will get out here."

"We're in the middle of the street, Master."

"The other motorists will have to make way."

His worried expression belied his feelings, but the goblin nodded.

The faerie creature was too stupid to understand the human world. Besides, my Mercedes waited in a parking structure only a short jaunt away. Once I'd reclaimed my possessions, dealt with Aquaylae and ensured the Sidhe trounced, I'd drive myself back.

A car tried to hit me the moment I stepped out.

Only my supernatural reflexes let me slip the sedan's hammer blow. The mortal leapt out of the still running car a moment later, not contrite, not apologetic, but indignant. "Stupid bitch! What the fuck is wrong with you?"

My mission to retrieve the sword imprisoning Mare was far too important to delay with injury or another death. Even so, the urge to teach the naïve a lesson about proper respect, especially of a lady, tempted me to tarry.

I placed a hand on the car's hood and will death into the machine. The act didn't manipulate life energy as Ignis might will control over flame through pyrokinesis. What I did was the opposite of manipulating life, and I have no idea how my power should be able to slay a machine.

The engine let out a groan of metal. Smoke poured from the hood only moments before fire licked out of the seams.

The driver's eyes widened. "What did you do? I'll sue you f—"

A troll-kin enforcer seized his arm. The driver jerked free and dove for the safety of his vehicle. The door locks clicked shut.

I eyed the flames flickering in and out of the engine compartment, raising a brow.

I needn't have given any thought to the man's lack of sense. My enforcer ripped the door from its frame. When the driver scrambled first to the passenger side and then to the back, more enforcers removed the doors.

"Teach him proper respect."

I hurried away, rushing despite the unseemliness of it. Grunts and pained profanities faded into the distance.

I considered the days discoveries on the run.

All phoenixes had limited control of their essence element. As life phoenix, I was the single most vital of all. It was my purview to grant the energy of life. It'd never occurred to me that control meant removal as well as granting.

It is fitting though. Who else should shoulder the responsibility accompanying the ability to draw life from those unworthy?

Pedestrians thickened to crowds. I fought my way along increasingly packed sidewalks. After a prolonged struggle, a repeat of earlier obstructions embrittled my temper. I reached a corner housing the Marriott Marquis. Across the street, the dumbstruck news anchor I'd seen on the television stared unmoving at his cameraman.

My old friend epitomizes everything I shall be as a Divine One.

Someone thrusted a sign into my face. "This is your fault, jezebel! You and the rest of these sinners brought the devil into our midst."

I took in the man in an eye blink. Catholic priest's collar, bullhorn and a sign staff adorned with fire and brimstone declarations.

"Whores, homosexuals and Satanists brought this evil. You'll burn for it! God will smite you for your hedonistic lifestyles."

I cocked an eyebrow. "You are mistaken, sir. The Creator loves all his creations, even when they err. That's why he sent a second host to protect you from hell and your foolish desires."

The preacher shoved his face into mine, spitting his vitriol. "My God is a wrathful God. He will punish you!"

My temper couldn't have ignited faster if I'd been a Pyri. The heinous wafer accosting me might have thought his sermonizing in service of my Creator, but his hateful speech did more damage than good as it incensed me.

I am a Shield of the Undying Light. It is not my place to judge.

"My good man, if you will refer to the Bible in—"

"Be silent, harlot! I will not listen to Satan's temptress pervert scripture with a forked tongue!"

"I haven't time for your willful ignorance." Essence leapt out of my fingers in writhing tentacles. "Ask the Author yourself."

For a moment, the touch of life essence enervated the preacher. New bluster rushed to his lips. I withdrew my gift, ripping out his life energy along with my own.

I left the corpse lay where it fell and pushed through the mesmerized crowd toward the hotel entrance. The scene beyond the glass doors stopped me short.

An army of pixies and fairies cleared away detritus as dwarves —not putti—rebuilt the scene. Half-ogres muscled people and objects around while elves touched wafers with magic and whispered new memories.

Why are faeries cleaning up the scene?

I snatched a passing fairy out of the air by one wing. "Why are you cleaning up?"

"Screw off, bird. I don't answer to you."

"Who do you answer to?" I demanded.

The fairy snorted, soiling my robes with snot-laden fairy dust. "We serve the Lady, fool, and if you know what's good for you, you'll let me go before—"

I pulped the creature and drew in its essence. A surge of magic accompanied the sweet addition to my strength.

Vilicangelus isn't here, all of this is Faery's work. To what end?

I grabbed a grendling, putting power behind the harsh whisper escaping my lips. "Tell me where my swords are!"

"T-the o-only swords t-they f-found were Champion blades," the moldy faerie stammered. "The knights claimed them."

Dolumii and Gherrian are here? Together? Working with Wyldfae?

An all-encompassing need demanded I slay the grendling too. He was too big to completely consume as was, and his body might draw attention.

I needed Dolumii's sword.

I needed to free Mare.

Challenging the Unseelie Knight while I was so vastly outnumbered doomed me to failure—new powers or not. Further reconnoitering of the hotel risked a like altercation. Both might undo the Sidhe's confusing but thorough coverup.

My next choices required wisdom and for that I needed to gather intelligence. I set the grendling down and gently dusted off his shoulders. "Thank you, sir. Have a nice day."

The grendling's stare lingered on my retreating back as I retreated toward my Mercedes. I'd observe from the old sanctum, formulate a plan, and take back my swords.

And I can retrieve more of my books.

Quayla

I trudged across one of the sky bridges exiting the Atlanta Marriot Marquis, lost in my own little world. Mortals crowded around me, celebrating beloved books and movies, comics and anime, dressed in a thousand lovingly-crafted cosplays. Laughter, excited chatter and shoulder-to-shoulder bodies pressed around me in a fetid, white noise cloud.

Awash in a sea of mortal adulation, I drifted like a bodiless specter. My soul hurt more than the lingering pain from my escape. I'd lost everything and everyone I loved in a single day.

Dunham Heffernan, CEO of Circlestone and Caelum's one-time boss had laid a trap. He'd captured Ignis, Caelum, and Terrance—the other phoenixes that made up Atlanta's Shield.

Well, the phoenixes that hadn't tried to kill me.

Right before I'd been suckered in by a wounded mortal in

Dunham's employ, our Shieldheart, our Vitae attacked me, forcing me to kill him. I'd escaped Dunham's prison through excruciating means none of the others—except perhaps Vitae—could replicate. Forced to flee rather than risk getting caught once more, I raced to the Marriott Marquis. If I could reclaim enough magical essence from another shield's corpse, they could be reborn into freedom.

The Marriott had been spotless. None of the carnage or destruction from fighting a hundred-foot kudzu elemental remained. How the property had been restored nagged from a corner of my distracted thoughts. Our boss, a divine phoenix renamed Summuseraphi was out of commission as was his superior Vilicangelus.

Yet, the Marriott looks fine. How is that even possible?

Dunham hadn't returned from the Marriott by time I escaped, so I had no idea if he'd monologue his master plan to the others. I hadn't spent a lot of time with the powerful man, but he'd never smelled of Sidhe taint like most of the Fae Kissed.

Even Caelum, our air phoenix and possessor of the best nose among us, had worked alongside Dunham without ever noticing the odor of faerie taint. Dunham could've been born with the druidic powers used to create the monster, but such things were rare and such people weren't the powerhouses Dunham had proven himself. Offspring of Fae Kissed occasionally inherited power without the cost, but I knew first hand Caelum's old boss was in cahoots with a powerful faerie.

One of the Dark Trinity.

I couldn't believe I'd been singled out by one of the most powerful entities in Creation. The Lady had told me Dunham— though I hadn't known who the Lady meant at that time—had been a seventh son of a seventh son. Mortals bred pretty well, but such children were rare—extremely rare as economic realities made such large families too expensive to maintain.

Talk about catnip for faeries.

Folklore attributed any number of special powers—good and

bad—to seventh sons of seventh sons. With just under two centuries worth of life, I'd met two—a young boy who lived in my first shield's territory and Dunham. I'd never witnessed any kind of magic from the boy, making it hard to judge their power.

The Lady and Dunham had made some sort of bargain. Sought for their potential, most seventh sons became Fae Kissed, bringing almost unilateral destruction for the Shields. Without a taint, there was no proof the deal had been a trade for Sidhe power, but they'd been working together cheek and jowl to capture my Shield.

If the Lady's warning meant Dunham, he wants me dead.

Fae Kissed were dangerous—even the corrupted like Emma who'd only bargained out of grief for the return of her deceased tabby. Knowledge of Faery was too dangerous even for so benign a wafer. If a Fae Kissed refused to surrender their boon and repent, we had no choice but to kill them before they could instruct other mortals how to get their desires granted.

The smell of a cookie store stroked my troubled soul with chocolate chip caresses. I didn't have any money. Even if I had my old ID, I couldn't have gotten anything out of my bank. My newest body was male, a difference not easily overlooked by even the most clueless teller.

If only I hadn't asked Dylan's memory be erased.

I wrapped arms around myself and trudged through the thronging masses out for a quick bite between panels. I'd requested a rewrite for Dylan, Mrs. Cox and Detective Foxner to protect them from the increasingly treacherous faeries around Atlanta. I hadn't wanted to lose them, but the death of Judith cemented the reasons to wipe away any ties to my friends and beloved Dylan. Judith died because she'd gone to my apartments. She'd been used as bait for yet another trap then slain to make the Lady's point.

If working in my flower shop was enough to put Judith on the Faery hit list, Dylan—the love of my very long life—had been in extreme peril.

The shop has a good supply of cash, but I'll have to break in.

I had cash stashed at my old apartment, but it was rent money and my personal dwelling was just as likely to be under surveillance as Caelum's. Once I'd been allowed off house arrest, I'd set up small caches throughout Atlanta—mostly clothes and maybe a few dollars. After meeting Dylan, having a helpmate made the caches less vital and I'd left them untended since.

No way to be sure if they're even there. I have to make a decision, to act. The longer I wait, the more places Dunham will stake out in hope of recapturing me.

Appendix A: Cast of Characters

Phoenixes:

Aquaylae (Quayla Buckler): A water phoenix assigned to the Atlanta Shield. Recently released from house arrest. Employed running a florist shop in eastern Atlanta. Dating Dylan Snyder. Preferred weapon: karambit knife

Caelum (Caelum Kite): An air phoenix assigned to the Atlanta Shield. Employed as Head of Charitable Projects by Circlestone Corporation. Preferred weapon: handgun or battle fan.

Ignis (Ignis Round): A fire phoenix assigned to the Atlanta Shield. Employed as a firefighter and arson investigator for the City of Atlanta. Preferred weapon: duo hilt bow and katana.

Mare: A water phoenix formerly assigned to the Atlanta Shield. Lost in a battle with Unseelie forced.. Preferred weapon: short swords.

Summuseraphi: A divine phoenix assigned as new praefectus of the shields of the southeastern United States. Formerly Lympha, Summuseraphi was recently elevated to divine status and placed under Villicangelus for training. Preferred weapon: chain blade.

Terrance (Terrance Wall): An earth phoenix assigned to the

Atlanta Shield. Employed at the Department of Motor Vehicles. Preferred weapon: cestus battle gloves.

Villicangelus: A divine phoenix assigned as overseers of the shields functioning in Southern Britain. Formerly overseer of the southern United States. Training supervisor over Summuseraphi. Preferred weapon: unknown.

Vitae: A life phoenix assigned to the Atlanta Shield as Shieldheart. Responsible for overall operations. Concerned about mortal deaths in her former shield, Vitae placed Quayla on house arrest. Preferred weapon: lajatang—bladed staff and baton forms.

Humans:

Detective Sabrina Foxner: Atlanta detective currently assigned to the robbery division. The former homicide detective is investigating the Howell Mill break-in.

Doctor Bradley Sky: Intelligent and enthusiastic junior assistant coroner working in Atlanta's morgue. His memory has been rewritten multiple times to remove discovery of the Fey.

Dunham Heffernan: CEO of Circlestone Corporation

Dylan Snyder: Quayla's bisexual boyfriend. Dylan is aware of Quayla's true nature. He's employed as an IT professional

Emma: Fae Kissed human who made a deal to resurrect her cat. Employed at Howell Mill Humane Society

Judith: Pessimistic and disinterested Korean college student employed at Ponds de Leon Flowers.

Mara: Employee of Camp Woof doggie daycare

Miri: Atlanta PD tech ops.

Mrs. Hadley Sage Cox: Quayla's sweet but nosey landlady. Superstitious with detailed knowledge of Fey folklore.

Nicolas: Owner of a hole in the wall grocery store near the Atlanta Sheild's HQ and Caelum's supplier for honey candy and milk used as currency in the Goblin Market

Pete: Owner of Camp Woof doggie daycare

Tommy: Doctor at Grady Memorial Hospital Long time friend of Bradley Sky.

Valerie: News anchor. Subject of lingering crush by Bradleh's friend Tommy

Viviane: Dunham Heffernan's executive assistant

FEY:

Grynnberry: A Seelie nymph. An informant that provides Quayla with intelligence.

Knight Dolumii: Knight Champion of the Unseelie Court.

Knight Gherrian: Knight Champion of the Seelie Court.

Lady Esloah: Knight of the Seelie Court

Oshyn: Half sized elf merchant in the Goblin Market. Provides brownie cleaning services.

Princess Mariene: Unseelie sovereign and royal court adjunct between the Seelie queen and the phoenixes.

Prince Vusolaryn: Seelie sovereign and royal court adjunct between the Seelie queen and the phoenixes.

Thatch: WyldFae representative for the Sidhe's Georgia Shire near Atlanta

OTHERS:

Anima: Monitoring entity assigned to the Atlanta Shield

TWISTED GALAXIES
MYTHS REBORN
MULTI-LAYER
CHARACTER-DRIVEN

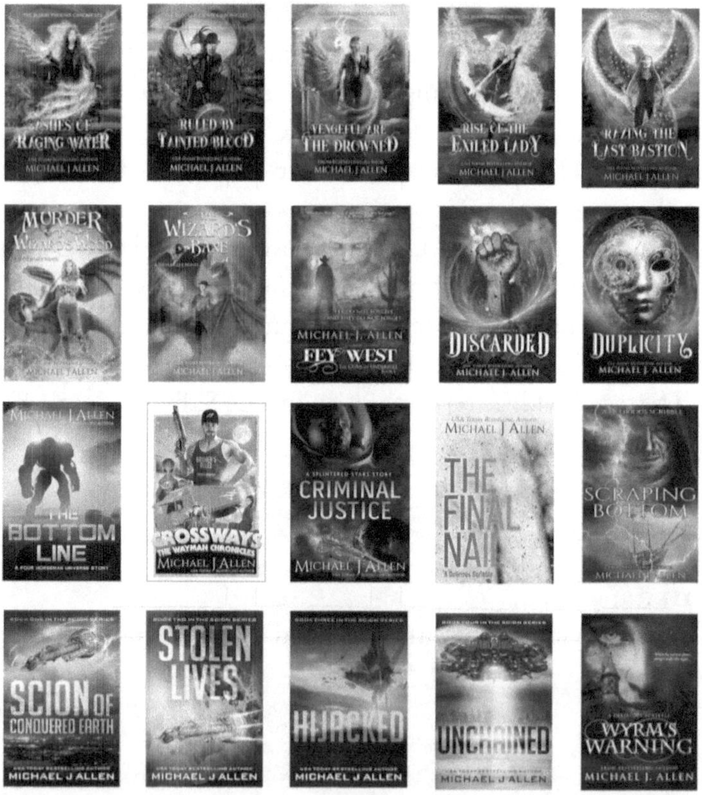

Acknowledgments

The second Blood Phoenix novels is in the can. I hope you've enjoyed the story so far. It's notable that Ruled by Tainted Blood is the first novel I've ever published as a USA Today bestselling author. Countless people supported us by buying Cursed Lands, and I can't thank any of you enough. Add to that my thanks to my collaborative authors for all the countless hours and dollars everyone put in to earn our rank on the list.

I'd like to thank you for joining yet another journey through my imagination. It's so wonderful having other people along to give my imaginary friends more people to entertain. Sure, there were some surprising moments—though maybe not as shocking as those to come. I also want to thank those of you that encouraged me. Through reviews, social media comments and emails, you've expressed you love – and sometimes hate – of what I'm doing. Thanks for keeping me motivated and pointing me down the paths you most want me to explore.

As I said in Ashes, Andrea Fodor put up with my nitpicking and perfectionism to create our covers, bringing life to Atlanta's Shield in both human and phoenix shape.

This rapid release schedule has put a lot of pressure on the people I trust to help develop the best books possible. Author T. Allen Diaz supplied more of his firefighting expertise. Trint provided information about a certain strip club, and Mike introduced me to DragonCon, fostering my love of the convention all these years. so many years ago. Billy and Scott, Rebecca and Sarah all contributed to the various stages of reading and editing, and

Tina, poor Tina, stepped up to take a hand in all of the editing phases when other members of my team had to bow out.

As usual, my final thanks go to the characters that trusted me with their story. Vitae especially opened up his heart—and a few throats—to bring the history of Atlanta's Shield into focus. You've got a hard road ahead, guys. Keep the faith...and you, please keep reading.

Thank you for being part of my journey.

Sharp Eyes: Thanks to Samantha W for catching some mistakes

About the Author

Photo credit: Jim Cawthorne

Michael J. Allen is a star-lord, goofball, and USA Today bestselling author of character-driven, multi-layer, full-spectrum science fiction and fantasy novels - pretty much whatever madness sprouts from his head... (Learn more at www.deliriousscribbles.com)

Let's Connect

I love chatting with my readers, and hope you'll join my reader groups. If you'd rather stay up to date without joining in on the fun, there are plenty of ways to follow along.

— Michael J Allen

Reader Groups:

Discord : https://discord.gg/WeM4bwq
Facebook: https://www.facebook.com/groups/dsreaders
MeWe: https://www.mewe.com/join/dsreaders

Follow the Scribbler:

www.deliriousscribbles.com

amazon.com/-/e/B0096GEILG

bookbub.com/authors/michael-j-allen

facebook.com/deliriousscribbler

goodreads.com/deliriousscribbler

instagram.com/thedscribbler

twitter.com/Thedscribbler